Thort's Epiphany

Thort's Epiphany

Carey Slay &
Cara Slay Coleman

ILLUMIFY
MEDIA.COM

DEDICATION

Carey:
To my family, with special thanks to my daughter. Her Elisha touch made my skeletal ideas come alive. To co-author with her is a gift that cannot be measured.

Cara:
To my Dad,
The past two and a half years have been a gift. The opportunity to work on a project with you has been many things; a season of learning, stretching, and growing, a season of listening, creating, and negotiating, a season of patience, providence, and perseverance, but most of all, this has been a season of appreciation for the opportunity to work one on one with you on a project that was a first for both of us. It has truly been an honor that I will ever cherish. I love you, Dad.

CONTENTS

PROLOGUE

The great angel Ramiel was dumbstruck. What had just happened? Why had his former servant gone along with such treason, and why had so many others followed him? What could they be thinking? The whole situation left Ramiel feeling confused and forsaken.

As he sat on the stone wall outside of the gate, contemplating, Joam approached. One look at his friend's face proved they shared the same sentiment.

Joam sat down next to Ramiel. "I can't believe any of this." "I just . . . There are no words to explain it," Ramiel replied.

"Why would the Father's light bearer ever think he could be like Him? He was a creature, not the Creator. This is lunacy."

"I know," Ramiel said. "Another question is, why follow him?"

Joam put a hand on Ramiel's shoulder. "I'm truly sorry, my friend. I know you must miss him."

"I just can't understand it on any level. One minute we were serving the Kingdom together, and the next, I'm here, and he's gone. Everything feels so broken and wrong."

"I know it may seem like that now, but our Lord will shed light on this for us. I'm assuming He may assign us as partners since He summoned us together. It would be a great honor to serve with you, Ramiel."

"Thank you, Joam. It would be good to have you around."

Moments later they were escorted by a beautiful spirit to the Chamber where they now stood. The King was speaking with His council members, and Ramiel and Joam waited to be summoned into the inner room. Anticipation of being with Him flooded them with a sense of joy and peace.

Noticing the two angels had arrived, the King gave a few more instructions to Kafziel, one of the council members, and then dismissed the entire group.

"Ah, Ramiel, Joam, so glad you both could join me this morning. Come over and have a seat."

"Thank you, Your Grace," Ramiel replied. "It's good to be with you. How may we serve You?"

"That is an excellent question, Ramiel. The Father and I recognize your service and loyalty, and that is why I summoned you here today." The King smiled at the angels, and a fresh sense of peace washed over them. "Before I talk about your mission, let me give you a little background. As you know, my Kingdom's authority has no end, not in Heaven or on Earth. The rebellion has resulted in your fellow servants being cast out of our Kingdom, Ramiel's servant and friend, being one of them. Their infractions were treason, pride, and jealousy for and against the throne. Your fallen brothers were burning with a desire to be independent and equal with Us. They embraced deceit as their very nature after being seduced and deceived."

"It hurt us, your Grace," Joam said. "We don't understand why they would make such a horrible and disastrous decision."

"There are many reasons. They believed We loved humans more than them. This jealousy was born from a lie. We love all Our creations. The division is painful and costly, yet we have a plan. We have always had a plan."

The King smiled at them before continuing. "My trustworthy servants, you have not seen the last of the fallout from this mutiny.

We knew this day would come. Humans are about to make a disastrous and eternal choice, just as your brothers did."

Ramiel and Joam both gasped. It was hard to believe this new creation would rebel just like their brothers.

The King expected their response, and he held His hand up to calm them. "Now, be at peace. As I mentioned, We have always had a plan. As dark as things will seem on Earth, my Word and my Blood will activate redemption and reconciliation with all of creation."

The angels shared a questioning glance and then settled back in their seats.

"This brings me to why I have summoned you here today. The two of you will play a key role in the master plan. I'll assign you as messengers and protectors. Your service will be required in the physical realm and in the spiritual realm. Do you remember Kafziel from my counsel?"

"Yes, we do," Joam replied, nodding.

"I'm teaming you with him throughout the mission. He'll oversee things here, and you will work on Earth. The specifics of your mission will come later, but I ask that you stand at the ready."

The King chuckled. "If you could only see your faces. Smile, my friends. The war has begun, but We know how it will end. Fear not, for I have overcome, and one day you will see the complete plan unfold. On that day we will celebrate."

"Your Grace, it is an honor to be chosen for this task," Joam replied.

The King stood. "Now go in peace, and keep your heads up. You will learn more about your mission soon."

After bidding Joam farewell for the evening, Ramiel strolled outside of the gate. A smile spread across his face for the first time since he had received news of the rebellion. The confusion and disappointment faded away. He had a mission, and when complete, there would be redemption. Hope consumed his spirit.

"Let's do this," he said, then took flight.

CHAPTER 1

THE BRIMSTONE BAR AND CHAIN

Couldn't a demon just get a drink? The days were long and swelteringly hot. Early evening felt like high noon there. Not a breath of air was moving, and everything felt stale and sticky as Thort flew into the perimeter of Hell Ops. He knew it was well past his appointment time to check in with Chief Despot, but he wasn't worried. He was one of the most acclaimed demons in his regime. In his mind, they were lucky to have him. He would report when he got around to it.

The Brimstone Bar and Chain was a smelly, sulfur-filled dive bar located just inside the gates of Hell. The beat-up, run-down establishment was across the street and one block down from Hell Ops. Hell Ops served as the pentagon for Hell's central intelligence service. They issued directives and mission assignments, so a constant stream of fallen angels was moving in and out of the area. The Brimstone Bar and Chain was a convenient spot to throw back a drink and swap war stories before heading out to the next assignment. Any time day or night, one might find upper-legion generals, heavily decorated fallen demons, as well as low, simple dark servants in the establishment.

The bar was staffed by lost human souls who, to their last breath on Earth, refused to acknowledge the Father. It was a miserable place to work. Being forced to serve the very spirits who had fooled them into spending eternity there was a bitter pill for the humans to swallow.

Thort could not wait to set foot into the Bar and Chain for a victory lap in front of the miserable plebes. A quick drink or two would grease the wheels before his report and his new assignment. Nothing pleased him more than to enter the bar, which would fall silent with hushed awe as his reputation preceded him. Only a few demons had risen to his rank and distinction, and Thort loved to remind everyone of that.

The door cracked open with a low, creepy moan, then stopped short. Thort peeked his wretched face around the corner to size up the room. He wanted his grand entrance to have maximum impact. Drawing attention to himself was one of his gifts.

The blight of an establishment was just as he remembered it. The pungent smell of rotting food and old urine mixed with smoke hung in the air like a thick fog. The strobing green neon light above the bar flickered on and off with a quiet whine. As the stench hit his nostrils, his eyes watered for a moment. Ammonia and sulfur burned through his nose and down his esophagus until he had to swallow to keep the bile from bubbling up into his mouth. It was putrid, but it was a welcome and familiar atmosphere.

Thort surveyed the room. Sitting at one of the reserved hightop tables, he noticed a couple of dark sketchy fellows. He could not make them out, but he knew that only the elite generals of Hell sat in that reserved section of the bar. They would usually be principalities and powers from some assigned region on Earth. Thort never passed up an opportunity to strut in front of the big guys. Who knew when someone might drop his name at a Hell Ops meeting and consider him for promotion?

Unfortunately, the rest of the bar was nearly empty. He would make another pass after his meetings. Thort wanted higher visibility, and it was important for the low ranks to see what a highly decorated demon of honor looked like.

He swung the heavy door open, and it struck the wall with a thud. Thort strode into the bar in all his dark glory. He was so dark that looking at him was like staring into a black hole. His face had chiseled smug features and a jaw set like stone. He stood much taller than most demons and wore a thick black cloak that hung down to the floor. His arms were almost covered with tattoos, with jet-black strips beginning at his wrists and extending up to his thick biceps. His burning yellow eyes glared straight ahead from under the hood of his cloak. When he was about halfway through the room, Thort threw his hood back, revealing a flowing, curled mane of jet-black hair. His entrance was quite a show, and almost everyone in the room took notice. His presence drew a level of fear and respect.

They respected him, but they hated him even more. A demon with a half-melted face sat at one of the low tables. Looking up from his gruel, he followed Thort across the room with his eyes. Only after Thort walked by did the demon groan with disgust under his breath and rolled his eyes.

Thort noticed a couple of faces he hadn't seen before at a round table. *Newbies, my favorite,* he thought. Passing by, he reached his foot out and swept out the leg of the smaller demon's chair. It tilted back and sent the demon crashing to the floor. The room erupted with laughter. Thort chuckled, not even bothering to look back.

The ruckus caught the attention of two demons in the reserved corner. Sorpine and Blastus, two highly ranked demons, had little appetite for the self-glorification of assignment demons like Thort. Paying attention to him would be like wasting time on the single thread of a tapestry. Principalities and powers were big-picture, authoritative demons with multifunctional assignments. Their influence weaved through a region or a people group with age-old deception and dark power. They only fraternized with other principalities and powers and reported directly to Satan himself. These dark, powerful emissaries controlled the most wicked places on Earth and were the most feared creatures in Hell Ops.

Sorpine glared up at Thort and scoffed in disgust. "How pathetic.

If his kind only knew how replaceable they were, they would gloat less. What an insignificant fool. "

"It's rather embarrassing," Blastus said. "Don't give him the honor of your attention. We can only hope he gets it out of his system and moves on."

"He will if he knows what's good for him," Sorpine said, hunkering back down over his drink.

Thort headed for the high stools at the bar, where only the honored demons were welcome. Before choosing a seat, he slapped his massive black fist onto the surface of a four-top full of demons. It scared them to death, sending grog sloshing out of their mugs and onto the table, where it dripped into their laps. Thort loved bullying other demons. He enjoyed smelling fear on them and having the power to choose who he would torment.

Alright, enough with the fun and games. Time for a drink, Thort thought, laughing. He needed to wipe his mind's slate clean, so he could focus his fury on his next assignment.

Choosing a seat, he looked down to inspect the fabric of his barstool. He tried to use his fingernail to pick off what looked like dried mucus, or possibly a squashed maggot. Finally giving up, he settled onto the stool.

Thort looked around to see if he recognized anyone sitting at the bar. Of course, he could trust no one in that godforsaken place, so he always had to consider the content of his discussions. Demons only cared about themselves and their next promotion. They kept a sharp ear out for juicy gossip that they could use against other demons or for their own glorification.

No one had polished or wiped down the copper counter of the bar since the BB&C had opened. It was tarnished black in places, with thick puddles that had long since dried into crusty brown-and-green layers of food, drink, and bodily fluids. Patrons just had to move their barstool to the least filthy spot and hope for the best. The vile stench of wet copper smelled like vomit and blood, blending well with the aromas coming from the sink of filthy old dishwater just behind the bar. The entire room reeked of excrement.

Hellhounds roamed freely, nosing around from table to table and weaving under the barstools. For years they had relieved themselves in the corners, marking their territory on the furniture and the walls. Occasionally, they engaged in a bloody scrap over the crumbs that fell from their masters' tables. Every mongrel carried a gnarly scar on its face, a missing tooth, or a clipped ear.

Thort's patience wore thin, thinking he might never get a drink. Finally, a short, haggard female soul approached. She was carrying a basket of the house chips and the dip trio. Setting the dish down in front of Thort without making eye contact, she pointed to each dip in turn. "This one is Graft, that one is Messalina, and this last one's Casanova. Can I get you a drink?"

"Bring me your tallest mug of Leech Ordure, you wretch," Thort replied. "And do it now! I've been waiting long enough." The woman cowered and then turned to fill his order.

While he waited, Thort grabbed a chip, dragged it through the thick, slimy Graft, then sat back with a long sigh. He was just starting to relax when he heard a voice. "Who do you think you are, walking in here like you own the place?"

Thort knew that voice anywhere. It was Fluto, a fellow demon whom he regularly ran into there. Fluto was one of the few demons whom Thort considered his equal. He enjoyed swapping gory stories about what crafty, spiteful things they had accomplished. Fluto, like Thort, was enjoying success after success with his human assignments. He was a highly decorated corporal whose dark pride in his accomplishments was even more evident than the stripes on his arm. As usual, Fluto was adorned in his full-dress blacks. Like Thort, he carried himself with an air of intimidation and demanded all eyes on him. His pride was evident in everything he did. Thort would never admit it, but he looked up to Fluto and fashioned much of his persona after him.

"You'd know exactly who I was if you could stop talking about yourself long enough," Thort replied. He kept his eyes fixed forward, pretending he couldn't bother acknowledging Fluto.

Fluto slammed his beer onto the bar, spilling some of it. Then he slapped Thort on the shoulder, way harder than necessary. "So, did you hear about Sphazo? Satan's lieutenants partially consumed him. They stripped him of his rank and placed him on probation from human assignments for a while."

Casting a nervous glance at Fluto, Thort grimaced. He had heard all about Sphazo's demise after losing his assigned soul, James. James was one of the original followers of Jesus, and the demons assigned to the apostles had very strategic, top-secret directives. Not even Thort or Fluto had access to that level of intelligence. As much as he enjoyed relishing in the demise of a fellow demon, it pained Thort to think of Sphazo. They had been sitting at that very bar the other day, measuring successes like two lying old fishermen. Now, look where Sphazo was. How did it happen so quickly?

"I heard a few rumors about it," Thort said, fishing for details. "What happened?"

Fluto scooted his stool closer to Thort, eager to spill the gossip. "He thought it would be a good idea to influence King Herod to have his assignment assassinated. However, his plan backfired. Now the followers consider James a martyr. His death has stirred up more problems than you can imagine. People are clamoring to hear the wretched news of how to gain eternal life. Sphazo won't get another assignment for centuries, if he even makes it out of the brig in one piece."

Fluto gulped down a huge swig of his drink and thought for a second. "If Sphazo gets reassigned, maybe they'll throw him a bone. Something easy, like a rich prince, already entangled with wealth. Hell Ops will never trust him with top-secret missions. Who knows? He will probably never make rank again."

Fluto laughed, loud and obnoxious. "Enough about Sphazo. I hear you're up for another black stripe. Keep it up, and you may be as mighty as me one day. Doubtful, but maybe."

Thort stuck out his chest and took a deep, satisfying breath. "Yes, another stripe. Soon they'll probably just have to give me one for every ten souls that I deliver instead of just every individual one. My arms are running out of tattoo space."

"Keep dreaming, my dear friend. You've always had a fancy imagination," Fluto replied. "Heard anything yet about your new assignments? Surely, your next one will be a slight challenge. I'll never understand why you get all the softballs. Pathetic." Fluto rolled his eyes and snorted.

"There isn't a soul alive who stands a chance when their name comes up for my assignment," Thort shot back. "Why Hell Ops hasn't promoted me yet is a mystery. My talents are being wasted with these individual mortals."

Fluto nodded. "Right, right. So, I hear—every time I see you. Anyway, who are the next unlucky souls assigned to the great Thort? I can't wait to hear about your next delicacies. I'm sure you will be relishing in the foils of their despair in no time."

Thort knew Fluto was being sarcastic. He rolled his eyes behind his closed lids and took a sip of his drink. "I have grown quite disinterested with it all. I won't bore you with the details. I barely even listen to who's up next. It's just one more piece of useless clay. They're all the same to me."

"It's rather mundane, isn't it?" Fluto replied.

"I know that these next unlucky souls are the beginning of some family line. I heard that Hell Ops is planning to assign me to many generations of the same family. Whatever it is, it must be important if they're putting me on it. I don't know. The pathetic soul's name is Paulk, and he's married to a sheepish gal named Sarah. Hell Ops is asking me to take them on as a couple. Finally, they realize that one soul at a time is a terrible waste of my resources." Thort threw back the last gulp of his drink and slammed the mug on the bar.

"Interesting," Fluto said, perking up a bit.

"The whole multi-generational thing will probably all have to change, though. When I single-handedly crush Paulk and Sarah, why will there be any need to stay on future descendants? Seems redundant. I don't know, but I guess I should head over and get the details before someone at Hell Ops gets their panties twisted."

The two demons stood up and headed for the door. Thort

glanced at Sorpine and Blastus. He wondered what they knew about Sphazo. The fallout from James's death looked bad on them as well.

Fluto hurled a few insults at lower-ranking demons on his way out. "Don't get too comfortable, you feeble frauds. We have business across the street. We'll be right back."

CHAPTER 2

PAULK AND SARAH

Peace may come from our lips, but its purity is only heart inspired.

Paulk walked through the front door to his humble home one afternoon in early June. The days were getting longer, and he was thankful. He had a lot of chores he wanted to finish before nightfall. His wife, Sarah, was kneeling in the kitchen in front of the fire. "How was your day?" Paulk asked.

"I haven't felt well today," Sarah said. "The same as yesterday."

Paulk rolled his eyes while she wasn't looking. "Do you ever feel well, Sarah? Are you sick, or are you just feeling anxious all the time?" He took off his outer tunic and hung it by the door. "I don't know what you're expecting. Things won't get better for us. We must learn to cope with what life gives us."

"I know, I know," Sarah replied. "I'm just tired. That's all." Not wanting to have the anxiety conversation again, she hoped her answer would satisfy Paulk, so he would drop the subject.

"By the way, I've arranged for us to attend a dinner meeting tonight. Do you have any food prepared that we could share at the gathering?" Paulk stated the question more like a demand. He knew that if he made the meeting optional, Sarah would certainly decline.

"A meeting? A meeting where?" Sarah asked. "I'm not going anywhere. Food to share? With whom? What are you talking about, Paulk? You never mentioned going out."

There was panic in her voice. Gatherings were extremely stressful for Sarah. She was not an outgoing person, and she always felt awkward speaking to people. She spent her days trying not to be noticed by anyone. A gathering with strangers was fuel for her nightmares.

"As you know, my cousin Peter is in town," Paulk replied. "He's been holding secret house meetings across Rome, and he asked us to attend one tonight. I would host the gathering, but I knew preparations would be difficult for you. I agreed for us to visit him at the home of Nahum and his wife. You remember where they live. It's not far. Several people will meet with us, and we should take food to contribute."

"Oh no you don't," Sarah said. "I know what cousin you're talking about. He's a follower of the one they call Jesus of Nazareth. He was one of his actual disciples. We aren't going anywhere near Peter. Do you know what might happen if they see us with him? What if they discover Peter is our relative? Forget it, Paulk. It's too risky to gather with those people. We're not going." Sarah sucked in a desperate breath before she continued. "People say horrible things about them. I've heard these people drink blood and eat flesh. Possessed people do that, Paulk. They also greet one another with a kiss. And who knows what else? The authorities could throw us in prison or even have us executed if they think we're his followers. Just last week I overheard a lady at the market say that the Romans were lighting Christians on fire and parading them around in private gardens like human torches. That could be us, Paulk. And for what? Just to associate with some dead Jewish radical?"

Thort sat at the kitchen table with his legs crossed, grinning. Sometimes he wished these useless clay beings could see his face, so he could laugh openly and scorn them. Holding the butt of his dagger with his jet-black thumb, Thort spun the blade as he listened to

Sarah's delightful pleadings. The assignment was a genuine gift from Hell Ops. It was almost like being on holiday. Paulk and Sarah's demise required minimal effort, mere babysitting.

Thort had already sealed their souls to darkness and death.

He rolled his eyes. *This assignment is a waste of my time. Can I get a slight challenge? I don't even need a strategy. They eat every lie right out of my hand like starving dogs begging for scraps. I could spend my limitless expertise on much more important missions for the kingdom. These fools already waste their days arguing and irritating each other. There's no threat here. Anyone from Hell Ops can see that. As entertaining as it is to watch them suffer and fail, can I move on already?*

Thort had spent the last several years planting seeds of fear, deceit, panic, and hopelessness in Paulk and Sarah. His lies had riddled their marriage with miscommunication, hurt, and resentment. Watching his plans come together was always amusing, but Thort had become complacent. There was no challenge to his assignments, no danger, no threat of failure. He longed for a promotion. Surely, Hell Ops would assign him to a whole territory soon. He deserved it, after all. Had he not proven himself? He had tied hundreds of souls to Hell, eternal death, and destruction. His reputation was renowned.

I was sure we would see some action after they crucified Jesus, he thought. *That riled up a few of his followers. Unfortunately, it didn't last long enough to have any real fun. I could make a short order of one of those disciples if Hell Ops would throw me a bone. Figures I wouldn't get to taste any of that disillusionment with my pathetic assignments. Of course not. I get weak, half-dead toys to play with. Fear, depression, and anxiety.* Thort spat on the ground in disgust. *How original.*

Thort's manipulative seeds of deception had sprung up like thick, choking weeds. Sarah had swallowed his lies and accepted fear without question. He had hoped a more challenging weapon would be required, but he was wrong. Fear had crippled her. *Boring,* Thort scoffed.

Paulk felt a hint of sympathy for Sarah, but he would never show it. Walking home from work, he had mulled over his concerns in his mind. Sarah was right about one thing: gathering with his cousin and his followers was dangerous. Anything could go wrong. He had talked himself out of the idea until he walked through the door. It was so odd. The words just shot out of his mouth before he knew what was happening. Now that he had mentioned it to Sarah, they had to go, didn't they? There was a lot at stake. Meeting Peter was unwise, but something was pulling at him. What was his cousin preaching? Why was his message so important? Whatever it was, they were willing to be martyred for it. Before he had time to over-think it, Paulk blurted out his orders. "We're going! Be ready to leave here at dusk."

Slimy mucous shot out of Thort's left nostril as he snorted in shock. His dagger fell to the floor as he lost focus on its spinning. Thort glared at Paulk with disbelief and hatred. Slamming his mighty black fist down on the table, he leaped to his feet. "Absolutely not! I know that, Peter. He is one of Jesus's apostles. If Hell Ops had given him to me, we wouldn't even be having this conversation, but they didn't. I can't control what happens with Peter, but I have control over the two of you. You're not going."

He looked over at Sarah, who was cowering in the chair by the fire, not saying a word.

Oh, no, I'm not going down like Sphazo, he thought. *Hell Ops assigned him to that disciple, James. He lost part of his scalp over that fiasco. The deplorable actions of other demons won't be my downfall. I won't allow my human assignments anywhere near a disciple of Jesus.*

Reminding himself that just a few moments ago he was pleading for some real action, a devious grin spread across Thort's face. "Well, looky here. I may have fun with you two after all. I won't get my hopes up too much, of course. You're both pathetic, and I won't need to pull out the reserve weapons. Fear works perfectly with you every time."

Thort considered his angle. He could always play on uncertainty and discouragement. Sarah was the obvious target. He fixed his eyes on her like a morsel of food to be devoured. Slithering out of his chair, Thort creeped up behind Sarah. The words dripped off his dark tongue like thick, putrid syrup. "Drink up, Deary. Remember who you are: a nobody. You've nothing to offer to anyone. If you were important, they would come to you. No need to leave this house. What if something terrible happens to Paulk or you? If he became injured and couldn't work, you both would starve. What if he died? You would be a widow forever. No one takes care of widows. Think about it, Sarah. Nothing's worth risking your lives for, is there?"

Sarah wept quietly, hunched over in her chair. Defeat wrapped around her like a heavy wool shawl. Fear moved in. She could feel it, like bile bubbling up from her throat. She knew where this was going. Sarah sighed, threw her head back, and sucked in a deep breath of sorrow. Her heart tightened in her chest as a panic attack loomed. The episodes were always similar, but this one was moving fast. She could feel it overtaking her. It would take several days for her to function normally again. She could not set foot outside of the house, much less meet with other people that night. The room closed in on her. The risk was so senseless. Paulk couldn't make her go. She would refuse.

After Thort finished weaving his web of deception, he opened his eyes and stepped back from Sarah like an artist stepping back from his masterpiece. He sensed the lies sinking into her spirit like the barbed hooks on a fishing spear. Thort stepped to the side, holding his hand out in a mocking invitation. He knew Sarah would soon retreat to the bedroom in defeat. She would stay there. This would all be over.

Sarah's bed beckoned her like a best friend. Time to disappear and be alone. She wanted to forget about Paulk, Peter, and the meeting. She didn't care if she ever met another person.

Sarah shot her husband a disparaging look and then stood to walk to the bedroom. Instead, her knees buckled, dumping her back down into the chair. A look of confusion spread across her brow. Staring at the floor in wonder, she took two deep breaths. A moment passed. She realized the dark was not closing in on her anymore. She could still focus on Paulk across the room. Each breath seemed to release the tightness in her chest. Puzzled, she sat up straight. What was happening? This was new.

Thort cast his dismissive glance from the bedroom back at Sarah. There was something peculiar. Her countenance didn't seem quite right. Instead of cowering, Sarah was gathering herself. Thort didn't recognize her demeanor. He leaned down over her. "What are you doing? Did you not hear me?" He snapped his long, knotted fingers beside her ear. Nothing. "What's wrong with you? Have you lost your spiritual hearing?" Thort was so surprised, he wondered if he were hallucinating. "What do you think you're doing? You're a coward. You can't even think for yourself. When you try, you always make the wrong choices. You're going to regret this. Nothing will go well for you or your husband tonight. Hear me now."

Fear had always worked like a charm with Sarah. What was going on? She had gotten out of his hands so quickly. One minute, she was under his spell. The next, she had effortlessly shaken the chains off. Thort shook his head in disbelief. He had not expected this at all.

Sarah's eyes were clear. She wiped her nose on her apron, stood up, and looked at Paulk.

Her husband stared back in amazement. Paulk had expected her to leave, retreating to the stronghold of their bedroom.

Sarah made direct eye contact with Paulk. She was not weeping. She stood strong and in control. "I'll be ready," she said. "We will take some fresh bread and figs."

Paulk's mouth hung open in disbelief. Then, gathering himself, he smiled. In his spirit, Paulk felt an unexplainable peace. He could tell Sarah felt the same way. Paulk stood and followed Sarah into the bedroom to wash up and get ready.

Thort was dumbfounded and furious. What had gotten into these two pawns? He realized he had better clear his head and refocus before any such meeting with Peter. Maybe a drink would help. He could make a quick trip to the Bar and Chain if he made it back in time for the meeting. Someone at headquarters might have helpful insight. Had he missed something in the regional briefing? There was one way to find out. Storming out of the house, Thort flew back to the Brimstone Bar and Chain.

Paulk and Sarah made the journey to Nahum's house later that evening. Sitting at a long table, they shared a meal. When the food was gone, Peter stood and gathered everyone's attention. "First, I want to extend my gratitude for hosting such a lovely meal. It's an honor to come together with you tonight. Nahum, thank you for your hospitality." Peter raised his wineglass in honor. "I see some fresh faces at the table tonight. Please let me introduce two of them." Peter motioned for Paulk and Sarah to stand.

After a brief hesitation, Sarah stood beside her husband, feeling every eye in the room on her.

"It brings my heart much joy to welcome my cousin, Paulk, and his wife, Sarah."

The others responded with smiles and words of welcome. Nahum lifted his glass. "We're so glad you came." Sarah's face reddened as she took her seat.

After dinner, the group listened eagerly as Peter recounted a few stories from the time he had spent with Jesus. He told them about Jesus's prayer over him and the other disciples just before His death. Then Peter recited the prayer from memory and explained how Jesus intended this prayer for them as well. He also told them that eternal life was real and available. Jesus sent a Helper to Earth after he left. This Spirit would live within them to reveal the love Jesus had for His Father and the love the Father returned to His Son.

Evening spilled over into night. The stories fascinated the group. They spent at least two hours asking Peter questions about Jesus and His teachings. He was gracious to answer, but then his attention became fixed on Paulk and Sarah.

"I have set aside some time to pray for each of you here tonight. As I mentioned earlier, the promises I have told you about are His gift to you. All Jesus asks for in return is your complete surrender. You can trade your life for His. Your life will pass away, but His life is eternal. You may choose life with Jesus or return home just as you are. The choice is risky, and it will cost you everything, but the return on your investment will have more value than all the gold and silver in the world."

Peter paused for a moment to give the people time to consider his offer. Lifting his head, he closed his eyes and asked the Holy Spirit to enter every willing heart in the room. The Spirit accepted the invitation. Jesus added souls to the Kingdom that night, including the souls of Paulk and Sarah.

Reluctance and fear fell away from them, and light shone where the darkness had been. Death became eternal life, and old things became new.

The Holy Spirit orchestrated Paulk and Sarah's attendance that night. What took place after Peter's prayer would alter eternity for thousands upon thousands of souls. The first generation of a great lineage stepped into their original design. Paulk and Sarah didn't know it, but their journey of faith was only the start of the divine promise, provision, and purpose they would experience.

Thort sat perched on the rooftop, dazed and confused. It felt like someone had hit him over the head with a mallet. He tried to remember how many drinks he had had at the Bar and Chain. He had not been gone long. His plan had been to return before Paulk and Sarah departed for the gathering with Peter. Unfortunately, Thort had lost track of time. He had gotten carried away by recounting his most recent victories to a lowly demon. Self-glorification always calmed his nerves. Thort had flown in just in time to witness Paulk and Sarah returning home from their meeting.

They had gone unsupervised.

"Idiot," he said, cursing himself. He could not believe Sarah had left the house and gone to a meeting. That act alone was against her nature. The roots of her anxiety must not have grown as deep as he suspected.

Thort wondered how long Paulk and Sarah had been away. He knew nothing about the details of the meeting. *Well, they're back now,* he thought. *I must keep a close eye on things. It won't be too difficult to draw them back into my snare. It was just one night and one stupid gathering. Nothing compared to a lifetime of scheming and deception."*

* * *

ONE AFTERNOON MONTHS after Paulk and Sarah's transformation, Nahum visited their home.

As the three of them sat at the small table drinking wine, Nahum explained that Peter had requested a private late-night meeting with Paulk. He asked that Paulk return to his home to receive a message from his cousin. He was to come alone and see that no one followed him.

"Is everything okay?" Paulk asked, his eyes wide with alarm. "Is Peter in danger? Why has he requested this meeting in secret?"

"Peter is fine. You don't need to worry about his safety. He told me you would ask a lot of questions." Nahum chuckled. "He also told me to tell you he would answer your questions at the meeting. Just be there."

"He will be there," Sarah assured him.

Surprised, Paulk looked over at his wife. Then he reached across the table and placed his hand on Nahum's shoulder and smiled. "She's right. You tell Peter I'll be there."

The next night, Paulk arrived at Nahum's front door, and Nahum opened it before Paulk could knock. Checking to see that no one had followed Paulk, Nahum ushered him inside and then led him toward the back of the house.

Paulk found Peter leaning against the hearth of a small fireplace in the back room. A huge smile broke across his face as Nahum and Paulk entered, and he stepped forward to greet them. "Cousin, it's so wonderful to see you." He embraced Paulk and kissed him on the cheek. "I must admit, I hardly recognize you from a few months ago. The Spirit has transformed you. You look amazing."

Paulk stood taller now, and the look in his eyes no longer conveyed worry and hopelessness. There was kindness and strength in his presence. Peter was thankful, and he soaked it in. Then he motioned to Paulk. "Sit with me here by the fire. How's Sarah?"

"I can't tell you how good we are, cousin. Where would I start?"

Peter smiled. "I understand, and it overjoyed my heart to see you delivered from bondage and walking in the peace of everlasting life."

"Nahum told me not to worry, but I'm curious to know why you called me to meet you in secret. It's so late, and Sarah is home alone. What could be so important?"

Peter paused and prayed a short, silent prayer before he replied. "Jesus revealed many things while he walked with us. He told stories. He performed miracles. Jesus was a walking, breathing example of what he came to give us here on Earth. He even warned us about going back to the Father, but we didn't have ears to hear. When they crucified Him, we weren't ready. Suddenly, He was just gone. We had abandoned everything to follow Him, so we didn't know where to go or what to do. When we saw Him the next time, He gave us a promise, and He asked us to wait. You and Sarah now understand how important that waiting was. He sent His Spirit to live within us."

"Yes, I know these things." Paulk was being patient, but what did that have to do with this meeting?

"My cousin, you and your generations to follow will each need this precious gift. Walking with the Spirit is important in your daily life. It will also be crucial for completing the destiny the Father has determined for you. He has chosen your family lineage for a special task, but it is going to require you to follow Him and trust His Spirit."

"A special task?" Paulk asked. "Why my family?"

"Only the Father knows why He has chosen you, Paulk. It's my belief that He foresees the fruits of His nature flourishing in your family line." Peter could tell that Paulk was struggling to understand what he had told him, so he grabbed Paulk by the shoulders and looked deep into his eyes. "He knows the beginning from the end. All I can say is, He chose you."

Peter turned and removed a rolled-up scroll from his bag. Then he turned back to Paulk. "Do you remember John? You may have heard me refer to him as 'the beloved.'"

"Yes, I do."

"John spent a lot of time with Jesus both before His crucifixion and after. He has remained diligent to record what he heard and experienced. It's miraculous what the Holy Spirit brings to his remembrance. We now have written accounts of Jesus's sermons, miracles, and prophecies."

Paulk fought back a yawn as he tried to focus. "That is all very exciting, Peter, but it's so late. What does any of this have to do with me?"

"When Jesus appeared to us after his death, He revealed many signs and wonders," Peter explained. "We didn't record some of those messages in our public writings." Peter held the scroll in front of Paulk's face. "Jesus commissioned John to write a sacred message. This manuscript contains that message. This scroll is to remain unopened and unread. Your family lineage is being charged with protecting this sacred manuscript until you receive further instruction."

Paulk was now wide awake. "You can't be serious. Is that all the information you can give me? Do you know what he wrote on the scroll?"

"The Holy Spirit instructed John to give this manuscript to me. Now that same Spirit has instructed me to give it to you, my cousin. I know my days of serving Him on this Earth are few, so I need you to listen. Take this home, keep it in a safe place, and don't open it. You must resist the temptation to read it or tamper with it. This manuscript will remain protected by your family until a messenger from Heaven arrives with further instructions. Pass the manuscript and the story of its origin to the next generation. Each of your descendants must understand the importance of this divine charge." Peter handed the manuscript to Paulk, smiled, then blessed his cousin.

Paulk stared down at the scroll, his mind swirling. *What is this thing? Why would the Lord choose me? All I'm supposed to do is keep it?* He had so many questions, but Peter offered no additional information. Paulk looked back at Peter and smiled. "I don't understand it all, but I guess I don't have to. I trust my Lord in everything, and I'll obey and trust Him in this."

Peter was proud. He hugged his cousin again.

Neither of the men knew it, but that hug would be their last on this side of Heaven. Paulk tucked the manuscript under his outer garment. On the way out, he thanked Nahum for setting up the meeting.

As Paulk made his way back home, in the distance he saw two Roman soldiers with torches walking toward him. He spotted a hay cart next to the horse stable and hid behind it. The guards didn't notice him as they walked by, arguing over a bet.

Paulk opened the front door to his home and shuffled inside, hoping not to wake Sarah. As he kicked off his sandals, she appeared from the bedroom.

"You didn't expect me to just sleep with your 'middle of the night' secret meeting happening, did you?"

Paulk walked over to the fireplace and threw another log on the smoldering coals. He pulled the scroll from under his tunic.

Sarah looked at it, her eyes glistening with curiosity. "So, I take it you got to see Peter? What do you have there?"

Paulk looked up at her and grinned. "Yes, I saw him. It was tricky, though. There were guards posted all around town. Nahum insisted we hold the meeting in secret, and now I know why."

Sarah tilted her head. "Why is that? What could be so important?"

He held up the scroll. "This. This is so important."

"I see it, but I don't know what it is." Then she realized Paulk's hand was shaking. "Why are you shaking? Are you okay?" Sarah asked.

Tears filled Paulk's eyes, and he shook his head without speaking. He had not realized how much his adrenaline was pumping.

"Come. Let's sit down."

He recalled the details of his meeting with Peter and explained to Sarah the instructions that he had received from his cousin. "We're to preserve it and keep it in a safe place. We will pass it down to our children, and they'll do the same to theirs. I don't know how long it will be in our possession. Peter told me to pass the manuscript to each generation until they receive further instruction."

Sarah's mouth fell open as Paulk spoke. Her mind was a blur of questions. "Wait, for what? Who wrote the manuscript? Why is it so secret? Have you read it?"

Paulk shook his head. "No, I haven't read it. I know that the Apostle John wrote it, but I don't know what it contains. Why did God choose us? I don't know that either, but I do trust Peter, and after the past two months, I believe I'm learning to hear and trust the Holy Spirit. I'm very confident about this, Sarah."

Sarah stood up and placed her hands on her husband's chest, looking into his gray eyes. "God has been faithful to us. Why should we doubt him now?" She took the scroll from Paulk's hand. "I guess we need to find a safe spot for this."

Thort paced outside Paulk and Sarah's home. *How could I have been so reckless? I should never have allowed these wretched souls access to someone like Peter. I don't know what's happening to me.*

Thort had been hyper focused on Sarah over the past few months. He thought she would prove to be the lower-hanging fruit of the two. Her fear and anxiety had always been his foothold. If he could regain control over Sarah, he would have them both. So far, crowd anxiety had not worked. She left the house daily for chores and fellowship. She even had new people she called friends. That complicated things. Fear for her safety had fallen flat. She didn't seem to believe or care about that anymore. Thort had attempted to wake her in the middle of the night, when his lies proved more potent, but she ignored him, rolled over, and went back to sleep.

Confusion and frustration overwhelmed him. Now, to add insult to injury, Paulk had slipped out of his clutches and attended yet another meeting with Peter. Thort rubbed his hands together, still pacing. *Who cares what that pathetic fool is doing? He only wishes he were important, like Peter. Look at him, running around like he is on a secret mission.* Thort turned to face the house. "You don't even know what they wrote on that scroll! If you were such an important part of the plan, don't you think they would have told you what it was about?"

Four days after Paulk hugged his cousin, they arrested Peter and sentenced him to death. Even though Paulk knew Peter was now with his beloved Savior, the loss hung heavily on him. Nevertheless, he knew he needed to focus on the instructions Peter had given him concerning the manuscript. Paulk had commissioned a trusted brother to help him seal the scroll. It might be many years before they received further instruction. The scroll needed to be protected. He and Sarah placed the scroll inside a bronze cylinder and sealed it with beeswax. Then they placed the cylinder into a clay capsule and sealed the lid by firing it seven times around the edge. The container was safe yet simple and unassuming.

That evening, Paulk and Sarah sat at their small table in front of the fireplace. The manuscript lay in its protective urn on the table beside Paulk.

As Sarah waited for the lentils in the soup to soften, so she could serve dinner, she cleared her throat. "There's something else I've been meaning to share with you. Things have been rather busy."

Paulk chuckled as he grabbed two small bowls from the shelf above the fireplace. "That would be an understatement."

Sarah looked at Paulk. "Doesn't it feel strange to think about our future generations when we haven't even been married long? It's just the two of us."

"It felt strange when Peter talked about it, yes. But at least now we know that the Lord will bless us with at least one child to carry on the family lineage."

Sarah stood up and walked over to Paulk, touching him on the shoulder. "Yes, my dear husband, now we know." She touched her belly with her other hand.

Paulk leaped to his feet, knocking his stool over. He grabbed Sarah by the shoulders as a tear spilled from her right eye, then threw his arms around her. As her feet left the floor and he spun her around, joyful laughter rolled out of his chest. God had been so faithful to him and Sarah. The first of His promises was to be a child.

Thort stood huddled in a dark corner away from the fireplace. He was in a state of shock, anger raging through his entire being. He spat on the floor and hissed. "Cursed be the both of you, and cursed be your offspring. You don't know who I am. Thort doesn't lose assignments to the enemy. I'll defile this family. You will cower again in fear. I will take your land, your home, and everything else you possess. You will fear for your lives and for the life of that unborn child. If I play my cards right, Sarah, that pathetic body of yours won't even carry that child to term. I'll assault your mind and spirit until you fall in line with my plan. I'll bring intimidation, betrayal, and unforgiveness, which will lead you back into stress, anxiety, and depression. I'll cause your newfound friends to spit on you and accuse you of blasphemy. Doubt and fear will increase. I curse any peace you may think you have found. Jesus, I know, and Peter, I know, but I won't take orders from the likes of you. You've been coasting, but that stops today. If you think I'll allow myself to be humiliated, you are mistaken. You've messed with the wrong demon."

After Thort's oath that day, he threw everything he had at Paulk and Sarah. He pursued every tactic he had promised, yet the Holy Spirit remained strong in the young couple. Fear had no fertile ground in which to grow. Peace and dependence on the Holy Spirit flourished in their home. Thort's death threats had failed too. In fact, Paulk and Sarah said they welcomed death over the denial of their Savior.

Thort's frustration mounted as Paulk and Sarah introduced many other households of Jews, and even some Gentiles, to Jesus.

Sarah gave birth later that same year to a son. Paulk named him Nebaioth. To Thort's horror, he grew up to know and love his Savior. The Spirit gifted him with the same peace and joy that the Lord had instilled in his parents. When Nebaioth was of age, Paulk shared with his son the story of the sacred manuscript and the instructions from his cousin, Peter.

Thort remained on assignment, but it felt as if someone had pulled his fangs, and his venom had no potency. His schemes could find no footing. If he gained any momentum at all, a repentant heart and a humble spirit seized it. Paulk and Sarah's home was a hostile environment for Thort. For the first time, he tasted defeat from clay beings.

When Paulk and Sarah passed into eternity, Thort knew he would have to answer for his losses, but he also breathed a sigh of relief. Finally, it was over.

CHAPTER 3
THE UNLIKELY ASSISTANT

Thort stood outside of the gate to Hell Ops in a daze. His meeting with Chief Despot could have been worse. The chief had gone light on discipline considering Thort's failures with Paulk and Sarah. Thort had been hoping to weasel his way into a different assignment altogether, but Hell Ops had other plans. They were giving him an opportunity to redeem himself, keeping him assigned to the family's wretched fruit. The chief was furious to find that Thort had been absent during Paulk and Sarah's initial meeting with Peter. Thankfully, he had not demanded to know where Thort had been because there was no appropriate excuse. Chief Despot didn't even bother asking Thort for details. When a demon brought forth a representation of true events, Hell Ops didn't give it much merit.

Thort's current assignment was straightforward. He hoped sealing the eternal fate of this generation would persuade Hell Ops to overlook his previous folly. All he needed was a fresh focus and renewed vigor.

Shake it off. You've got this, he told himself as he shuffled away from the gate. *It's easy. Don't get rattled now. It was an off assignment.*

You're bad—terrible, in fact. You always have been, and you always will be.

Catching a whiff of rancid garbage, Thort's attention was drawn across the street to the Brimstone Bar and Chain. He wondered if he could slip in under the radar and grab some grub and a quick drink. Maybe he could catch up with his fellow demons without having to explain himself. He hoped the rumor of his failures hadn't rippled through the ranks already.

He opened the door to the bar and slipped inside. Almost on cue, Sorpine and Blastus locked eyes with him from across the room, glaring at him with a hateful sense of knowing. Sorpine and Blastus knew. If they hadn't recognized him before, he was on their radar now. Blastus was the principality who ruled over the region where Peter had ministered. Hell Ops had given him special permissions to use dark forces to lean on the region. His mission was to prevent an uprising of faith at all costs.

"He has a lot of nerve showing his face in here," Blastus seethed. "That waste of space is lucky I don't dismember him right here and feed him to the hounds."

"Eh, not worth the effort," Sorpine said, waving his hand in dismissal. "Remember, it was just one lowly couple. It's not like they were key targets or anything. Let it go, Blastus."

"Yeah, well, he'd better get his house in order. He won't make a fool out of me. I've worked too hard in that region. Much has been required since they nailed Jesus to that tree. I have far too much invested there to risk further penetration because of the stupidity and ignorance of one demon." Blastus cast another glare at Thort before he turned back to his drink.

Thort was thankful when Blastus broke his stare. For a moment, he thought there might be a confrontation, and then there would be no flying under the radar at the Bar and Chain that day or any other day.

Just as he had expected, Thort found Fluto hanging out at the bar. He was deep in conversation with two other demons. Thort eased toward them, taking a seat at one of the empty tables. He didn't want to interrupt Fluto since he had nothing to brag about. He knew Fluto would try to humiliate him just for kicks.

The leftover dip tray from the last patron was still on the table in front of him. He swatted the flies away. There was no telling how long it had been sitting there, but he would take his chances. A few broken chips were left in the basket, and they would satisfy until he could order a drink.

Before he could wave down the bar wench, Fluto snuck up behind him, dug his talons into the sides of Thort's rib cage, and yelled into his right ear. Thort jolted and braced himself to keep from falling off his seat. He would never get used to Fluto's unnerving greetings. Fluto cackled like a hyena as he stood over Thort.

"Seems like I've heard some things about you. Let me think. What was it?" Fluto rolled his eyes toward the ceiling and placed his finger to his lips, pretending to think. "Oh yeah, that's right. Demotion! Demotion might be in your future. Is that true, Thort? It can't be." Sarcasm dripped from his tongue like sap from a pine tree.

Thort knew better than to engage with such condescending humiliation. He shoved a chip loaded with Graft into his mouth and chewed. He gagged, then choked it down to keep from spewing it out of his mouth. The leftover dip had been sitting out too long and was rancid.

Realizing that Thort would not take the bait, Fluto decided that if he couldn't entertain himself by chiding his colleague, he could at least strut his own accomplishments to rub it in. He took a swig of his drink and then leaned in close to Thort's ear. "I don't mean to brag, but my current assignment from Hell Ops may just get me promoted *again*. Yep, I see another black stripe in my immediate future."

Thort swallowed the contents of his mouth with a disgusted gulp. "Fantastic. I'm sure you'll tell me all about it," he said, rolling his eyes.

Fluto squared his shoulders with pride and walked around to the chair opposite Thort. He tucked his cloak behind him and straddled the chair. "My pathetic human assignment knows only one god, and his name is greed. The guy cherishes his earthly belongings and is always longing for more. It's important that he always has just a little more than his neighbors. In a stroke of genius, I encouraged him to lie and cheat his fellow business partner, so he could take a larger portion of the profits for himself. So far, I've found that his taste for material wealth knows no bounds. Easiest human assignment I've ever had. It's as easy as playing a tune on my flute as I march my assignments straight to Hell, one deceived wretch at a time."

Fluto paused and relished in his glory. He loved hearing himself repeat the stories of conquest. "Anyway, enough about me. Unless, of course, you'd like to hear more." A spiteful grin spread across his face as he pointed his mug at Thort. "How is it going with you these days? You're looking a little pale. You feel alright?"

Thort shrugged. "Eh, I've been better. My new human assignments are descendants of the leeches I lived with before. They make me want to vomit, just like their parents did. I can't seem to get Hell Ops to throw me a bone. You'd think they would recognize my previous accomplishments and reassign me to something more important, but no. They're intent on assigning me to these married couples. They don't seem to realize that when there are two of them, the enemy is twice as likely to be in their midst, disrupting my every tactic. These two are worse than their ancestors. They're following the same narrow road as their parents and grandparents, blinded to any distractions I might bring. All the while they seem to experience this nightmare of a curse they call 'joy.'"

Thort looked to see if that word registered on Fluto's face. It didn't. "Are you familiar with this 'joy' thing?" Thort continued. "There's no such feeling or experience in Hell that I can identify it with. Whatever it is, it seems to grow in them like some supernatural gift from the enemy. They draw strength from it, and it makes it hard to penetrate their souls with anything else. Fear doesn't seem to stand a chance when it encounters joy. It always seems to manifest when they talk about the resurrected Jesus. They meet with other sect members with no fear of being caught. I've planted the seeds of mistrust, gossip, slander, and even envy, but it's like I'm sowing into shallow, rocky soil or something. Nothing has yielded even a morsel for Hell's consumption. I think that joy must be a secret weapon from the enemy that I have received no intelligence on. Having to listen to them talk, smile, and laugh makes me want to puke."

Fluto held up his hands and chuckled. "There's no way they can be all that happy, pure, holy, and unstained. You've missed something somewhere, but that isn't surprising. There aren't many of us who can succeed all the time."

Thort rolled his eyes. "I don't know what I was expecting from you. It's not like you would ever be helpful."

"Helpful?" Fluto put his hand over his heart, faking surprise. "Thort, that hurts. How could you say that? When have I not been helpful to you?"

Thort knew better than to respond and draw more mocking sarcasm from Fluto. "Just forget it."

Fluto thought for a minute. It went against his nature to offer advice or assistance to his fellow demon, but he decided there wasn't much at stake. Thort was on the descent in the ranks and posed no threat of competition for him. He cleared his throat and assumed a more serious tone, "Look, there's always a crack somewhere, and that's all you need to gain a foothold. You know, from there, work toward the stronghold. What are some methods you may not have considered? You can always set more obstacles before them during the day. You said they were blind to distraction, but have you tried to convince them to do some good things outside of what the enemy has commissioned them to do? If it were me, I would exhaust them with 'worthy' causes. Steal time away from the enemy's work, and convince them to say yes to every supposed good deed. Cause them to become overwhelmed and confused. Before you know it, they'll be ready to walk away from it all. Whatever that 'joy' thing is, you can suck it dry with trivial busy work. Lure their focus away."

"I've tried that and more, Fluto. You don't know what I've been up against," Thort shook his head, his exasperation growing.

Fluto smirked. "Tell you what, loser. How about I take a brief field trip and shadow you for a day or two? My human assignments babysit themselves in misery regardless of my presence. I suppose I could entertain myself by watching you flail around for a bit. Maybe you can learn how things get done around here. You seem to have lost your touch."

"By all means! Someone else needs to see the rock I'm up against with these people. I can't find a crack. As much as it pains me, I'll take any advice you have to offer."

With that the two left the bar. Fluto was looking forward to this. His current assignment had become quite boring, and this diversion would give him an opportunity to toy with Thort, pointing out his every failure and possibly even throwing in a trick or two to trip him up, just for laughs.

CHAPTER 4
DURANE AND AMIRA

Joy never seeks a hiding place.

As Thort and Fluto approached the home of Durane and Amira, Thort pointed at three young boys playing in the dirt patch behind the hut. "Those three little brats are the offspring of my current human assignments. The enemy saw this couple deliver not one, not two, but three descendants at once. This should have taken the life of at least one of them, if not all. Instead, here they are, healthy and whole, playing in the dirt and being trained up in the same way as the ones who came before them. More headache for me, times three."

Thort and Fluto spent the afternoon observing Amira and the boys as they interacted together. Thort thought about what subversive tactics might work best to interrupt the family and change their focus. It wouldn't be too difficult to change their sense of purpose. It would look small now, but the trajectory would expand over time.

Hell Ops had trained Thort to employ a sense of hopelessness to turn assignments and their family members to despair and ultimate darkness. This family seemed content, which didn't benefit him.

Thort overheard Amira speaking to the boys that afternoon about joy. He didn't understand it, and he could not comprehend how it brought such strength to his human assignments. He and Fluto assumed it must be the opposite of hopelessness, which was something Thort did understand. If joy was the root of their peace and happiness, his top priority was to disrupt it.

Durane was Nebaioth and Deborah's son. The authorities had imprisoned Nebaioth for most of Durane's life growing up. They arrested him for teaching about Jesus Christ's death and resurrection. The authorities arrested many Christians, as such people were now called, for spreading the so-called "Good News." They faced long prison sentences with little hope of release.

After their father's imprisonment, Durane's mother, Deborah, became the biggest influence in Durane and his brother's life. Durane had grown up witnessing the supernatural joy that his mother showed as she raised her children as a single parent. Given her circumstances, she could have lived a life full of anxiety and depression, focusing on her hardships. After receiving her salvation and being filled with the Spirit, however, her joy overshadowed any hopelessness that she ever felt.

During his childhood, a family friend had taught Durane how to smelt and work with precious metals. After his marriage to Amira, he had found an opportunity to use his skill on the island of Cyprus. Following the destruction of the temple in Jerusalem a hundred years earlier, many people from Durane's country had moved there. One of his cousins, John Mark, had even traveled there with his uncle, Barnabas. After Barnabas passed away, John Mark stayed to carry on the ministry. It was nice for Durane and Amira to have local family connections on whom they could rely.

Early that evening, Durane stepped through the door to his small two-room house. It took him over an hour to walk home from work each day, so by the time he made it there, daylight had already given way to the evening. His muscles were sore, and he felt a dull ache in his back as he shrugged off his outer garment. His arm still stung from the burn he had sustained that morning at work. He looked down at his filthy feet. Another blister was beginning on the heel of his foot. His left sandal had never fit right. He would have to see if Amira had any more salve that he could use to soothe it. It had been another long, hard day at the silver smelter. He was thankful the Cyprians had moved the operation several miles from the mine after a huge earthquake. He praised the Lord that he didn't have to work at the mine like many of his friends did. That work never got easier. It was the same tedious job, hauling the same heavy load to the same drop-off point for twelve long hours day after day. That work wore on the body fast. Durane realized God had directed his steps, even as a young boy, toward his trade. He had a natural talent for the craft. Durane was thankful, but his days were still long, full of hard work, and the journey to and from work added to his exhaustion.

He looked over at Amira, who was rocking back and forth, humming to herself as she mended one of his tattered tunics. Durane took a moment to admire her silhouette in the candlelight, noting how beautiful she was. Every day it reminded him of how God had miraculously brought her through the pregnancy and birth of their triplet sons. To his knowledge, no woman had ever survived the birth of triplets, nor had all the babies been born alive and healthy. God had been so faithful to him. Amira was a good wife, and their home was a loving place. He could hear the boys out back. It sounded like they were playing that stick game again. He couldn't remember what they called it. It was almost time for them to come in and clean up. It would be dark in no time, but Durane believed it was best to let the boys release as much energy as possible before they all crowded into their small home for the night.

Amira looked up at him and smiled. "How was your walk home, dear?"

"The great thing about my walk home each day is that it gives me time to clear my head and talk to the Lord about what is weighing on me," Durane replied. "Today I was praying for Jessie and Matthew and our other Christian friends who remain in prison. Sometimes that can seem so hopeless. The Lord reminded me that His presence is with them even there. I remember my mother telling my brother, Michael, and me the same thing when they threw our father in prison. She would say, 'In His presence there is joy, and each day that joy brings strength to everyone who believes in Him.' To be honest, I didn't understand that kind of joy as a child. I couldn't imagine being happy about being in jail or happy about having to raise a family alone. Today I realized that I often think back to the difficulties that my mother lived through with joy in her heart. When work gets hard or I think things aren't fair, I'm reminded to be thankful. I have you to come home to, and we have a warm home and food on the table. I also have two good feet to walk to and from work. That reminds me; I need some of that salve you made up for my blisters."

Thort had grown weary of all of this "joy" talk. It was time to make a desperate move. What would Fluto think of all of this? Now was his opportunity while he had the couple focused on Durane's blisters. "You know, you should be *doing* more," he said. "There are so many opportunities out there for the two of you to serve your God. You haven't earned the right to call yourself blessed yet, have you? You don't deserve what you have, but you should at least try harder. Don't you want God to be proud of you?"

Thort knew the simple task of suggestion could go a long way. If he could pitch "good works" as a sort of currency, he could have them busy trying to earn the enemy's favor and maintain their salvation. This maneuver was tricky. Thort had to be sure that he pointed them away from the enemy's assignments and toward tedious, time-consuming tasks that played to their sense of selfworth. If only he could convince these two that good works would earn them a place in the enemy's kingdom. Perhaps then he could steer them away from the enemy's real purpose for their lives.

Thort looked over at Fluto. "Like our training manual always says, sidetracked is always better than on track."

As Amira applied salve to Durane's foot, an idea popped into his head. "You know, maybe we should set aside a few nights a week to visit Jessie and Matthew at the prison. And not just them but all the inmates. I know nights are busy with the boys and all the house chores. Dinner and Old Testament lessons take up most of the evening, but I feel like we aren't doing enough. We could encourage them and pray with them. Even though it would be hard to fit it in, I think it's important that we take this on. It's a good idea, it would be a good work, and I'm sure they would appreciate it. I know it would make the Lord proud. Don't you think?"

Amira nodded without looking up as she considered Durane's idea. It sounded like a good thing, but she knew that committing to anything, even good things, without being led by the Holy Spirit may not be fruitful in the long run. If it wasn't God's direction, it could be draining and not bring life to either of them. She prayed in her spirit, and after a moment, she felt sure she had her answer.

"Durane, I miss Jessie and Matthew too. I think about them all the time and hope they're holding out well. I believe Jesus is with them right now, just like He's here with us. His joy brings them strength even tonight as they sit in their cell. When I close my eyes, I can see them worshiping God like Paul and Silas did in prison. Matthew's sister stopped me at the market yesterday. She visited them last week and said she had never seen her brother so happy and full of joy. She said his countenance was bright, and he was so excited to tell her about the people he had gotten to pray with in prison. Jessie even spoke to one guard about Jesus and prayed for his daughter, who was born crippled. Neither of them had experienced hunger or thirst. In fact, Matthew said that the King's presence is always with them, and their physical needs are being met daily. Amazing!"

Amira finished with the bandage and then stood up and wiped her fingers on her apron. "Jessie and Matthew are in a different season of life. They're doing what God has called them to do, and He is providing for them while they do it. You and I are in our own season. God blessed us with three boys, and our commission right now is to bring them up to know God and to understand who He wants them to be. God has provided work for you that provides for our family, and I'm so thankful. We need to focus on what He has for us in this season and devote our attention and his resources toward that. It's enough. We're all so blessed not because of what we do but because He paid the price. All He wants in return is a relationship with us."

Amira paused, wanting to offer her husband a concession. "That said, what would you say about setting aside a day to visit Jessie and Matthew? We can take the boys and go as a family. It will be good for us to see what God is doing at the prison. It's important we set aside our lives for the purpose God has for us in this season."

Thort could feel the sweat pooling on his brow. Listening to this was hard enough, but listening under the judgment and condemnation of Fluto was even worse. He needed to show strength. "Oh, no you don't!" he shouted in the spirit realm, hoping to plant his ideas in whoever was the most vulnerable. "Look around you! Amira and the boys shouldn't even be here. He has given you so much, and you do nothing in return. You talk about being blessed. You should focus more on what you're *not* doing. What are you giving back to your God? When He recognizes how selfish you are, you'll lose everything. You owe your lives to Him. The least you can do to show your gratitude is to help other people." Thort looked over at Fluto and grinned, nodding for emphasis.

Fluto just sat there, waiting to see if any of Thort's words would find purchase.

Durane thought it through, considering what his wife had just said. He was still feeling a tinge of guilt for sitting in the comfort of his own home while his friends sat across town in a cold, filthy prison. Matthew's sister said they were fine and were being provided for, and in return, they were at least ministering to others in the jail. Durane was doing nothing. "I just want to feel like we're doing enough to serve Him. He has provided so much, and most days it feels like the only people we care about or focus on are living under this roof." He stood up and looked around.

Several minutes went by and Amira felt led by the Spirit not to say anything else but instead to let her words sink in. She trusted her husband to hear from the Spirit too. Eventually, he left the room and walked to the back of the house to change his clothes and clean up for dinner.

About a half hour later, Durane returned to the kitchen, resuming their conversation as if he had never left the room. "We must understand what God has entrusted us with. In this season of life, He has given us three healthy, growing boys to teach and raise in a godly home. Thank you for reminding me that our responsibilities here are our heavenly assignments. It's another reason that I love you so much." He placed his calloused hands upon Amira's shoulders. "As godly parents, our job is to ensure that we impart all the truths we have learned to our children, especially in these trying times. Our boys are ours to treasure, to teach, and to prepare for His return. This commission is crucial to the Kingdom. It's of utmost importance. We ensure that laughter and joy fill this household every day. Our children must know the strength that only the Holy Spirit can bring to them. There's much work to do to prepare for His return, but you're right. We must not take on tasks that keep us from our commission. I know God will equip us for everything He asks us to do. Thank you for your obedience to the Holy Spirit. Sometimes it's easy for me to think that all good things are God's things. I trust that our family will be up to any task He puts before us, and regardless of the circumstances, we will continue to serve Him."

His eyes wide, Thort turned to Fluto. "Now do you understand what I'm up against? How am I supposed to work with this? Hell Ops can't think I have any chance against souls like this. They draw on the enemy's Spirit, and the weapons supplied to us by Hell Ops are useless."

What Fluto had just seen and heard left him speechless. As he stared at Durane, he would not admit it to Thort, but he could think of no hellish response. "I'm glad my greedy merchant is eating at another table because you've got a real problem, my dark friend. I'm not sure what that 'joy' thing is, but I don't see any black stripes in your near future, pal. Perhaps you should brush up on the forty-seven-page chapter on misery in the manifest from Hell Ops again. Apparently, everything you ever thought you knew has slid out of that one good ear and made you useless. I know one thing: you best be luring those children into one of Hell Ops's false religions. If they grow up this strong and defiant, you'll be lucky to keep your head. Come to think of it, I'm not sure I should be seen associating with such a pathetic loser like you. If Hell Ops thinks I'm helping you, they'll assume I'm a failure too. I knew this was a bad idea. I have way too much at stake, and to be frank, I hope you fail. More glory for those of us who deserve it. Make sure your little pests stay as far away from my human assignments as possible. This day never happened. I don't want to associate with you in the bar or anywhere else. This dumpster fire is on you. I'm done with you!"

Fluto left before Thort could respond. Instead, he was left to ponder what he was going to do about these assignments from 'Heaven'. He felt the color fade out from his complexion. This was beyond humiliating, and he knew Fluto would throw him under the bus back at headquarters the first chance he got. His situation couldn't get any worse, or so he thought.

CHAPTER 5
JERUIT AND JANIS

There had been a recent shift in history. The Roman Emperor had decided to change its policy toward Christianity. An agreement known as the Edict of Milan gave Christianity legal status and a reprieve from the persecution that Christians had suffered under over the centuries. The Church had grown exponentially since the first apostles walked with Jesus. Now being a follower of Christ was legal.

Thort paid little attention to the business of the growing Church over the years. He had his hands full with the sixth generation of Paulk and Sarah's descendants. If only he could go back and intercept them before that first meeting with Peter, the ensuing centuries could have been different. He had been paying the price ever since.

Generation after generation had been an impenetrable fortress of failure for him. Thort had spent the last 250 years hurling darts of misery and despair at the family. He had wielded the weapons of depression, distraction, anger, confusion, and even dabbled with the idea of murder and suicide. The family members had countered every offensive strike with love and peace. Not to mention, joy had been a liability in every one of his assignment households since he first landed on the roof of Paulk's miserable mud hut. Even after years of witnessing it, he didn't understand the incredible strength that joy brought to believers. Thort could find no cracks, no holes, just the sure foundation of the enemy's presence in which the insufferable believers took comfort. None of that mattered, though. He couldn't give up. This time his arrows would hit their targets. This generation would make the turn. They had to—for his sake.

Jeruit and Janis arrived back at the family home from Cyprus late one evening in September. They were returning from Janis's mother Bethany's celebration of life. It had been a unique experience. There had been no mourning or ritual lament, which was standard for a funeral service during the late antiquity. A large gathering of people had attended the celebration.

After the first few hours of the wake, it was clear something was different. The gathering shifted from a grieving loss to a celebration of the eternal destiny of a spiritual giant. After the first twenty-four hours, people went out and returned with food and supplies to feed the attendees. They ate and drank and fellowshipped with one another as if they were at a wedding instead of a funeral. Family members and friends from the church shared testimonies as they remembered Bethany's legacy. Dozens of new believers came into the faith right there at the family tombs as the funeral attendees glorified God. No one grew tired or distracted as the Spirit moved among them, touching one person after another. The funeral gathering lasted three full days and nights.

Janis emptied her arms of everything she had carried home and took a deep breath. "What a weekend!" "You can say that again," Jeruit replied.

Janis stared toward the back of the house and then walked from the main living space into the hallway. When she reached the farthest room on the left, she pulled the curtain back from the doorway of what had been her mother's bedroom. She had not been in the room since Jeruit had taken her mother's body from the bed four nights ago.

Jeruit followed her in, wondering how his wife would react to the moment. The room was so quiet, so empty. He knew Janis would need to process her grief as everything settled. It was time to return to normal life but without her beloved mother. Janis had always been very close to her mom, even more so in the dusk of life, as she had nursed Bethany's every need in that very room. The two had a bond that would leave a vacancy in Janis's life.

Janis sat on the edge of the bed and ran her hand over the linen bedclothes, which were still pulled back and tousled. "Mom remained faithful to God throughout her life. If she could only have seen the celebration over these last three days. What joy it would have brought her."

Her voice was steady, but Jeruit could not help noticing the tears welling up in his wife's eyes. He laid his hand on her shoulder. "I haven't met any other person who loved her Lord as much as your mom did. It manifested itself this week for sure. She touched so many people during her life and now in her death. It was amazing to watch tears of loss transform into hope and joy. I know you will miss her. We all will, but I'm so thankful to have these past few days to think back on as I remember her. I've seen nothing like it, and I know it would make her happy."

"It was incredible and such a way to honor her," Janis said as she wiped her cheek with her hand. "Looking back on my early childhood, I recall so many times someone would visit her, mostly women, who needed her advice or counsel. People would just show up at the house. She didn't turn anyone away. She would pray with them and sometimes even stay in their home with them for days until they felt better or received direction from the Lord. Her gentleness and kindness have blessed this family and so many others. She never gave in to darkness or despair. She knew it had no place in the lives of the redeemed, and people recognized that authority. Mom spent her life serving the Lord with joy and determination. Nothing ever seemed to take that from her. Even when she lost my little brother at birth, she found rest in knowing that God's plans were higher. My mom trusted Him in everything, and if I take anything away from being her daughter, I want to walk in faith like her."

Thort was standing at the foot of the bed, listening. He had hoped the sadness of the empty room and the dirty bedclothes would win back some of the territory the enemy had taken over the past few days. There was no way he could bring himself to be in close proximity to that funeral. He tried, but the atmosphere was so toxic when so many other believers showed up, he had to flee. He knew he would have to deal with the fallout later when he could breathe and see straight again. The three-day bender at the Bar and Chain was taking its toll on his senses now. It had not been smart to take off like that with so much at stake, and now it felt like coming in after a tornado to survey the damage. Thort would never realize the gravity of what had taken place in his absence.

As he listened to the couple reflect, he recognized strength in the place of sadness. "Are you serious?" he yelled, looking at Janis. "You can't be. Your mom is dead. You will never see her again. Your children will forget her, and so will you. No one will remember anything she stood for. I don't care what all of you fanatics did over the last three days. Nothing will ever bring her back from the dead."

He waited for a moment, only to realize his words hadn't fazed either of them. "What's happening here?" he asked. No one answered, of course. Then he stomped his foot on the floor, cursed, and fled into a nearby field to process his thoughts.

Fluto is gone, and he was no help at all, he mused as he paced through the tall grass. *No one cares about my treacherous luck with this never-ending family. No other demon has faced this level of opposition repeatedly like I have. Why do I deserve this? What did I do?"*

He kicked a large stone hidden in the grass. His small toe would have completely separated from the rest of his foot had the skin and torn ligament not held. Thort hissed as he stumbled to one knee. Pain bolted through his leg, but he welcomed the torture. At least he could feel something besides hopelessness and abandonment. He continued with his disgust and self-pity throughout the night, wearing a path in the field as he stomped back and forth. He cursed, gnashed his teeth, and threw stones at imaginary foes as his tantrum progressed.

After Thort had finished letting off steam, he stopped. *Time to regroup,* he told himself. *This affront is going to stop here and now. The family only thought they had tasted the weapons of my warfare. Time to pull out the big guns. Anger will come to my aid. Who knows? Maybe I'll even let murder make an appearance. No one comes back from murder. I just haven't put in the proper effort with these pawns. My mind hasn't been thinking clearly lately, but the fog is lifting. I'll triumph over this generation, and my victory will ring from every hall at Hell Ops. Before this is over, Fluto will be coming to me for advice. My successes will set a standard for demons to study for ages. Won't that be the day? I can't wait to laugh in Fluto's ugly, pretentious face!*

Thort's pace picked up with his excitement. He rubbed his hands together and devised a new plan. *Let's kick it off with some false accusations. Who doesn't love a little injustice? Let one thing lead to another, and then it won't be hard to convince someone to kill for it. I may even see if a hound of Hell is available for an assist. Perhaps Shadie Nawg is not on a current assignment. I'll have to check."* Thort stopped pacing and clapped his hands. *Oh, I have a plan now!* A smile spread across his face as he played the whole thing out in his head. He hadn't smiled in so long it made the muscles in his face ached. After a moment, he shook his head. *Enough of that. Bleh!* Thort bolted out of the field and flew off to Hell Op's kennels.

Jeruit worked as a silversmith in the small town of Ioannina in Greece. His master's shop was well renowned in the community, due in large part to Jeruit's craftsmanship. He had worked diligently as an apprentice, and his integrity was evident in every piece he put out. He never took a shortcut, even if it meant taking twice as long to produce. The townspeople knew this and would wait patiently to make sure Jeruit was the smith who worked on their items. He was a skilled master.

Argento, the shop's owner, had a great deal of respect for Jeruit. Over the years he had given him more and more responsibility, even entrusting Jeruit with the tasks of opening and closing the business each day. Argento also gave him full artistic liberty, something that wasn't afforded to the other employees. He had even promoted Jeruit to foreman over his peers a few years back. Jeruit didn't take his responsibilities lightly, and he served his boss as if serving the Lord.

One week after Jeruit attended Bethany's funeral, Argento approached him in the shop with several ounces of silver. A wealthy patron had asked that Jeruit forge the silver into a piece of fine jewelry. He had even offered double the price if Jeruit completed the piece in a timely manner. Jeruit disliked giving the wealthy man's request precedence over the other customers, but Argento was adamant. The customer had left a note with some specific requests. He required that Jeruit work independently on the piece to ensure its quality. This would not be the first piece that Jeruit had crafted for the man's wife, and now he wanted her to have an authentic custom ensemble. Argento handed the silver nuggets to Jeruit in a small brown calfskin pouch along with the patron's written instructions. Jeruit got permission to start on the piece first thing the next morning. That would give him some time that evening to brainstorm and make a sketch of his ideas.

Argento prepared to leave early that afternoon, as he had become accustomed to, having Jeruit available to finish up and close the shop. He listed off for the one hundredth time the closing procedures. Even though Jeruit had closed the shop time after time, he knew Argento felt better if he could walk through the steps every time. He nodded as if he were making a mental note of each step. Satisfied with his routine, on his way out, Argento pointed to the pouch sitting on the workbench. "First thing." "Got it, boss. First thing," Jeruit replied.

That afternoon, like the last several weeks, had been busy at the shop without Argento to field the walk-in customers. Each time a customer came in, they would ask to speak with Jeruit instead of one of the other workers. Jeruit had to speak to new customers, retrieve pieces from the back, manage the furnace, and try to focus on the piece on which he was working. Every time he settled into work, someone would walk in and ask for his help. He never got overwhelmed, though. As good as he was with a hammer, he was also great with people. He had a knack for listening and discerning what someone was looking for. People loved to stop in and speak to him, even if they were just passing by.

Amelia was a nine-year-old Molossian hound who lived at the shop. Argento had gotten her as a pup to serve as a guard dog. That was a joke in the shop. Amelia was the most compliant and loving dog anyone had ever been around. She served as an amazing companion to Jeruit. The customers all loved her and brought her treats when they stopped by. Since she lived at the shop full time, it gave Argento a peace of mind when they locked up the shop for the night.

Amelia stood from her bed and stretched.

Shadie Nawg was the hound Thort had borrowed from the Hell Ops kennels. He had been waiting all morning for Amelia to awaken from her nap. It was time to suggest a visit to the front of the shop for a tasty treat. Argento had closed the door from the back area that led to the shop on his way out. Shadie Nawg made sure Amelia grew impatient and bored, pacing the back area with no one moving in and out to greet her. He even reminded her that her breakfast had been a little light with Argento in such a hurry that day. After being such a noble watchdog, the least they could do was feed her properly.

Suddenly, Jeruit opened the door to the back area, and Amelia jumped up and put her paws on his apron. She felt relieved that they had not left her alone forever.

"Down, girl. Easy. I love you too, but I have a lot of work to do this afternoon," Jeruit said as he patted her on the head.

Amelia jumped back onto all fours and licked his hand as she watched him go into the back storage area. Before Jeruit came back through, she padded through the door and into the front shop area, past the anvils, and over to Jeruit's workbench. The contents on the table were out of her reach, but an interesting leather cord was hanging off the edge of the table. She had a strong, muscular build, but her legs were short to sustain her solid frame. She heaved up onto her hind legs and sniffed around to see where that interesting smell was coming from. The fresh calfskin pouch with the silver inside lay on the work surface.

Amelia was an incredibly obedient dog, but she had an affinity for freshly tanned leather that made her forget her senses. She tugged at the leather tie binding the pouch and then pulled the pouch down to the floor. Remembering the harsh scolding from Argento the last time she got hold of a pair of leather shoes, she carried the pouch to a more remote location. She knew better than to snatch things from the tables, but she was bored—she had been locked up all morning, after all. She headed to her hiding place to chew the lovely leather uninterrupted by anyone who might notice what she was doing.

Shadie Nawg walked tall beside Amelia with a look of satisfaction as she carried the pouch in her mouth. Amelia didn't sense Shadie's presence, but the damage had been done. *That was easy,* the hellhound thought. He had served his master well.

Amelia had a remote hiding place where she often retreated, especially when children visited the shop. She wasn't a fan of high-pitched squealing or having her ears tugged, so she sought solitude in an unfinished area behind the cellar door. It was always open, so the area behind it was private. No one ever glanced back there. Thus, she had stashed an assortment of treasures in that spot over the years. She sniffed them upon entering, admiring her trophies. The calfskin pouch would never survive to achieve such. Given an afternoon of uninterrupted time, she would devour the pouch completely. The contents were of no interest to her. The silver pieces fell out one by one through the gaping hole in the leather's side. Amelia pawed the silver pieces to the back of the nook. The silver laid there, covered in dust and over nine years of dog hair.

Shadie Nawg stood watch until his job was complete. He had done little except make a few suggestions to his canine assignment, but it had worked like a charm. Surely, a rancid treat would await him when he returned to Hell Ops.

As Jeruit walked through each of Argento's closing procedures for the night, he called out to Amelia right before he locked the front door. The leather pouch was long gone, but Jeruit didn't notice when he cleaned his workspace and replaced his tools. Hearing his call, Amelia jumped up and ran toward the front shop area. Jeruit smiled at her when she appeared. "Good girl," he said. She was dependable and faithful, coming whenever Jeruit called.

The next morning, Jeruit unlocked the shop before daybreak. After opening the windows for light, he looked around the shop. He always liked to be the first one there in the morning to get things ready for the day's business. After lighting candles, feeding Amelia, and gathering his tools from the back shop area, he started the fire in the furnace. Jeruit had to get right on his new project, so his other customers' jobs wouldn't fall too far behind. He was glad that Argento would be back to run the front of the shop that day.

Jeruit had laid awake the night before considering what he might do with the wealthy merchant's silver. Many times inspiration would come to him late at night as he awoke and acknowledged God in the silence. He was excited to get started on his fresh ideas.

Jeruit went to the workbench, only to realize the pouch of silver was missing. He searched the area for it. *I remember it being here yesterday morning,* he thought. *I wonder if Argento stopped by in the evening and took it with him. I know it was here when I locked up last night.*

Jeruit looked everywhere in the shop, even in a few unlikely places. Then he headed back into the storage area and even checked the cellar. He stopped to pat Amelia on the head. "Where did it go, girl? You don't know, do ya?"

After searching everywhere, he started on something else so as not to waste the morning. Argento had to have the silver. There was no other explanation.

Later that morning when Argento came to the shop, he noticed Jeruit was working on some armor that wasn't due for another week. The jewelry was a priority. The nobleman had promised to stop in and check on the progress in a couple of days.

Jeruit looked up from his work. "Argento, good morning. Hey, did you stop by last night, by chance, and remove the silver pouch from my workbench yesterday?"

Argento gave Jeruit a puzzled look. "No, of course not. I left it here for you with the patron's instructions, and I haven't been back to the shop until this very moment. You know that time is of the essence with that piece. Why would I take it?"

Jeruit stared at Argento, a sinking feeling in his gut. "It's not here. It wasn't here when I came in this morning, and I've searched everywhere for it."

Argento's eyes nearly popped out of his head. "It must be here! Don't be ridiculous. What have you done with it?"

Jeruit walked Argento through the events of the previous day, ending with checking on Amelia and locking the front door.

"Then you mustn't have locked up properly!" Argento said. "I assume there were no signs of forced entry when you arrived today?"

Jeruit was taken aback by the tone of Argento's voice. "Yes, Argento. I unlocked everything this morning when I arrived. Everything was as it should be, and Amelia was here just like every morning," he replied, his tone turning desperate.

Exasperated, Argento shook his head. "This is our biggest project of the year, Jeruit. What we will make from this will feed our families for months, not to mention replace some of these old tools that are so worn and useless. You know how important this is to me and to this business. And now you have lost the silver. What am I to make of that? What am I to tell the patron when he comes to check on your progress?"

"No, my brother, you must believe me. I've never abused your trust, and I never will. I left it right here on the bench."

"Yes, you've said that repeatedly. However, if you locked up properly, and there were no signs of a break-in, that leaves only one scenario."

Jeruit's eyes bulged with disbelief. "You don't think I would steal from you, do you? I would never."

Argento looked at Jeruit, feeling sheepish. He was right. Never in all the years working for him had there been a hint of wrongdoing of any sort. Jeruit was a devout religious man, and he and his church members followed a strict moral code. Stealing would be a clear violation of that code. This made little sense, but Argento had no other explanation.

"You leave me no choice, Jeruit. I'll have to tell the patron something, and telling him we lost the silver won't cut it. The only other option is for you to pay to replace it. As much as it pains me to say so, if you can't replace it, you'll have to be arrested. I won't tolerate theft."

"Argento!" Jeruit exclaimed. "I didn't take the silver, and you know I can't pay you, my brother."

Jeruit put his hands on his head and walked back to his workbench, looking again for the silver. "I can't steal from you, not only because it would be a disgraceful thing to do but also because my Father in Heaven would be disappointed, and I can't bear that possibility." He sat down in defeat, cradling his head in his hands.

Thort stood leaning in the shop's doorway, holding Shadie on a leash, their chests bursting with pride.

Things are finally working out for me, Thort thought. *I'm not sure why I didn't try this angle sooner. This false accusation will probably bring unjust imprisonment and financial and emotional hardship to the family. Jeruit will taste anger as he rots in prison, and his family will starve with no provider. Brilliant.*

Thort reached down and patted Shadie's head. "Who would have ever thought that something without a soul could bring such relief to my spirit? Good boy." If a hound could smile, Shadie Nawg would have done so.

Thort looked over at Jeruit. He could feel the despair from across the room. It was like a welcome salve to his weary ego. *Today marks the turning point. My failure with this wretched family is over. I can now bring about doubt and mistrust. Fear will make another appearance as I snatch away their livelihood. I'll attach the title of "thief" to their reputation, and those who knew them as devout followers of the enemy will now see the sham it is. This community will now discount any influence that Jeruit had. I'll even plant anger in his children, sealing them into the dark-*

ness. They will hate Argento and even grow to hate their father for aban-doning them. All joy be damned."

Later that morning, there was a loud rap on the front door of Jeruit's home. It startled Janis from her work. Who could it be in the middle of the day? She hoped there hadn't been an accident at the shop. As she stood and moved toward the door, the Holy Spirit comforted her.

Opening the door, she saw Argento standing there. She smiled. "Good morning, Argento. It's good to see you. How can I help you?"

Argento had no time for pleasantries. He felt bad enough as it was, and he needed to push through without emotion. "Janis, Jeruit has stolen a very expensive amount of silver from the shop. He has refused to admit this guilt or repay me for my losses."

Janis stumbled back, trying to keep her balance. She couldn't believe what she was hearing. "What? You must be mistaken."

Argento could not bear to make eye contact as he continued. "A wealthy patron entrusted several precious nuggets of fine silver to be crafted into jewelry by your husband. He had the silver yesterday, and now it's gone. There's no evidence of a burglary at my shop, so that leaves Jeruit as the only culprit."

Janis pulled her hand away from her mouth and reminded herself to breathe. "This can't be. I don't understand. Where is Jeruit?"

Argento paused for a moment and turned toward the public building. "He's in jail," he said, his voice devoid of emotion.

"Prison? Argento, you know my husband, and you know our family. We serve God, and we would never betray Him for any material wealth of this world. Search your heart. You know my words are true."

"Your husband will stay in prison until I get the silver back or until someone pays for it to be replaced," Argento replied. Then he leaned across the threshold. "Should I have the authorities search your house? The silver could be here, I suppose. Are you protecting it while pretending your husband is above reproach?"

Janis realized Argento was beyond reason. He had no previous infractions to base these wild accusations on, but he was intent on his narrative. "If you won't give my husband the benefit of the doubt based on years of proven integrity, there is nothing I can say to sway you from this thinking. I must excuse myself and go to him."

Argento glared at Janis. "They have thrown Jeruit into the dungeon in the center of town. They stopped arresting you Christians for preaching your religion, so there was plenty of room. I used to wonder if there was something to your faith, but now I know people are inherently greedy, and nothing changes that. People only serve themselves, and now that my business is suffering the consequences, I'll see that your family does too." He tightened the belt around his tunic and then turned to leave without saying farewell.

Janis headed toward the center of town with her daughter, Agnes, in tow. Girls could not attend school in Greece, but her son, Lucius, would be at school for several more hours. She would have to explain to him later.

When Janis and Agnes reached the jail, Jeruit told her about the false accusations and vowed he didn't know where the silver was. His explanation was unnecessary. Janis never doubted his integrity for a moment. They both knew they could not repay Argento for the silver.

As Jeruit spoke, reality set in for Janis. The responsibility of raising the children and providing for them in Jeruit's absence would fall onto her. It was heavy and surreal, but strangely, hope surrounded her at that moment. So much unknown lay ahead, but she found herself wrapped in the arms of Jehovah Shalom. She knew the truth; God would never abandon them. Although she could not see it, she knew He had already made a way for them.

CHAPTER 6

LUCIUS

Forgiveness is an indescribable fragrance to the soul.

Months and then the years went by. A dark, cold dungeon offers no hope, so Thort focused little on Jeruit, believing his fate would take care of itself. Janis remained grounded in his enemy's brainwashing no matter how many lies Thort taunted her with. She was too strong in her faith; he decided she was a dead end. Instead, he turned his primary efforts on their son, Lucius. Thort saw great potential in him. He was young, passionate, and impressionable, and these were components he could work with. His plan was to start with anger and, over time, shift toward revenge and possibly murder.

Lucius was only twelve years old when his father was thrown into prison. One morning he left for school, and when he came home, his dad was gone, and so was the life he had known. Twelve was an impressionable age and a season when he needed his father's influence. The sudden turn of events confused Lucius. He could not understand why they had arrested his father and thrown him in jail with no proof of guilt. Lucius found it hard to believe that Argento had so suddenly turned on their family over money. Lucius had played under his father's workbench in that shop for so many days as a boy. He loved when Argento, who was like a second father to him, would give him minor tasks to help around the shop. All of that had ended for nothing.

Lucius wrestled with his feelings toward Argento. Emotions flooded him daily as he passed by the shop on the way to the stables. He could see through the front window as the workers buzzed about the furnace and swept the floor.

One day, Lucius caught sight of Argento inside the building. He was standing behind the front counter with his son, a young man about the same age as Lucius. He had been his friend and playmate as a child.

Well, look at that. Teaching the kid the business. How perfect, Lucius thought. Anger rose in his chest. Argento would never get what was coming to him. He had continued with his life and business, and his children had a father who came home to them every day. They always had food on the table and new clothes to wear. They never had to wonder if God would come through for them this week. Argento had carried on with no understanding or care that Lucius's entire life had been twisted upside down, and Lucius hated him for it.

After his father's imprisonment, the family's needs forced Lucius into a man's share of work in addition to his studies. At first, he was eager and willing to do anything to make things easier for his mother and sister. Over time, however, he came to resent the theft of his childhood. There was nothing fair about it. He was the man of the house now, and he had enormous shoes to fill.

"Lucius, you don't speak to us much these days. Is everything okay?" his mother would ask.

"Fine, Mom. Everything is fine," he would reply.

Some nights, Lucius would lie awake in his cot staring at the thatch ceiling. He had often imagined himself meeting Argento in a private alley after dark. His mind had rolled through all the scenarios, from what he would say to the man and even what he might do. Even if he never got the chance, his imagination helped him feel like he had some control over the injustice that he and his family had suffered.

Thort visited nightly, standing by the bed while Lucius lay awake. He watered and fed those precious seeds he had planted years ago. He also introduced new feelings of self-entitlement and resentment.

"You don't deserve this. It isn't fair," Thort would hiss in the darkness. "All you ever do is work to put food on the table. A man your age should be looking for a wife of his own. Instead, you're forced to provide for your father's family. Someone should pay for these years of injustice, and it shouldn't be you."

He continuously lied to Lucius, telling him that a god who really loved him would never let this happen. Thort remained patient and diligent, waiting for the perfect time. His narrative was a slow-burning fire that he hoped would one day roar through the ages of defeat with this family. He just had to stay the course.

Meanwhile, Jeruit remained in prison, year after year. Miraculously, despair never set into his heart. The prison they housed him in no longer held Christians since the new laws made it legal to worship God and spread the gospel. This made room in the jail for actual criminals. Jeruit lived among some of the worst. There were thieves, corrupt politicians, and even murderers in his company. Jeruit had many opportunities to share the redemption story of Jesus with his cellmates. Some paid him no mind, but others accepted the message of salvation. The opportunity to be a witness in such dire conditions strengthened Jeruit and gave him hope every morning.

Jeruit also earned the guards' trust and respect over the years. Many would come to him for advice and prayer about different circumstances going on in their lives. In return, the guards allowed Janis and the children to visit him more regularly, a privilege that was not afforded to most prisoners. Janis visited weekly with encouragement about how God was sustaining the family and how the ekklesia had stepped in to help meet their needs. The children would come when their schedules permitted. Lucius had not been to see his father for several months. Work and school consumed most of his time.

As time went by, Jeruit continued to share the gospel inside the prison, and life went on outside for the family. God met each of their needs, but things were difficult.

Conditions in the dungeon were awful. There was no daylight, and the food provided was only enough to keep the prisoners alive. The guards had blessed Jeruit over the years, sometimes providing him with leftover provisions from their own table.

Eventually, the living conditions of the prison took their toll, and Jeruit developed scurvy. His body was failing fast. He had sustained a slight injury to his lower leg that, under normal circumstances would have healed with no issue, but he developed an infection, and within a few weeks was fading.

He could not remember the last time Lucius had visited. Jeruit knew the situation had been hard for his son. He also knew Lucius was not just busy with work. His absence spoke of a much deeper problem, and it worried Jeruit. His time in his earthly body was ending, and he wanted to know his son would be okay when he was gone.

The next time Janis visited, Jeruit requested a private meeting with Lucius.

Thort listened that evening as Janis informed Lucius that he needed to head over after dinner and meet with his father. The demon rubbed his scaly hands together, drooling over his impending triumph. *Tonight could be the perfect night. He will be alone after dark. There won't be many people out. He must walk right by the silver shop on the way to the jail. Argento will surely be there closing the shop. There will be no witnesses and no hindrances. I've got him now!*

After dinner, as his mother had requested, Lucius headed out of the house, turning down the road toward the prison. He had walked that road so many times with his mother and sister. Lucius didn't feel like going, but he knew his father was not well, so he had not argued. It seemed odd to be summoned alone, and he sensed urgency.

His mind wandered to Argento as he walked the road from his home to the first turn. He had entertained so many fantasies over the years about avenging his father and feeling the glory and satisfaction that would come along with it.

Thort followed just behind Lucius, barely able to suppress his anticipation. "Wouldn't your father be so proud if you resolved this whole thing before he died?" Thort suggested. "Once he's gone, there will never be justice. They will never clear his name or his reputation. Your mother doesn't care about the truth, so that leaves you, Lucius. You're the only one who can right this wrong."

Thort kept pace as he continued to whisper in Lucius' ear, quivering with delight. He was so close that he could almost taste it.

Lucius reached the road where he had to turn and head toward the center of town. The silver shop was located just beyond the houses in the distance where the trade market began. Lucius could just make out a faint light spilling out of the front window into the street. The thought of Argento entered his mind, and hot anger spread up from his chest.

We would not be here if it weren't for that ungrateful fool. It would be my dad in there closing the shop and then coming home to his family. Instead, he lies rotting across town in a dungeon.

Lucius couldn't quite make it out, but something was on the road in the distance between him and the silver shop. It was blocking the road, and people were milling around it. As he got closer, he realized that a produce cart from the markets had overturned in the street, blocking traffic in both directions. Fresh fruit was scattered all over the road. People had gathered around the overturned cart and were salvaging any food that wasn't damaged. The owner of the cart was pulling barrels into the street to load the fruit, since his cart remained disabled.

Lucius knew if he was going to visit his father before the jailer closed things for the night, he would have to detour through another part of town.

As Lucius turned off the main road and took a shortcut to the adjacent street, Thort seethed. "No way. No way! A fruit cart? This can't be happening. It's just a few spilled melons. Where are you going?" He stomped and jumped in front of Lucius, his head spinning with fury, but he couldn't manage to get out an intelligible thought.

Lucius took the detour.

Jeruit had always held the heart of his young son. That affection and admiration had never faded, even as Lucius grew into a young man. Lucius respected his father and loved him deeply. Many godly men from the ekklesia had influenced him over the years in his father's absence, but no one could replace his dad. His reluctance to visit was not out of resentment or a lack of love for his father but because it broke Lucius's heart to see his dad in such a terrible state.

The jailer ushered Lucius in to see Jeruit, who was sitting on his bed. A huge smile broke out on Jeruit's face as he stood to meet his son. They embraced through the iron bars. "Good to see you again, son. There are few things that bring as much joy to my heart as the sight of you."

They spent some time catching up, and Jeruit inquired about how Lucius was holding up. On previous visits, Lucius had tried to remain strong. He wanted his father to know he was doing a good job of taking care of his mom and sister. Of course, Jeruit had never doubted his son for a second.

This night was different. There was a presence in the room that broke through the walls Lucius had been hiding behind. Knowing that his father's time on Earth would soon end, Lucius opened his heart and revealed his desire to hurt Argento. He also talked about how angry he was and how he had no way to release those emotions. Lucius was completely transparent with his father on every level.

Evening stretched into the night. The jailer, who had become quite fond of Jeruit, allowed the visit to continue for as long as needed. Jeruit listened patiently to every word his son spoke. He had sensed the Lord's presence the minute Lucius walked through the front door of the jail, so he knew it was going to be a special night for them both.

Jeruit had spoken to Lucius about Jesus throughout his life. He shared the stories of deliverance and faithfulness of his parents and grandparents. Lucius had always listened to the stories, but that night, the message hit differently.

Jeruit opened his mouth to speak, but the words that came out were not his words but the words of the Holy Spirit.

As his father spoke, Lucius's anger and fear melted away. He fell to his knees. With tears streaming down his face, Jeruit prayed and witnessed the Spirit of God enter his son. There was no peace like that peace, no joy like that joy.

There was much rejoicing in the dungeon that night. The two cell mates who had come to know the Lord after meeting Jeruit rejoiced to hear the news, and each of them prophesied over Lucius.

It was getting late. Jeruit didn't want Janis to wonder where their son was, so he moved on to the last bit of business. "Lucius, listen closely to me. I thought I might get released from here and return to you and your mother and sister, but I feel in my spirit that this won't happen. My body is weak, but that doesn't matter. We're eternal, son. Physical death has no hold over us. When you return home, share the good news of your experience with the Lord tonight. I have a good idea that you won't even have to tell your mom when she lays eyes on you. She and I have prayed for this moment. Tell her you're ready to hear about the manuscript."

Lucius looked at his father, his eyes wide. "What manuscript?"

"I want you to sit down with your mother and Agnes. She will tell you about a special container that holds a manuscript hidden in our home. She will tell you everything that you need to know, which isn't much, but it is eternally important. Our Heavenly Father entrusted our ancestors to protect an ancient piece of writing. We have carried it for five generations. It's a duty that none of us have taken lightly, and I trust you won't either. Now go see your mother. I love you, son."

Jeruit reached through the prison bars again and embraced his son for what could be the last time. He hoped eternity would feel different than it had in that miserable cell. He didn't want to wait too long to see his family again.

As Lucius made the trek home late that night, he had forgotten about the blocked road earlier, so he took the usual route. When he turned the corner, the silver shop came into view. At that moment, he knew something had changed inside of him. He no longer felt anger as he thought about Argento. As he walked by the business, he even reached out his hand and spoke a quiet prayer of blessing. It was the most incredible feeling.

The overturned cart and all the produce were all cleaned up. The only evidence it had ever happened was the partial rind of a melon that lay in the grass beside the road. But that wasn't the only thing Lucius saw.

At that moment, the Spirit gave him a vision. In his spirit he saw a small pile of trash in the back corner of Argento's shop. He had a vague recollection of the nook from his childhood wanderings. In that pile of dog hair and old forgotten garbage, something caught the light. He reached down in his vision and picked it up. It was silver, several pieces of pure silver, in fact. Lucius could hardly wrap his head around what the Spirit was showing him. Then the vision ended.

The moment it did, he ran as fast as he could to Argento's house and pounded on the front door.

Argento peeked out to see who it was. Townsfolk had made Argento aware that Lucius's father was sick and dying in prison. *He is here to kill me for having his father imprisoned for all these years,* he thought.

"Argento, I know you're home," Lucius said. "Please, I beg you! Don't deny me this audience. I have a request and I promise I'll do you no harm."

Argento waited in silence for a moment. He knew he owed the boy this much. He had always carried a measure of guilt, knowing that the accusation of theft went against everything he had ever known about Jeruit. But the fact remained: the silver had gone missing and was never recovered. Knowing he could not be too careful, he armed himself with a dagger before he went to the door. If Lucius tried anything, he could defend himself.

"What is it, boy?" he asked, his voice gruff.

"Please accompany me back to your shop. I have something I need you to see. Call the local guards to meet us there. You have my word; you have nothing to fear from me."

Argento couldn't imagine what Lucius was going on about, but he hesitantly agreed. He summoned the guards, as requested, and then walked with Lucius to the shop. As soon as Argento unlatched the front door, Lucius walked straight to the back storage area where Amelia used to sleep. A new, much smaller hound laid there now. Argento lit a candle and followed.

"Argento, can you please ask your dog to move?" Lucius asked.

Argento grabbed the dog by the scruff of the neck and pulled him back. Lucius reached down into the dark and raked his hand through the pile of dog hair. Just then the candlelight reflected on something shiny in the rubble. Everyone saw it. Argento gasped, and the guards both straightened. Lucius stood up holding the pieces of lost silver and handed them to Argento.

"Argento, even though you knew my father was a good man, you did what you had to do. I want you to know that neither I nor my family wish you any ill will. Until this very night I have carried a burden of unforgiveness toward you for what happened all those years ago. Tonight, I prayed with my father and asked Jesus to forgive me for this, and I surrendered my desire to see justice for him. On the way home, Jesus showed me a vision of this pile of rubble. Now not only has He has restored my heart, but he has also restored your silver and my father's reputation."

Argento could hardly believe what he had just witnessed. He was relieved to acknowledge what he had always known about Jeruit. He had never been a thief.

The guards looked at him, awaiting instruction. "Quickly, go and have Jeruit escorted to his home," Argento said. "I'll pay for whatever medical treatment can bring him comfort in these last days of his life. I'll also be responsible for the expenses incurred by his family upon his death and burial. He must spend these last days with his family in his home."

After the guards departed, Argento turned to Lucius, tears

streaming down his face. He asked him to explain the gospel and this Spirit who had given Lucius the vision. Their conversation lasted until dawn and ended with joy and celebration, as Argento's name was written in the Book of Life.

Because of that moment, the city of Ioannina became known as the sacred city of silversmithing. It bears that honor even to this day.

The next week was a blur. News had come in the early morning hours that Jeruit had passed away. Since then people had been in and out of the house, bringing food and helping Janis prepare for the funeral. Even the jailors who had guarded Jeruit for many years came to offer what they could. Jeruit would have a proper Christian burial surrounded by family and friends who had known the truth of his innocence all along.

After the funeral, Janis shared the story of the manuscript with her children, telling them how John had written it and handed it down through Peter. She also told them about the special instructions for its preservation. After going through the history, she relayed what a responsibility and honor it was to continue safeguarding the sacred treasure.

"Beloved children, now that you know all about the secret mission our Lord gave to our family lineage, I want you to listen carefully," Janis said. "Your earthly father has left us, but the God of Abraham will continue to provide. Our God is YAHWEH-JIREH. He will never leave us or forsake us. Even though he who is in the world has brought great harm to this family, God has always been faithful to us. We root our faith in the understanding that our provision exists in Him. This faith is a shield that protects us from anything the enemy might throw our way. The evil one's intent has been to destroy us and our legacy because we are all aligned with Jesus. He caused me for a time to believe that your father was our sole provider. That was a lie. He wanted us to be victims and blame others for our circumstances. He wanted us to wallow like pigs in sorrow because we could not change the outcome of events. The good news is, and forever will be, that our Savior, Jesus, has overcome the world. That means that we are not victims. Our Father knows every hair on our heads and goes before us to make a way where we see no way. We will continue to counter evil by remaining faithful to the one who made that way for us. We will trust our Holy Savior in every situation, no matter how difficult. This is the legacy of our ancestors, and we carry this forward to future generations. Your father may not be with us anymore, but the joy of our Lord will be with us forever. From this we will gather our strength and continue the responsibility of guarding His sacred scroll."

Thort sat listening to the account of his utter failure, which at one point had seemed to be in the bag. Had he ever been close at all? Was he lying to himself? Not only had he failed to destroy the next generation of this family, now almost the entire town of Ioannina was falling into the Enemy's hands. The testimony of Jeruit and Lucius was spreading like a wildfire. Thort couldn't decide whether he was feeling defeat or rage. Did he feel like hopeless surrender, or was he being stirred to a new level of resolve?

Suddenly, he exploded into a hateful rant. "I had them in my claws! I had this family on its knees. How could all my hard work fail just because that sniffling kid ended up in the wrong place at the wrong time? How can I damn forgiveness, faithfulness, and joy in this clan for eternity? Hell Ops must have weapons available to eradicate these infernal holds on me. I know someone is holding out on me. Someone must want to see me fail. I need help. No one will help me. And here I am. It's time to attend the generational meeting and new assignment briefing to find out the name of the next brood of cursed bipeds. I don't even know why I need to show up to hear about the next blight on my existence. They will never let me enjoy a tour of duty off from this family. Apparently, this is my eternal curse. With each passing generation, I can feel the darkness fleeting from my spirit. My strength is draining with each failure. I fully expect Hell Ops will notice this time. I don't even feel the sneers and jabs anymore. The pain of listening to my assignments die to themselves to follow the enemy is like a branding iron to my chest each day."

Thort was out of energy. He plopped down in the dirt in front of Janis's home, empty and beaten. *Darkness, oh darkness, where is your rest? The eternal light in this family is draining, and I must find respite,* he thought.

He didn't have time for this wallowing, but he didn't care. He knew he needed to get his act together, and eventually that night, he did. Tomorrow he would have to report to Hell Ops.

CHAPTER 7

HELL OPS GENERATIONAL DEPLOYMENT BRIEFING

The next morning, Thort reported to Hell Ops Central Command for the Generational Deployment Assessment. Demons came to such assessments either to celebrate success or to suffer punishment for failure. Thort used to look forward to such meetings, but now he had come to dread them. Before Hell Ops issued new assignments, a progress report was to be submitted to Hell Ops command, and each demon had to go through a generational exit review. Eternal soul losses were especially heinous to the Department of Destruction.

Demons had to sit for an assessment interview that would go on their official record. Failure led to severe repercussions, including torture, mutilation, or even exile.

Thort's assignments had suffered six generations without sealed deaths. However, at each interview he had managed to slither his way out of severe punishment. Like all demons, he had a natural gift for lying. Deception rolled off his tongue so fluently that he could even lull Chief Despot into believing his next victory was just over the horizon.

One thing Thort could not hide with his sly words was the fact that his spiritual complexion was fading with each defeat. The deep black color that had defined his chiseled features had faded. To look at him was like looking through a clouded or scratched lens. His appearance seemed blurred and out of focus. He had noticed it a few generations back, but so far none of the officers had taken notice or asked about it. Would this briefing be the one? He had come adorned in his formal black cloak, just in case. He hoped it would not draw even more attention to him. Demons believed others paid just as much attention to them as they did to themselves. Self-focus was a borrowed tactic that often worked well on human assignments too.

As Thort walked down the long hall to the forum, he planned scenarios of interchange with his superiors in his head. He rehearsed the responses for each of them. Distracted by his dark thoughts, he didn't notice the stares and sneers of his peers as he walked through the double doors.

Thort wanted to remain unnoticed, so he took the sixth seat in the second row from the back. He glanced toward the front of the room and recognized Fluto and a few other demons seated in the front row.

Of course, Thort thought. *They can't wait for another day to be glorified among the ranks. I'm sure we'll all get to see the chiding bow and humiliating grin as Fluto's name is called over and over during this putrid ceremony.* Thort fought to swallow the bile that had bubbled up from stomach. He threw back his hood and settled down farther into his seat. He loathed Fluto and detested his constant success, which he earned only because his assignments were handpicked, spoon-fed softballs. The gloating was unbearable. That foolish demon didn't know what a challenge was. They had never assigned him to generations of a family devoted to the enemy. Had Fluto ever even smelled the hopeless stench of everlasting peace and joy?

As Thort glared at Fluto, he let his imagination play out a wishful dream of reversed roles. Fluto was sitting in the back hiding while Thort's name was called repeatedly from the podium instead. *If only the tables were turned. You would fall faster than you thought was possible,* he thought.

The meeting started with the "Pledge of Allegiance to Death,

Hell, and the Grave." Thort suffered through the meeting by relentless daydreaming. It seemed like the endless doldrums of award announcements grew longer with each generation. How could Thort be one of the few demons who had not tasted the sweet flavor of glory for six generations in a row?

Hell Ops gave black stripes out to the demonic fallen who had produced the broadest paths of confusion, those with the most integrated upside-down pyramid schemes, those who had woven the most creative web of deception, and to those who had inspired the most suicides. At the end of the ceremony, they awarded the Belt of the Dark Arts to the one demon who influenced the most humans away from the enemy.

After the ceremony was the generational celebration and feasting, known as the Feast of Debauchery. Officers in charge and those who were to be recognized on stage were the only ones invited. Everyone else was to report to the holding barrack to wait while the others relished in their accomplishments. This holding period was its own form of torture. It had become a custom for the victors to see to it that their party lasted well into the week while they held the defeated demons in a prison of their own shame.

Thort looked around the dark, musty barrack as he and the other failures were herded in like cattle. He swore it seemed like there were fewer and fewer in there with each generation. That made it increasingly difficult to remain unnoticed. His only saving grace was the fact that everyone in there was utterly ashamed, so they barely made eye contact, much less spoke to one another.

The worst part was the agonizing anticipation of the impending progress report interview and assignment. These were the last requirements of the briefing process and were the parts that Thort dreaded most. He would report to Chief Despot and sift through the gritty details of his previous assignment, explain what went wrong, and then try to convince his superior of his plans for success with the next assignment. After a thorough grilling, which may or may not cause a court martial, he would get his next human assignment and expected performance requirements. Thort recalled having barely made it out of the last report process with his limbs intact. His fate would not be the same in this cycle, and he knew it.

He pulled the cloak back from his forearm, staring at his deathly graying skin as he wondered if he would have his arm at all by the end of the week. The thought wrenched his gut. There had to be some escape from this.

His mind drifted to Janis and Lucius. He envied the security and provision they enjoyed while living unified with the enemy's spirit. What did that feel like? He snapped himself out of it, glancing around as if someone may have noticed him indulging in such a ludicrous thought. What was he thinking? He had plenty to answer for already. No one could know he had entertained a brief fantasy about serving the enemy. *Good grief. Get it together,* he scolded himself.

The feast lasted an unprecedented eight days. The defeated demons knew to report to their chiefs when the door clicked open and swung out toward the Assignment Wing. They stood up from the filthy floor, gathering themselves with what strength they had left after going for days without food.

Thort felt his heart roll up into his throat. The time had come. He drew the hood of his cloak over his head and then dragged himself off to meet his dreaded fate.

The wing was long and lined with door after door of interrogation rooms. Each door had a number and a file holder with the name of the demon reporting to that briefing. Thort moved toward the door he knew so well. The sight of it induced a new level of dread in him. He grabbed the door handle, sucked in a hesitant breath, and turned it. The door squeaked open with a deviant whine.

As Thort's eyes rose to meet Chief Despot, he gasped and rocked back on his injured toe, almost losing his balance. There at the desk sat another demon, one he vaguely recognized but could not place. He knew his face showed his confusion as he stood frozen in place, trying to decide if he had entered the wrong room.

Newly promoted Chief Maltreat huffed at him. "What are you waiting for, moron? Are you lost? Sit down, and let's get this over with. I can barely breathe after eight days of eating and drinking.

Sitting here waiting for you is already giving me a headache. I have sixty-six other demons to depose today, and you're over there acting like you've never done this before."

Thort sat, still stunned, but he didn't open his mouth.

Chief Maltreat rattled off the required military jargon to begin the interview. He scoffed under his breath while announcing Chief Despot's recent promotion. He glanced through Thort's file, not noticing any details. It was apparent he just wanted to get through the meeting and rubber stamp it.

"I see that Jeruit and Janis were your last human assignments. Then you were also responsible for their immediate offspring. Hmm . . . okay . . . whatever . . . whatever . . . boring . . . blah, blah . . . wait! Hold on a blasted minute. You *lost* them? You lost them all! I was expecting to see at least some minor victory. Lucius was in your clutches. What the Hell happened? You couldn't even employ murder when you had the chance?"

These were condescending but rhetorical questions. Maltreat didn't even look up from the file for answers. "Wow, I can tell you're going to be an absolute imbecile to work with. Just my luck. How did Chief Despot get a promotion? It certainly wasn't by standing on the shoulders of the likes of you." IIe slammed the file shut and tossed it across the desk in disgust. It slid off the desk and onto the floor. The pages came crashing out at Thort's feet in complete disarray.

Thort bent over and gathered the file's contents. As he picked up the progress report labeled "Paulk and Sarah," self-loathing washed over him. Those two were where this nightmare had begun. Oh, the effort he would have put into them had he known where this would all lead. Thort muttered something unintelligible as he gathered up the evidence of his recent failures. So many red marks, so many footnotes.

When he leaned back up from the floor with his file, he noticed Maltreat focused on another report on his desk. He acted as if he had forgotten Thort was still in the room. After a couple of seconds of awkward silence, Thort cleared his throat.

Chief Maltreat snapped to and looked up from his report. "Oh,

Thort is it? I forgot you were there. I was just looking forward to seeing who I have coming next. All I can hope for are at least a few I can count on. My career depends on you fools. You won't humiliate me in my command." He glanced back at Thort's file. "I'm going to be honest. I couldn't care less about your past and where you came from. I don't care where you've been and who we have assigned you to. Chief Despot handled your progress, or lack thereof, and now he's gone. I don't want to hear your pathetic excuses for failure with these last assignments. They don't affect me. But as of now, you're mine. I'll share your glory, and you will pay dearly for your failures. We won't have these boring little exit interviews high command wants documented by every generation. I *don't care* about the details. All I care about is you looking good and me looking better. Got it?"

Thort stared at him, his eyes glazed over in disbelief. Was he really getting a pass? Was he going to walk out of there unscathed with another chance to defend himself? What a turn of events. He blinked. "Yes, sir. I won't disappoint you, sir."

"Yeah, right," Maltreat muttered. "Anyway, I have your next assignment here." He used the thick yellow talon on his right index finger to unseal the black envelope. Opening the page, he scoffed and rolled his eyes. "So much for that! You're so stupid, you don't even merit a reassignment." He tossed the paper across the desk. "Know this. Your family assignment may not be changing, but the expectations are! Chief Despot may have put up with you rolling up here full of excuses every generation, but I won't. You bring me a progress report of victory at the next briefing, or I'll let you decide which two body parts you no longer need. Are we clear?"

"Yes, sir." Thort snatched up the report and scurried out the door. Maltreat's threat overshadowed any feeling of relief he felt. He escaped with his hide this time, but it would be the last grace extended to him.

Thort waited until he had left the building before pulling the assignment papers out of his cloak. It would be best if he just vacated the premises before someone else spotted him. Based on what Maltreat had said about the new assignment, it would not be good news anyway. He glanced down at the first page as he departed the western perimeter.

Human Assignment: Oppert and Brea (immediate descendants of Lucius and Helen)
Earth Location: Ioannina, Greece
Earth Year: 445 AD, a.k.a. Post Redemption.

Thort didn't even take the time to read the historical presentation or suggested operational tactics information on the next pages. He simply rolled his head toward the sky as if searching for some unknown entity who could intervene in his situation. After a moment, knowing that no entity, neither spirit nor flesh, was coming to his rescue, he crumpled the papers, shoved them into his cloak, and took flight for Greece.

CHAPTER 8

THE BISTRO IDYLL

Ramiel and Joam sat opposite each other in the booth. The beautifully decorated Bistro Idyll was situated right inside the gate of the Celestial City. The little diner was a glorious spot where angels often gathered to enjoy a meal after returning from missions to Earth. Ramiel and Joam had met there many times when on assignment together.

That day, Councilman Kafziel had sent them there to wait for a special assignment. This was not the typical order of operation. They usually received assignments at the general briefing, but they were always flexible. Being a messenger of God to His beloved required it. Joam and Ramiel didn't know how long they would have to wait or who would come with the assignment, but the Bistro Idyll was a perfect place to relax while they waited.

The Light beamed in through the cut glass of the window, casting a brilliant rainbow-like essence around the room. Ramiel closed his eyes and felt the warmth of the Light. No matter what time of day it was on Earth, it was always a crisp and brilliant state of perfection in the Celestial City. He smiled and took a deep breath. The smell of honey and smoke wafting from the kitchen was intoxicating.

Their server, Aurelia, walked over and greeted them with a beautiful smile. "It's so wonderful to see the two of you together again today."

"You too, Aurelia," Joam replied. "It's always a pleasure."

"Can I get you anything to drink while you consider what you might like to have, or are you ready for me to put something in for you?" Aurelia's voice sounded like the tone of a beautiful wind chime. Joam and Ramiel felt the warmth and hospitality that she exuded.

"Sure thing," Joam replied. "How about two glasses of the finest wine?" A silly smile broke out across his face as he cut his eyes at Aurelia.

Aurelia chuckled, even though she had heard this joke countless times. It was always such a joy to serve her brothers, and she enjoyed their company, no matter how dry the humor was.

"I'll have to check in the back. I think we ran out of the very finest last night, but we may have someone who could help us with that." She winked at them, then floated off toward the kitchen.

Before the angels could even strike up a conversation, Aurelia reappeared with two golden goblets of a sweet-smelling elixir that made the finest wine on Earth taste like drinking sand from the Sahara. "It just so happens that we have an endless supply of exactly what you ordered. You know, the owner is quite the vigneron." She winked at Ramiel.

The angels smiled, and Ramiel lifted his goblet toward his friend. "How is it that no matter how many times I enjoy this, it never dims on my tongue? It's as if I taste it for the first time every time."

The two toasted and raised their goblets to their lips. They didn't have time to swallow the wine before they became aware of the King's presence.

The atmosphere of the diner shifted as He moved into the space. Joam and Ramiel transitioned from the booth and bowed low to the floor.

"Rise, my favored sons. I see you ordered from my vineyards a fine vintage indeed. We enjoyed crafting that one. I trust you are enjoying it."

Ramiel realized he had been so caught up in the Lord's presence that he had forgotten to swallow. He choked the wine down, overwhelmed with honor to be a servant in the Kingdom.

It was almost impossible, even for spirit beings, to look at Him. He was so brilliant, and it took Ramiel a moment to catch his breath. "Yes, my King, we were so excited about being asked to come and receive these orders. We didn't know that you would deliver them yourself. Pardon us, Your Grace. It takes a moment to gather our composure when you are so close."

The King beamed at them with love. "It's good to visit with you today. I'm as excited to deliver these orders as you are to receive them. Now rise, my friends, and pay close attention. I have an assignment for the two of you that is of the utmost importance to all my people."

The two angels glanced at each other as they rose from the floor.

"There's a family on Earth who I have chosen to be the guardians of a very important manuscript. This manuscript contains my words. My beloved John dictated them from my mouth years ago. This family has been charged to protect the sacred writing until the Father's appointed time. Events in human history now require a shift. The manuscript will need to be hidden away on Earth and protected for several centuries. The family has waited patiently, generation after generation, for the next instruction and I'm sending the two of you to deliver it."

The King turned to Joam. "Joam, you will see to it they place the manuscript in the place I have prepared. I'm commissioning you to guard it until the proper time in creation's history."

He turned to Ramiel. "After delivering the message to the family with Joam, you will report back to me. I have an assignment that is also crucial to this part of eternity. The situation is delicate. Only you and the three of Us will have knowledge of your mission until it comes to pass. This assignment will bring you and all my other creations much joy and celebration. I can't wait to tell you about it."

The three of them took a seat in the booth, and the conversation lightened a bit as the King shared a few more minor details with the angels. He inquired about what they had been working on and where they had been, as if He didn't already know. It was His joy to hear their stories in their own words. As they finished their wine, He smiled and stood up.

Upon leaving the bistro, the King greeted the employees and chatted with the other patrons, patting them on the shoulder or commenting on their meals.

When He left the building, Aurelia appeared with Joam and Ramiel's meals packed and ready to go. She smiled at the angels. "I assume you need to be getting on. I had the chef pack these for you."

"So, I take it you overheard?" Joam smiled at her, feeling her anticipation.

"I hope this is about what I think it is. What an honor that He is sending the two of you. I packed a few extra treats in there for the road. I can't have you hungry out there."

Joam took the bag from Aurelia and smiled at Ramiel. Being in the King's presence was always overwhelming, but that day's surprise visit came with such a sense of honor. The two could hardly believe He had chosen to commission them for the task. The mystery of what was unfolding was a marvel to them, but they were so thankful to be a part of His plan.

The bell on the door chimed as they stepped out of the diner.

Ramiel turned to Joam. "I guess we'll eat our picnic on location."

"You're right, my friend. Greece awaits." They were gone in an instant.

CHAPTER 9
OPPERT AND BREA

Kindness should never be random.

The city of Ioannina had become quite the little hamlet since the days of Jeruit and Lucius. The silver business was still thriving. Some of the more independent citizens had settled on the outskirts of town to the north near Lake Pamvotis, enjoying the extra space to grow crops and raise their own animals. The children enjoyed living by the water, swimming, and learning to fish. It was a simple life. The peaceful settlement had been a safe place to raise a family. The occasional brown bear sighting was the height of local danger. Many of the villagers were the descendants of Christian families, and they had always had a benevolent attitude. Sharing with those who had less and looking out for one another's interests had worked well for the community.

However, over the past year, numerous strangers had passed through the area, with many of them begging in the streets. Not all the migrants were harmless. Some were looking for people or unattended possessions to take advantage of. Choosing to live outside of the city meant the villagers didn't have Roman guards for protection or to maintain order. Farm equipment mysteriously disappeared.

Eggs and grain were stolen, and even livestock would go missing in the night. It had forced families to isolate more and keep to themselves, looking after their own possessions. Members from some of the wealthier families took turns standing watch at night to be sure no strangers moved through and helped themselves.

Christian families still met in homes on the Sabbath and shared amongst themselves, but the fear of loss had replaced the overall sense of safety and community. Almost everyone avoided strangers as they passed through the settlement as a general precaution. Engaging with a migrant typically evolved into them lingering and eventually stealing from the vulnerable before moving on, never to be seen again.

Brea was the second-born daughter to Lucius and his wife, Helen. Her older sister, Simona, was outgoing and talkative, always a part of everything going on in the community. Brea loved her sister and admired her unhindered social involvement, but Brea had a more quiet and observant spirit. She also had a strong sense of discernment regarding people and their intentions.

Brea was married to a kind man named Oppert. They loved their home, their children, and their fellow believers. They were known for their unbiased generosity in the community. If the wheel fell off a wagon in town, no matter who owned it, Oppert would turn up with his tools and a smile to help. Brea made the best homemade bread anyone had ever tasted. Her secret ingredient was wild garlic, but no one could figure it out. People had often encouraged her to sell the bread for extra income, but sharing it for free brought joy to her heart. Brea never accepted payment. They had many friends in the city and were considered elders in their church home. People felt comfortable coming to Oppert and Brea for advice and spiritual guidance.

It was almost dusk on a cold evening in January. Oppert was looking forward to wrapping up the chores, so he could go inside, warm up, and enjoy the stew he had been smelling all day. He could already taste Brea's bread dipped in that lovely concoction of venison and potatoes. It was a family recipe that had been handed down. He loved that Brea's family was so meticulous in their heritage. They took great care to pass down traditions, artifacts, and history from one generation to the next. He figured they probably had more historical information than the city's museum. His own family had never paid much attention to the advice or history of previous generations. He didn't even know his own grandfather's name, so he relished being part of a family with such a rich heritage.

Brea was working inside their small adobe hut, putting the finishing touches on dinner. Her favorite part of baking was the egg wash at the end that made the perfectly browned bread shine with a delicious luster. She hoped the children realized it was getting late and had already started back from the lake. It would be a shame for the bread to get cold before they made it home.

Oppert heard footsteps approaching down the road. He didn't look up, assuming it was the children returning from their adventures at the lake. *I just hope they didn't get wet today. It's much colder than it was last week,* he thought. When the footsteps stopped at the edge of their front walkway, Oppert looked up from the wheel he was working on. Two enormous men were standing there. Both of them were wearing cloaks, their heads covered in ominous mystery. Just as he moved out of the barn to approach them, Brea stepped out the hut's front door.

Thort had been standing in the barn with Oppert when the strangers approached. He could smell them long before he saw them. "What in the world is this?" he asked.

Following Oppert out into the yard, he recognized them immediately, even in human disguise, but he didn't know what they were doing there. He remembered Joam from his time of creation. And Ramiel . . . that was a long story.

When Thort had first fallen, he was malevolent. He could manipulate a human psyche like no other demon, but now he had become more of a thorn than Thort, the great deceiver. His black spirit was noticeably fading. He wondered if Ramiel would even recognize him.

What could this be about? he wondered. *Who are they here to see?*

He hoped that their sheer size and the fact that they wore such ominous cloaks would instill fear in Oppert and Brea. His fellow demons' hard work was paying off all over the village. Almost no one would even make eye contact with a stranger, and everyone knew better than to offer them anything.

He seethed as the two approached, wishing there was a way he could distract Oppert so they would pass by undetected. Brea and her disgusting discernment would be nearly impossible to fool if she had any dealings with them.

Before he could conceive a decent plan, the strangers were standing on the front lawn, and Oppert was headed toward them. "Ugh. here we go," he hissed. He moved out in front of the barn but noticed that Ramiel recognized him immediately. They held intense eye contact. There were a lot of memories there. Thort knew he had better keep his distance unless he wanted to be exposed and run out completely. He hoped he could at least hear what they were talking about. What plans did the enemy have that would warrant an official visit from not one heavenly messenger, but two?

The larger of the men removed the hood of his cloak. "Greetings. I am Ramiel, and this is Joam. We mean you no harm, and I hope we didn't alarm you approaching in the late evening like this."

Oppert walked over and stood between the strangers and his wife. "I'm Oppert, and this is my wife, Brea. What can we do for you on this chilly evening?"

Joam, who had been staring toward the barn, stepped forward. "First, we would like to thank you for speaking to us. The folks at the last hut we passed went inside and closed all the doors and windows. We had not even attempted to approach them. In fact, we have received similar treatment from everyone we have encountered since we left the city limits."

Oppert nodded in understanding. "Yes, there have been more than a few strangers moving through this area with ill intentions over the past several months. Thieves and beggars roam around looking for things to steal, so the neighbors have become more guarded and less hospitable to strangers."

Ramiel nodded. "Ah, dangerous times I see, and yet you and your wife remain open to strangers? You didn't rush inside when we approached."

Brea stepped up and stood beside Oppert. "You're large men. I know you could do us harm, and we could do little to stop you."

Joam looked at Ramiel and then back at Oppert. "So, there are many who would rob and steal from you in this land. Would wisdom not dictate a more cautious approach to strangers?"

Oppert shrugged. "We're children of the most high God, our protector. Everything you see here belongs to Him, so we fear no loss of it. If you take something, we know He will provide for us. If you hurt us, we know He will take care of us. We don't live in fear, and we refuse to close ourselves off from people we have been commanded to love as Christ loved us. We can't do that from behind closed doors."

"Has your Lord always protected you?" Ramiel asked. "Have you seen much loss?"

Oppert cleared his throat. "Although we have been taken advantage of in the past, our Lord has used us many times. Even in our suffering, we have been blessed to minister to those who needed water, bread, or a place to lay their head for the night. We know that the physical needs of these strangers can often lead to a conversation about the Living Water and the Bread of Life that can sustain us forever. Introducing our Savior Jesus to many of those passing by has led to eternal life for some. No possession is more precious than that."

Oppert took another step forward and offered his hand to Joam. "The fact is, you never know who you might be entertaining, and we trust the Lord for His wisdom and direction in all things."

A warm smile spread across Brea's face. "If I discern correctly, you mean no harm to our family. Therefore, our home is open to you."

To Thort's disappointment, but not surprise, Oppert and Brea were open and hospitable with their words and body language. He could only hear in part what was being said.

"Why would they come using this disguise? What are they trying to prove?" he mumbled to himself. "Yeah, yeah, we get it. You never know who you might be entertaining," he mocked. "Shut up, Oppert. You make me sick."

He looked off into the distance. *Oh, fantastic. Here come the kids.* Thort chuckled to himself as he watched little Midsam run. His younger sisters were faster than him. *They can't even say you run like a girl, you little sissy boy. What a pathetic excuse for a human male.* Thort made a mental note to keep pushing that narrative on the little squirt. *If I can call his masculinity into question as he matures, perhaps I can steal his identity, convince him that God must have made a mistake. All the other boys aren't short and skinny, lacking strength and agility. Even if it just keeps him focused on himself and confused, that will bene-fit me.*

Ramiel glanced behind him to see the children returning from the lake.

"Don't worry Mom!" the oldest one yelled. "We didn't get very muddy today. It was too cold to go near the water." When they ran up behind the two strangers, they stopped and greeted them. "Hi. I'm Midsam. People call me Sam, and these are my sisters, Beta and Circe." Sam was indeed a small boy for his age. He didn't enjoy being the same size as his younger sisters, and he could not wait to get a little older and, hopefully, hit a growth spurt.

"Mom, are they having dinner with us tonight? Can they please?" little Circe begged.

Brea turned to Joam. "It's almost evening, and I've just finished preparing dinner. Please stay and share a meal with us. My husband has procured a fine skin of wine that we've been saving for special guests. Let us refresh you on your journey. You're also welcome to sleep in the stable out back overnight. I'll have Beta fetch some fresh blankets and put them out for you." Brea turned to the children. "You kids, hurry inside and wash up. Then prepare two extra place settings at the table for our guests."

Joam and Ramiel looked at each other and smiled. They could only imagine the wine and how it would taste compared to that they had just a few hours ago at the Bistro Idyll, but the family's kindness warmed them, and they could see why the King had chosen them.

"Thank you for offering. We didn't want to impose but to share a message with you. However, we accept your hospitality. We have stored your kindness and generosity for you in the Father's house. Mercy and kindness are Kingdom gifts freely offered to all who are in need. You've found favor in the eyes of your Lord, and He is well pleased. Fear not, for Eloah will be with you always and in all things, as you have said."

Oppert stared at the strangers with a look of slight confusion, but Brea smiled knowingly, then motioned them in the door.

Thort watched as the family followed Ramiel and Joam into the home. *Wouldn't you know it? Why can't you just offer them some water and send them on their way? Oh, no. Invite them to dine with your whole family. Oh yes, and break out the excellent wine, of course. Great idea!* Thort's most fluent language had always been sarcasm. He knew it would be impossible to get within earshot without retaliation. He was also aware that Ramiel and Joam were two angels he did not want to mess with.

Thort was in way over his head yet again. Oppert and Brea were not run-of-the-mill Enemy-fearing bipeds. Something heinous was going on, and he had to get on top of it before things got out of hand. If he didn't report this sort of intelligence back to Hell Ops, it would be his head. He needed backup. But whom could he trust? Certainly not Fluto or any of his cronies.

He made up his mind to head over to the Bar and Chain since this night was completely blown anyway. He could return in a few days and eavesdrop after the messengers left and put together the gist of the story. Right now he had to find help.

As Thort flew to the Bar and Chain, he mused to himself. *Through the centuries, since the death of Jesus and my assignment of this family, I haven't delivered one soul to the gates of hell. Not one! Something is going on with me, and I can't put my finger on it. With every new assignment, I tell myself this is the one, that I can turn this all around and redeem myself. I must believe I can still deceive, lie, and destroy these human assignments. I just need to figure out what worked best for me before, when I was at my peak of darkness. Most of my successes were from the arsenal of fear and unforgiveness, but those seeds have found no purchase here. If I'm to destroy this lineage, it must collapse from within. I must divide the family against each other: husband against wife, children against their parents, blood against blood. It's true; all my fiery darts from the outside tactics against them have failed, but if I can convince them to throw darts at one another, a house divided against itself can't stand. The Son of the Enemy said those words Himself.*

Brea had just crossed the threshold of the house when she turned back and squealed with delight. "I knew it! I knew it when I stepped out the front door. You're here about the manuscript, aren't you?"

Oppert looked at his wife with amazement. "Honey, can we let them get in the door first?" He hadn't thought about the manuscript in years. He remembered the meeting when all the detailed information and history had been relayed to him after he had joined the family. Oppert also remembered how excited he had felt to be a part of something so important and yet so secret. Could it really be possible that the time had come for the scroll's contents to be revealed? He couldn't wait to hear what the strangers had to say. "Let me take your cloaks. Sam, grab the wineskin from the cellar, and be careful with the goblets."

Brea walked over to the counter and was pleasantly surprised to discover that the bread was still warm. She ladled the stew into the bowls, happy to see that there was plenty to feed the seven of them, even though that morning she had carefully measured out the ingredients to feed five.

Oppert prayed over the meal, and they enjoyed the delicious food and each other's company. The children always loved it when they had visitors. They enjoyed learning where people had been and the interesting things they had seen. Each child took turns drilling Ramiel and Joam with every question they could come up with. The strangers' answers astonished them. How could two men have seen and experienced so much in one lifetime?

After dinner the children cleared the table and headed off to their bedroom, their minds reeling from the stories they had heard.

Oppert filled the goblets again, and the four adults sat at the table in the soft candlelight.

"So, am I correct to assume that you're here about the manuscript?" Brea asked. "Do you have further instructions for us? My father told me we were to wait for further instruction. Forgive me for being so forward, but I sure would like to know what's in it. I hope the time has come."

"One day you will know exactly what's in it," Ramiel replied. "On that day, all of creation, all humanity, will rejoice that Peter entrusted it to you and your family."

"You're correct in part," Joam added. "We're here on a mission concerning the manuscript but not to unveil its contents. If it makes you feel any better, the contents are unknown to us as well."

Joam paused and took a sip of wine, which made Brea squirm in her chair with anticipation. "The King himself has sent us to you. Your family has been loyal and trustworthy in protecting the manuscript, but now it will be hidden away from your possession. The King has determined a safe place where the manuscript will be hidden, protected, and preserved. I'm here to ensure that you find that place where people won't uncover it by accident. Understand that your commission has not ended. He will restore the manuscript to your offspring."

Brea and Oppert sat there speechless, staring at the angel.

"I, Joam, will guard the manuscript's resting place until its next revelation. Rest assured, the manuscript will remain in its original form, sealed and safe. Not one finger will touch it outside of your lineage until the King orders its destiny. I know that the Holy Spirit is now testifying to you that my words are true."

Brea took a breath and considered what she was sensing in her spirit. She felt the Holy Spirit speaking quietly inside, confirming Joam's words. She reached over and took Oppert's hand. "What he says is true. The Holy Spirit has confirmed it. We must make preparations."

Oppert was dumbstruck. Angelic messengers from God were sitting at his dining table. He knew that instruction would come one day, but it had been several generations since anyone in the family had done anything but protect the manuscript. Now it was time to follow the next set of instructions.

Joam continued, revealing the detailed instructions to the couple. He would accompany the whole family, including the children, to the island of Patmos. They would leave in two days' time to meet the boat and sail there. They would find arrangements made and their needs met at every point along the journey. Joam didn't give any information about the actual hiding place. That would come when the family arrived at the location.

Ramiel agreed to stay behind and take care of the house and the animals while they were gone and answer any questions about the family's whereabouts.

The next morning, the children could hardly contain their excitement about traveling. They had never been farther than the Ioannina city center, so it was going to be a tremendous adventure. Oppert briefed Ramiel on the farm animals and the daily schedule. Brea packed as lightly as she could for five people. Then she retrieved the manuscript from the family vault where it had spent its last twenty-four years. She baked bread all day, so they would have some to take and to share along the way.

The party left the following morning before daybreak, full of anticipation and excitement. The children soon grew weary on the journey. They were so thankful that they got to come, but they had never spent so much time on the water, and after they sailed away from the coast, there was not much to look at. They passed the time listening to stories about their ancestors. Brea told them about events dating all the way back to Paulk and Sarah when the manuscript was first given to the family. No matter how many times the stories were told, they were always full of intrigue. It was incredible to hear how God had provided and sustained their family over and over again. He had been faithful to His Word.

Joam enjoyed listening to the stories as well. It was so refreshing to experience a human family who lived in the light and love of their Savior.

After four long days of sailing, they finally made it to the coast of Patmos. Walking on solid ground again was a relief. They had not experienced hunger or sickness while at sea, but they were eager to arrive at their destination. Joam helped them carry what supplies they had left as they departed the boat. To their surprise, he guided them to a series of caves not far from where they had docked.

How is this hiding place so secret if it's right here, so close to civilization? Oppert wondered. He knew better than to ask, though. Joam had instructions straight from the King. Who was Oppert to question that?

They walked past several caves large enough for a grown adult to walk into. Sam wondered if people lived in them. Perhaps animals lived there. He wondered how long the caves had been there and what had created them. Maybe they had once been under the ocean. Sam had so many questions. He contemplated them silently as he and his family followed Joam deeper inside.

After walking through the myriad of caves, Joam stopped on the threshold of one particular tunnel. He glanced behind him with a broad smile and then entered. Oppert followed and then the others. What they thought would be a dark, cold, wet cave was anything but. A skylight allowed a direct beam of sunshine in from the top. The sun shone down on a beautiful, vigorous waterfall that spilled over from a hidden underwater source behind the rock structure. The sun's gleaming light reflected from the falling water all around the cave in an ever-changing array of colors. The sound of the falling water was so peaceful as it landed in a small pool and then careened off farther down into the system of rock formations, out of sight.

Brea wondered if they were the first people to witness the splendor.

They all stood there for a moment. Then Oppert started searching the room for what must be the perfect hiding place for the manuscript. Nothing jumped out at him. The waterfall covered the short length of the far wall, so there was nothing there. The other three walls didn't appear to have a secret space or anything. He looked back at Joam, awaiting further instruction.

Joam stepped forward until he was standing in front of the waterfall. He stretched out his hand at the top of the water as it fell. His hand created a parting in the curtain of water just large enough to reveal the mouth of another much smaller cave. This one was a mere crawlspace and disappeared.

Joam motioned for Sam to come closer. Then he bent over and put his hand on the boy's small shoulder. "Midsam, I know you have been wondering why I asked you to come on this long journey with your parents. I also know that you have wondered your whole life why God made you so small when other boys your age are so much taller." Joam looked into Sam's wondering eyes and smiled. "Well, great stature is often found in a child of God, and you were built for such a time as this. The King has chosen you to place the sacred manuscript into its hiding place. Your sisters are too young, and your parents are too big. It's your hand that will be the last to touch it until God calls your family to retrieve it."

Sam looked up at Joam in disbelief. "God created me just like this? Just for this?"

"He did, Sam. He needed *you* for this day. You won't always be a small boy, though. You will grow in stature, strength, and spirit, following God all the days of your life."

Sam looked at the waterfall. "How will I know where it goes when I get in there?"

"God himself has prepared this place for you," Joam replied. "Crawl into the tunnel. When you find a fork in the path, take the narrower of the two. When it seems like you are approaching a dead end, look to your right at the cave wall. You will see an etching there, a picture of a Lamb. Under the etching, you will find a hole in the rock veiled by a small piece of the finest linen. Behind that linen veil, you will find a blue amulet made of gemstone not yet discovered by man. Remove it, and place it in your tunic, then deposit the manuscript in its place and crawl backwards the same way you came in. Do not be afraid, Sam."

Joam motioned to Brea for the manuscript and then handed it to Sam. "The King himself prepared this spot. Until today no person has been in that space except for Him." Joam smiled at Sam. "When you see it, you will know it."

Sam took a deep breath and then turned his gaze away from the mighty angel and toward the tiny cave.

* * *

Thort remained completely unaware of the transaction between the angels of the Lord and Oppert's family. He never knew they left. Upon his return from the Bar and Chain, he found the family back on the farm working just like any other day. He heard no part of the conversation about the manuscript and nothing about the safe hiding place that Jesus had prepared in advance.

Thort was too self-consumed in his own failure to pay attention to his big-picture problem. Instead, he remained hyper focused on the micro problems in desperate hopes of ensnaring the family. It was a vicious cycle that he had been repeating itself since his first assignment with them.

CHAPTER 10

ROYYE AND ANDREA

Goodness is a gift that never needs to be wrapped.

Although the heavens had been quiet for hundreds of years since Jesus's resurrection, the traditions followed by Simon Peter's cousins had not diminished. Generation after generation grew on a foundation that became sure and firm, a foundation where the Holy Spirit found favor and empowered them in the physical and the spiritual realms.

Each preceding generation passed on the stories and instructions about the secret manuscript to their descendants. The amulet remained with the family as a symbol of God's promises and their responsibility.

The family had enjoyed a successful trade in metalwork, especially with silver. Every man in the family, including sons who married in, learned the trade. The community recognized and respected the family's integrity for generation after generation.

The Middle Ages in Europe were an active era in the spirit realm. Christianity was spreading in grassroots form. Charlemagne came into power and strove to unite all peoples under his domain into one kingdom. Then he converted his subjects to Christianity.

The forces of darkness were also working overtime, struggling to cling to any hope of destruction and dominion. Hell Ops assigned many principalities and powers to the region. An intricate web of deception involving witchcraft and demonic interaction with humans was at play.

Thort had been desperate to rope in another demon to assist him after the visit from Joam and Ramiel. He was getting the sense that this family meant a lot more to the Enemy than Hell Ops was aware. He knew he needed backup, but he didn't want to draw unwanted attention to his failures or to make things worse over the next several years. Thort suspected he was being followed, spied on. Was Hell Ops building a case against him? If so, why draw it out? He was a complete failure. His paranoia compounded everything and gave him a constant sense of impending doom.

More and more often, he would daydream about going AWOL. What would it be like to be free of this pressure and constant measurement of success and failure? The never-ending circle of scheming and laboring for nothing was like a weight on his neck, suffocating him with each passing decade. He felt his spirit slipping away as if someone were amputating him limb from limb with a butter knife. Something had to give.

Many years had passed since Joam had led Oppert and Brea's family into the cave. The family had been on a slow migration from Greece. The metal trade led them to the Harz Mountains of Germany. Thort had reluctantly followed.

Royye and his wife, Andrea, enjoyed a comfortable life serving the Lord. Royye ran the family business, and Andrea raised the children and served tirelessly in the church. They had used their resources to serve others, and God had blessed them. Their home was a bustling headquarters, with people coming in and out for meetings and fellowship.

Andrea's uncle, Deib, was a frequent visitor in their home. Deib had become a widower at a young age and had become a bit of a vagabond. He had not coped well with the loss of his wife and child, both of whom had died during childbirth. He was not a follower of

Jesus, and he carried a great deal of bitterness and resentment toward those who were.

Andrea longed to see Deib walk in the Way, so she was always benevolent and hospitable toward him. The family never looked down on him or treated him with pity. He would stay in their home for as long as he wanted, being fed and ministered to until one day he would leave for an indefinite amount of time, only to turn up again months later.

Andrea suspected Deib was in a considerable amount of debt because of gambling. He had never gotten a solid foothold on life after his loss. Sorrow ruled him. During one visit he would spend extravagantly on meaningless purchases, and during the next he would show up having not had a meal for days.

A few shady gentlemen came calling one evening in search of him. Andrea was thankful to be able to tell them that she didn't know where he was. It was then that she suspected Deib was in some serious trouble. She knew that only God could save him from the dangerous lifestyle into which he had fallen.

The following spring, just before the family's annual heritage celebration, Deib turned up looking worse than ever. He had lost at least thirty pounds, and someone had roughed him up. Andrea asked about the wounds and bruises on his body, which were in different states of healing. Deib was always aloof, never answering questions directly and dismissing any attention that the family tried to give his state of affairs. However, Andrea knew by the look in his eyes that things were different, worse.

As she prepared the room for her uncle that evening and chose a few of her husband's clothes to give to him, Andrea prayed that Deib would come to the end of himself no matter what that looked like as long as he still had breath in his lungs and a right mind in his head to make a choice. She prayed that God would grab him out of his sorrow and despair and give him ears to hear. There had to be hope. She knew joy would only come to her uncle when he submitted his life to the Lord.

As they laid in bed that evening, Royye spoke up. "Honey, I know you love your uncle."

Andrea braced herself. She knew this conversation was long overdue.

"But how many more times will we let him back in? He comes, he eats, he stays for who knows how long, only to be gone without so much as a thank-you. As a true heir, he should work shoulder to shoulder with me. He learned the trade just like all the other men before us and was once a brilliant artisan. Instead, he sweeps in for his share of the profits without ever lifting a finger."

"We can't even imagine what he has been through since Corren and the baby died," Andrea replied.

"It has been twenty-two years, Andrea!" Royye exclaimed, then caught himself. He didn't want Deib to overhear, but his passions were rising. "Yes, his wife died, and he never met his son. It's awful, but at what point are you expected to move on and live your life providing for yourself and not living off everyone else?"

Andrea knew his words were true. Deib had had plenty of time to work through his grief and get back on his feet. She knew she had played a complicit role in his irresponsible lifestyle.

"He can stay until after the celebration," Royye said. "He needs to be here for the naming ceremony anyway. After that I feel like we need to consider more of a tough-love stance. If he has gotten himself into trouble, we can't afford to tarnish our reputation or that of the business. He will never be self-reliant if we just carry him all the time."

Andrea rolled over without replying. She knew Royye was right. It was time to make some changes. She just didn't want those changes to drive her uncle away forever without knowing he would experience eternal life. She hoped that maybe the heritage celebration would provide an opportunity for him. He would hear the stories of God's miraculous promises and provision for their ancestors. He hadn't attended the festivities in many years.

With no wife or descendants of his own, Deib felt like an outcast.

It was bitter to hear of God's provision for his ancestors when He hadn't seen fit to preserve his branch of the lineage.

The next morning, Andrea rose early. She had a lot to do to prepare the family for the celebration. It had become quite the event, and she looked forward to it every year. The family would come together for a weekend. Those who were not local would stay in their home for a few nights. They would feast, play games, laugh, and catch up. But most importantly, they would spend one evening telling the ancient stories of their ancestors. They would explain to the children how they had passed down the manuscript from generation to generation, beginning with Peter. They taught the children about the visitation of the angels and the promises given when the scroll was hidden. Andrea would bring out the amulet along with a few of the other precious heirlooms she possessed from her grandparents and great-grandparents and show them around. The young children always marveled at the stories and asked endless questions about who lived where and how they had gotten to Germany. Each year when she passed the amulet around, a reverent hush fell over the family. Knowing that Jesus himself had touched that very stone was incredible.

This year would be the most important. The family would take on a surname. People were now traveling more from village-to-village trading. Distinguishing families by name was becoming a necessity, so the family had voted to adopt a patronymic surname. Royye would announce the name they had chosen at the celebration.

While Deib's niece scurried around and readied everyone for the celebration, he spent the next few days mostly sleeping. He would awaken to eat a bit, maybe bathe himself, then return to his room for hours at a time. This was wearing thin on Royye, who observed everything that Andrea and the others were doing to prepare for the celebration.

Thort hung tight over the next few days. He would fan the flame each time Royye glanced toward the guest room or saw a chore around the house left undone. Building up layers of aggravation and disappointment was easy, as Deib did nothing to contribute. Thort was hard at work to divide the household ahead of the celebration. Andrea's kindness was working against her now, and Thort hoped this seed would grow.

Thort was also certain he was being watched. Twice that week he had caught a glimpse of someone following him. The first time was when he was flying in from a visit to the Bar and Chain. It was only for a second in his periphery, but he was certain he had seen someone—or something. The second time was when he was tailing Royye home from work. Whoever it was, he had followed them all the way home. The suspicion was getting to Thort. He had conjured up every scenario for who would be following him and why. If Hell Ops was so concerned about his comings and goings, why didn't they just call him in for questioning? What was with all the low-profile spying?

Andrea worked through the list she had made to keep her on track. She washed and prepared the special dishes, and she planned which flowers and herbs she would choose from the garden to adorn the tables. So much went into the family gathering, but she loved making it special and watching the family enjoy themselves with everything prepared beforehand, so no one had to spend the entire weekend working.

On Tuesday afternoon before the big weekend, she remembered she wanted to check the table linens to make sure all the stains had been removed before storing them last year. She also wanted to hang them outside and let the creases fall out before they decorated the tables. Andrea had a beautiful hand-carved cypress chest in her room where she stored her precious belongings, including the family heirlooms and the amulet. She could hardly wait to present the lovely items once again at the telling in a few days. She opened the chest, removed the linens, and counted to make sure they were all there. Under them they stored the heirlooms. Some were in little boxes or stored inside of sections of bamboo reeds. Others were wrapped inside protective clothes. She looked at each one. Her eye caught on her great-great-great grandmother Brea's old bread bowl. It was one of Andrea's most prized possessions. Every time she saw it, she imagined what Brea's hands must have looked like working in that bowl, kneading flour into dough day after day. Inside the bowl, wrapped in cloth, was Andrea's mother's silver bracelet. Andrea rarely handled it, but she prized it in her heart. It was one of the few things of her mother's that she still owned. As she ran her thumb over the bracelet, she thought about her younger sister, Alma, who would be arriving soon with her family. She wondered if Alma would appreciate having something passed down from the family. Perhaps she would present her with Brea's bread bowl during the family celebration. She knew it would mean a lot to Alma. Andrea also hoped to ask her uncle to share some stories that she and Alma may not yet have heard about his childhood while living with their mother. Andrea always loved to hear about her mother as a little girl.

Before she closed the chest, she lifted out a few other items and then, out of habit, checked on the amulet. It was right where she left it last year, wrapped in fine linen. She smiled, thinking of the weekend and how everyone would enjoy once again hearing the stories and passing the amulet around. She closed the chest, grabbed the table linens, and headed off to keep working on her list of tasks.

The rest of the week rushed by. They made the final preparations and set everything as the weekend festivities approached. They hoped it wouldn't rain like last year, so they could use the outside patio area instead of crowding into the house.

Royye walked outside the night before the guests were due to arrive and gazed up at the clear sky. He could see every star, and he thanked God for pleasant weather and prayed for safe travel for his family members and asked for a blessing over them during their fellowship together.

Thort stood over Royye, perched on the roof of the house, and rolled his eyes in disgust. How could this man pray after spending all week in irritation and building anger toward his uncle-in-law? Thort would never understand how these people could turn so quickly from darkness with just one glance at the heavens. Royye's prayer irritated Thort, but he didn't panic. He knew that the next few days would be full of opportunities with all the bustle of the guests.

Just then a quick flash caught his attention out of the corner of his eye. If his mind hadn't been training to notice it, he would have thought it was a fault in his vision or a trick of his mind. But he couldn't dismiss it. It was there. He had seen it over and over enough to convince him this was more than a trick his mind was playing on him out of paranoia. His spy, his watchman, his pursuer, or his huntsman had to be revealed. "That's it!" He cried and darted off the roof toward the being.

* * *

WHEN MORNING CAME, people started to arrive. It was such an exciting time for everyone. Andrea laid fruits and nuts out in the kitchen for people to graze on as they arrived throughout the day. The women caught up and enjoyed the new baby who had recently been born to Royye's youngest cousin. The men formed a bit of a competition outside, seeing who could chop wood with the most precision in one swing. It was a beautiful day.

Andrea glanced out at the men and noticed that Deib wasn't among them. She rolled her eyes. "I'm sure no one even thought to wake him and invite him out to be a part of the game," she mumbled to herself as she headed back toward his room. She knocked on his door and called out, but there was no answer, which was typical. Deib was famous for sleeping like a stone in the middle of the day. She cracked the door and called out to him, but there was still no response. As she entered the room, she noticed the bed was disheveled and the linens were strewn across the floor. She also saw crumbs of whatever Deib had eaten over the last few days. The room was gloomy and smelled stale. There was no sign of her uncle. He was gone.

"Not again!" she exclaimed. "Why would he leave today?"

Her sister-in-law walked up behind her to see who Andrea was talking to. "Oh, honey, this room is a mess."

"Yes, I'm aware. Uncle Deib has been staying with us for several days, and this is his room."

"I'll be happy to help you clean it," her sister-in-law said. "Where is he now?"

"Apparently, he left in the night—again. I had hoped he would stay for the celebration and the naming ceremony. It saddens me, but he comes and goes at his own leisure, and it's been wearing thin on your brother these days. Don't worry about this mess. Go back and enjoy that baby. I'll have this fixed up in no time." Andrea scurried her sister-in-law out the door and back toward the kitchen.

The day went on flawlessly. Everyone arrived with no travel issues. The weather was so nice that they spent the day outside enjoying the sun.

It wasn't until late afternoon that Royye passed by the kitchen where Andrea was preparing the evening meal and asked about Deib.

Andrea hadn't wanted to bring it up until she had to. She laid down her knife, wiped her hands on her apron, and pulled Royye out of earshot of the guests.

"He left, Royye. He was gone this morning when I checked on him. It's okay. We knew he would leave eventually, and now we don't have to worry about him spoiling the weekend." She was trying to land the news gently. She knew Royye would not take it well.

As she spoke, Royye's face reddened. She knew it was coming. "You can't be serious!" he exclaimed. "Today? Today he's gone? You've fed him for almost two weeks, seen to his every need, and today he decides it's time to go?" Royye was fuming. At this point, he didn't care if the guests heard him. He was so tired of being taken advantage of that he couldn't think straight. "Deib had better hope he's long gone because if I see his face today, it won't go well with him, Andrea! I'm done. This home is not open to his comings and goings any longer. He has spent the balance of my hospitality. He is a liar, and he uses you, and I won't stand for it another day!"

Andrea tried to squelch the fire that was burning in her husband. "We don't have to deal with this now. He's gone, and we have many things to be thankful for. Look around you. God has blessed us beyond measure. We must not let this steal our joy. Take a deep breath, then go back outside. Enjoy this weekend, and let's celebrate God's goodness."

The red slowly drained out of Royye's face. Andrea's words always had a soothing mercy. All he had to do was listen. She was right. God had surrounded their family with so much to be thankful for. Why had he let that man get under his skin so easily? What were they out for his being there, some food and a few dirty sheets?

He kissed his wife on the forehead and thanked her for everything that she was doing. He was so grateful for her.

"Look at it this way," she said, smiling. "Now that his room is free, we won't feel so crowded in the house with the other family."

Royye smiled back at her, acknowledging that simple truth.

The rest of the evening and next day went smoothly. Everyone settled in and was enjoying the weekend.

On Saturday afternoon, Andrea went to gather the items that they liked to share with everyone as they told the stories of their heritage. She had been running a few of the stories over in her mind as she prepared to share them the next day. She kneeled beside the chest and opened the lid.

Immediately, she lost her breath. Someone had ransacked the trunk. All the neat little storage boxes and protective cloths had been tossed around. The silver bracelet was missing, and so was the pocketknife and the prayer shawl. The bread bowl was overturned on its side. She was afraid to pick it up. "Surely, it's not broken. Please, Lord, don't let it be broken," she whispered as she riffled through the empty cloth and containers. She knew who was responsible for the missing items. Tears welled up in her eyes as she reached the bottom of the chest and found the old square of fine linen. The amulet was gone.

When Andrea informed Royye about the robbery, it surprised her that his reaction was not more irate. He handled it with a great deal of self-control.

"I knew there was something off with your uncle this time. I know you love him, but I've never been comfortable around him. Every time he visits, he has taken advantage of you and the family's generosity, and now we have lost so much. The family valuables are all gone. I'm sure he has peddled them off for pennies to settle some debt he owes."

"He just doesn't have the light of Jesus in him yet," Andrea replied. "We expect our friends and relatives to be just like us, but without Jesus and the baptism of the Holy Spirit, they are blind in darkness like we all were once. I hate the loss of our family's possessions, and I hate that I don't have them to pass on to our children, but you and I both know there are many more things we pass on that are eternal and those are so much more important." Andrea knew she had to make an explanation to the family about what had happened to the heirlooms, especially the amulet. How could this turn of events play into God's plan? She wiped her tears and stood up.

Just then, her sister knocked on the bedroom door. "There's an officer at the front door asking for the two of you," she said.

Thort had been shivering with anticipation all morning. So much had transpired since the night before. He could see a freckle of darkness at the end of the incessant light tunnel he had been in for so long. Another demon by the name of Nag stood by his side with confidence as the two glared down at the policeman at the front door.

The night before had been a busy one. When Thort scurried off to find out who was tailing him, he had caught a faint blur. There was another one of those quick flashes of light. He thought it was so strange. Nothing from Hell Ops omitted light on any level.

He snuck over to the barn with all the stealth he could muster. He stood with his back against the barn's front wall holding his breath and listening for any movement. After a solid two minutes, Thort heard another faint shuffle. Without hesitation, he leaped around the corner, ready to fight. For a split second, his eyes chased the shadows back and forth and up and down. Then he saw it.

There by the tree was crouched a short, stocky demon shrouded in a cloak. Nag was startled by the sudden sight of Thort, who towered over him.

"Who in Hell are you?" Thort demanded.

Nag gathered himself and uncovered his head. "It's me, Nag. I'm here on assignment."

"Well, now that's obvious. Why did Hell Ops assign you to me, and why have you been hiding?"

"Assigned to you? What are you talking about?" Nag's face declared he was confused. "I vaguely remember your face, maybe from the Bar and Chain, but I don't know who you are, and I'm certainly not assigned to you. Demons aren't assigned to other demons, you moron. Are you lost?"

"No, I'm not lost. I'm right where I'm supposed to be. This family is my territory. Don't lie to me. I've seen you tailing me several times. You aren't fooling anyone."

"My current human assignment, Deib, is a pathetic fool, but so far has proven to be quite the simple task, so I come and go at my leisure. I just look in on him from time to time to make sure he stays on track. This is the first time I've run into you, so whoever you say is following you must be a figment of your imagination. If you have seen me in passing, it's simply because our assignments are in the same vicinity, not because I have any interest in you," Nag said in disgust.

"Whatever. I picked up on you tonight, and here we are." Thort breathed a tremendous sigh of relief, but he was still not convinced that Nag was telling the truth. One could never trust another demon.

"So, I'm assuming they assigned you to Deib's niece? What's her name?"

"Andrea. But she's married to Royye, and I'm assigned to both as a couple."

"Well, any relative of Deib must be as easy an assignment as he is. That's obvious since they assigned you two at a time."

Thort's head almost exploded with rage. If he could have shot fire out of his eyes and incinerated Nag on the spot, he would have.

"You don't know what you're talking about," he hissed, pacing back and forth in frustration. "Honestly, I don't even understand how this Deib character can be related to this family. Hell Ops assigned multiple generations of these vermin to me, and I've seen no headway for the realm in decades."

"Huh, that doesn't seem right," Nag replied. "Deib has been a pure delight since the death of his family irreparably damaged his life."

"Good for you. I'm so glad your mission is so simple that you barely have to pay attention," Thort shot back, malice dripping from his tongue.

"Maybe you're doing it wrong," Nag said, dismissing Thort's anger. "Perhaps I can show you a thing or two." A condescending grin spread across his face.

The blow to Thort's pride punched him in the chest like a jolt of electricity. Was this meager dwarf of a demon offering to show him the ropes? If Nag had only seen Thort in his glory days when his very presence was like a black hole, sucking the very life out of things as he passed by. Nag didn't know who he was talking to. But Thort had to admit, he was no longer the same demon. Nag was talking to a demon who, after years and years of being bled dry by these incessant bipeds, bore only a shadow of the darkness he once displayed. At this point, Thort was willing to take advice from a bullfrog, but it didn't hurt his pride any less. After an uncomfortable silence, to Nag's surprise, Thort met his eyes with a humiliated, almost pleading look.

Andrea knew the officer was there about her uncle. She just didn't know if he was there to arrest them for assisting a criminal or to inform her that Deib was in prison, had hurt someone, or worse. She said a quick prayer under her breath as Royye opened the front door.

"Officer, I'm Royye, and this is my wife, Andrea. How can we help you this evening?"

A few of the family members huddled behind them to see what the disturbance was about.

"Would you please step outside?" the officer asked as he straightened himself and adjusted his stance to look more official.

Andrea turned to the family behind her, holding up her hand

with an assuring look and a polite smile. The couple stepped out into the front of the house and closed the door.

"I understand you have a relative by the name of Deib," the officer said. "Is this correct?"

"Why, yes, we do. Deib is my wife's uncle. He has been staying with us for a short time, but he was missing this morning when we went to check on him. Do you have news, sir?" Royye wasn't sure he wanted to know the answer to that question.

"He was found early this morning by a fisherman on his way to work. He was unconscious in a ditch beside the road. His injuries are extensive, so we are not sure how long he was lying there. He briefly regained consciousness and gave your names as his family contact. He said he was attacked by strangers and mugged. We have him in a holding facility at the jail awaiting medical assistance, but we need to know if you agree to cover his expenses."

Royye turned to his wife. Andrea hung her head in silence. She felt sad, hurt, and relieved all at once. "Of course we'll cover his expenses, whatever he needs." She grabbed Royye's hand and squeezed it. "I need to see him immediately. Can you take us there?"

Back inside, Andrea reassured Alma and the rest of the family. She also gave a few directions about continuing preparations for the celebration. Then she and Royye left with the officer to visit her uncle. She hoped he would be conscious and could speak to her when she got there.

Upon their arrival at the jail, the guards ushered them to a holding cell with a single cot. There lay Deib, covered in a ratty blanket issued to him by the jailer. His legs were bloody, and one was apparently broken.

Andrea rushed over and kneeled by his side, looking into her uncle's face. It was barely recognizable with the swelling and dried blood clinging to his beard. The stench coming off him was hard to bear, but she rustled his shoulder and attempted to stir him.

"Deib. Deib, are you awake? It's Andrea and Royye. Deib, can you hear me?" Andrea shook him as hard as she thought she should, not knowing the extent of his injuries.

Deib woke with a painful jolt and shuffled his body away in fear before he realized who woke him.

Andrea wasn't sure what she had been expecting from her uncle. Perhaps regret or a sense of shame. Could his vulnerable posture be the open door she had been praying for to reach him finally? She searched his face as he opened the one eye that wasn't swollen shut.

Deib dashed her hopes when he made eye contact. He rolled his eyes in disgust and murmured a curse under his breath.

"Deib, thank the Lord you're still here with us," Andrea said as she placed her hand on his shoulder.

"Don't start with that, Andrea," Deib winced and said. "You can see I'm lying here half dead, and yet you still want to 'thank the Lord.'" Deib wasn't interested in a conversation or any sort of lesson his niece may have prepared for him.

Andrea's eyes filled with sorrow. "Oh, Deib, what has happened to you? Who did this to you and why?"

"Not that it's any of your business, but I was off to settle an affair, but before I got there, the sorry crook sicked his thugs on me. They beat me, took everything I had, and left me for dead. Yet here I am. Thank the Lord," he said. Although speaking was growing more and more difficult from the stabbing pain in his chest, his voice was still full of sarcasm.

"Were you off to settle your affairs with the family heirlooms that you lifted from our home?" Royye asked.

"Royye, you do realize I'm part of this family too, right? You act like I stole something that I had no right to. It's quite simple. The family had resources and I needed resources," Deib coughed and blood spat out from his lip.

Andrea had heard enough. Her blood was boiling, so she took a deep breath and called on the Holy Spirit to guide her next actions lest she finish her uncle off herself. Her family had given and given to this man. She had stood up for him time after time, knowing he didn't deserve it, knowing he could never repay her family, and knowing that he would probably never turn his life around.

Andrea felt like she was at the end of herself when the Holy Spirit whispered in her ear. "Remember now, it is what He did for you. It's the greater love. It's His love that He put inside of you. All He asks is that you lay your life down." She nodded in understanding, then took a deep breath and lifted her eyes to meet Deib's.

"I want you to know that what you did was very upsetting to me and our family. You took precious items we all inherited from our parents and their ancestors. Those possessions are now gone forever." She paused, and Deib rolled his eyes again, bracing for the tongue lashing he knew was coming. "But the things of this world will pass away," she continued. "We won't pass away, Uncle. Those heirlooms were just symbols used to tell a story. The real prize, the most precious treasure, is that our names are written in the Lamb's Book of Life. Not one item on this Earth is equal to that gift, given freely to us even though we don't deserve it."

Andrea rose to her feet, dusting herself off. "Now, I hope our family's resources have freed you from the threats of your debtors. I forgive you for taking them without the family's permission, and we will pay for your medical needs. I love you, and I'll never give up on you." She tucked her arm under Royye's and reached up to kiss him on the cheek.

Deib remained stoic throughout his niece's speech. He refused to listen to the gospel being displayed before his very eyes, instead hardening his heart. Nag had worked hard on his greedy heart and held it fast. Deib didn't care if he lived or died at that point as long as he didn't have to listen to anymore of his family's self-righteous rhetoric.

Before they left, Royye made arrangements for Deib's care. On the way home, he held his wife and thanked God for a woman who was so alert to the Holy Spirit's leading. She recognized what mattered in this life and was even willing to wash the feet of the one who had betrayed her, who had betrayed their entire family. What a testimony. A feeling of appreciation for what Jesus had done for them overcame Royye.

Upon arriving home, Andrea found that Alma and the family had been hard at work, cleaning the house and continuing to prepare for the celebration. She didn't have to lift a finger. Tears of appreciation fell down her face as she walked through the house. Every floor had been swept and every bed made. She walked down the hallway to the bedroom where Deib had been staying and found it perfectly clean. All the bedclothes had been replaced, and the surfaces had been wiped clear of dust and clutter. The window shade was lifted, letting sunlight stream into the room. In the center of the bed, the sun caught a shiny item, and the light gleamed deep blue back at her in a beautiful shimmer. It was the amulet, right there on the bed.

Alma wrapped her arms around her sister's shoulders. "I found it under the bed when I was changing the sheets. He must have dropped it on the way out."

Andrea's breath caught in her throat as the tears welled up again. "He dropped nothing. This is the Lord's work." She smiled.

Thort stayed with Nag at the jail after Andrea and Royye departed for home. It was so refreshing to watch Deib hold tight to the darkness even in the face of a ridiculous barrage of self-righteous flaunting. Oh, how Thort longed for the taste of victory he had just witnessed. It had been so long.

As Deib took his last breaths, Thort witnessed Nag absorb the darkness that he had invested in his assignment. His form became more defined and crisper to the eye.

Nag relished the moment, knowing that Thort was looking on with envy. There was nothing more honorable than escorting a human assignment to the gates of Hell at the end of their time on Earth. Sweet victory and the promise of promotion loomed as Nag luxuriated in the moment.

It was painful to watch, but Thort had an idea. "Hey, I think I'll go with you when you report on this assignment," Thort said. "What would you say to a bit of a tag team moving forward? I must give you credit for finding the crack in this family. Perhaps you have other angles that we can work on together. We can request a partnership from the chief. What do you think?"

Nag threw his head back and laughed. He didn't really object to the request, but he could not resist a theatrical attempt to capitalize on Thort's pathetic self-loathing. "Works for me. I don't mind a rehabilitation project now and then. Maybe you'll pick up on things quickly, and I can earn a special task stripe for mopping you up off the floor."

Thort rolled his eyes in disgust.

The family grew quiet as Andrea approached the center of the tables facing each other. It had been a wonderful day filled with games and family stories, ending with a delightful feast. News had arrived late that afternoon of Deib's passing, but Andrea did not let it shadow the day.

"Before we get to telling the tale of the amulet, we want to make an announcement," Andrea said. "As you all know, we decided this year to take on a family surname to help distinguish our family from others in the region. We prayed and asked God for a name that would honor Him and point back to the legacy that He has been a part of in our family heritage."

Andrea held out her hand for Royye to join her. She took the amulet out of a pocket in her dress and placed it in his hand. Royye looked at his family as he spoke. "From now on, we will be known as Petrus. I'm Royye Petrus, and this is my wife, Andrea Petrus. We're honored to be a part of this family and to share this name with all of you. This word means 'rock.' We have all read what Jesus said to our ancestor, Peter, after he identified his master as the Christ and the Son of the Living God. He said, 'Upon this rock, I will build My church; and the gates of Hell shall not prevail against it.' We're that Petrus."

Those were the last words Thort heard before he departed with Nag back to Hell Ops: "And the gates of Hell shall not prevail against it." His ears almost bled when Royye uttered the words. Shock and betrayal rattled around in Thort's brain as he flew next to Nag.

What was this setup? Who had pitted him against an invincible force? Suddenly, Thort wasn't so afraid of reporting back to headquarters. Instead, he was angry. Someone back at Hell Ops had some serious explaining to do!

CHAPTER II

CALLING FOR BACKUP

Thort skidded into town with a renewed sense of entitlement. Had they denied him pertinent information that would explain all this generational nonsense? Why had higher-ranking officials classified this information, and why had they not assigned more resources to this mission? He had so many questions.

For so long he had felt like a miserable failure, hiding in the shadows, hoping not to be recognized for generation after generation, only to repeatedly fail and lose to the Enemy.

He didn't plan to wait for any debriefing meeting. He was going to barge right into Chief Maltreat's office, plop down in a chair in front of his desk, and demand some answers.

As he ran the questions through his mind and practiced what he would say. He almost forgot that Nag was by his side. He was thankful to have someone to back up his story, especially since Nag had been connected to the family and witnessed firsthand how bleak the situation was. Surely, Hell Ops would not deny him additional resources moving forward.

Chief Maltreat forced Thort and Nag to wait in the lobby for a full day. He didn't appreciate unannounced visits, and he was not interested in rearranging his daily schedule for a couple of low-ranking officers demanding his time. Maltreat always gave off the air that he was swamped with top-secret Hell Ops business. In truth, he was just making Thort and Nag wait. He loved a good humiliation.

Five minutes before the offices were too close for the day, he strolled out of his office and glanced over at the demons sitting against the wall.

"Oh, Thort, Nag, I forgot you were there," Maltreat said.

Thort was seething.

Maltreat wandered over to his secretary's desk and asked if there were any messages. He knew there were none. He had been in his office doing nothing all day. No one was looking for him except for Thort.

Maltreat turned and acted as if he were heading out for the day without further acknowledgement.

"Sir." Thort cleared his throat. His tone was riddled with indignant loathing, but he didn't want to be shut down before he was given an opportunity to explain his case.

Maltreat kept walking as if he heard nothing.

"Chief Maltreat! We have been waiting to meet with you, sir!" Thort yelled after him.

Maltreat turned with a look of ignorant wonder on his face. "I'm sorry, the offices are closing now. You'll need to report back first thing tomorrow. Hopefully, I can fit you in."

"Sir, we have important information that we need to discuss concerning a current assignment," Thort said. "We can't continue maneuvers until we have further intelligence and instruction on how to proceed."

Maltreat rolled his eyes. He wanted to send them away and make them wait for him another day—maybe several days. Thort couldn't just barge in like this. Unfortunately, Maltreat was also concerned that the report might be important. What if something urgent was happening, and he just blew it off? Maltreat didn't want to catch the wrath of anyone higher up the chain, so he motioned them into his office with a short-tempered sigh of annoyance.

Thort spent the next half hour giving a brief account of his dealings with the newly named Petrus family. He didn't go into detail, aware that the complete story would paint him in a horrible light. Maltreat had warned that their next meeting better not include more reports of failure.

Thort also explained his encounter with Nag. As much as it pained him, he even had to brag about Nag's success with Deib, though he had to speak slowly to keep himself from gagging.

Giving glory to someone other than himself was contrary to his nature. When he felt like he had given as much information as was safe to do so, he reported what he had heard Royye Petrus say when he announced the family's new name.

For a fleeting moment, Thort thought he saw a look of disbelief—or was it confusion?—on Maltreat's face. He was still trying to read his response when Maltreat stood up and ushered them back out into the lobby. He instructed them to wait and then went back into his office and slammed the door.

Thort and Nag stared at each other in confusion. What had just happened?

"So much for demanding answers," Nag said, chuckling. "You really showed him."

Thort was in such a state of shock that he didn't even notice Nag's mocking tone. Maltreat's response was totally unexpected. Surely, they owed him some type of explanation. At the very least, they had to instruct him on how to proceed.

Meanwhile, behind his office door, Maltreat called his lieutenant commander to brief him on the meeting with Thort and Nag. He spent over an hour speaking with his lieutenant commander and other officers, including General Screwtape, on the call. The consensus was that the Hell Ops Intelligence Agency had heard this name used before when Jesus addressed Peter prior to his crucifixion, but there was no interpretation of its meaning. The fact that it was being brought up again centuries later with a random family deciding on a surname was reason to take note, but they didn't understand the affiliation or the definition of the term. No one at Hell

Ops knew what the words "On this rock I will build My church" meant.

Maltreat had nothing meaningful to say to Thort and Nag, but he knew he had to address them, so he called them back into his office.

"Thort, your missions are assigned with stringent attention to classified intelligence and based on the strengths you are expected to be proficient in to succeed. That you have been so incompetent for so long and still have your head on your shoulders is a mystery to me. Some unseen mystic must be protecting your existence. I should strip you of the right to walk through the gates of this realm right now. As you both know, we give intelligence to you on a need-to-know basis. If there is anything you need to know to succeed with these assignments, we have included it in your briefs." Maltreat paused for effect.

"Sir, I have a question," Thort said, realizing he was treading on thin ice. Maltreat nodded, giving him permission to proceed. "Have they have assigned me to a multi-generational suicide mission?" Thort asked. "Is there any hope of victory?"

Maltreat leaped up, knocking his chair over in the process, and slammed his hand on his desk in rage. "There's *always* hope for victory! We don't work for darkness in vain! We expect you to succeed every time we send you into the field. Do you think we're just here for fun and games? We seal humans' fate. We see that they *never* taste eternal life! Could there be a more vital mission?"

Leaning over the desk, Maltreat pointed his boney talon in Thort's face. "Your failures over the centuries are glaringly apparent. This office won't stand for another disgrace on your behalf. I can't think of the proper words to threaten your existence if this folly continues."

For a minute, Thort thought that the six hairs on top of Maltreat's head were going to ignite. "I take this mission seriously, sir." Thort realized he needed to backtrack and change course. "I simply wanted to make sure that we had properly briefed you on all the intelligence gained from the front lines. Would you consider assigning Nag and me as partners moving forward? He sealed his previous assignment earlier this week, and the situation with the Petrus family seems delicate and of utmost importance to the realm."

Nag had remained silent throughout the discourse. He knew better than to wade into the fray with Maltreat.

After the chief glared at them both for a very uncomfortable amount of time, he waved his hand in dismissal. "Fine, you may work as a team. How many idiots does it take to bring a human soul to the lake of fire? Now get out of my office, and come back at your regularly scheduled time for generational assignment." He opened the door and pushed them out. They staggered back into the lobby, and Maltreat slammed his door behind him.

The meeting hadn't gone as Thort had pictured it in his head, but at the very least, he wasn't alone anymore on this seemingly impossible mission.

"Need-to-know basis," he muttered as they walked across the street to the Brimstone Bar and Chain.

"Oh, get over yourself," Nag replied. "You've got me now, and I never fail. So, that means this family is finished. Whatever the enemy has been scheming ends with the next generation. In a few years, you won't even remember this meeting. Now let's go grab a brew, and stop being so dramatic."

CHAPTER 12

RELLY AND WYEITA, SIMON AND ALVIDA

Patience walks beside wisdom.

For 500 years, the dark kingdom had been busy at work. Orders from Hell Ops were to present Christianity as just another useless religion, followed by a few crazed fanatics. The tactics and the mission maneuvers issued were bent on diluting the power of the gospel. The end goal was for the Church to be lulled into a deep sleep. Many things that should not have been forgotten were lost. A kingdom full of greed, lust, and idolatry had subverted the message of the Kingdom of God. Fossilized institutions had replaced the Church, and they lacked the power and potency that the early Church enjoyed.

Despite the widespread status of the religion calling itself Christianity, the invisible Church was still very much alive. The Father saw that a remnant of believers, true in their faith and willing in their service, were preserved and responsible for furthering Earth's redemption story.

The Petrus family remained central to this calling. During these dark ages, a stranger who had been traveling through Europe gifted the family with a printed Bible that was translated into Latin. The

Petrus family, notorious for passing down family relics and legacy stories, added the Bible to the valuables. Patriarchs and matriarchs read the Bible aloud to the family, from the youngest to the oldest. The Holy Spirit provided the much-needed revelation and direction over those dark years. God honored His word to preserve them.

Like their ancestors, Relly and Wyeita Petrus had received many spiritual and financial blessings. They had resources well above and beyond their physical needs and enjoyed the ability to seed into the Kingdom with regular financial contributions. There was no greed found in them, and God had used their family as a vessel to bless others and further the gospel message in their region.

God had also blessed the couple with two daughters and seven sons, the eldest of which they named Simon. He grew up hearing the scriptures read aloud from his youth. Simon was aware of his family's legacy and how God had sustained them throughout history. He knew about the historical importance of the amulet and the manuscript. He had never experienced need or hunger in his life. All the Petrus children enjoyed easy childhoods, free of sickness or a need for work outside their home.

Simon was a loving, independent child. When he was young, he loved helping Wyeita with his younger siblings. He also took a special interest in helping the elderly members of their church congregation, but he didn't get along as well with other children his own age.

Simon grew to be a handsome, tall, strong young man. In the later part of his teen years, he became a bit more self-absorbed. His sense of entitlement grew, and he considered his wants and desires over almost everything else in his life. He was never blatantly disrespectful to his parents, but he interacted with them as little as possible, telling them what he knew they wanted to hear to get them to leave him alone. There was an insatiable hole inside of Simon's heart.

Relly, Simon's father, was concerned about his son's behavior. He recognized the unspoken distance between them when it first began at age thirteen, but he was not sure how to address it. He had tried many times over the years to engage with his son. It was difficult with nine children, but he was desperate not to lose his eldest. Relly had arranged hunting and fishing trips for just the two of them, but Simon showed no interest. Relly also took extra initiative to include him in conversation or to ask questions to show his affection for what might interest Simon, but nothing seemed to appeal to his son.

More recently, Relly had offered Simon a position at the family business. Simon was of age to work for a wage, and Relly knew how smart and capable his son was. The position was one with some moderate authority over the craft workers and responsibility for daily output. Relly thought the opportunity might create a sense of ownership in Simon, encouraging him to develop a healthy work ethic. The attempt had fallen flat, though. Simon failed to show up to work on the second day, embarrassing his father.

The simple fact was, Simon didn't care about hunting, fishing, or cooking his own food. He didn't care about having a conversation with his father, and he certainly didn't care about working or taking on responsibilities. Why did he need to work? The family had more than they could ever need, and he was the firstborn heir to the fortune.

Simon had a few things he enjoyed. His friend Gorce had grown up with him and had been his only close friend since childhood. He and Gorce had entertained themselves by being the school bullies growing up. They enjoyed making fun of and pulling harmless pranks on the children of lower social status or those with lesser physical abilities. Simon didn't have a natural-born empathy for others. He would not physically hurt anyone. The cruel jokes and targeting of others were merely for his enjoyment.

Simon's parents were highly respected in the community, and their benevolence had helped many of the town people, so Simon's cruel actions went mostly unmentioned. His peers knew his reputation. Hence, Gorce was the only one who stood by him as a friend.

As Simon and Gorce got older, maturity turned them from schoolyard games to darker interests. The two were highly interested in females. No self-respecting young woman who had grown up with the boys would have anything to do with them, but there were ladies who would spend plenty of time with a young man—for a price. Simon had been involved with several prostitutes over the course of the last six months, but the more he engaged in it, the less it seemed to satisfy him. He became emotionally detached from everyone, and physical pleasure was fleeting. He and Gorce were on a dangerous path with little care for where it was taking them.

Thort, currently on assignment to Relly and Wyeita, had been spending most of his time tagging along with his cohort, Nag. Simon was Nag's current human assignment, and the weapons he had been using seemed very efficient. It was refreshing to witness a firstborn Petrus in self-destruction mode.

However, something strange was going on. Thort could have sworn he was still being watched. He assumed Nag had been the presence he had detected and then discovered. Hell Ops had granted permission for them to team up, so it made no sense for someone from headquarters to still be spying on him. The issue didn't seem too threatening, but it certainly rode in the back of his mind as a mystery worth looking into.

Thort trusted that Simon's ultimate demise would be the death of hope for his parents. All those long nights spent praying together for a son who couldn't care less about what happened to him or how his actions hurt anyone else made Thort giddy with anticipation. He hoped someone from Hell Ops was watching him. Whoever the spy was would be a firsthand witness. Thort and Nag's partnership set the course for a splendid success. It thrilled him to have had such a brilliant idea, and he couldn't wait to see this generation play out.

One morning in early spring, Simon woke up with a throbbing headache. He and Gorce had gotten drunk and stayed out all night. Simon knew his parents would be worried, but he considered himself a grown man now. He didn't need to answer to anyone about where he had been. Simon just hoped his father would not give him too much grief when he returned home for more money.

Simon stumbled out of the brothel around noon and strolled to the marketplace to use the last of his money on some lunch. Gorce was not around, but he figured they would catch up later. He sat at a small table by himself in the shadow of the overhanging building of the butcher stand. The sun hurt his eyes, and his head was pounding. He sniffed himself. Whew. Simon knew he needed to head home and clean up, but who would be there in the middle of the day? What day was it, anyway? Would he have to answer all the questions that his nosey mother or one of his annoying siblings asked? Could he get in and get out without being picked to death by his family? He pondered his evasive maneuvers as he choked down some crusty bread and a glass of cheap wine.

Across the street, the gate to the herb market swung open. Simon glanced up from his misery and forced his eyes to focus.

Time stopped.

He watched her as if in slow motion. Soft brown hair tucked behind her ear on one side, revealing her beautiful profile and flawless olive skin of her face. A bundle of lavender tied with twine fell from her basket as she turned to close the gate. Simon watched as she gathered the skirt of her dress to pick it up. She moved with such grace and poise in an effortless fluidity that had Simon spellbound. All he had seen was her profile, but he longed to look into her eyes and know her name. Simon wanted to know everything about her. He didn't care what he had to do or how long it took. He would meet her. He would learn everything about her. And he would marry her.

Dumbstruck, Simon stumbled out of his chair and shuffled across the traffic path, weaving through the people, his gaze was locked on the beautiful girl. He stumbled in front of a woman carrying a baby and then barely missed being run over by a man with a large fruit cart. Simon continued without even noticing the man yelling behind him.

He had not considered how awkward it would be for him to approach this woman out of the blue and stop her on the street with nothing to say. None of that crossed his mind when he placed his hand on her shoulder to get her attention.

The woman turned to look at him, and it was just as he had imagined. Her eyes were as deep as a spring bubbling up from the ground but as warm as a balmy summer day. Although she was a bit startled, her face spread into a welcoming smile. Simon knew he wanted to spend the rest of his days looking at her. She radiated with a beauty that took his breath away. In the second that it took for his eyes to take in her face, his mind had run the gamut and confirmed he had never seen anything so perfect.

She waited for him to speak, but he just stared at her. Her eyes widened, and she tilted her head in question.

This was awkward.

When she saw that the man was clearly in some sort of trance, she spoke. "May I help you, sir?"

Simon remained silent for another painful moment as his ears took in the voice that sang a song to his soul. Then he snapped out of it, lost. "Um, oh yeah. Excuse me. Um, I'm sorry. I, uh, saw you from across the street . . ."

She smirked and waited, but he said nothing else. Realizing he was struggling, she decided to help him along. "Oh, yes. I dropped the lavender. I thought I had secured everything before I left the counter, but it slipped out as I passed through the gate."

"Yes, the lavender," Simon said, his voice overly loud. "I hurried over to help you gather it, when I saw it had fallen, but by the time I got there, you had already picked it up, so . . ."

"Oh, yes. Well, thank you. I got it. I'm all good now. Thank you for trying to help, sir." She paused, giving him a chance to offer his name.

Simon's mind was still swirling, and he missed the hint. He found himself just staring at her in bewilderment, not knowing what to do or say.

"I'm Alvida," she said. "Do you have a name, sir?"

Simon blinked twice and then snapped out of his trance. "Simon! I'm Simon, son of Relly Petrus. My father is a silversmith here in town. My family has been around this area for ages. I'm sure you've heard of us."

"Well, Simon, son of Relly Petrus, my family is new to this area, and we have not heard of Relly Petrus or his silver business. It has been awkward but somewhat nice to meet you. Thank you for trying to assist me with my wayward lavender. I must be off now. Speaking to strange men on the street isn't my usual course of action." She smiled as she turned to leave.

"Wait! I must see you again," Simon said. Only then did he realize how inappropriate he was being. "I apologize, Alvida. Would it be permissible for me to see you again?"

"My father would not approve of our talking like this. I respect my father and would only agree to meet if you had his permission." She glanced down at his wrinkled clothing, noting his disorderly hair. "And I seriously doubt he would grant it to you."

"May I ask him? I would love to have the pleasure of your company, and I'll request permission from your father. I'm sure when he hears my family name, he'll agree."

Although his tone was rather presumptuous, Alvida thought Simon was cute in a clumsy but innocent sort of way, so she gave him permission to seek her father's approval.

Later that day, Simon asked Relly to go with him to meet Alvida's father. He had always fallen back on the excellent reputation of his family when he needed it, and he certainly needed that good name now.

Relly sensed that his son was trying to use him, but he was interested to see who had drawn Simon's attention so thoroughly. Rumors had been trickling in about his son's actions around town, and he didn't want to face the reality that he knew in his heart was true. He was just happy his son had included him as a part of his life that afternoon. Relly and Wyeita hoped this might be the interruption in Simon's life they had been praying for.

The meeting didn't go well for Simon. Alvida's father was completely unimpressed. The family name carried no weight with him, nor did their wealth. Simon seemed like a pretentious boy with no ambition, bent on riding his father's coattails. He could go around demanding his wishes elsewhere but not in this home and not with his precious daughter. Alvida and her family loved and worshiped Jesus. They served the Lord with their lives and trusted that God would make Alvida the wife of a God-fearing husband.

That was of utmost importance and well worth waiting on. Nothing about Simon seemed right. Simon's request to see Alvida was denied.

After the unfortunate meeting with Alvida's father, Simon fell into a deep depression. He grew even more distant despite his father's attempts to comfort him. Simon could not get Alvida out of his mind, and the fact that he could not use his family name to get what he wanted felt so unfair.

Simon was inconsolable and listless. He turned back to Gorce and his reprobate lifestyle. No person or substance could drown his sorrows. He was empty and broken.

Thort and Nag toasted to their brilliance and good fortune. "Finally!"

All hope seemed lost for their son, but Relly and Wyieta never gave into that false reality. Instead, they fell back on the anchor moments throughout their lives and the lives of their parents and grandparents to steady them. God had been so faithful throughout the generations. He would not give up on them now. Simon was their son, whom God had gifted to them. They had raised him up in the ways of the Lord. There was a purpose for his life, and they trusted in the love of the Father for them and for their son. Relly and Wyieta Petrus called out to God, and God heard their cries.

One night, as Simon lay draped across the foot of the bed, half dressed and in a drunken stupor, he fell into a deep sleep. As he slept, the room illuminated with a bright light. Simon was startled awake as a man appeared in the room. Terrified, Simon fell out of bed and onto his face, unable to look upon the man.

"Simon," the Son of Man said, "you have always chosen your own path. The one you are currently on leads to death. That is not the path that I purchased for you. It's not my intention that you die but that you taste life everlasting in my Father's Kingdom. The choice is, and has always been, yours. That choice lies before you tonight."

The Son had barely finished speaking before Simon shouted his reply. "I choose You! I choose Your path! I know I need You, all of You. My life is in ruins, and I'm the one who caused it. I don't deserve You, but I'm so sorry." He was sobbing uncontrollably, still on his face, afraid to look up.

The Son leaned down and helped Simon to his feet. They embraced, and warmth washed over Simon's being.

Simon didn't know how long they stood there, but when he pulled away from the embrace, Jesus looked him in the eye. "Go back to Alvida and her family. You will tell them of this visitation. You will ask for her hand in marriage, and I will bless your union."

Simon's eyes widened in shock. "But her father has already denied the courtship. My family name carries no weight with him, and I have squandered that name anyway. I've thrown it to the pigs. I don't deserve Alvida, and I don't deserve her father's blessing, much less Yours."

Jesus nodded. "You're right, Simon. You don't deserve Alvida. She is pure and lovely."

Tears welled up in Simon's eyes.

"But I'll make you holy as I am holy. You will be delightful in your wife's eyes and in the eyes of the Lord. Your family's name is righteous. Yes, you have used it to serve yourself in unrighteous acts. I'm the Lord of your fathers Paulk, Durane, and Jeruit, the God of Oppert, Royye, and your father, Relly. I've preserved your lineage and will continue to do so with you and your offspring. Your family will go by a new name. You were Simon Petrus, named for your ancestor, Peter. The name you will give to your new wife is Pathrose. My Father will bless you and Alvida with a long life and with many children. I ask that you cling to my commands and freely love and forgive others as I have forgiven you. Instruct your children and their children's children to follow me. Teach them stories about your family's legacy, the amulet, and the manuscript that you have been taught."

Simon nodded in understanding.

Finally, Jesus said, "And Simon, this is very important: tell them to always be ready."

With that, Simon awoke.

The next several days were a blur. New life was pumping through Simon's veins. He felt like a completely new creation when he awoke from his dream. He had no sense of apathy or need to satisfy lustful imaginations. His life had purpose and hope. He didn't know exactly how that hope would play out given Alvida's father had already denied him any formal contact with his daughter, but the words had been spoken, and he knew they would not return void.

Simon shared the dream with his parents. He would never know the rejoicing of their souls as they listened to how God had answered years of prayers in one miraculous visitation. Relly and Wyeita agreed to pray for Alvida and her family. They assured Simon that God would go before him.

One week after Jesus visited Simon in his bedroom, he sat across the table from Alvida and her father with sweaty palms and a lump in his throat. Speaking to Alvida for the first time was scary and awkward. With his parents by his side, Simon recounted his dream exactly as he remembered it. He added nothing to it nor took anything away from it. When he finished, a hush fell over the room. For what felt like an eternity, all he could hear was his heart pounding in his chest and his own breath rushing in and out of his lungs. He calmed himself as he waited for a response. He felt an unexplainable peace in his heart.

Alvida's father was stunned. His eyes bulged out of his head as he turned to his daughter. He could not believe what he was hearing. The only thing more shocking than Simon's story was when he looked over and saw the look of confirmation on his daughter's face.

Alvida stood up and placed her hand on her mother's shoulder and looked first at her father and then at Simon and his parents. "I too have had a visitation," she said. "I knew exactly what Simon would say today when he knocked on our door. Everything he said here is true. I'm to be his wife, and God will certainly bless our union."

CHAPTER 13
HELL TO PAY

Thort and Nag again found themselves in that dreaded lobby awaiting another meeting with Chief Maltreat. There had been no words between them. Thort sat picking at an oozing scab on his left forearm. Sticky black blood ran out from the old wound and dripped onto the floor. His eyes were wide open, glossed over and fixed on nothing. Thort knew he should feel fear or at least have some anxiety about what was waiting for him behind that office door, but he was numb. Time stood still in his mind. He knew he was breathing because he could sense his chest moving, but his mind was transfixed in a deep hole of nothingness, thinking nothing, feeling nothing, caring for nothing.

Thort looked down at his arm. What had once been a strong, well-defined weapon of chiseled muscle and bulging veins was now a feeble, faded, and weak excuse for an appendage. Skin just hanging from the bone. It was ashen and dry as if his very life had dehydrated out of his body in the scorching sun. His chest was sunken, and his shoulders slumped forward, reducing his height by at least eight inches. His stature gave him the appearance of having a spinal deformity. The once mighty and brutal Thort was now a mere shell of a demon who seemed capable of being blown into mere particles by a stiff wind. And, what was worse, he didn't care if he was.

He and Nag made no eye contact. Impending doom hung thickly in the space between them. Both were aware of their impending demise, but Nag, unlike Thort, squirmed in his chair as they waited. He cursed himself under his breath for falling into such a trap. How did he, in just one generation, go from accepting an achievement award and a promotion to awaiting a sentence on his very life? "What was I thinking? I never should have tied my fate to a demon so beneath me," he muttered. "It would have been wiser to stick to myself. I should have known I was the only one who could get things done correctly. Why did I listen? How could I be so stupid?" Nag punched himself in the temple. He realized his pride had blinded him with visions of glory and rising through the ranks to be placed in power over legions. He had to believe Hell Ops would not hold him responsible for the negligence of one flailing lowlife demon who had lost all ability to discern right from wrong. Perhaps Maltreat would call him in first and give him an opportunity to explain that this wretched turn of events was not his fault. Maltreat must know Thort bore complete responsibility for Nag's poor performance. Free from Thort, Nag was still valuable to the darkness with an exceptional ability to ensure eternal death for his future assignments. He just needed to rid himself of the miserable puke who sat slumped next to him, taking up space. Nag's mind raced through the possible disciplinary actions they might take against him. Would they strip him of his rank? One stripe, maybe two? Two would be harsh. A generation in the brig? Surely, they wouldn't maim him over this, would they?

Nag remained lost in his internal decision tree when the door to Maltreat's office opened. Two towering demons stepped out and descended on Nag, grabbing him by the underarms. They yanked him to his feet and dragged him into the office, throwing him across the room like a ragdoll. The door slammed shut, and the two thug demons stood like stone pillars outside of it.

Thort stared at the demons, his face expressionless and his mind like thick mud. *Scary. That was scary, right? I should be afraid. I'm next. Why am I not afraid? What's wrong with me?* he thought.

He wasn't sure if Nag had been in Maltreat's office for three minutes or three hours, but suddenly, the door swung almost off its hinges and slammed against the wall so hard that the doorknob punched a hole in it. The two thug demons entered the office and dragged Nag, kicking and screaming, from the room. Thort made brief eye contact with Nag as they manhandled him through the lobby and into the hallway. The look in those eyes was haunting: shock, desperation, and a terrible gaze of finality. Nag's screams turned into sobs and pleadings. He cried out to Maltreat and the demons who carried him. He cried all the way down the hallway as they dragged him, flailing and scraping his talons along the floor and the walls and anything he could grasp to buy him more time.

Nag's desperate pleadings grew fainter until the iron door at the end of the long hall slammed shut. Then everything fell silent—but only for a moment.

Suddenly, Thort jolted in his seat, his blood curdling in his veins. The sound of a thousand rabid coyotes in a bloody feeding frenzy echoed through the hall. A guttural scream of torture tore through the iron door and permeated every space in the building. Every demon's blood ran cold when they heard it. That scream meant only one thing, and they all knew what it was. An ending, but not one that would come quickly. It was a devouring that would scar every creature within earshot. All Hell was forced to hear it unfold. Thort had never heard a human or a demon cry out like that. Just when he thought it had to be over, it got even worse. It sounded like a fresh team of assailants had descended on Nag. They sounded like hyenas, laughing as they tore flesh from bone. The screaming increased, and the entire building quaked.

Thort's head throbbed. He clawed at his temples, covering his ears so his brain wouldn't explode. The walls of the building shook, and the lightbulbs in the fixtures blinked on and off. Tiles dropped out of the ceiling, and dust filled the air.

For a moment, Thort thought the building was going to implode and the ground open beneath it, sucking everything into its mouth in a single gulp. He slid out of his chair and huddled on the floor against the wall, anticipating his immediate end.

Through clenched eyelids, Thort saw a flash of brilliant white light. He closed his eyes again, not daring to look.

Ramiel stepped into the room.

The screaming stopped.

CHAPTER 14
STEVEN, AVON, AND KATI

Hope defies darkness.

Kati Pathrose ran as fast as her little seven-year-old legs would carry her. The tall grass of the meadow swiped at her legs and swept through the bottom of her dress as she ran. The boys were pulling away. She hiked up the skirt of her dress, freeing her legs to run full throttle. She knew she was just as fast as those boys. They knew it too, and she would not let them think any differently today.

The dress was slowing her down, but Kati had been intent on wearing it. It was her favorite dress. Her mother, Avon, had intended for her to wear the dress only on special occasions, like church services and weddings. Kati had plenty of common clothes to wear for school and playtime, but those dresses were shorter, plain, and boring.

This dress was beyond special. It was long and flowing. It was also a shade of blue that Kati had only ever seen in the sky on a perfect spring morning. It fit perfectly across her shoulders with an open neck in the back. Avon had adorned the entire neckline with a row of tiny white beads that billowed in a pattern that looked like perfect little puffs of clouds. The dress had a beautiful wide satin sash that tied high around her waist and made a beautiful bow in the back. It flowed all the way to her feet in a perfect A frame. The underskirt provided just the right amount of bulk to the bottom to keep it off the floor when she wore her shoes. It fit perfectly. Kati felt taller in the dress, like a beautiful young lady instead of a little girl. In fact, Kati was a princess in that dress, a princess who ruled a beautiful kingdom and held court in a grand hall. Wild horses grazed in the fields around her castle, and when she felt like it, she would ride the white one around town, checking on her people and making sure everyone in her kingdom had food and was happy. Kati had a wild imagination, and whenever she wore that dress, it put her right in the center of her magical kingdom.

Kati and Avon argued every morning after breakfast when it was time to get dressed for the day. Kati begged to wear the blue dress, and Avon would explain, yet again, how many hours she had put into making the garment and how special it was.

"If you wear it every day, it will get ruined and won't be special anymore. Then when you need a beautiful dress, you won't have one. You'll have to wear your linen dress and apron to church. How would you like that?" Avon had said these words more times than she could count since she unveiled the dress to her little girl three weeks ago.

"Please, Mom," Kati begged. "I promise I won't leave the house with it on. I just want to play princess in my room for a bit. Please, Mom! Please!"

"Kati, I know you won't play in your room for ten minutes before you go outside with your brother and Thomas. It's a beautiful day outside. You should just put on your play clothes. There will be plenty of days for you to wear your dress."

Avon was tickled that her daughter loved the dress. She had poured herself into making it, painstakingly measuring and remeasuring the fine cloth before cutting and then triple stitching every seam to reinforce the garment's strength. The beadwork had taken many nights sitting by candlelight. She had gone to bed with aching fingers more times than she could remember, but she wanted those tiny beads sewn on perfectly. This dress was the very garment Avon had dreamed of having as a little girl, and she had hoped Kati would love it just as much as she had in her mind.

After weeks of tedious toil, Avon was not disappointed. Kati squealed with delight when her mother brought the dress out of the back room on her birthday. She had begged to try it on immediately, and she would have worn it every moment of every day if Avon had allowed it. Even though it was irritating to go through the same argument every morning, it still gave her great pleasure to know that Kati loved the dress.

That morning the conversation had gone as it had every other morning and had ended with Kati reluctantly putting on her play dress. She sat on her bedroom floor with her legs crossed and her fists on her chin, downcast with a pitiful look on her face. Today, Kati would be a mere peasant girl who would have nothing magnificent to do but play with her dumb older brother and his goofy friend.

Avon smiled at Kati and winked as she left the bedroom and returned to the kitchen to clean up after breakfast. "You're a princess every day, my love," she called back over her shoulder. Kati huffed.

Avon had busied herself all morning with housework. They had pulled most of the remaining potatoes from the garden yesterday, so she was scrubbing them down and preparing them for storage. She looked up from the basin she was washing in and glanced out the kitchen window to see her husband, Steven, working with the ox in the garden. He had started at daybreak to take advantage of the cool of the morning. She knew he would come in any minute to clean up and get ready to head to work.

Avon smiled as she thought of Kati pouting in her room. The child was headstrong but obedient, and Avon was thankful for her. She thanked God for the blessings of her family. It had taken seven long years to get pregnant with Kati's older brother, Jude. God had shown her a vision of her two children shortly after she and Steven had married, but the years had been hard while waiting on children. Month after month it seemed like the couple would never have a family of their own. Steven realized that it may just be the two of them, and he had come to terms with it, but Avon had kept the hope alive.

Later that evening after Steven returned from work, Avon and the children sat by the fireplace and listened as Steven read their new Bible aloud before bedtime. Avon was sewing a patch on both knees of Jude's pants. "Apparently, when you're eight years old, you need shoes on your knees as well," she said, smiling down at her son.

Just under the foot of Avon's chair in a special hiding place under a floorboard were two sacred items: the amulet and a tattered Latin Bible that Steven's ancestors had handed down from the Middle Ages. Seldom did either item come out of hiding. The Bible was so frail that they kept it wrapped in a linen cloth to preserve the cover. The ink had faded in many spots, but they could still make out most of the sacred scriptures.

Now that the Gutenberg Bible was being mass produced, the family had a new copy to read from. As soon as the children were old enough to speak, Steven had created a game for them that encouraged them to memorize scripture every week.

That night the children practiced their memorization verses, and Steven read a passage about King David from the Psalms to them. After the reading, the children asked who David was, what he did, and why God loved him so much.

Avon smiled as she rocked in her chair. What a blessing her family was.

The following morning, Kati slipped out the back door. It was another beautiful day, and she wanted to feel the sunshine on her face. As she emerged from the shadow of the house, she spun around on her tiptoes, admiring her shadow on the ground. Kati had started out in her play dress without complaint. About an hour later, however, she had slipped the new dress on while her mother was distracted doing the laundry. She just *had* to wear her princess dress for a few minutes. Kati wouldn't mess it up. She would take it off before she went to play and then hang it up beside her bed.

Kati spun around again and looked up at the sky. She was sure that her dress and the sky matched perfectly.

Thort was leaning up against the backside of the house with one foot perched on the foundation, his arms crossed as he stared at the ground. He rarely entered the house these days. What was the use?

After all this time, he still didn't understand what had happened back at Hell Ops the day they consumed Nag. Thort assumed he had blacked out after the burst of bright light, and he didn't even remember opening his eyes. His first recollection was waking up on his next Pathrose assignment, dazed and confused with a sense of an indefinite period of lost time.

His "rescue," if one could call it that, had done nothing to improve his mental health or his emotional state. He had not heard from Hell Ops, and he knew he would never hear from Nag again. Thort shuddered as he thought about his former partner. He could still hear those screams in his mind. Never had he imagined they would execute a demon over the loss of one soul. All he could imagine was Simon Pathrose must have been someone important, someone whose loss to the enemy had triggered some cataclysmic shift in all of eternity. If that was the case, why hadn't he and Nag been told what they were dealing with beforehand?

Thort didn't understand why he was still alive. All he knew was he was back on assignment with the same hopeless family and no new intel or schemes for success. He didn't care. He didn't care what happened to the Pathrose family, and he didn't even care what happened to him. Thort found nothing satisfying. He had nothing to look forward to, and nothing piqued his interest day in and day out. So, he just stood there, leaning against the same house in the same spot, waiting for . . . what?

Many times Thort had watched Kati play in the backyard with her vivid imagination and competitive spirit. It was like watching a particular ant in a long string of ants move along, wondering if it would make it back to the anthill or not. It wasn't overly interesting, but he found himself slightly bent toward her, so he watched her come and go. She was young and understood little. A harmless biped.

The back door swung open, and the demon turned his head and watched as the young girl strolled into the sunlight. Thort wondered what it was like to have her whole life in front of her without a care in the world and with no knowledge of angels, demons, anxiety, fear, death, war, or destruction. *Oh, to become like a little child,* he mused.

"Hey, Kati! You know you're not supposed to have that dress on!" Jude yelled from the front side of the garden. "Mom is gonna be mad."

"I'm not wearing it. I just tried it on. And it's none of your business, Jude!" Kati yelled back at her brother.

Just then Thomas ran up from behind and tagged Kati on the left shoulder. "You're it!" he yelled, then ran past her before she even registered he was there.

"Run, Jude! She's it!" Thomas yelled to his friend.

"No fair! I wasn't ready!" Kati said.

Thomas glanced back at her, still running. "Too bad because you're it. Come and get us!"

Kati lunged forward, but Thomas was just out of reach. *No way is he gonna to get away with this,* she thought as she tore after him.

Thomas caught up to Jude, and the boys darted out through the garden. The ground was soft but had some hidden holes where the potatoes had been. Jude almost lost his footing right before they made it back to the edge of the tilled soil.

Kati was hot on his trail, and she took a swipe, but Jude ducked out of her reach.

The end of the garden opened into a wide meadow with tall grass that ran down to a stream from which the family hauled their water. Thomas and Jude split up to give themselves more of a chance. Kati was fast, and they knew she would catch up to one of them. Kati pursued Thomas, since he was the one who had tagged her from behind. As he approached the middle of the meadow, Thomas sidestepped and then darted back toward the house. Jude made a similar move. Kati wasn't expecting the sudden change of direction, and it took her a moment to pivot. She turned back toward the garden and took off with all of her might. Her dress dragged through the tall grass, slowing her down, so she hiked it up. It was at that moment that the reality of her impulse decision to chase the boys while still wearing her dress hit her.

"I can't run in my dress! Stop!" Kati yelled.

"I don't know why you wear that thing. It doesn't matter. You can't run, anyway," Jude said as he regrouped with Thomas, still running toward the garden.

Kati couldn't give up. The boys would not get the best of her. Holding her dress, she ran as fast as she could up the small hill until she reached the garden's edge. The boys had stopped just on the other side to taunt her. She caught her breath and then took off across the garden toward them.

Kati had taken about six steps when she stepped into a hole left behind from digging up the potatoes. Her foot sank into the ground and sent her hurtling forward. She caught herself with her hands, so she didn't eat dirt, but she felt an intense pain in her shin as she slid across something sharp and finally came to a stop, lying face down in the soil.

Kati laid there for a second, assessing her pain, and then she sat up. Looking back, she identified the source of her pain. Her father's pitchfork was lying in the field beneath her. Two of its prongs had ripped through her dress and scraped across her leg. Not only was her dress torn and covered in dirt, blood was also seeping through the fabric, forming a slowly spreading circle of deep crimson. Kati lifted the skirt and was relieved to find that her injuries were minor, though they were bleeding profusely. She pulled back the remaining skirt of her dress, so she wouldn't get any more blood on it.

Jude and Thomas rushed over when they saw her fall. Thank goodness she had not screamed or cried, which would have brought Avon out to check on them. The boys helped Kati to her feet.

As she stood there, sniffling, she realized the skirt underneath the satin belt had torn away from its seam. The triple stitch stood no chance when her knee came down on the skirt, and her torso pulled the bodice forward.

Sorrow filled Kati's heart, and tears welled up in her eyes as she looked up toward the house. Her beautiful blue princess dress was destroyed.

Thort's interest was piqued as the children approached the back door. Kati limped, supported by the two boys, looking as if a horse had dragged her down the road. Her dress hung shredded and covered in mud and blood.

Now, this might be interesting, he mused. *Looks like the baby ant might have some explaining to do. I think I might join them in the house for the fallout. Why not? I don't have anything else to do.*

When Steven came home from work that afternoon, Avon explained what had happened in the garden.

Kati was sitting in her room. Avon had cleaned and then bandaged her leg. Then she hung the ruined dress in the closet of her own bedroom. She took supper to Kati early and instructed her to rest until her father got home.

Kati's afternoon had been filled with tears of regret. The pain of her wounds had already subsided when her father entered her room at dusk.

"Kati, honey, are you okay?"

"Yes, Daddy. I'm fine. My leg doesn't even hurt anymore." She sniffed and wiped her nose on her arm.

Steven sat on the bed in front of his daughter. "Then why are you still crying, sweetheart?"

"My dress. I messed up my dress," Kati said, sobbing. "Mom told me not to wear it, but I wanted to. I knew I wasn't supposed to, but I changed clothes and went outside for just a minute. I forgot, I ran, and then I fell, and now my dress is ruined."

Steven placed his hand on Kati's shoulder, giving her a moment to calm herself. "Why don't you clean up and then come see me by the fire?"

After a few minutes, Kati joined her mom, dad, and brother by the dwindling fire.

"What are you doing, Daddy?" Kati asked as she sat down beside him.

Steven looked over the top of his spectacles. "Do you remember what we were reading about in the Bible last night?"

Kati wasn't ready to talk about her fall or the incident with her dress, so she welcomed the diversion. "The part about King David."

"That's right, Kati, the part about King David. Tonight we're going to talk about hope. Do you know what that is?"

"I think so. Maybe. But I'm not sure."

"Well, David spent his whole life hoping in God, trusting His words and having faith that God would protect and defend him. I can read some of these passages to you if you like."

"I always like when you read to us," Kati said as she snuggled in closer to her father.

Steven read several passages from the Psalms as the family sat in the fire's light. He gave context for what David was going through when he wrote the passages and asked questions to engage his children's minds as they imagined being like the great king and trusting in God. After the last of the passages he had marked to read, Steven closed the Bible and looked down at Kati.

"Do you hope your mother can fix your dress?" he asked.

The question caught Kati off guard. Oh, how she would love for her mother to fix her dress, but she didn't know if it was beyond repair. "I know that if my dress can be fixed, Mom can do it. So, I do hope she can fix it. Yes." She paused and looked at the floor. "I also know that I don't deserve for her to fix it. I wasn't supposed to be wearing it at all. My dress is ruined because I didn't listen to her."

"You're absolutely right, my dear," her father replied. "You don't deserve it, and I would like to talk about that for a minute." Steven looked at Avon and then back at Kati. "You know, David was a mighty king whom God chose for Himself. Even his own family didn't pick David, but God did. You would think that David must have been close to perfect for God to choose him. He had to deserve it, right?"

Kati thought about it for a second and then nodded. "Yes, he must have deserved it."

"Kati, your dress was a gift from your mom and me. Your mom

made it for you because she loves you, and she knew you would enjoy it. She even knew that you were going to want to wear it every single day, but she gave you the rule that she knew would preserve the dress, so you could wear it and enjoy it and not damage it. You broke that rule because you wanted what you wanted. Tonight, you sit here without a dress, and you deserve that."

Steven paused to let his words sink in. "You might wonder what your dress and King David have to do with each other. You're going to be surprised to find out that the great King David, chosen by the Lord, made some silly decisions from time to time too. He went after things that he wanted and disregarded God's rules. He messed up, just like you did today." "So, he couldn't be king anymore after that?" Kati asked.

"Actually, no. Someone came to David and helped him see what he was doing wrong, and David repented. He knew that he needed to make things right with God. He hoped God would forgive his sins and restore their special relationship."

"He didn't deserve it, but he still had hope?" Kati asked, glancing at her mom.

"David knew God was his provider, his protector, and his redeemer," Steven replied. "If anything could be made right, it would be from God. David had faith because he understood God's nature, and his hope was rooted in that." Steven put his arm around his daughter. "You said that if anyone could fix your dress, it would be your mother. Why do you say that?"

"Mom made my dress, and I know that she's the best seamstress in town. My dress is ruined, but I know Mom can fix anything."

"Well, honey, that is faith, and her mending the dress is what you hope for."

Steven explained hope in more detail, giving his family other references in the Bible. Then he talked about how their hope was found in Jesus's love and righteousness. Finally, he prayed with Kati, leading her in a prayer of repentance.

Thort had been skulking near the back door of the room, eavesdropping on the exchange.

"Oh, good grief. Blah, blah, blah. Faith, hope. Hope, faith, love. Who cares? Hope all you want, kid. The dress is still in shreds, and I don't know what any of this has to do with King David. The only thing I can ever hope for is not to be devoured by my boss and his cronies back at headquarters. Why don't they just give this blubbering kid what she deserves and get it over with?"

The words were barely out of Thort's mouth before he realized the irony of what he had just said. He certainly had not gotten what he deserved. And why was that? He had no faith or hope of redemption. Why had someone delivered him from the same fate as Nag?

Thort lost track of the rest of the conversation while he focused on his unanswered questions. He snapped out of his thoughts when he noticed Avon step back into her sewing room for a moment and then reenter the room.

Avon handed Steven a package wrapped in sackcloth. Stephen unfolded the cloth and revealed the bodice of Kati's dress. Avon had folded it just above where the sash wrapped around the waistline. Kati shuddered as she remembered the stretched seams that pulled thin through the beautiful blue fabric, tearing down the front.

Then Steven lifted the dress out of the cloth covering, revealing a new creation. The bodice was the same, but the tattered seam had been removed, and a belt of golden-threaded filigree transitioned from the bodice to a beautiful flowing skirt of brilliant yellow fabric. The old tattered, bloody skirt was gone. The dress had been made new. It was perfect.

Kati couldn't hold back her tears. So many emotions came all at once. Joy, thankfulness, peace, and love coursed through her as she threw her arms around her mother's legs.

"When you look at the yellow in this dress, I want you to remember the story of hope," Avon said. "When we repent and turn back toward God's heart, He doesn't give us what we deserve. He redeems us and makes all things new because of the sacrifice of His Son, Jesus. This is what we build our hope on. I love you, Kati, and I'm so pleased that you love your dress. Now I know that you will cherish it and take care of it as you should. I take great joy in lavishing you with good things, as does God."

Kati threw her arms around her mother, hugging her. Avon smiled. "Now it's time for bed. You and your brother go get cleaned up, and I'll be in soon to tuck you in and say your prayers."

Steven was still reading when Avon came in to join him. She was used to this. Her husband spent countless hours in the Word, and the couple enjoyed deep conversations as they chewed through the scriptures together.

He smiled at his wife of almost fifteen years. "You get them to bed?"

"Yes. Said their prayers and tucked them in."

Avon sat down next to Steven. "So, what has you so captivated that you have let the fire almost go out?"

Steven looked over at the embers in the fireplace. "Oh, sorry. I hadn't noticed." He added two logs to the hot coals. As he sat back down, he picked up his old Bible again. "I never paid much attention to this verse in Psalms: 'Why are you cast down, O my soul, And why are you disquieted within me? Hope in God; for I shall again praise him, My help, and my God."

Avon thought about it as she waited for further explanation. When none came, she prodded her husband. "What about it exactly?"

Steven looked down at the worn pages. "It sounds like his soul is arguing with itself. Why are you cast down? Why are you disquieted?"

Avon nodded. "Yes, but he also urges himself to put his hope in God."

Steven closed his Bible and turned to look at Avon. "I think David is preaching to himself. He was a great man and a great king, but with all that happened to him with Saul and then later after he became king and experienced so much war, I don't think hope came naturally to him. I believe he was preaching to himself and understood he had to put his hope in God. He had to depend on the Lord constantly in the face of hard and seemingly hopeless circumstances."

Avon nodded again. "Sounds right. So, what is hope to you, my dear?"

Steven smiled, knowing his wife would not accept a quick offthe-cuff answer. "I'm no scholar, but I know faith, hope, and love are all tied together, and I don't think they can be separated."

"I agree with you, but you didn't answer my question."

Steven smirked. "Kati said she hoped you could fix her dress and was confident you would. That's how she defined hope."

Avon pondered her young daughter's answer, admiring its simplicity. "I'm no theologian or scholar, but to me hope is a confident expectation and desire for something good in the future."

"Well stated, my non-theologian wife," Steven replied, smiling. "Kati was confident, knowing you could fix her dress, and she desired that she would have a dress to wear again in the future."

"And she has it," Avon replied proudly. "Not only is it repaired, it's also new and even better than what she expected. Our Father works like that too."

Steven leaned toward Avon and touched his lip with his finger. "To me, hope sometimes seems to get lost between faith and love, but it's there because genuine hope will never waver. Hope is rooted in our faithfulness to God and our love for Him. Without hope I don't think faith can exist. I know that doubt is the enemy of faith, and if we have no hope in the future, our doubts have no expectations for anything good. Hoping is not wishing. Thankfully, because we have a risen Savior who is coming again, we can agree on what King David said. Our hope is in God and in nothing else."

Thort sat listening, pondering their words.

CHAPTER 15

A MISERABLE REFLECTION

The mud that Thort sat in was cold and thick with filth, but Thort didn't seem to notice. He sat steeping in his solitude one cold day in late January. Time seemed to be standing still lately, with nothing to separate one miserable day from the next. Generations had come and gone as he lay in complete apathy. He couldn't remember what it was like to look forward to something or even dread anything. There was no emotion left in his being, no feeling, no care, and no hope.

Thort had heard all about hope all those years ago, sitting by the fire with little Kati Pathrose and her father. It was like being forced to stand outside of a candy shop, drooling at the window, but never to be allowed inside.

It had been a long time since he had stopped reporting his misfortunes and failures to Hell Ops or expecting anyone to come after him for it. He had given up caring about who was following him. He still caught sight of the stalker every now and then, but his curiosity and will had faded like his complexion.

After his unexplainable escape from Maltreat's office that day, his dealings with headquarters had been brief and strangely uneventful. He came and went for his assignments for a while, but they were always the same: Pathrose generation 116, 117, 118, and on and on and on. He couldn't understand why Hell Ops had pardoned his repeated failures, letting him walk away unscathed for generation after generation. Something had changed the day Nag met his doom. Some unknown force had rescued Thort from his deserved demise, or had it? Maybe he was so useless that Hell Ops could not be bothered to do away with him. He was no threat, and he was certainly no use to anyone. What darkness he had left in his spirit would not satisfy a hound pup. Nothing made sense anymore. So, he stopped reporting, stopped explaining, and stopped promising. The only thing he had not stopped doing was following the next Pathrose family and the next. Thort would have ended his own existence long ago if that had been an option for demons.

Instead, he had witnessed generations of Pathrose families walk upright, pleasing the Lord until his ears and eyeballs seeped with infection. He had puked up the contents of his belly so many times that the acid ate away at his throat and stung with every swallow. Nothing quenched his thirst or took away his hunger. His complexion was now little more than an ashen gray hide. His cloak was thin and tattered, full of holes and barely capable of flight. The only reason he could take flight at all was because his body had withered away to bare bones with skin pulled over them. At least he assumed he could still fly. He couldn't remember when he had last left this mud hole.

That day he found his mind wandering over the events of the last few centuries. He had been with several more generations of Pathroses since little Kati. Two more recent families stuck out in his mind.

He remembered when he was first assigned to Kelly and Carla, who married young. Carla had spent her childhood dreaming of being a mother. She had helped raise her siblings and many of the children in their church community. She had a God-given nurturing spirit, and children loved her. She had the nickname "baby whisperer" at church. Even a baby with a terrible case of colic could find rest in Carla's arms.

Kelly had grown up with Carla and knew that being her husband would mean being the father of many. He was more than up for the challenge. He loved children too, and he had a tremendous gift of patience. God had spoken to him as a young man, revealing that he would, in fact, be the father of several children. That was part of what made him fall so deeply for Carla. He loved watching her with the little ones.

Five years went by after their wedding, and every day people would tease and inquire about what was taking Kelly and Carla so long to start their brood. No one knew how deep those words cut into Carla's heart. She and Kelly had started trying to conceive almost immediately, but so far they had failed. They lost seven babies to miscarriage, breaking her heart a little more each time.

Infertility had broken other marriages and banished hope in people forever. Thort had high hopes for Kelly and Carla early on. As each year passed, he panted after each loss. He felt assured that their inability to have children would lead to Kelly and Carla's ultimate demise.

What Thort had not counted on was the young couple's faith. Kelly's faith in God's promise to him had never faltered. He comforted his wife and assured her that God would be true to His word, just as had been with Abraham in the Bible.

Thort's head throbbed as he remembered the disgusting details.

Kelly and Carla had held fast to their supernatural faith in God. Ultimately, the couple became the parents of over twenty-four children through adoption. They were also the founding members of one of the biggest orphan outreach ministries in Europe. Thort had watched helplessly as they opened their hearts and their home to child after child, even when there was no apparent provision for their family. They took one step of faith after the other over the years, showing loving kindness to unwanted and discarded children, shaping the future of hundreds of families as they showed them the love of Christ.

Thort had stopped counting the ripple effects of Kelly and Carla's service to the Lord. It was mind-boggling. As he sat there, he recalled a prayer that he had heard Kelly pray over his family one night. The words bounced around in his head like a ping-pong ball.

"Heavenly Father, we honor you in this house, in this family, in our hearts. You're our abundance in all things, and all glory belongs to you. Thank you for meeting our family's needs today. Our lives belong to you, made for service to you and no other. As we grow in your love, we pray for your heart to be our heart as we minister to one another and with one another. Father, be our priority as we touch this generation of kids. Our faith is in you, Lord. Blessings and honor to you and your Son, Jesus, for it is in your Son's name we pray."

Faith was such a foreign idea to Thort. There was nothing like it in the dark realm. Faith, just like hope and love, was a concept that Thort had spent his entire miserable existence hearing about from the Pathrose assignments. Even after tens of generations, he still had no capacity to understand it. He had heard Kelly and his ancestors repeatedly say that "the righteous live by faith" and one is "saved by faith." "Faith is the reality of what is hoped for and the proof of what is not seen." But these concepts were lost in his mind, and the confusion they brought sent him soaring from one volatile emotion to the next, ranging from fiery rage to self-loathing.

Thort had to admit that somewhere in between those emotions, jealousy and longing were also present. Why couldn't he experience those things and enjoy the benefits of a creator who loved and cared for him? Why had that been reserved for such feeble creatures as humans?

His mind drifted to Nathan and Christine Pathrose. When he was first assigned to them, he had not given it much thought. They were Pathroses, after all. Would any of them fall?

The only difference with this family was that they had been the recipients of a tremendous windfall of wealth. Generations of Pathrose had come from a long line of silversmiths. The business flourished over the years, enjoying a reputation for some of the finest metallurgy in the world. Nathan's father had negotiated the sale of two of the company's divisions. The company had grown so much that it needed to be downsized to maintain its integrity. The buyout had been lucrative, and Nathan inherited a great fortune when his father passed.

Thort took notice and hoped that trusty old mammon would deliver for him. Greed was such an easy tool to work with. Of all the Pathrose families, this one delivered so much promise. Rich men rarely, if ever, inherited the Kingdom of God. Riches and greed were something that Thort could work with.

It pleased Thort when Nathan took some of his wealth and moved his family into one of the city's wealthiest communities. Not only would money be at his disposal, so would all the wealthy neighbors whose lives were so heavily entangled with earthly things. He had checked the registers, and not one soul throughout the entire community followed Yahweh. Thort tried not to get his hopes up, but this seemed like such a straight shot. For the first time in many generations, Thort believed he might be the deceiver he had once been pre-Pathrose.

Nathan and Christine were an instant hit with their neighbors. With their outgoing personalities and wealth, everyone wanted a seat next to the Pathroses at the dinner club. Something about Nathan and Christine drew people in. People didn't understand it, but it was the Spirit that lived in them, beckoning people to "come see."

Instead of being ruled by mammon, God used Nathan and Christine's wealth to place them in a strategic spot to reach people who seemed out of reach. God worked through them to tear down idols and restore marriages in the community. A small group held weekly meetings in the Pathrose home and became a hub similar to how the ancient church had functioned. The pursuit of money and power melted away, replaced by a desire for service and sacrifice.

What Thort thought would be his easiest job soon turned into a landslide of redemption in a circle of people who had been all but locked into eternal death and destruction. *So much for believing that mammon would rule the family and the day,* he thought.

This defeat was the catalyst that landed Thort in the puddle of mud in which he was wallowing. Just like all the other times that these memories and thoughts flooded into Thort's consciousness, he shook his head as if to shake them away. Each generation of Pathroses had scarred him with a sense of loss. One pounding after another had come until he lost his sense of worth, his honor, and his feeling of self-righteousness. He no longer cared what other demons thought of him. That concern had left him long ago. He had no pretense that he would ever taste victory again. He no longer could do anything right. Every assignment they gave him was a promised defeat. Every breath he took and effort he made was a waste. The once proud demon hardly associated himself with the darkness anymore. He didn't deserve it.

Thort gazed down at the water on the mud's surface. The reflection that stared back at him was hard to look at. Utter misery. How far he had fallen from his days of glory, parading around in the Bar and Chain. He didn't recognize himself at all. He had to look away.

Ramiel stood just out of sight from Thort. He didn't even have to use stealth to conceal himself anymore. Thort had given up centuries ago on trying to figure out who was following him, so Ramiel stood watch with little effort, waiting for the Master to step in and reveal what all of this was about.

Ramiel and Thort had been close friends before the Father had cast Thort out of the Kingdom with the rest of the rebels. Ramiel would never understand Thort's decision, and it pained him to watch his misery unfold.

Ramiel had a lot of questions. Why had an angel been sent on a mission to guard a demon? Why had his partner, Joam, been ordered to stand watch in an abandoned cave, guarding something that only one family knew existed? It was all so intriguing. It had to be tied to the promises. The idea made his heart leap in his chest. Ramiel was curious, but he never questioned His Father's loving plans, and was always honored to carry out any mission his Creator sent him on.

So, he waited.

CHAPTER 16

JAMES AND VICTORIA

Faith is where the impossible disappears.

James Pathrose was the son of Codill and Keren Pathrose. His father had been a third-generation pastor who was called late in life to the mission field. God had used Codill and Keren mightily in South America. Through their service, they claimed over 100.000 souls for Jesus in a little over a year. The family served the people in South America for seventeen years. Codill and Keren planted many churches, and those churches still thrived and multiplied. God had supplied every need and equipped their ministry far beyond expectation. Because of Codill and Keren's ministry, South America now had more Christians than any other continent in the world. It was a great harvest that came from small seeds planted by two older members of the faithful Pathrose family who said, "Yes, send me."

James was an older teenager when he joined his parents on the mission field, but he had experienced a lot before he moved to South America.

From the time he was a young boy, James had been sensitive to the spirit realm. He could sense and sometimes even see things that his family members and friends could not. It had scared him as a young boy the first time it happened. He could remember it like it was yesterday.

A sound had woken him from his sleep. James was on the top bunk, his older brother Eli underneath. James was five years old, and Eli was ten. James had just talked his brother into giving him the top bunk, which he was proud to claim as his own. The room was tidy. With two boys sharing it, they had to keep their clothes and toys put away in order to use the space. There was a tricycle in the room, stored in the far-left corner. James had already outgrown it, but the trike had been passed down from his older cousins to Eli and then to James, so the family was reluctant to get rid of it. He had not ridden it in over a year, but James often used it as a prop in his imaginary war games with his toy soldiers. James had left it out a few times in the rain before his mom finally brought it inside for safekeeping. As a result, the front wheel had a slight squeak when it turned due to rust.

That night, James awoke to the familiar sound of his squeaky tricycle wheel. He laid there for a moment, staring at the ceiling, trying to come out of his haze of sleep, his mind wondering if the sound was real or if he had dreamed it.

There it was again. He sat up, knocking his head on the ceiling. He forgot he was on the top bunk. Placing his hand on this head, he looked down, and there in the middle of his room was the tricycle. It was moving, and there was something on it. It was hard to make out in the dark, but it seemed like a shadow, just a little darker than the room. It reminded him of a troll or some type of creepy dwarf. It terrified James, and he stared at it from his bed, his eyes wide and his entire body trembling.

Squeak, squeak, squeak . . . The little trike kept circling and circling while James sat there frozen with fear.

It had been a long day for Thort back then. He had ventured over to the house of Codill Pathrose, his current assignment, late that afternoon. He wasn't sure why he still felt a responsibility to look in on them from time to time. He had run out of arrows in his quiver long ago. He knew the visit would make him sick, just like it always did, but he still came now and again. He couldn't believe that this had gone on for so long and that these people were so set on following the Enemy with no cracks in their resolve.

He had sat at the dinner table and then listened to Codill read from the Bible to his two sons afterward. He watched James, the little one, pick his nose and stare at something in the distance.

How is it they don't even pay attention, and yet it seems to still seep into their little skulls? Thort wondered. *There's no way that a five year-old boy can understand any of what his father is reading from that dumb book.*

Thort had also sat and listened as Keren prayed over the boys before bed. She prayed for protection over their minds as they slept and for the Lord to reveal himself, even in their dreams. Thort spat on the ground.

"Seriously? Even while they're asleep they're untouchable? Foul play!

The boys had been tucked in and lights off for a couple of hours. Thort was miserable. He sat on the tricycle in the corner, his chin resting on his fist.

I'll never understand why I'm so hated, he thought. *What did I ever do to deserve this punishment? Why must I be damned to endure this family for eternity?*

Deep in his own thoughts, Thort pushed off from the floor and pedaled the trike around the room, muttering to himself. "There must be some reason I'm still around. There must be something I can do to feel useful again."

Thort didn't notice little James staring down at him from the top bunk.

When he heard the squeaking of the wheel come to a stop, James finally built up the courage to look back down from his bed. The creature sat still for a moment, mumbling. He didn't notice that James was awake. After what seemed like an hour to James, the dark spirit stood up. He was much taller than he looked sitting on the tricycle. His misshapen spine caused him to hunch and move as if he had no will. The creature dragged his foot as he walked toward the bedroom door, but he never opened it. He just passed through it and then disappeared.

James stared at the door in disbelief. He had never seen anything like it, and it terrified him. But then, when he saw how weak the creature seemed, his fear subsided. It didn't seem like it could hurt him, but his five-year-old mind had no idea what it was.

James had seen into the spirit realm several times during his life, but he would never forget that first time. He had seen angels in his dreams, and he had caught sight of Thort twice, but he didn't know the demon's name. James witnessed the principality who was overthrown in South America when God moved through his family in that region. Because of his experiences, James thought about angels and demons a lot more than the typical person, even as an adult.

He was married now to Victoria, a beautiful God-fearing woman whom he had met on the mission field in his early thirties. She was a gift from God, and he enjoyed sharing his experiences with her. Victoria was one of the few people he had told of his visions who didn't think he was weird. She had never seen anything like that, but she believed her husband's accounts.

It was mid-January, and James and Victoria were sitting in the backyard looking up at the stars. The stars were so much easier to see in the winter. The crisp night air felt like it was alive.

The couple was older now. Their children were all grown and married, and they even had grandchildren to love. Their youngest grandson, Spencer, stayed with them during the weekdays while his parents worked. He had just learned to walk, and James and Victoria were so happy to help teach him and watch him grow.

Life was mostly quiet and comfortable for the couple. They had followed Jesus and enjoyed a lot of prosperity and peace. Most nights, they found each other's company satisfying, even in complete silence. Other nights, they would get into deep discussions about what they were hearing from the Lord.

James looked over at Victoria and smiled at the sight of her silhouette, staring up at the night sky. He reached for her hand. "The stars are beautiful, aren't they?"

Victoria nodded. "Absolutely. It seems like you can see more of them in the winter. Don't you think?"

"It does. Imagine all the ones that we can't see, trillions of them." James paused. "Looking at the stars always makes me wonder about all the other things around us that we can't see." Victoria nodded but didn't respond.

"I often wonder what's going on in the spirit realm. I wonder if Hell really understands that it will never taste victory. Do demons know they're fighting a losing battle, or are they just ignorant?"

"Why are you thinking about demons?" Victoria asked, turning to him. "That seems odd."

"Oh, I don't know. I think about them a lot, actually. I know it sounds baffling, but I wonder if demons realize Jesus will come for His Bride soon. Do they know they're on the losing side? I can't imagine what that would feel like. If it were me, I would want to defect, even if it meant becoming a prisoner of war."

"James, that is insane," Victoria replied. "I don't know much about demons, but I don't think they have the option to change camps and follow God again. They don't call them fallen angels for nothing. The Father cast them out and has separated them from His presence. Even worse, they have devoted themselves to perpetuate the separation of the human race from the Father. All their energy is pointed toward destruction."

James looked over at his wife. "Exactly! Demons must see that they're on a sinking ship. All signs point to the King's return, and sooner rather than later. All I'm saying is, humans realize they need a Savior. Humbling ourselves is necessary to receive redemption, and once we do, He gives it to us freely. I'm sure glad you and I had a choice." James paused, and Victoria thought maybe he would leave it there, but he didn't. "I just wonder if they do too."

Victoria scoffed, prompting a smile from James. "You know me, honey. I'm just thinking out loud."

"Your imagination is something else, babe. Even I am at a loss for words on that topic." She patted James's thigh and then stood up. "I'm headed in to put away the books and toys from the weekend.

Toddlers are like little tornadoes." She chuckled at the thought of Spencer's energy.

Victoria was used to such conversations. Her husband had seen things that she had never seen, and that gave him a different perspective. They had had a lot of bizarre chats over the years, but this one might have topped them all. Secretly, she hoped he hadn't mentioned this idea to anyone else. She knew James's theology was out there, but she loved him, and she knew Jesus did too. Anyone else might think he was crazy.

"A redeemed demon," Victoria muttered as she walked back to the house, shaking her head and smiling at her husband's crazy thoughts.

CHAPTER 17

DREAM A LITTLE DREAM

James usually listened to his wife's advice. Many times her words of wisdom had set him, as well as their entire family, directly on the Lord's course. Victoria often saw things in the natural world and understood them well before they came into clear focus for James. His perspective had always been different. He loved that he could share his experiences with her no matter how strange they were. She kept him grounded, and he opened her world to the things she could not see. They trusted each other to hear from the Lord.

James knew he sounded like a lunatic with his question about demons earlier, but he could not get the crazy thought out of his spirit. Victoria never brought it back up, but he could tell that she had dismissed the idea early on. A good night's sleep was just what he needed to clear his mind. So, he retired early. He drifted off before Victoria even came to bed.

Not long after he fell asleep, a touch on his shoulder startled him. He sat straight up, wide awake.

An entity was standing before him, filling the room with bright light and saturating every shadow. The background sound of the fan faded as if he had entered a slow-motion dimension of time, and the room fell silent.

The being who had touched him stood gleaming in great stature. His height superseded the ceiling, and yet he was completely visible.

James's eyes could not adjust to the light. He held his hand in front of his face to shield them and squinted at the burning eyes that stared back at him.

"James, my name is Ramiel, and I bring you a message from the King," the being said.

James jumped out of bed in sheer terror and fell to the floor. He rubbed his eyes until they finally adjusted to the light. James stared up at the larger-than-life figure, towering over him.

"Don't be afraid, James," the angel continued. "I'm not here to harm you. Rise."

James hesitated. Ramiel was frightening, and no matter how many times he had seen a spirit being, he had never gotten used to it. Eventually, he gathered his courage and stood up. He glanced over at his wife, who was fast asleep. *How in the world can she sleep through something like this?* he wondered.

"Listen and do not speak," Ramiel said. "My Lord has heard your question concerning those who were once among us and cast out."

James's mind was suddenly filled with swirling thoughts. Was this real? Was he dreaming? Had his crazy thoughts been heard? Had he committed heresy? He opened his mouth to speak, but Ramiel raised his huge hand to stop him.

"At birth, our Lord gave you a gift of supernatural sight, but until now you have only used a small part of it. Now because you have inquired, my Lord will allow you to see into His Kingdom here on Earth for a special encounter. Listen carefully to me, James. Soon you will meet a fallen creature who was once much like me. You've seen him before, but you didn't know what you were looking at. He chose to betray our Lord and Father. This creature now goes by the name of Thort. When you meet him, you will notice that he is very weak, but he was not always this way. He has served Satan with loyalty and ushered many souls to eternal death since his fall. He was once a brutal force for darkness, wielding powers of deception. However, our Lord has set him aside for unknown deeds of heavenly significance. All the generations who have gone before you have tasted of his malicious works. He has toiled endlessly over the generations to ensnare and deceive all of those entrusted with guarding the sacred manuscript and then the amulet that is now in your possession, yet none of your ancestors have ever asked what you asked tonight. Our Lord knew your thoughts and was listening when you spoke to Victoria. Your question points to our Lord's fulfillment and divine plan for Thort and for you. What you will be a witness to will usher in the end of an age as well as the beginning of His glorious Bride's place in eternity. Your question was God's will, and He will see fit to answer it. Soon you will meet your family's generational deceiver, Thort. You must be careful to speak only what your Lord speaks through you during this encounter. The Holy Spirit will guide you. Pray now for discernment. You will need it. The divine interaction with Thort will be unique. The Father has never used a human in this capacity before. As you know, He has preserved and protected your family over the years. He has always had grand plans for your line. Now He has heard your question, James, and you will witness a part of those plans as they unfold in the coming days. Speak of this to no one, remain in prayer, keep your eyes open, and be ready."

With that the great Ramiel disappeared, and the room returned to normal.

James could hardly process what he had just heard. It was a lot to take in. He couldn't remember if he had blinked the entire time Ramiel was speaking. Still startled, he closed his eyes for a moment to take it all in, replaying the words he had just heard.

Standing there in the dark room, he looked over at his wife in undisturbed slumber. His legs felt like they didn't have bones in them as he slid down onto the edge of the bed. It was like the moment after one awakens from a vivid dream when they are trying to decide which reality is real. But he had not slept through this one, nor had he awakened. The room was so dark and normal now. His mind tried to introduce the idea that he had imagined the whole thing. It was so surreal.

What a night, James thought. He took a deep breath and then crawled back into bed next to his wife. He still could not believe Victoria had slept through the encounter. He contemplated waking her to tell her about it, then decided against it. As he pulled the blanket back over him, he didn't think he'd fall asleep again that night. Surprisingly, however, he fell asleep almost immediately.

CHAPTER 18
A MEETING BY THE WATER

James awoke the next morning with all the details of the previous night clearly in his memory. He was still grappling with his thoughts, trying to decide if Ramiel had really been standing in his bedroom or if he had dreamed the entire exchange. It didn't really matter. Either way, one of God's messengers had visited him, and the anticipation of what was to come was palpable in James's heart.

He had so many questions, and he yearned to share his encounter with Victoria. He would love to hear her thoughts and share his excitement, but he remembered Ramiel's instructions. His faith was going to have to be sufficient for the days to come. He began to pray and ask for discernment. He didn't know what was coming, but James surrendered himself to be used by his Lord and agreed to speak only His words when the time came.

Several weeks passed. The vivid details of the visitation from Ramiel faded in James's memory, but the instructions remained as vivid as ever. He spent time in prayer each day. He looked at things differently and considered things more carefully in anticipation of the message being fulfilled. Every day was a new opportunity, and every moment held great potential. He would be ready when the time came.

On March 15 that year, James took the day off from work. It was his and Victoria's birthday. Since they shared the same birthday, they always planned a special date night each year. He had made a dinner reservation earlier in the week at her favorite Italian restaurant. He planned to pick some wildflowers from the property for her instead of buying the overpriced commercial ones. He knew it would be more special to her if he gathered them himself.

James and Victoria owned a beautiful property. Their home sat on the cleared portion of a 114-acre plot. When they cleared the land, James left several large hardwood trees for shade and beauty. He managed the backside of the property, which was woodland. It was beautiful, and James was very proud of it. Victoria had chosen this piece of land because of the stream that flowed through the woodlands. It was a spring-fed tributary that fed the major river about two miles away. The stream was anywhere from eight to twelve feet across and never more than just over knee deep. Its banks were mostly sand and pebbles. The stream snaked back and forth through cedars and oak trees, all the way across the length of their property. James worked regularly to tend the bank and fight back the overgrowth, so they could enjoy the stream. He often brought his grandson, Spencer, down to catch tadpoles and skip rocks. It was an oasis right in their backyard.

It was early spring, and James knew the hyacinths would be in bloom down by the stream, closer to where it opened into the river. Victoria was out running a few errands before their date, so he left her a note and headed out the back door.

It was an overcast day. The weather was mild, and the breeze smelled of clean laundry on the line. It was so peaceful down by the stream, and he wished he took the time to enjoy it more often. He spent most of his time working down there to keep it accessible.

James had a favorite oak tree he loved to sit under. On a whim, he grabbed his Bible on the way out. If he happened upon the right flowers soon enough, maybe he would have a few moments to sit and finish reading the book of James.

As he strolled down toward the water's edge, he took note of what things needed to be tended to the next time he was down there. He was looking over at some thorny vines that had sprung up from the base of a tree and were winding their way around the truck toward the sky. *Good grief, those things grow fast,* he thought.

Just then, something rustled down by the water. James jumped at the sound. He assumed it was a deer or a raccoon that had been down taking a drink when he approached. It was common to run across wildlife down there, but he had never encountered anything dangerous.

He hurried past the trees, hoping to catch a glimpse of the animal before it scurried off. Just as the stream came into view, he spotted it. It was not a deer or a raccoon or any other kind of animal. It was a man. James's thoughts ran wild. *Who is it? Is someone squatting on my property?* James was ready to approach the man and find out, but then he wondered if the man was dangerous and maybe armed. Should he approach or go back for some help?

James moved in closer to assess the situation, though he remained cautious. He had no weapon to defend himself other than his Bible. As the man came into view, James recognized he was battered and beaten up. Some of his wounds looked old. The scars had long healed, leaving his skin thick, leathery, and deformed and his clothes tattered and filthy. He also had fresh wounds that appeared to be festered and infected. His eyes were milky. It looked as if he were completely blind in one of them. The man even appeared to have what looked like severe birth defects. A missing ear and a grossly elongated leg with a calloused club foot were some of the first things that stuck out to James. But the most bizarre part of him was the man's complexion. James couldn't decide if he was just that pale or if he was seeing through him, like an apparition. It was hard to focus on him because his form had no distinct lines.

The man and his clothing were several miserable shades of gray, not black and white but gray like dead flesh after it had been left in the water. James squinted and tried to focus, but it was like the man was fading before his eyes. He didn't move. James would have thought the man was dead if he hadn't heard him stir earlier.

Clearly, this man was no threat, so James approached him. "Excuse me. Hello there."

The sound jolted Thort from his miserable thoughts. He wiped away the string of drool that ran from his half-open mouth to his chest and looked up toward the tree line where James was approaching.

Who is he talking to? Thort wondered. *Did the woman or the kid come down here while I was sleeping?* Thort looked all around him, searching the stream and the trees, but he saw no one else.

James waded through the stream toward the man, though he kept enough distance between them to lunge back across the stream to safety if the man tried to attack him.

"Hey, you there," James said, raising his voice.

Thort frowned in confusion. *Seriously, who is he talking to? He can't see me, can he? No biped has ever seen me. He can't possibly be talking to me.*

"Sir, I think you can hear me. I didn't mean to startle you. Are you alright? Are you blind? Are you able to speak?"

Thort was astonished. This man could clearly see him. Feeling emboldened, he decided to respond. "Who are you to address me?"

"Well sir, I'm the owner of this property that you're trespassing on, and I wondered if you might be lost. You look hurt."

Thort lurched back on his hands and dug his heels into the mud. "You can see me? You can hear me?"

James stepped closer. "Yes. Why would I not be able to see or hear you?" Just then a lightbulb turned on in James's head.

Thort fumbled to his feet. "I'm not of flesh and blood or clay from this Earth."

James's heart jumped in his chest as he recalled his dream and realized who was standing before him. "It wasn't a dream. It was real!" he cried.

"What?" Thort frowned in bewilderment. "What did you say?"

"Oh, nothing. Sorry, I wasn't talking to you."

James's mind was racing like no other time in his life. *What a moment this is,* he thought. *What an opportunity.*

"Wait! Who else are you talking to then?" Thort asked. He was so confused.

"Um, no one. Just you," James replied. He remembered the angel's instructions about speaking only the words that the Lord gave him when this moment arrived. He closed his eyes and took a deep breath, calling on the Holy Spirit to guide him. Then he gathered himself and spoke with solid assurance. "You must be the one Angel Ramiel spoke of. You're one of the fallen stars. You're called Thort."

Thort tilted his head in disbelief, his eyes wide. "You know Ramiel? How do you know him? And how do you know my name?"

James nodded. "Yes, I know him. He visited me and told me about you, Thort. And sure enough, here you are."

Thort's world was spinning, but before he could reply, James continued. "You see, I was talking with my wife, Victoria—who thought I had lost my mind, by the way—about whether a fallen angel could be restored if they asked for forgiveness. I was just chewing over the idea of redemption. Well, not really redemption but the possibility of fallen creatures like you being reborn or remade. After our discussion, Angel Ramiel appeared to me." James paused and took a breath. "Sorry I'm talking so fast. I'm really excited to see you."

"You're excited to see me?" Thort's forehead crumpled into a roadmap of disbelief.

James waited to see if the idea of restoration had landed or passed right over the fallen star's head. A lost being who had once served his Lord and now served his greatest enemy was standing— well, barely standing—right in front of him. This being had walked beside every one of James's descendants and strived to destroy them. James recognized amazement and confusion on Thort's face, but he proceeded without hesitation.

"Can I ask you a question?"

Thort glanced down at the ground and then looked off into the distance. "You can ask, but I might not answer."

"As I understand it, you've been deceiving, harassing, tricking, intimidating, falsely accusing, lying, cheating, and seeking the destruction of my family and the Pathrose ancestors before me all the way back to the time of King Jesus's resurrection. You've schemed against every generation and attempted to use every demonic weapon against us. Am I right?"

Thort said nothing. He just stared at the ground, scratching the side of his face, and shifted off his aching foot. He couldn't escape the feeling of being exposed. What he wanted to do more than anything was take flight and disappear from there forever. But where would he go? Hell Ops? The Bar and Chain? There was no safe place left for him.

After several moments of silence, Thort scowled up at James. Getting no verbal response from Thort, James continued his questions. "Why? What did the king of all liars promise you?

"You knew my Lord Jesus before I did, and you knew Him in His divine state. What did He do to you that caused you to side with darkness? Can't you see that you and all the other fallen made an eternal mistake? You knew my Father has prepared a horrible place for you, a place of eternal separation from Him, the one who made you. Then your puppet master used you to deceive God's chosen. How has that worked out for you?" James gave Thort a once-over. "Judging from your appearance, I would say not as well as you had hoped. Just look at yourself; you're pitiful. What do you have to say? Speak, demon."

Thort could take no more questioning. He held up his crooked, deformed hand as a sign for James to cease with his questions. This interrogation was humiliating but true. His hand dropped, and he hung his head in exasperation. He wanted to speak, but the words stuck in the back of his throat like thick mucus. A few more awkward moments passed, then Thort took a deep breath.

"Looking back," he croaked, then paused to clear his throat.

"Looking back, I can still feel the excitement of my service to the Creator and the union with the others in the Celestial City. But my eyes left Him and fell away as I and others like me looked toward Satan. Serving the Father was no longer fulfilling what I desired. I wanted to be given authority over my brothers and receive glory for myself. That desire became my quest, and Satan became my new lord. Now I know that my brothers and I were deceived. We were told by the great deceiver that with enough hard work and dedication, we would ascend to the Father's throne and rule. God never offered that honor to us."

Thort looked up at James with a furrowed brow and hatred in his eyes. "Instead, He offered it to you useless clay beings. We couldn't believe it. *You* would rule and reign with the King of Glory. What was that about? There was no way I was going to stand for such an injustice. So, I joined the darkness and committed my existence to the extermination of those whom the Lord had chosen to love and accept over me."

"For centuries I disposed of you useless humans that Hell Ops assigned me to. For a long time, I enjoyed great power and walked with my head held high, exalted among my brothers. Then one day they assigned me to a simple man named Paulk. I'll spare you the gruesome details, but my dilemma started with Paulk and his pathetic wife, Sarah."

"Your dilemma was my family?" James asked. "The Pathrose family?"

"Yes, the Petrus family, the Pathrose family, whatever," Thort hissed. "Throughout each generation, they resisted my every effort using His holy tactics against me. Not once was I able to distort the truth, steal their joy, or wreck their peace."

Thort pointed his talon at James. "Through the ages, your family and the followers of your King Jesus cannibalized every false religion that Hell Ops supported. I lost every Petrus and Pathrose generation assigned to me. Now I'm fated to become food for a hundred fallen ones. They will destroy me and feast on me because of my failures, and I'll deserve it."

"That sounds, well, justified," James replied. "So, it seems you have accepted your fate, knowing there is no escape?"

Thort looked around to see if anyone else was listening. Then he leaned in closer to James, lowering his voice to a whisper. "I made a mistake and followed the usurper. I know that now. After watching your family for generations, I'm convinced there is only One whom I was created to serve. They have forbidden my lips to even mention His name except to curse Him. My greed and self-righteousness blinded my eyes and my spirit, and I refused to acknowledge His heavenly sonship. The Son of God brought a truth into this world that your ancestors fully accepted. No weapon in the Hell Ops arsenal can compromise that truth. Your family forced me to endure, to face the truth and the Word, yet Hell Ops continued to deceive me. They told me I could defeat it, and I believed them, but in truth, I never had a chance. Look at me, my failure with each generation caused my darkness to fade. Now I know that this truth is invincible. I followed the wrong leader, and that choice has led me to certain destruction. I deserve nothing less."

Words came forth from James's mouth, though not from his mind. "You're right about one thing. You deserve nothing less." James paused and leaned closer to the pitiful gray demon. "But what if I told you there was another way?"

Thort scoffed. "Another way to do what, die? No, that is the way in Hell. See, we can't create anything, so if anything is to grow or become more powerful, it must draw from something else. My fellow demons will consume me and use me for their own self-exhortation. It's humiliating and painful, but I assure you, there's no other way. I'll go the same way Nag did; I'm sure of it."

James looked up at what had been a dark and dreary sky all morning, but had suddenly become cloudless and bright. "Let me explain something to you, Thort. Darkness, no matter how dark or how long it stays that way, can't exist in the light. I always find light in forgiveness, self-control, faith, love, hope, and joy. You've experienced many divine lights. The Pathrose descendants have shown you many forms of fruit that come from being filled with the King's

Spirit. They used many weapons of warfare against you that had no equal. It's like spiritual radiation. They exposed you to too much light. The darkness within you had nowhere to hide." James pointed to Thort's arm. "That would explain your fading."

"I guess spending the afternoon here with you will probably be the end of me then," Thort said, then stared down at the flowing water in the stream. Oh, how he wished he had not been so foolish. What would his existence have been like? Maybe like that of his old friend, Ramiel.

Thort's thoughts were clear, but it was still hard to transfer the words from his lips. "I know this is my end." He paused and took a deep breath. "Somehow before I'm devoured, I must bow down . . . and ask for forgiveness from your Lord and Savior. I know He won't hear me, but even if it's in vain, I must beg for His forgiveness."

James closed his eyes, and a smile stretched across his face. He was so thankful for this day. He knew that his face-to-face encounter with this fallen angel was the only one of its kind in all of history. A fallen star was asking for forgiveness. Would the Lord allow it, and why now? Throughout God's word, James had never read of anything like this. No one had ever even discussed it. He had just witnessed the epiphany of the ages. How would God respond? What was the purpose of this remarkable repentance saga? James didn't have any of the answers, but he was okay with that.

In an instant, James opened his eyes and discovered he was in his red recliner in the living room. A vase of purple hyacinths sat in water on the end table next to him. The sun was fading outside as the back door swung open.

"Honey, I'm home!" Victoria called. "I could use some help with these groceries!"

CHAPTER 19
THORT AND AADIEL

James was gone from the creek bank in a flash, almost before Thort could get the word "forgiveness" out of his crooked mouth. In that same instant, he found himself face down in the mud with Ramiel's foot on his neck. Thort attempted to spit the mud from his mouth as he tried to reckon with the abrupt change of company.

Ramiel was experiencing several emotions at once. He had to admit his enjoyment. He had waited a long time to stomp on this idiot after all he had done. Ramiel had taken Thort's betrayal personally. After all, they had been friends. They were created together and had worked and worshiped together. The betrayal cut deeply. Ramiel had imagined the circumstances much differently when he faced Thort again, but it turned out the Lord had a unique plan for them both. The prospect filled Ramiel with wonder.

After a moment of spitting and sputtering, he allowed Thort to roll over. Thort gasped for breath as he looked up at his old friend turned foe.

"Get up," Ramiel growled, grabbing Thort by the neck and yanking him to his feet. "My Lord has sent me to inquire about your condition, as miserable and pathetic as it may be. State your position plainly, you wretched, paltry demon."

Thort wavered on his feet. His legs could barely support his puny weight. Finally, he gathered himself and stood as erect as he could. Seldom did demons tremble, but Thort could not control his muscles. As he stood before Ramiel, his dark mind filled with images of how he was going to be destroyed. Perhaps his dark fiends would have nothing left to consume after all.

"Speak, deceiver!" Ramiel thundered.

Thort's bladder released as he began to stammer. "My condition . . . my condition . . . my state of nature . . . is fallen, sir. It fell on the day I followed the deceiver."

Ramiel nodded. "I won't ask you for an explanation because I know there isn't one." Thort hung his head.

"My Lord listened as you spoke with James today and then sent me here. Apparently, you have something you would like to say to Him."

Thort lifted his eyes and met Ramiel's burning stare.

Ramiel surveyed Thort's depraved, skeletal form. "I see you must not be very good at what you do. The Father has witnessed your failures. What you didn't know was His sovereign hand was on a selected family, protecting and preserving each generation. You could never penetrate the grace found in them. You never had a chance, and now look at you."

"Yes," Thort replied. "Hell Ops's weapons were useless against them. They knew all along we could never win, but they lied to me over and over!" Thort wheezed and hacked, coughing up what sounded like a major organ. "I knew it, too," he said, spitting.

Ramiel glared into the faint existence that remained in Thort's eyes. "You've deceived many, and for a time you were successful. The Pathrose lineage was His light for generations. You should know that as they came to a full realization of your purpose when they died, most of them felt a measure of sorrow for you, Thort. You were fighting against Jesus's Spirit, which was so strong in them, so your tactics were useless. It was Him who rendered you weak and aimless in your efforts. The fruits produced by His Spirit allowed them to touch the untouchable on this Earth. The King wrote their names in His book with His blood, and now they live in His house."

Ramiel looked down at Thort's arm. His flesh was paper thin and feeble, it appeared to be blowing away with the breeze.

Thort pondered Ramiel's words for a moment before responding. "Out of fear I haven't reported to Hell Ops in a long time, but if I did, my report would be that through the generations I've witnessed a coming glory, which I know we can't stop, a Bride making herself ready. They followed Him with a furious love that brings me here today, defeated and finished."

Thort was feeling weaker by the moment. He knew he had little time. Something in him was changing, softening, weakening, repositioning, and exposing a vulnerable untouched truth. It was numbing and excruciating all at once. Truth, something Thort had rejected and fought against since the day he had decided to rebel. But here it was, truth, staring him in the face, shining through the molecules of his existence, laying his faults bare. Thort felt a frantic sense of urgency for his last words to be heard.

"Ramiel, I can blame no one. I chose this path. Me. I turned away. I chose deceit and destruction over truth and submission. I know my eternal fate is sealed. There's no question about what will happen to me. The king of liars will devour the darkness left in me, and I deserve nothing less. I have no excuse, no argument or rebuttal. My decisions and actions deserve an eternal punishment that my dark spirit won't allow my mind to put words to. I don't even deserve to be heard today, but Ramiel, I need you to deliver a message to your Lord. My last words will change nothing, but I need you to witness them, to repeat them."

Ramiel said nothing to Thort's plea. He offered no promise.

Thort stumbled forward and grabbed Ramiel by the forearm, his voice fraught with desperation. "This truth has not proceeded from my lips since we were cast down. Your Lord Jesus is the King of Kings and Lord of Lords. Please tell Him I'm sorry. I'm sorry for my part in the insurrection, I was wrong to follow the king of liars, wrong to take my attention and adoration away from the Creator. I should never have served another over Him. Greed and covetousness blinded me, making me desire to be more than He created me to be. I've deceived, lied, manipulated, stolen and misdirected the thoughts of His sheep. I've created division, chaos, injustice, and confusion. I was wrong—about everything. From the first thought of self-service to the last thought I just had, I've been wrong, and I'm sorry. No words on Earth or in Heaven can describe the depths of my repentance. Please tell Him for me, Ramiel. I need Him to hear it."

Thort turned his face toward Heaven. "Forgive me! Please, please forgive me, Father." Burning tears seared the thin hide that was pulled tight over his cheekbones. Then Thort fell face down in the mud beside the stream, the life having left his body.

Never, in all eternity had a heavenly or demonic spirit just ceased to exist. Thort's once proud and mighty black spirit now laid in a pungent, unidentifiable heap of gray steaming matter beside the water's edge.

Three minutes passed. Then Ramiel took two steps back and lifted his face to the heavens. Closing his eyes, he took a deep breath. All was quiet and still until the Creator began His work. Suddenly, a great wind arose out of the east. The heap of gray goo began to move and shift. As the wind blew, the mass began to take form, and color and light burst forth from it. A sweet aroma replaced the stench of rot. Through the light, the shape of a new being erupted out of the heap and began to move. His skin was firm and without blemish. His facial features were properly proportioned with a strong jawline, and his hair fell in soft brown curls above each of his ears. The new being's eyes were a piercing emerald green. A bright blue garment adorned his body.

Ramiel reached down and offered his hand.

The newly created being rose to his feet. He was much taller than Thort had been. He stood on his muscular legs and gazed down at his massive feet. A look of wonder filled his countenance. His ever-widening eyes beheld a myriad of bright colors and fractals of light around him. He took his first cleansing breath, and his new spiritual body radiated and filled the atmosphere with joy and awe. He looked at the angel standing in front of him.

Ramiel had witnessed thousands of universes spoken into existence, but he had never seen something like this. No one had. He stood looking at what had once been a treasonous, pitiful, demonic deceiver, now a new creation.

"The Almighty has destroyed the dark and fallen spirit, Thort. The Creator has orchestrated something new. You, my friend, are one of a kind. No longer Thort, you are now Aadiel. You were destroyed and then remade, and now you are alive again. Listen with your new ears, and hear the truth. As Thort you strove to devour the Pathrose clan. You were their greatest enemy, and yet one of them dared to ask a question that had never come to my Lord's ear. James Pathrose said, 'Would God restore a fallen angel?' Aadiel, our God sent me here with His answer. He will never restore you to the glory He adorned you with at the time of your creation. However, our Father has heard your heart and your request to be forgiven, and I was a witness to it. We are spirits, not flesh and blood like humans. Therefore, redemption is not the place of grace for you. Jesus shed His precious blood for them, not for us. Yet in His sovereignty, God has mercifully recreated you."

Sound erupted from Aadiel's newly created vocal cords. He spoke with a voice as strong and smooth as burnished bronze, catching even himself off guard, "How? How can this be?"

Ramiel was beaming. "The impossible has become possible today only through our sovereign God's love. His unexplainable mercies are new every morning. Aadiel, the Pathrose family exposed Thort to the fruits of a sacrificed life. You would not be here if not for Thort's assignment to them. Thort's failures led him to a posture of submission and a request for forgiveness. He died the moment his request was uttered. The message of repentance was heard, and Thort's acknowledgement of the justice he deserved moved the Father's heart. As a result, Thort didn't receive that justice. Instead, our benevolent God has given you a portion of that promise that has set aside for every human who claims Him as their Lord."

Tears streamed down their faces as they embraced. It had been so long, and Ramiel had missed his friend. The chasm between them had been bridged.

"Your God is love," Ramiel said as he pulled back. "Your God is merciful even to the fallen stars. Aadiel, you are proof that He is a restorer of an unimaginable breach."

Ramiel took another step back from Aadiel and cleared his throat. Aadiel sensed his demeanor stiffen with formality. "Now for your first assignment. You are to report to the middle northern gate of the Celestial City. There, you will meet one of God's most loyal servants. His name is Kafziel. Listen to him carefully, as he has as much to teach you. He will also brief you on your coming assignment."

As soon as Ramiel's finished speaking, the great angel vanished.

Aadiel staggered back, still in a state of shock. His mind was crowded with wonders, so many thoughts and questions. Never in his wildest imaginings had he considered a new beginning. He glanced down at the mud he had been lying in earlier that morning when he encountered James and was overcome with thanksgiving. Praise be to his Master who had chosen to split his existence in two. Lifting his head to the heavens, a wide smile spread across his face. Testing his newfound strength, Aadiel exploded into the air.

CHAPTER 20

KAFZIEL AND THE DIVINE COUNCIL

From the mud to the Celestial City, Aadiel suddenly found himself at the middle north gate. It was like taking a step back in time. He remembered this place, but it felt surreal to see it again. The sight of the great wall filled him with many memories of the city's beauty and grandeur. Would he ever enter the city again? He had so many unanswered questions, but he felt no anxiety or fear in his spirit. The gate's massive height matched the walls as it rose so high that Aadiel could not see the top. He remembered how those tremendous pearl gates could open or close with just a nod from the guardians who stood at each entrance.

Standing in front of the gate, Aadiel glanced in both directions along the great wall. He wondered where he was supposed to meet this special angel. *This is where Ramiel told me to meet him, right?* he asked himself. There was no administration building around and no one to ask.

Suddenly, he felt a tap on his right shoulder. Aadiel turned but saw no one. Then he looked over his left shoulder and saw a portly being with a playful grin on his face.

"Gotcha!" the being said as he doubled over and chuckled from deep inside his belly.

Surprised by the stranger's behavior, Aadiel snapped to attention. He didn't know who the jovial fellow was, but his rank was probably higher than his own.

"Uh, excuse me, sir. My name is Aadiel, and I'm . . . well, I'm new here, sir. Ramiel sent me to report for my first assignment. I'm to see Kafziel."

"Relax, Aadiel. I know who you are," the being said, still recovering from his laughter.

"Um, okay. Could you point me in the direction I should go to meet Kafziel?"

The ancient angelic being smirked in amusement at Aadiel. "Come with me, kid."

"Yes, sir," Aadiel replied, then followed behind the strange being.

After a few steps, the being looked back at Aadiel. "No, come up here beside me. Walk with me."

Aadiel hurried to join the strange being.

"You remember I told you to be at ease, right?" He chuckled again.

Aadiel wasn't sure how to respond.

"I'm Kafziel, kid. I promise you can be at ease. I don't bite."

Aadiel wondered if Kafziel knew how ironic that statement was. "Sorry, sir. I just want to show my respect."

"There's no need for pageantry with me, Aadiel. I know you respect me and this place and everyone in it. We do things differently here. I know it's been a long time, but you'll get used to it again soon. I promise."

The two walked along the wall in silence before Kafziel spoke again. "I have much I want to show you and teach you about the Kingdom and your new home. But before we get into that, I'm going to need to restore your memories. It will be a lot for you to take in, but it's important for your new assignment. We'll fill you with all you need to serve Him. I promise."

"You promise a lot, uh, sir," Aadiel replied, stumbling on his words.

"Kafziel. Just call me Kafziel. And yes, I promise a lot. Today you will get a small taste of the Father's promises. It will be my honor to tell you about them and help you remember things that have passed. as well as inform you of some of His plans."

Aadiel couldn't help but think back on his dreadful meetings at Hell Ops and how differently this briefing was going. Kafziel was such an odd one. He was quite short for an angel, and he wore a simple brown tunic tied around the waist with a sash that looked like a bolt of lightning. His hair and his beard were long and tousled. He walked with the carefree gate of a happy-golucky hobbit instead of a commanding angel. But he carried an assurance that could have only come from being in the Father's presence. Aadiel couldn't get a clear read on the guy, but he didn't mind. He was thankful to be there under any circumstances instead of where he deserved to be.

Without another word, Kafziel veered toward one of the surrounding wheat fields. When they reached the field, he pulled a few of the heads of grain and popped them in his mouth. As he strolled through the field, he looked back at Aadiel. "I know all about you, Aadiel, but you know very little about me, so let me tell you some things. I'm a loyal servant of the Kingdom like you, but I'm also one of the sons of God who serves on His council. He has given me the responsibility of introducing you to your new surroundings, restoring many of your memories, and bringing you up to speed before He places you on assignment."

Aadiel tried to hide the look of astonishment on his face. *This guy? A son of God?* he thought.

"I know what you're thinking," Kafziel said. "but many things are backward in His Kingdom compared to the ways of Earth and the fallen realm. You will learn this as you reacclimate to this place. Anyway, let me catch you up on a few things that will help revive your memories."

Kafziel leaned his hand up against the trunk of a beautiful tree and motioned for Aadiel to take a seat on the grass.

"Where to start? Where to start? Let's just go all the way back, shall we? I know you remember the rebellion. There were three specific occurrences related to it. In the first one, Satan desired to rule and reign above the Father. He despised the Father's love for his new children. Many like you chose that path and swore your allegiance to darkness. That choice, of course, ended your residency here and pitted you against humankind in a feeble attempt to overcome the Kingdom."

Aadiel nodded in agreement. "Feeble indeed."

"The rebellion continued, and Satan pitted himself against humanity in the beautiful garden with the two special trees. What a wonderful place it was in the beginning . . ." Kafziel trailed off as he became lost in memories. "The Father's desire to fill the entire Earth with all the glories in that garden was halted that day, but only temporarily. Brethren of mine, fellow sons of God, also fell. Many of them had relations with women on Earth, resulting in unholy offspring. The Earth was so rampant with rebellion and evil that the Father chose to cleanse it with a devastating flood."

"Those were joyous days for the dark realm," Aadiel said. "I remember them well. Hell was so proud of the Nephilim. There were even reports of an impending surrender by the enemy. Hell Ops assured us we had filled the planet with wickedness. The flood caught everyone off guard."

Kafziel chuckled. "I bet it did. The flood cleansed Earth of everyone who had denied the Father's love."

He turned and leaned back on the tree, folding his arms. "Third, there was Babel. Seventy of those fallen sons who once proudly served our Lord beside me attempted to destroy humanity again. As a result, God disinherited humanity, scattering them to the wind and confusing their language."

"I have never heard of anyone at Hell Ops being referred to as a son of God," Aadiel said.

"Oh, I'm sure they disavowed that title immediately, but you might recognize the title 'principalities and powers.'"

Aadiel nodded. "Oh, yes. That makes sense. Sorpine and Blastus were referred to as principalities, powers, and rulers. They often visited a bar outside of Hell Ops. They were the chief spirits there. So, you're saying they were once sons of God and on His counsel with you?"

"Correct. Now their primary goal is to worry, harass, injure, confuse, frustrate, and kill humans. All of this to get back at God for kicking them out of Heaven and sealing Satan's fate in Hell and, eventually, the lake of fire."

"That's a lot of rebellion," Aadiel said. "And I was there for all of it. I know it broke the Father's heart."

"But there was always a plan," Kafziel said, a grin playing across his lips. "The Father selected a people for Himself. He called them out of that wilderness and confusion. They're a peculiar people who will one day, because of the greatest act of love ever imagined, become a Bride to His Son."

"It would appear that I have spent the last several centuries with some of those peculiar people," Aadiel said.

Kafziel stooped so he could look directly into his pupil's emerald eyes. "Aadiel, you were duped. All of those who fell have been a part of the ongoing rebellion. They think it's about winning and losing battles. What Hell Ops doesn't know is their time of thievery and deception is drawing to an end."

"An end?" Aadiel asked.

Kafziel bopped him on the nose with his finger. "Yes. It appears our Lord recreated you just in time. You will be the perfect instrument to shine a light on His plan. Now get up, kid."

Aadiel jumped up and ran after Kafziel. "Wait. Instrument? What do you mean?" He thought it was so odd how the little angel could talk about such deep and important things concerning the Kingdom and all creation one minute and then be so strange and aloof the next.

He caught up with Kafziel and walked beside him for several moments in silence. When it was apparent Kafziel wasn't going to offer any more details about God's plan or Aadiel's role in it, Aadiel spoke.

"Am I at liberty to ask questions?"

"You're at liberty to do whatever you wish. What would you like to know?" Kafziel replied.

Aadiel thought for a moment. "Why does God need a council? After all, He already has His Son and Spirit."

"Ah, good question, kid. You're paying attention." Kafziel smiled. "You're correct, the Father has Himself, His Son, King Jesus, and the Holy Spirit. However, He created many other sons to serve in His assembly, His council, and His courts. He created a Divine Counsel to carry out the kingdom's administrative tasks in Heaven and on Earth. The Father is Elohim, God, but he created other servant elohim, called sons of God, to serve His new creations, the offspring of His human family. The Father instructed us to carry out the divine plans of His Son, their Creator. He gave us liberties and a free will to accomplish His purposes. To do that, we can use our own thoughts and ideas to fulfill God's divine directives."

"So, you can use whatever methods and ideas you desire to achieve His perfect plan?" Aadiel asked. "You have that freedom."

"Yes." Kafziel stopped walking and turned to Aadiel. "But the Father has always directed the end result. You see, He has given every created being free will, knowing it could produce spiritually unhealthy and even deadly fruit. Nevertheless, He created us this way because He didn't want His created beings to serve Him out of duty but out of willful, loving obedience. You asked why he needed a council. He didn't. He didn't even need humankind. The Trinity has no needs, but They desired a family and were willing to risk the pitfalls of free will for an eternal family whom God would love and who would choose to love Him."

"Okay, I understand," Aadiel said. "I have one more question, though. You didn't rebel. Why?"

"The Father's human family, like those you know from the Pathrose clan, serve Him out of love for what He has done for them. In the same way, we serve Him out of loyalty. We don't know the dimensions of love He has for His human family, but we do know that He was willing to send King Jesus to Earth to die for them. We know Jesus stepped out of the Godhead to become Emmanuel for them. Although we can't understand that love, we comprehend that our creator deserves our loyalty. With free will, we choose to serve Him and Him alone. There are many like me on the council whose loyalty never wavered and never will. We understand that He loves humanity above everything because He gave everything for them. We also know He created us for a special dual role. We get to serve Him and His Bride. It's our highest honor."

"And now it's my honor as well," Aadiel replied.

Kafziel placed a hand on Aadiel's shoulder. "That's right. But enough of the history lessons for now. Let me show you to your resting place."

He turned and walked back toward the city wall. "You never get tired here. I'm not sure why we call it a resting place. But, hey you have one."

Aadiel followed, his mind churning with thoughts. *What's a resting place? I never had a place of any sort in Hell Ops.*

After a short walk, they arrived at a lovely jasper-walled house attached to the city's north wall just past the third massive pearl gate. The grounds surrounding the house were like a perfectly maintained garden. Fresh-smelling herbs and beautiful flowers bloomed under the welcoming shade of trees beside the front porch. A small crystal-clear brook ran under the house from the city wall. The brook wound past the walkway to the house, around a tree, and through the beautiful flower garden. Aadiel followed it as it flowed over smooth stones, creating a gentle waterfall in several spots before it flowed back under the wall. Steps led up to a beautiful blue door with an onyx handle. The house was built on a foundation of twelve layers, each one adorned with brilliant jewels, making them unique.

Aadiel stood there in awe, taking it all in. The sounds, the smells, and the colors were all so welcoming. He couldn't believe this place could be for him. His eyes were wide with amazement as he turned to look at Kafziel.

"Ha! How about that? The door matches your robe. Cool," Kafziel pointed out. "Looks like that may have been planned on purpose." He winked at Aadiel and then chuckled.

Aadiel walked through the garden, touching the beautiful flowers. He put his hand on the trunk of a tree just to make sure it wasn't all some grand illusion.

"When you aren't on assignment, this place will be yours to enjoy," Kafziel said. "You may wonder why it's out here instead of inside the city." He paused to clear his throat. "You won't be permitted inside the city. This is a consequence of your rebellion, but because of your humility, you will have access to the living water that flows from there. Out of the Father's great mercy, you will forever enjoy this outer court, but because of your betrayal, you will never enter the Celestial City again."

"I understand," Aadiel replied, his voice solemn.

Then, in true Kafziel fashion, the angel flipped back to his playful, quirky self. "Well, here ya go. Good luck." He turned to leave. Looking back over his shoulder, he waited for Aadiel to respond. "It was a joke! Come on. We don't have luck up here. That's something that they use back on Earth, along with indecision and procrastination."

"Oh, yeah . . . Okay," Aadiel replied, striving to act like he got it.

"I'll be by in the morning." Kafziel reached out and touched the front lapel of Aadiel's blue robe. "Tomorrow, I want to talk about these clothes and introduce you to some folks, so don't sleep too late."

Kafziel paused again as if waiting for a response. Then he smiled. "Joking again. Who's sleeping? No one sleeps here." Kafziel laughed at himself. At least he thought he was funny.

Aadiel couldn't wipe the awkward look off his face, but he smiled back and waved goodbye. *What an odd little angel,* he thought. He was thankful for Kafziel's joyful character, though. It had helped break the ice and made him feel welcome and more at ease in his new environment. Aadiel wondered what the other council members were like. He had remembered and learned so much, and he was excited about what tomorrow held.

He turned and walked up the steps of his new home, took a deep, satisfying breath, then opened the beautiful blue door.

He's right, Aadiel thought. *The color does match my robe.*

CHAPTER 21

LESSONS LEARNED

The next morning, Aadiel opened his front door and took a deep breath. His senses were still getting used to the splendor of the place. He sat on the solid silver chair on his porch. Its seat and arm cushions were the same beautiful blue as his robe and the front door. He inspected the chair in amazement at the resources and the craftsmanship that had gone into making it. *A silversmith must have poured his life's work into this chair,* he thought.

He gazed out into the garden, still in amazement at its supernatural beauty. He wondered when Kafziel would return to continue his orientation. As he sat, his ears tuned in to a multitude of vaguely familiar sounds coming from over the city wall. Sounds he remembered from before he was thrown down mixed with sounds he had never heard before. His memory was hazy, but certain aspects of those beautiful sounds came to the surface.

Then out of the corner of his eye, he noticed movement. Two identical fairy-like beings came skipping by on the road that ran past his house. He recognized them and was surprised when he recalled their names from memory. "Carley and Casey, is that you?"

The twins stopped and looked over at Aadiel, then turned back toward each other with a surprised smile. They walked through the garden toward the front porch as gracefully as if they were floating.

"My blue robed friend," Casey said, "Aadiel, is it?"

"That's my new name, yes," he replied. "I remember you two. You always made me smile. It blesses me to see you again. You seem different now than when I knew you before, though."

Carley nodded. "Well, much has transpired since you saw us last. We have had a lot of adventures. We even had a brief assignment on Earth in human form."

"Really?" Aadiel said. "That sounds exciting. Were you both assigned together?"

"There was a young family on Earth. The Father had assigned us to them previously but in our heavenly form. We watched over the man and his wife from the day they were married, and we often communicated directions to them to guide their decisions. Then one day we received a blessed surprise. We were being assigned earthly bodies to go down and be a part of that same family. We were twin sisters." Carley smiled at Casey.

"How fascinating," Aadiel said.

"While in our earthly bodies, our tongues were tied," Carley continued. "It was difficult to speak clearly, and our hearts and voices were sometimes misunderstood. Our words were always clear to each other and, of course, to the Father, but humans often had difficulty understanding us. We had to lean heavily on our spirits to communicate His messages of love while we were there. It was a delightful challenge that we enjoyed very much."

Casey bounced up and down while Carley spoke. She couldn't wait to chime in. "Our earthly bodies were physically limited as well," she said. "It was challenging to do even simple things like run and climb and jump while we were there, but it was all worth it!"

"What an odd assignment," Aadiel said. "Why did you need to do that?"

"Our time with them was a special gift from Heaven. We had the honor of teaching the family one on one about the Father's love and how He loves the Son and where the family fit into that story. It was the most creative assignment. We will always be thankful for those memories."

Aadiel smiled at them. "And look at you now. You're back here, skipping and dancing around. Speaking of which, can you explain what sounds I'm hearing from over the wall? There's a rhythm coming out from the city. It's so beautiful, and I can remember parts of it, but there's so much more."

"Oh, you mean the music," Casey said.

"The music?" Aadiel asked.

"The music is composed of many sounds. If you listen closely, you will hear the 144,000 saints singing praises. There are six winged birds of the most spectacular color who fly through the city and ring out new tones every day. We call them the Holy Flock."

"Don't forget about the rainbows," Carley added.

"Ah yes, the colors you hear are all the rainbows from the first promise all the way through those scheduled in eternity."

"I didn't know you could hear colors," Aadiel said. "But then I didn't experience a rainbow when I was here before. It's incredible."

Casey nodded. "The crystal waterfalls pay tribute to King Jesus as well. A trained ear can distinguish the River of Delights from the glories of the Lord."

"The music here is pure and eternal with a love that is unfiltered," Carley said. "You bask in it, but you never get used to it because it's new every moment. Casey and I like to walk around the outside of the wall sometimes to experience the sounds from out here."

"Nothing here gets old," Casey added. "Darkness is unknown. Celebrating, feasting, serving with our King Jesus, and dancing with the Holy Spirit is our eternal blessing."

"I hear it all," Aadiel replied. "Thank you for explaining. It means so much more to me now. The music is so beautiful that it refreshes me from inside. It lifts me and gives me a sense of great anticipation."

Carley grinned. "It should. The music is full of celebration and preparation."

"Preparation for what?" Aadiel asked.

"On Earth Jesus taught His followers to pray 'Thy Kingdom come, Thy will be done, on Earth as it is in Heaven,'" Carley explained. "The Father will answer that prayer soon. The Kingdom here and all its glory, the King, and His Bride are about to culminate on earth!"

Casey put her hand over her mouth and leaned in as if to tell Aadiel a secret. He leaned down to listen. "I think it's going to happen soon, and I think that might be why you're here."

"Wow." Aadiel stood back and looked at the twins in astonishment. The depth of their foreknowledge and understanding was amazing.

"So, where are you headed now?" he asked. "Back inside the city?"

"Now that our tongues are loose, we have the great honor of welcoming every new saint coming to the eastern gate. Our words are no longer misunderstood. We speak the following words clearly to everyone who enters: 'Well done, good and faithful servant; you have been faithful over a few things, our Jesus will make you ruler over many things. Enter the joy of your Lord.'"

Casey bounced with excitement. "The greatest words a saint will ever hear are ours to proclaim!"

Carley put her arm around her sister's neck. "Speaking of proclaiming, we should get to it. We don't want to be late."

As the beautiful angelic twins skipped off toward the eastern gate, Casey glanced back over her shoulder. "It's so wonderful to see you again, Aadiel! All praise to the Lord most high."

He sat back down in his chair, thinking about what he had been told. He spent the rest of the morning bathing in the endless sounds penetrating the thick jasper walls.

He wasn't sure how much time had passed when Kafziel strolled up.

"So, I see you met Carley and Casey."

Aadiel smiled. "I did, and it was amazing. I remembered them from my time here before, but this morning they opened my eyes and my ears in ways I didn't think I could see or hear. I guess there's something to the old saying 'He who has ears let him hear.' Now I can, and it's incredible!"

"Good, good, my friend. We have a long day ahead of us. Things to do. People to meet." Kafziel turned and headed back toward the road behind the house.

Aadiel hopped down the steps and hurried to catch up to him. Kafziel smiled and turned his head toward Aadiel as they walked. "I can't wait to see your face when you experience all that the King has in store for you. Meeting you and having the pleasure of showing you around has been so much fun. I always enjoy the new creations, but you're one of my favorites so far."

"Why, thank you, sir. I'm enjoying my newly created self as well. Moment by moment, I'm more overwhelmed with thanksgiving and praise for what He has done for me. I'm really excited about today too. Can you tell me where we're going?"

"The north gate," Kafziel replied.

Aadiel hadn't been there long, but he knew enough to determine they were walking in the wrong direction to be headed to the north gate.

Noticing his confusion, Kafziel chuckled. "Nothing gets past you, does it? Yeah, yeah, we're taking the scenic route, but I thought it would be nice to show you a few things on the way. Besides, what else do you have to do today?"

"Nothing, sir."

"I get a kick out of the new ones who arrive here daily. They're so used to the construct of time. Then they get here and realize there is no yesterday and no tomorrow. Here there's only today. You know the Father doesn't wear a watch, right?"

"I hadn't ever thought about it," Aadiel said, wondering if he would ever get used to Kafziel's strange manner and sense of humor, if one could call it that.

As they walked, he took a deep breath, experiencing all the beautiful new fragrances around him. The perfumes that wafted in on the cool breeze were ever changing, and just when he thought he had identified one, it would change. All of his senses were alive and thriving.

They were approaching another gate when Aadiel heard a new sound unlike any of the ones Carley and Casey had introduced him to that morning. An even brighter light shone through the openings in the gate. Aadiel picked up the pace, overwhelmed with anticipation of what he would see.

When he rounded the corner of the gatepost, the beautiful sound of children laughing, singing, and playing overtook him. Through the gate he saw white-robed children, so many he couldn't count them. They were dancing and playing beneath a huge waterfall that was raining down crystal water. It appeared to wash over them, yet it didn't touch them. The children lifted their hands and raised their voices in unison, saying, "Ra'ha, Ra'ha." He stood in awe as their voices were amplified, growing louder and louder until he felt them in his entire being. It was as if their praise saturated everything and multiplied itself repeatedly. He looked up and saw the source of the light, dancing with love and life above the children, who stood beneath Him. His light reflected off them and penetrated far beyond the gate. Aadiel's heart leapt in his chest at the sight. He dared not blink, so he wouldn't miss a moment of the heavenly spectacle. Their powerful chorus shook the ground beneath his feet.

Kafziel waited without speaking, allowing Aadiel to take it all in. With tears of joy in his eyes, Aadiel turned to his diminutive companion. "Who are they?"

"The Shepherd's lambs," Kafziel replied. "All of those precious white-robed children belong to the Great King and Shepherd, Jesus. He left the many and went to find the ones who had been lost. These are those ones. What you hear is the sound of them lifting their voices to their Shepherd and Savior, Jesus."

"But why were they lost?" Aadiel asked as he stared at the children, spellbound.

"These children didn't live out their intended purpose on Earth. They were unwanted, undesirable, and sacrificed to the idols of selfishness and greed. Their parents considered them an inconvenience and deemed them unworthy of life. Satan deceived some parents into thinking that these children never lived at all."

Aadiel clapped his hand over his open mouth in awe, his mind full of words but his mouth unable to speak any of them.

Kafziel continued to stare beyond the gate. "They may have been unwanted on Earth, but here the great Shepherd took them by their tiny hands and led them through the valley of the shadow of death and brought them here. Now their existence brings honor and glory and joy to Him forever. Their voices shout with new praises and every offering is different and new. The Father turns His attention fully on each one of them as they praise His Son. He dances above them to honor His Son's love for them. That is the glorious light that you see."

Aadiel stood speechless, looking at the children as Kafziel's words sank in. He wanted to stand there for eternity, listening to their voices and relishing in the love and trust that radiated through the opening in the gate.

Kafziel jolted him out of his daze with an elbow to the ribs. "There are no favorites inside, but these are His favorites. Now, let's go, kid."

"Can't we stay longer?" Aadiel pleaded.

"Things to do. People to meet," Kafziel said over his shoulder.

Aadiel took one last look back at the children. He yearned to stay, but he knew there were endless wonders to see. Even though he would reside outside of the city, he would never grow weary of the surrounding treasures.

As they continued their journey around the city's great wall, questions swirled through Aadiel's mind. He wanted to take advantage of the time he was being given with Kafziel, so he finally spoke up. "Why am I clothed in blue when everyone inside the city wears white?"

"Oh, for the most splendid purpose, my friend," Kafziel replied as he kept walking.

Aadiel waited for Kafziel to continue, then grew tired of waiting in awkward silence. "Well, what is it?"

"I could tell you, but I'm not going to," Kafziel replied.

"Oh, that's helpful," Aadiel quipped. "Well, I have another question that I hope you will answer."

"Shoot, kid," Kafziel said.

"Why me? There are legions of demons, principalities and powers who wielded far more dominion than I ever did. In the end, I was miserable and inept in every fiber of my existence. There were no admirable or remarkable qualities in me. Why am I here? Why was I remade? Why me?"

Kafziel stopped dead in his tracks and turned to face Aadiel. All the quirky humor of his character was gone. "Look at me," he demanded.

Aadiel sensed the tone of importance and met Kafziel's burning gaze with trepidation. It was in that moment that he truly saw Kafziel as a son of God and understood who he was.

"Now close your eyes," Kafziel instructed. He placed his hand on Aadiel's right shoulder and his other hand over his closed eyes. Then he spoke with booming authority. "Recall all the days of vile victory you tasted from the multiple generations as you schemed, cheated, lied, distracted, and deceived the saints of the Pathrose family. Recall each deception that you and your masters concocted. Now, remember your failures from each and every attempt."

Aadiel's head ripped back on his shoulders as it threw his mind into a new realm that caused him to relive the past two thousand years all at once. He trembled like a lost child, not knowing where to go or what to think. He not only witnessed the victory of each Pathrose, he also relived each of his lies. Every deception flooded his psyche all at once. Again, he felt the dishonor of his fallen state. Two thousand years of failures swirled through his head in a twisted mind warp. Each memory brought a fresh sting of defeat and regret. His knees threatened to buckle, but Kafziel steadied him.

"You were Thort, the deceiver, for many centuries. Throughout your hellish failures, you often asked, 'Why me?' Now you stand before me still asking the same question. They robed you in utter darkness. In your defeat, that darkness faded into an ugly gray, but you remained marked by the master you served." Kafziel finished casting the memories. "Now open your eyes."

Aadiel regained his strength and peeked out through his eyelids. It took a moment to adjust to the light after experiencing so much darkness.

Kafziel took hold of Aadiel's lapels. "There are no coincidences here. This blue robe, which now marks you, is the color of extremes. It represents powerful associations of the past. There's no greater extreme than God and Satan, God's love and Satan's hatred, God's eternity with His followers and Satan's eternity with his. You, Aadiel, are also an extreme. Once you were Thort, but now you are Aadiel. Once you were lost, but now you are found. Your satanic master assigned you to a lineage who ultimately asked an unimagined question about forgiveness. That question led to your death as Thort and to a new life as Aadiel. What your satanic master meant as evil has been turned into a good that will be far above anything you can conceive. The blue robe represents the extreme associations with your past and present state, and it will be used in a divine and powerful way."

Kafziel reached down and tugged on the robe's cuff. Aadiel lifted his right arm. There, embroidered into the robe with golden thread, were the words "Trust, Power, Loyalty, and Purpose."

Aadiel gazed back at Kafziel, burning with a deeper understanding than he had before. He felt completely new! The gravity of this new reality filled him with thankfulness. He would live up to the words inscribed on his cuff. He would live up to his blue robe.

As if on cue, Kafziel winked at him. His quirkiness was back. "Like I said, kid, there are no coincidences around here." He turned and continued down the road as if nothing had happened. "Now stop wasting eternity. Get with it, alright? How long are you going to keep them all waiting?"

"What? Waiting? Who? Who's waiting?" His mind still spinning from his recent revelations, Aadiel shook his head to clear it and then ran to catch up.

CHAPTER 22

FAMILIAR FRIENDS

As the pair approached the great northern gate, Kafziel pushed Aadiel forward and then disappeared.

Aadiel saw a group of people gathered just outside of the gate. They were laughing, hugging, and milling around, greeting each other with such affection. It was apparent that they all knew and cared for one another. *Who are these people?* he wondered. *Are they the ones waiting for me?*

As he approached the crowd, Aadiel realized he knew exactly who the people were. He recognized Simon Pathrose first. Oppert and Brea were standing together near the front. He even recognized little Kati, even though she wasn't little anymore. There were mothers and fathers, cousins and brothers, grandfathers, and great nieces. The amazing group of people were the Pathroses. Aadiel's memories resurfaced like boiling water in his brain as his eyes fell on each family member. He remembered his previous life and how he had attacked, deceived, and worked against them. Strangely enough, at that moment he was overwhelmed with feelings of thankfulness and honor. Aadiel was so proud of each of them. He felt honored to be in their presence. As he took in each familiar face and considered his history with each generation, it hit him. It was their faithfulness that had brought him to his knees that day in the mud by the stream. He had witnessed these people hold fast to their faith and understanding of who they were in Christ for generation after generation. They had stood against the enemy and his weapons, and they had not faltered. Thort had spent the entirety of his assignment with them foiled and yet amazed at how this lineage had been protected and preserved. Love and adoration spread through his spirit as the people looked at him and smiled. Overcome with emotion, Aadiel's knees buckled, and he fell down and wept.

From the middle of the crowd, two men strode to the front. They each grabbed Aadiel by an arm and helped him to his feet.

"Stand, my friend," Lucius said.

Although he was on his feet, Aadiel still felt like a heavy weight was pressing down on his shoulders. It was difficult to stand in the presence of the two great saints.

Jeruit had been the humble and hardworking silversmith whom Thort had tried to destroy by hiding the precious silver that his boss had commissioned him to work on. Jeruit's son, Lucius, had evaded Thort's evil intentions for his life when he chose forgiveness over anger. Even Jeruit's boss, Argento, had been softened and introduced to the Kingdom through the sacrifices and obedience of these two men. Aadiel felt like he didn't deserve to stand among them.

"How joyous a moment is this?" Jeruit said to Aadiel. "To see you standing here clothed in righteousness after where you've come from. I would say that I've seen it all now, but I know that's impossible when I serve the King whose mercies are new every morning." Jeruit smiled at his son and chuckled. "When I heard what had happened to you, my heart leapt, and I couldn't wait to meet you. We all wanted to meet you." He motioned to the crowd of people who were now hushed and focused on Aadiel.

"I don't know what to say," Aadiel replied as tears streamed down his face.

"It has all been said, my friend," Jeruit replied. "The Father's decision to call you out of great darkness and restore you in order to bring glory to His Son says everything that needs to be said between us. He protected each of us throughout our lives on Earth. He covered us with His gifts, His fruit, and His armor. You could do us no eternal harm, and we take great delight in meeting you in your restored state. We are thankful that you are now able to continue your assignment with our family."

"Continue?" Aadiel said, his face full of bewilderment.

"Oh, yes. Your work is far from finished, Aadiel. You will resume your assignment to our people, but you won't seek their destruction. Instead, you will assist them and bear witness to the Father's brilliant design and purpose in this age. You may think you've already seen great things, but what's to come will be unlike anything you or I have ever witnessed."

Lucius turned to face Aadiel. "Do you remember the manuscript? The one Peter gave our family in trust?"

Aadiel nodded. "Vaguely. They hid it from me centuries ago, but until this moment, I hadn't given it any more thought. I never knew what was in it, and I just assumed it was some family story or folklore that had been long since forgotten."

"Soon you will understand it is so much more than that," Jeruit replied. "You're right. We did hide it from you, but it was never forgotten. Our descendants have carried an amulet through the generations as a marker and a reminder of our commission. Each generation has been faithful to communicate the responsibility to the next. Our family has been miraculously preserved and protected as we carried out this significant task. The time has come for the retrieval of the manuscript."

"This will be your first assignment as Aadiel," Lucius said. "You remember James, right?"

"Why, of course I remember, James. He's the reason I'm here. I hope I'll see him again soon."

"It just so happens that 'soon' is today." Lucius smiled at Aadiel. "You will assist James and his grandson, Spencer, as they take a journey to retrieve the manuscript. You will remain in the spirit, of course, as you always have, but they'll need your help to retrieve it. It has been hundreds of years since the small hands of Sam Pathrose placed that manuscript behind the linen veil. The Earth and the waters have shifted considerably, but the treasure was never at risk. You will see what I mean when you join them on Earth."

Aadiel beamed with excitement and anticipation as he thought of seeing James again. Spencer had been only a toddler when Thort took his last breath. How old would he be now? How many Earth years had he been here outside of the city? Aadiel had a lot of questions, but he knew he would get answers soon, and he was ready.

"So, should I go now?" Aadiel asked.

"Yes," Jeruit replied. "But before you go, there's something special that I would like to give you."

Aadiel's eyes widened with wonder as Jeruit reached into the pocket of his tunic and pulled out a beautiful necklace made from fine silver. From the chain hung a brilliant medallion that caught the light as it spun, casting an endless hue of colors across Aadiel's face.

Jeruit placed his hand on Aadiel's shoulder. "You won't recognize it now, but this very silver was used against me in your scheme to destroy my family. It was lost for a time and intended for evil. Then that story was redeemed when the silver was miraculously revealed to Lucius. This earthly element carries with it a history of redemption and forgiveness. What Hell meant for evil was turned into much good. That's why my son and I thought it would be the perfect symbol to represent you, Aadiel."

Aadiel's eyes puddled with tears yet again as Jeruit placed the chain around his neck. He looked down and took the medallion in his hand. On one side of the beautifully crafted silver was the outline of a star. The star was broken and separated down the middle. Over top of the broken star, there was a lower case "r" written in beautiful calligraphy. It was embellished and stood out from the broken star, creating a 3D effect.

"The broken star is me," Aadiel said, speaking his realization out loud.

Jeruit nodded and then lifted Aadiel's chin, so he could look into his eyes. "Aadiel, you are now known to us in eternity not as Thort, the fallen one, the broken star, but as Aadiel, restored and forgiven servant of the Most High."

Aadiel ran his thumb over the raised letter. "But this letter, what is its significance?"

"The 'r' stands for 'renunciation.' When you asked for forgiveness, you renounced your previous choices and turned yourself in. God heard you, and He responded." Jeruit paused to let that information sink in. "That's not all. Flip it over."

Aadiel flipped the medallion in his hand and looked at it. The surface was a perfect mirror, revealing his reflection.

"You see, in the process of refining silver, we heat it over the hottest of coals. During the process, the impurities inside the ore rise to the top. To remove the impurities, a silversmith blows hot air across the surface until what remains is pure silver. This process is repeated over and over until the silver becomes a pure precious metal that can reflect like a perfect mirror."

Aadiel looked down at the mirror as his image stared back at him.

"You, my friend, are an 'imager,'" Jeruit said. "Every time you see your reflection, be reminded that you are the image of God's sovereign move. He refined a crushed spirit and breathed His breath across its impurities. Your existence mirrors His mighty love and shines that image back for all created beings to witness. Wear this medallion to proclaim to all of creation what you are and what our Father has done for you. Our God is loving and merciful even to the stars. You are proof that He can restore even an unimaginable breach."

Aadiel threw his arms around Jeruit. His heart was bursting with affection toward him and every person in the crowd. He didn't know if he had the capacity to experience the emotions that were coursing through him at that moment.

Lucius put his arm around the two as they embraced. "Glory to God in the highest!" he exclaimed. "Aadiel, you've been restored! God has shown His goodness and mercy to you!"

After a few moments, the cries of celebration faded away.

"Thank you. Thank you, all," Aadiel said, addressing the entire group.

Lucius patted his shoulder. "Okay, you should get going now. It's time to begin your assignment."

CHAPTER 23

THE RETRIEVAL

James sat in his recliner, reading. Victoria was out for the morning. She led a small group at the church on Tuesdays and Thursdays and then went to lunch with the ladies from her group. He knew he probably still had a good two hours before she would be home, so he had taken advantage of the empty house. He worked through his devotion before picking up the fiction book he had been reading about the end times.

In his left hand, he played with the blue amulet that his mother had given him before she passed. She never let him play with it as a boy, only showing it to him and his brother on special occasions when she would share its story and talk about the "one day soon" that they would be given further instruction. He had always been fascinated with its deep blue color. As a boy, he had wondered what sort of material it was made from. About ten years ago, he took it to a gemologist to find out. It turned out to be a blue benitoite, one of the rarest gems in the world, only discovered in 1902. According to what he had learned, benitoite gems are formed at Earth's plate boundaries in super-cold but extremely high-pressure environments. The two extremes came together to form a beautiful creation. Astonishing! He had always kept it in the safe with their other valuables but decided last week to retrieve it to show his grandson, Spencer.

Spencer was a mere ten years of age but mature beyond his years. He had a passion for history, geology, and archeology. He was always asking questions when they spent time together, so James was constantly on the lookout for an article or a documentary they could read or watch together. Spencer loved to hear stories of the family's ancestors and was enthralled with the story of the manuscript and how it traced all the way back to Jesus's disciples, John and Peter. James had decided last week to tell Spencer all about the amulet and the instructions concerning it. Usually, this information was shared with a family member when he or she became a young adult. Spencer's father had heard the stories many times and was there when James discovered what the amulet was made of, but James marveled at how Spencer had listened yesterday, soaking in all the stories as if he were twenty or even thirty years older.

James's eyes were moving across the words of the pages of his book, but his mind was wandering. Realizing that he had not comprehended the last page and a half, he glanced at the amulet, turning it over and over in his palm. He thought about all the hands that must have touched it over the centuries, all the families who had guarded it to ensure that it found its next rightful trustee. Now here it was in the palm of his hand. So much history packed into such a small stone.

James's stomach growled, and he looked over at the clock on the wall: 12:45 pm. With Victoria gone for lunch, he would have to fend for himself. He groaned as he pulled himself out of the recliner and stretched his back. He figured he would go into the kitchen and heat the leftovers from last night's chicken and dumplings.

As he passed the front door and headed toward the kitchen, he noticed a delivery truck pulling out of their yard. He hadn't heard the doorbell ring like it usually did when a delivery was dropped off. He unlocked the front door to check for boxes, thinking Victoria must have ordered something.

There on the welcome mat in front of the door lay a single yellow envelope with the names "Spencer and James" written in purple ink. James furrowed his brow. What kind of delivery was this? There was no shipping label or return address. It couldn't have come from Amazon. He had ordered nothing for Spencer. He stooped over and picked up the envelope, then looked up and down the road in both directions as if someone might appear with an explanation of where the envelope had come from and what it might contain, but he didn't see a soul in either direction, and all he heard was the song of a bluebird as it shuffled out of the nesting box on the big oak out front. James closed the front door.

Forgetting all about his empty stomach or the leftovers in the fridge, he returned to his recliner, filled with curiosity. Turning the envelope over, he found it was sealed in pressed wax. The envelope had the initial "R" stamped on it. One name rushed into James's mind, Ramiel.

Ramiel was the angel who had appeared to him in his room the night before his open vision by the stream. Could this be a message from him? James chuckled at how quickly his mind leaped to that possibility instead of considering all rational explanations first. Maybe the supernatural was becoming natural to him.

He broke the wax seal and removed the envelope's contents. It was an old hand-drawn map with a note clipped to the front. The note had three short words written in the same purple ink and the same handwriting as the single letter outside the envelope: "It is time."

James removed the paperclip and laid the note beside him on the recliner's arm. His hands shook as he studied the aged mudbrown map. He wasn't familiar with the formations of the landmasses and bodies of water listed, but he recognized the names of the places from his studies with Spencer. They had studied the geographic locations of the ancestors of the Petrus line in ancient Greece and Cypress. James recognized the Isle of Patmos immediately and reached over to his Bible on the end table. Flipping to the maps in the back, he held the hand-drawn map up next to the beautifully colored and decorated one in his Bible. The handwritten map was much more crudely drawn, of course, and focused on a much smaller portion of the geography, but he could deduce that it was the same region.

Could this be what he thought it was? The blood rushed to James's face as he grabbed the simple note to study it.

"No way," he said. Of every Petrus and every Pathrose, was he the one who had been chosen to go on the anticipated adventure to retrieve the manuscript? Before he had finished running the possibilities through his head, he knew the truth. "It's time," he said. A grin spread across his face when he thought of Spencer.

* * *

SPENCER STARED out the small window as the wheels of the charter plane touched down at Leros and Kos with three smooth bounces. James had rented a local charter from Athens, so they only had a short ferry ride to the isle for the last leg of their trip.

Spencer was beside himself. Not only was this the first time he had ever flown anywhere, he was on a literal treasure hunt with his grandfather in an ancient world was more than his little mind could conceive. They had spent the last two weeks studying maps and combing through family archives and diaries to learn as much as they could about the amulet, the manuscript, and the topography of the island where they were going. James thought he remembered most of the stories of his ancestors, but it was intriguing to read back over the accounts of people like Paulk and Simon. He appreciated Andrea's detailed writings. She had ensured that the entire story of the manuscript and the amulet were recorded for future generations. He could tell that she had taken many shorter writings and assembled them all in one place, providing a wealth of information. Victoria had transferred photocopies of everything in the family archive over to digital format to preserve the integrity of the ancient documents. They didn't need to be handled anymore and were now stored in an airtight case. James had everything he needed on his laptop and the amulet safely placed in Spencer's leather marble bag.

"Off we go, kiddo," James said to Spencer as he unbuckled his seat belt and gathered their belongings. "Grab your backpack. Your compass and flashlight are in there, right?" "Yup!" the boy replied.

As they walked off the tarmac, James smiled, watching Spencer jump and skip with excitement. He twirled around and faced his grandfather. "Now we get to ride on the boat!"

Considering the anticipation that James was feeling, how much greater would it be for a young boy? James took a moment to thank the Father for this opportunity. Then he drew in a deep breath that filled his spirit. It was an amazing feeling to know he was walking the exact path destined for him, and he was so thankful to have his grandson with him to experience it all.

Not knowing much about the island, James had booked a cave tour with a local tourism company. He knew from the family stories that the manuscript had been placed inside a cave, so it seemed like a logical place to start. Plus, it would give them an idea of what the island and the rock formations on the beach were like. He had Ramiel's map as well, so he knew what part of the island they needed to target. Even though he didn't have every detail worked out, he knew they were not alone, and he trusted the revelations would come.

James was right. They were not alone. Aadiel, now officially on his first assignment with a Pathrose, had been waiting on the tarmac when the plane touched down. When he caught sight of little Spencer, his heart exploded with joy. He was so tall. How could this kid only be ten years old? Spencer skipped right past Aadiel without a thought. Behind him walked James, carrying all the luggage as well as Spencer's backpack, which he had left behind in his haste to exit the plane. James's kind face was a welcome sight. Aadiel was overcome with a desire to run up and wrap his arms around him. Oh, how he hoped he would get that opportunity at some point.

Right now it was just an honor to be there and to be a part of what was about to take place. Aadiel loved this assignment. It was like being with his own family, even if they couldn't see him.

Ramiel had briefed Aadiel about the manuscript, the map, and the location of the hiding place. He was not to interfere with the process but only to assist when needed. He was amazed that he had not noticed such an important manuscript while he was with the family before. How self-absorbed he must have been not to recognize its value and the importance the family had placed on it. Ramiel had told him of God's provision and protection placed over the family in order to preserve them and the scroll. If he wanted to, Aadiel could get his mind all twisted trying to figure out how this could have happened to Thort. Instead, he had accepted that the family, the manuscript, and all his failures were part of what had brought him to this place. Smiling at the little boy on the tarmac, he was thankful he was now serving the Pathrose family instead of destroying them. Aadiel took a moment to thank the Father for this amazing opportunity. He drew in a deep breath that filled him completely and then turned to follow James and Spencer.

After a quick stop at the hotel to drop off their luggage, the ferry to Patmos was short and much not nearly as exciting as Spencer had expected. They met up with their tour group at the pier and, after some instructions, got onto a bus headed for the Holy Cave of the Apocalypse. The location wasn't even a cave anymore. Throughout the years, it had attracted many chapels, monasteries, and small churches who had created an unusual architectural ensemble around the original site. Obviously, it was the most famous cave on the island, but the guide had assured James that he and Spencer would have plenty of time to explore the hills and other less popular cave systems during the tour. James didn't mention to the guide why they were there or what they were looking for.

That afternoon after James and Spencer had eaten the picnic lunch provided by the tourism company, they checked in with the guide to let him know what direction they were headed and then double-checked what time they were to return to the bus. James was grateful that the guide seemed very laid back and showed little interest in their desire to strike off on their own.

The boy and his grandfather ventured off from the manicured grounds of the holy cave and followed a crude path that ran by a small, clear stream of water flowing from the top of the hill. James knew this was not a well-traveled path. In fact, it looked as if someone may have just walked it for the first time early that morning or maybe the night before. He could tell because the tall grass was not cleared away but simply laid down in the direction they were walking. He couldn't identify any clear footprints, but something had moved through there. It reminded him of the small game trails that he had on his own property back home, which the deer and other animals made as they walked to and from the stream to drink.

"How do you know we're going the right way, J-Daddy?" Spencer asked.

"Well, for starters I have the map, and I know we need to head down from this knoll and toward the beach area. When you're looking for something, it's always smart to follow a stream or a river. Do you know why?"

"So, we know how to get back?" Spencer asked.

"Good thinking. Yes, so we can backtrack along the water to return where we came from. Also, a water source will usually lead you to civilization if you're lost. And if you're hunting, it's good to scope out the local water source to see how the animals move in and out of the area. There are a lot of good reasons to follow a water source when you're exploring nature."

"We aren't hunting animals, though," Spencer replied.

"No, but we know that there was a waterfall near the cave where the manuscript was hidden long ago. We also know they accessed the cave from the beach. Water starts at its source and flows to the lowest area. Even though springs of water down in the ground often dry up, move, and shift over time, the primary source from above is always available." James stopped and dipped his hand in the crystal-clear water. Spencer did the same.

"Feel that?" James asked. "It's cold. This is spring water."

"I bet the Apostle John even drank this water when he lived in that cave," Spencer said.

"I hadn't thought of that. Good point," James smiled back at him. "Anyway, we're going to follow this stream and see where it goes."

The path took them winding down the side of the hill toward the larger rock formations off in the distance. They came to a place where the water seemed to disappear into the ground. But James could hear water moving under the rocks. He stood up, puzzled as to what to do next, when he noticed that the grass was still laid out past that area and wound around to the bottom of the next group of boulders.

"This way," he said, taking Spencer by the hand.

Aadiel stood looking up at them from the large rocks. He had walked their path early that morning. The angel Joam was waiting there, standing guard as he had for centuries. It overjoyed him to see Aadiel in his new state. The two of them caught up for a short while and then Aadiel relieved Joam from his assignment.

Aadiel was so proud that James had so easily found the path. "Here they come," he said as he turned and walked into the rock formation. He was waiting at the unassuming entrance to the cave when they rounded the corner.

To look at the formation of rocks from any distant direction, one wouldn't know there was anything there. It didn't take James long to find the entrance, though. Behind one boulder, he and Spencer had to shift sideways to enter through a slim keyhole between the two rocks.

The cavern they entered was nothing like it had looked when little Sam and his family were there. Earthquakes and storms over the centuries had reformed Earth's surface and shifted the landmarks. The cavern was dimly lit and littered with small boulders, rocks, and gravel. The only movement in the room was the dust they had kicked up upon entering. There was no sunlight shining in, nor was there a waterfall like Oppert and his family had witnessed when they were there. However, some ambient light came from an unseen opening in the rocks beyond what they could see, so they weren't in total darkness. James heard water moving somewhere within the inner structure of the cave. He asked Spencer for his flashlight and turned it on. James looked all around the cave in search of a clue as to what to do next but found nothing.

"Could we be in the wrong cave?" Spencer asked.

"We certainly could be, I guess," James replied. "According to the map, I know we're in the general vicinity. I sort of just assumed things would reveal themselves the way they have so far, but I have no more leads, kiddo."

After doing another sweep of the room with his flashlight, James looked back toward where they had entered. "Let's step back outside for a moment, so we can see better."

They stepped out into the sunlight, and James pulled the old map out of his back pocket. He felt like they were in the right place, and another glance at the map verified that. He didn't know what else to look for, and they were running out of time before they had to catch the bus back for the tour.

Aadiel stood with them at the mouth of the cave. They were not aware of his presence, but he had been there all along. He watched as James studied the map and looked back toward the cave, puzzled.

"Ask for help," Aadiel said. "You've been obedient, but you can't do this alone."

James folded up the map. "Spencer, I'm going to be honest: I'm stumped. I thought we were in the right place, but I don't know what to do next. Maybe we should come back tomorrow."

Spencer looked up at his grandfather. "Maybe we should pray and ask God to help us."

James's head lolled forward, and the sting of shameful realization washed over him. "Yeah, kid. Maybe we could do that."

In the rush to plan everything out, he had completely forgotten about prayer. He had all his bases covered—the flights, the tour, the diaries he had studied, all the work he had done to familiarize himself with the island, and, of course, the map. He had taken care of it all, but in his haste, he had forgotten the most important thing of all.

James slid the bag from his shoulder and kneeled on his left knee, smiling at his grandson. "Unless we become like a child," he muttered.

"What?" Spencer asked.

"Nothing. I was talking to myself," James said. "Do you know how happy I am to have you on this trip with me, Spencer?"

Spencer smiled. "Yeah. I know you wanted us to do this together."

"Thanks for reminding me." James pointed to the sky. "He wants us to do this together. I wouldn't want to do this without you, even though I could. It's the same with God. He can do anything, but he wants to do things with us. Thank you for reminding me, Spencer. Now let's take a moment to see what He wants to do here. Something tells me that will work out much better."

Spencer kneeled next to James, and they prayed together. James repented for rushing out in haste and for expecting everything he had planned to go well. He thanked God for the child next to him who had called him back to prayer and reminded him that they were not alone.

"Lord, we're so thankful that you want to do things with us because we want to do things with You. Now we ask You to show us what to do. Light our path, Father. We trust you completely. Amen."

"There you go," Aadiel beamed as he looked down at James and Spencer. "That's the Pathrose faith I remember. Thort never had a chance. Not a chance."

As James finished speaking, they were hit by a gust of wind. The sun still glowed in the sky, and there was no apparent storm blowing in from the coast, but the wind was strong. James stood up and grabbed his bag. Slinging it over his shoulder, he took Spencer by the hand and headed back toward the cave. The wind blew against the rocks behind them, kicking up sand and dust from the beach, which beat against their skin like tiny bullets. It forced them back to the cave. James motioned for Spencer to hold his shirt over his eyes to protect them.

As they stood against the rocks, the mighty wind blasted them. Although his face was covered by his shirt, James felt the sand beneath his feet shifting. The ground to the right of the cave sank as if it were being sucked straight into the ground by an unseen force. James looked down to see the edge of the rock formation just as the sand sank into the ground, revealing an opening. James grabbed Spencer and pulled him back, so he wouldn't fall into the shifting sand. The Earth swallowed the sand until there was an opening in the ground about three and a half feet in diameter. Then as suddenly as the wind had begun, it faded.

James and Spencer stared at each other. Neither of them could believe what had just happened. As they peered down into the dark hole in the ground, James recognized the sound of water falling inside. He wasn't sure how they were going to get down into the crevice. It only appeared to be large enough for someone Spencer's size, but James didn't feel comfortable sending the boy down alone, not knowing if the ground had fully settled.

"What do we do now?" Spencer asked.

"I'm not sure," James replied, "but God didn't bring us this far to leave us hanging."

James and Spencer couldn't see him, but Aadiel was standing inside the cave just below the opening. All he could see when he looked up were the silhouettes of the man and boy with the sun just over them in the sky. He knew the cave was dark, and they would need to see to move any farther. Aadiel stepped just out of the opening and took his medallion in his hand. Positioning it just right, he caught the light of the sun and projected it directly toward the cave wall where the water fell from the rocks above. The light shone brighter than any lantern could have and illuminated the whole room. Aadiel smiled and looked back up at James and Spencer.

"Wow! I can see the entire room," Spencer exclaimed. "The floor isn't that far down, and I can climb down most of the way and drop in."

James was still hesitant. "That hole is too small for both of us. Are you sure you can see where you would land? More importantly, will you be able to climb back out afterwards?"

"Of course!" Spencer exclaimed. "Daniel taught me how to climb, remember?"

Daniel was Spencer's much older brother, who loved to free climb mountains as a hobby. He was extraordinarily tall and strong with a passion for the wilderness. Spencer loved to visit his brother, and when his growth spurt started at such a young age, he had begged Daniel to teach him to climb. The two had spent some time at an indoor climbing wall and even taken a couple of outdoor treks to do some light climbing. Spencer was proving to be a natural, just like his brother, but his mom always made sure they took precautions in the learning process.

James raised his eyebrow at Spencer. "Your mom would kill me if she knew I was letting you climb down into a cave by yourself, but I know this is not just any cave. I need you to be really careful, Spencer, and I need you to communicate with me the whole time you're down there." James reached into his jacket pocket and took out the marble bag that held the amulet. He pulled the blue gem from the bag and handed it to Spencer. "Put this way down deep in your pocket."

"Wow, look at that," Aadiel remarked. He had just noticed something for the first time. As Thort, he had seen this amulet many, many times. He remembered when Andrea's uncle Deib had attempted to steal and sell it. He never really knew what it was or why it was so important to the family, but at that moment, he knew.

The blue benitoite was the same deep blue color as his robe, the same blue as the door of his home.

"What do I do with it?" Spencer asked.

"The amulet has served as a marker for the manuscript, a memorial piece held in trust by our family. Today you will bring the manuscript back into our keeping. When you find the manuscript, retrieve it, then put the stone in its place. And remember, communicate with me the whole time you're down there, okay? Let me know what you see and what is happening."

"Oh, J-Daddy. I'll be fine. Don't worry about me." Spencer grinned at James. Then, stooping down, he descended into the cave opening feet first. His foot found a solid first step, and he dipped his head down to find the next until he finally reached the cave floor. It amazed him at how well lit the room was. He saw beautiful colors dancing across the face of the rocks as if light were shining through a prism.

"It's so cool down here!" he yelled back up to his grandfather.

"What do you see?" James asked.

"It's like a secret room. There's a waterfall next to me. I can't see where the water comes from, and it just disappears down into the rocks at the bottom."

Aadiel still held the medallion in one hand, reflecting the sun's rays into the room. Reaching over, he stuck his other hand into the mouth of the waterfall. The waters parted. "There you go, buddy."

"Oh wow! There's a tunnel behind the waterfall! It just appeared! I can see it!" Spencer could hardly contain his excitement.

"It just appeared?" James replied. "What do you mean it just appeared?" James wished he could be down there. Getting all the details from a ten-year-old wasn't how he wanted to do this. But it was obvious Spencer was not alone in this task, so James trusted that God was taking care of him and would show him the way.

Spencer ascended into the small cave behind the waterfall and crawled through it. Unfortunately, the falling water drowned out his ability to communicate back up to his grandfather as he moved deeper into the cave.

Back outside, James called out to Spencer, eager for an update. "Bud, what do you see?" There was no answer. "Spencer? Buddy, I need you to talk to me." He placed his ear to the opening. There was no response. James stood up. "Oh, this is not good. What have I done, sending him down there alone?"

Meanwhile, Spencer had been scooting through the cave tunnel with ease, but the opening was beginning to narrow just ahead. He could see where there had been some erosion, causing the tunnel to be partially blocked. As he crawled closer to the caved-in area, he called back to his grandfather. "J-Daddy, I'm coming up on a caved-in spot. I'm not sure what to do." He paused, turning his head back to listen for further instruction. He couldn't hear anything but the sound of the water falling behind him. "J-Daddy?" Nothing.

Spencer crawled ahead a few more strides to see if he could make out the area behind the erosion. Peeking around the rubble, he saw a fork in the tunnel. What looked like the main route was to the right, and then to the left was a much narrower opening littered with debris and adorned with cobwebs. Spencer called back to James again, much louder this time. "I don't know which way to go. J-Daddy, can you hear me?"

Seven minutes had passed since James last heard from his grandson. A cauldron of acid was building up in his belly as scenarios swirled through his head. *How long do I wait? Nobody even knows where we are.* James glanced back toward the tide splashing up on the beach, panic overtaking his mind. *How will they even get to us, and how will they bust this rock open to rescue him?* He realized how reckless he had been, following what he believed to be a divine leading.

"Spencer!" James leaned and yelled again down into the mouth of the cave, every ounce of his worry evident in his desperate cry. "Spencer, please son, answer me." Hearing no sound, he stood again, his eyes fixed on the cave opening as he backed away from it. Waves of dread were washing over him.

Spencer had no idea what to do. He couldn't hear his grandfather for instruction, and his ten-year-old mind couldn't make a decision. He turned, sitting upright, and leaned back against the side of the tunnel. He knew he should turn back. His grandfather was probably worried since he hadn't been able to hear or communicate with him. He glanced again at the two paths beyond. The looming cobwebs draped across the path on the left made him shudder. *It can't be that way.* "J-daddy, I don't know what to do. I need help. I can't do this by myself," he said, knowing he couldn't be heard, but the sound of his own voice still comforted him. He sat for a moment longer, inhaling the cave's stagnant air and listening to the faint sound of the falling water behind him. As he sat there, he realized that beyond his confusion about which way to go, he was not experiencing any fear or anxiety. Here he was, a small boy lost in an abandoned tunnel inside a cave on the other side of the world from his home. He should have been terrified, but he trusted what his grandfather had told him and believed this was his part in a bigger story. He, Spencer Pathrose, was the one meant to be there, in this moment, for that task.

Taking one last look back toward where he had crawled in, he squinted his eyes and cemented his resolve. He crawled forward and straddled the eroded portion of the cave. He had to shuffle sideways to maneuver through. On the other side, he didn't even pause to think. It was as if the decision portion of his mind was on override. Spencer crawled headlong into the narrow left opening. His hair collected the shroud of ancient dust-laden cobwebs like a runner proudly claiming the winning ribbon at the end of a race. *This is the way. I know it is.*

James sat with his back against the rock formation, his arms folded over his knees with his head hanging limp. Tears burned his eyes, and his mind raced like a scared mouse in a sticky trap. With the minutes passing, his imagination had already jumped from his statement to the police, to apologizing to his son and daughter-in-law for putting their son in peril, to the flight back to the States and the empty seat next to him. Terror ripped through the synapses of his brain in a chain reaction, setting fire to every thought. Helpless.

As Spencer walked toward the sunlight pouring through the opening of the cave, he picked the layers of sticky cobwebs from his hair. He paused for a moment to look back, knowing he would never be there again. It was possible no human ever would. In his right hand, he held the clay cylinder. Excitement bubbled up as he pictured his grandfather's face when he showed it to him. As he placed his foot on the first stone of his ascent back out, he shielded his eyes with his hand and looked up. "I got it!" he yelled.

Aadiel smiled.

CHAPTER 24

THE GREAT HARVEST

Having returned from his first assignment, Aadiel strolled through the garden in front of his home reflecting on the last few days, particularly his most recent adventure. He had so enjoyed his first assignment back on Earth with James and Spencer. He could not believe the difference he felt from the last time he had seen them. Fear, disappointment, anxiety, and dread had turned to joy, peace, fulfillment, and a sense of belonging. He was so proud of them and longed to see them again soon.

Later that morning, Aadiel was scheduled to meet with Kafziel for further instruction. He wondered what his next mission would be. Would he meet the future generations of the Pathrose family? Whatever it was, it would be his great honor to serve them.

He headed out early for his meeting. There was still so much to see and learn outside of the Celestial City. He enjoyed exploring and meeting other spiritual beings on his walks.

That morning he walked to the western side of the wall. He had not seen or experienced very much on that route, and he had plenty of time before meeting Kafziel. As he strolled, he enjoyed the sounds and smells of the surrounding paradise.

Off in the distance, a large, beautiful meadow caught his eye. He saw lovely rolling hills with different crops and produce growing in perfectly manicured patches. From a distance, it looked like a masterfully crafted quilt with different textures and colors.

As he walked closer, he saw someone bent over working in one of the many patches. His curiosity piqued, Aadiel had to know what was growing in that field, so he walked out to meet the person and inquire.

As he entered the meadow, he realized the patchwork of crops consisted of many trees, shrubs, and plants. There were gorgeous flowering trees of different colors, tulips, and rose bushes that had been pruned and were in full bud. He also saw sturdy fruit trees, hardy bushes, stalks of grain, and low-lying plants whose crops lay underneath the rich dark soil. Thick, ancient vines were woven through trellises. Someone had meticulously arranged every variety of fruit and vegetable-bearing plant and tree in that patch of land. Aadiel realized that each crop appeared to be fully ripe and in season for harvest. *There must be a team of people who work these fields,* he thought. Everything was so immaculate. Aadiel looked around but saw only the one worker.

Not wanting to startle her as he approached, Aadiel cleared his throat and called out a greeting. "Excuse me. Good morning. I couldn't help but notice this beautiful field of crops. I had to come over for a closer look."

The woman stood up and swept her hair from her eyes, smiling. "Well, hello, Aadiel. I wondered when I would see you here. I knew you would come for a visit at some point."

"You did? You know me?" Aadiel replied, puzzled.

"Yes, I know you," she said, then bent back over to her work. "And I have everything you will need right here."

"Everything that I'll need? How do you know what I'll need? And need for what? I don't even know what I need." Aadiel shook his head in confusion. "Come to think of it, I don't even know who you are. Should I remember you?"

She stood back up. "It's possible you might remember me but

probably not. As Thort, you would have been far removed from this field or any of its yields."

The woman tucked her trowel into her apron pocket, removed her right glove, then walked over to Aadiel. "My name is Eve. I'm the tender of Gardens of His Complete Righteousness. On Earth they also knew me as Eve, one of the first tenders of His Garden in Eden."

"I can't remember ever seeing or experiencing anything so healthy and beautiful as this place," Aadiel said. "How do you take care of it all on your own?"

"Here in the garden, I represent the human creation, but I'm never on my own. The fruits you see here are cultivated by the Holy Spirit. He is the Sower, the Harvester, and the Giver of these precious gifts. He was here earlier this morning. You just missed Him."

"Oh, wow," Aadiel said, glancing back in the direction he had come.

"You see, in the beginning we were working with the Father to make all of Earth as beautiful as this," she said, holding both arms out to indicate the entire garden area. "Unfortunately, the original plan was interrupted. Allow me to show you around, and I'll explain."

Aadiel grinned. "Absolutely."

As they walked side by side, Aadiel was overwhelmed with the kindness and generosity he felt from everyone he met there. He hoped he would never get used to these new, refreshing feelings. He took a deep breath of the fragrant breeze that wafted against his face. The experience was indescribable, as if he was smelling the ripe produce of every tree, shrub, vine, and flower all at once.

"The breeze here is so nice," he said. "It was one of the first things that I noticed when I arrived. It seems to be constantly blowing. So pleasant."

"Uh, huh," Eve replied with a wide grin. "There's always light here too. It's the perfect environment for growing things."

Eve pointed toward the city. "You see, the Light is Jesus who is sitting at His Father's right hand just beyond those walls. King Jesus is the only Light needed here. No darkness, not even shadows, exist. He is the Light."

"It's beautiful," Aadiel said.

"And that breeze you feel is the Life of the Holy Spirit. It flows from Him and saturates everything in the realm. His life is inside every element. So, everything you see and touch here, including me and you, are wrapped in the eternal life provided by the Holy Spirit."

Aadiel looked down and touched his forearm. "So, the light comes from Jesus, and the life comes from the Spirit."

Eve approached a rose bush. She took one of the brilliant red blooms in her hand, pulled the shears from her apron, and clipped it off with a long stem. "And then there is God, the Father of all things. From Him comes love, the greatest of all fruits."

Eve took a few steps and then turned to face Aadiel. "I stand in the middle of it all. On Earth, I rejected the original plan and chose death. But God loved me so much, he sent the Light, His Son, Jesus, to die in my place. Then Jesus gave me His Holy Spirit to bring me back to life. Now here I am, restored by the Light, the Life, and the Love, the Holy Trinity. It's an unbroken circle of giving," she said as she handed the rose to Aadiel. "And it is what makes everything in this garden so perfect."

Tears of remembrance welled up in Aadiel's eyes as he gazed over the garden and allowed Eve's words to penetrate his new spirit. "My mind is recalling the days of my original creation. How could I have walked away from Them, from all of this, for darkness?"

Eve looked deep into Aadiel's eyes. "Believe me, I understand what you're feeling."

She motioned for Aadiel to follow as she started down a path that wound around the base of a small knoll. The clearing was positioned at an altitude that allowed them to overlook the city.

The view was stunning.

"Wow!" Aadiel exclaimed. "What is this place?"

"This is the Memorial of Free Will," Eve replied. "It's also a garden."

Aadiel turned his attention away from the city. Behind them a wild, unkempt patch of crops grew. It was nothing like the well-tended fields they had just left on the other side of the hill. It boasted several species of wildflowers and flowering shrubs that bore copious amounts of small, underdeveloped fruit. Twisted trees and untrained vines with low-hanging nuts and fruit covered the side of the hill. Berries grew along the ground from vines full of thorns. Huge thistles popped up throughout the foliage, and every plant, bush and tree were fighting for real estate among the weeds and overgrown briars, yet there was beauty in complete chaos.

They stood there for a while as Aadiel took in the sight.

"I'm afraid this garden will be much more recognizable to you. I know you remember the weapons you had at your disposal when you served the darkness."

Aadiel nodded in reluctant remembrance. "I do."

"Hell Ops cloaked these weapons, presenting them as beautiful and enticing gifts when you used them against your assignments. You presented the weapons as harmless in the beginning to deceive and trick people into choosing to walk against the Father's will. The bounty of this garden is beautiful but only to the eye."

Eve pointed to fruits of a thorny red vine that had weaved around the trunk of a tree. "You see those berries over there? That is turmoil." She pointed to some wiry bushes beyond the tree. "Over there, you will recognize confusion and restlessness. They don't seem too bothersome, do they? That grassy plant that looks similar to wheat is distraction. Thort used that one many times. They have come out with several genetically modified varieties of that one over the ages. The blue-and-white ones near the back are a newer strain they call social media distraction."

As they continued to stroll through the bedlam of foliage, Eve pointed out agitation and bother, distress and interruption, lies, discord, hubbub, and pandemonium. There seemed to be countless species and subspecies of every variety, all bearing beautiful fruit.

"What is this here?" Aadiel asked, pointing to a blossom with a deep blue throat.

"That one is especially heinous. It has stolen more souls from the Kingdom than any other poison," Eve replied. "That one is self-pity."

"Oh, I certainly remember that one. We had that available in an elixir. Nag used copious amounts of it on Andrea's uncle Deib. He was so full of it. Had the thieves not murdered him, I believe Nag could have convinced Deib to take his own life. It worked wonders on him, but Andrea and her husband Royye were immune to it."

"That's because the Spirit filled them with His goodness," Eve replied. "They loved others the way the Father loves. There's no room in your heart for self-pity when you see yourself as He sees you. Your only response is to love Him and serve other people."

Eve continued to walk through the memorial, pointing at different plants. "As you will remember, each of these poisons cause mild infections at first, but soon they get much worse. Minor injuries become festering sores and open wounds that never heal, eventually crippling all that was good. The weapon is used to deceive the creature and pull him or her away from the Father's eternal presence. It gets darker and colder. What you see here is just a representation, a memorial. Plants like this grow in abundance outside of the Kingdom, as you well know. Sin is progressive. It begins small and hides in obscurity, waiting for the next opportunity to grow into eternal darkness. On Earth, these grow aggressively. You used them to catapult a person into lust, bloodshed, blasphemy, envy, wrath, pride, anger, and ultimately, death. Your end game was eternal separation from the Light, Life, and Love. All sins are not the same, but all are dangerous. We're aware of every weapon used by Hell Ops to lead creation far from the Father's will."

"Unfortunately, I recognize every one of these," Aadiel said.

Eve nodded. "From what I understand, you were unsuccessful with them for quite some time. That Pathrose assignment really threw a cog into things for you."

Aadiel sighed but didn't respond. He spotted a small bed of colorful flowers that grew in a concentric cluster, almost like a bouquet. The blooms started out yellow, then turned gold, orange, and eventually black in the center of the bouquet.

"What are those?" he asked.

Eve approached the cluster. "These are the deadliest of all. These were used to lure many of the sons of God and a host of fallen angels." Eve pointed to each color of bloom in succession. "The wispy yellow flowers on the outer part of the cluster are temptation. Those blooms touch the golden pedals of desire. Unchecked, that leads to the dark orange flowers of covetousness, and the black flowers of the inner circle are domination."

"Oh, my stars." Aadiel gasped and took a step back from the plants as if they were going to jump out at him.

"There is only one I AM," Eve said, her voice full of authority. "There are many who desire to be like Him, but there is only one true God. Remember, Aadiel, this garden is a memorial to all, planted here so it can be seen by all the city's inhabitants. His sheep on Earth are still subject to these temptations. We were all given the same free will. We were free to follow the Holy Spirit and enjoy the fruits from this garden or become a slave to sin and partake from the garden over the hill. These fruits bring death, and those over there bring life. The Father has always wanted all His creation to serve Him willingly in love as He has loved them. He gave us free will, and it came at an enormous price."

Aadiel's mind was spinning. Memories and thoughts bombarded his consciousness as he stood there staring at the fruits of his previous existence. Seeing them grow here and hearing Eve explain everything reminded him of his former dark self and being separated from God's presence. He was not experiencing condemnation but thanksgiving and praise. He thought about the significance of free will, and he contemplated what Eve had said about the Trinity and how the Son died for those who were deceived.

"If only humans could see the two groves this way, the choice would be much easier," he said.

Eve nodded in agreement. "Yes, you're right. Now that's out of the way, let's get back to my mission. Come with me." She headed back down the path, motioning for Aadiel to follow.

Eve stopped at the entrance to the path that ran through the middle of the Gardens of His Complete Righteousness. "I tend the Lord's fruit, and the Holy Spirit gives it to everyone who chooses to follow Him. The grove also feeds those in the Celestial City, His fruit nourishing them in eternal abundance."

Eve started down the path, brushing her hands across the tops of the wheat in the patch to her right, plucking off a few of the heads. "In this garden, everything is true. There's no trickery. These are the fruits of pure, abundant life. You saw what grows back in the memorial garden. Those weapons are used by the darkness. What you see here are the spiritual weapons available to the children of the King. These fruits are His answer to the enemy's attacks."

Eve pointed her thumb back over her shoulder. "All the deceit, lies, and frustrations lay cloaked in beautiful color and present a hollow promise. Those fruits caused your downfall." Then she pointed down at the ground where they were standing. "All these fruits were a part of your restoration. The members of the Pathrose family, from Saint Peter to Sean, the one you are about to meet, know that these fruits combat the enemy's tactics. While on Earth, they were unwilling to settle for pretty fruit that brought no life. Thort witnessed those choices over and over. It was fruit from these very trees that brought you to repentance, Aadiel. The eternal sustenance of these fruits is the treasure of our Father's heart."

"I'm more overwhelmed every moment I spend here," Aadiel said. "I have no words. How long will it take me to understand everything?"

Eve reached up and pulled a fruit resembling an apricot from a nearby tree. "Here, try this. It tastes like patience with a hint of understanding."

Aadiel took a bite. The fruit was so fresh that juice ran down from his mouth onto his blue robe. "Oh, my. This is incredible."

Eve continued toward a small potting shed at the front of the property. "As I mentioned, the Holy Spirit was here with me this morning. He has put together a special harvest for you and Codill Pathrose. Do you remember him?"

"Boy, do I ever. He was James's father. He and his wife caused me more demerits than I can count during their years in South America. Their success on the mission field was the great shame that sent me into permanent hiding from Hell Ops."

Eve stepped inside the potting shed and came back out bearing a picnic basket covered with a white linen cloth. "Take this with you. Kafziel has your instructions. You and Codill will soon be on assignment together, and he will need these." She stepped forward and offered Aadiel the basket. "It was wonderful to see you again, Aadiel. Your existence brings me joy, and joy is one of my favorites."

CHAPTER 25
THE GIFTING

Aadiel flew in, landing on Sean and Nancy Pathrose's front porch. He was excited after all of these years to meet back up with Codill Pathrose who was waiting there for him in spirit form.

"Peace, my friend," Codill said.

Aadiel bowed in honor of the missionary saint. "Peace to you, Codill."

Codill was holding the picnic basket that Eve had prepared. Kafziel and Ramiel had briefed the two before they left. Aadiel marveled at what an opportunity this was. Standing beside a great saint and the ancestor from a previous century, ready to serve the next generation of Pathroses.

"It has been such a joy to watch Sean and Nancy," Codill said. "They remind me a lot of Keren and me when we first got started. Service in missions requires a great deal of reliance on the One sending you. Only the Father can help you love a people group you have never met. Understanding where your spiritual bounty comes from is the key."

"I remember working tirelessly to sabotage your financial means while you were in South America, hoping you would give up on your work," Aadiel replied. "Fortunately for both of us, you never fell for it."

Codill nodded. "There were plenty of times that we were at the bottom of the barrel, but the provisions always came through. The mission field is not a place for the faint of heart."

"Sir, I'm truly sorry for my efforts to make things difficult for you," Aadiel said.

"We worked in a continual state of 'unknown' in those early years. We didn't know where we would live, how long we would be there, or if our work was even making a difference. Although things were unknown to us, God knew every detail. When Keren and I left our earthly bodies, we knew there was still so much to be done. It has been our great honor to watch the harvest of souls come in. God worked mightily with the seeds planted from such meager beginnings."

Aadiel chuckled. "Those meager beginnings sure brought a lot of trouble for the kingdom of darkness. We also watched the harvest of souls come in. It was because of your ministry that I was banished from Hello Ops. There was no way I could show my face there, having been responsible for Codill Pathrose."

Codill laughed. "God was always faithful. All He asked for was our yes. Everything else was Him. Thinking back, I bet your efforts were quite frustrating."

"Is this type of mission the normal mode of operation?" Aadiel asked. "Is it normal for my kind to be put on assignment with a saint?"

"Let me stop you right there," Codill replied, chuckling. "First of all, you're one of a kind, so I'm not sure what you mean by 'your kind.' Serving is what we all do in the Kingdom. As the Son served us, we serve one another. My wife and I carried a mantle of authority as we labored in the mission field during our lives on Earth. The significance of me being here today is to pass that mantle on to Sean and Nancy."

Aadiel nodded. "Okay. Still trying to catch up."

"No service to the Father is odd or out of place. He is sovereign and constantly creating. Don't worry about trying to catch up. Just be ready. As you serve, you will increase in kingdom transparency and will know the needs of those you are serving without them having to ask. Remember, one person can put one thousand to flight and two can rout ten thousand. It's an honor to serve Him together. In this mission we serve not only in multiplication but also in His perfection and power."

Aadiel looked back at Codill. "Perfection and power? I understand perfection, but—"

"Yes, the timing of your renewal is perfect, and soon you will witness a power that few have ever experienced."

Aadiel smiled. "That's exciting."

"You have no idea," Codill replied, a huge grin on his face. "Follow me."

They walked from the foyer, through the living room, and into the small kitchen. There at the dining table, a young couple was looking over a stack of papers.

"Meet Sean and Nancy Pathrose, the last of their name."

Aadiel gasped in surprise. "The last?"

Codill nodded. "Our Father has called these two to a remote village known as Aria. The message of the life of our Savior and King has not touched that place. It's the last place on Earth that has not heard the Good News. Sean and Nancy have been called to reach this village with His love. Their mission will fulfill the scriptures and complete the Father's mercy on Earth."

Aadiel gasped again, covering his mouth with his hand. "Can this be what all of creation has been groaning for?"

Codill smiled, his eyes were full of excitement and anticipation. "All of creation, my friend. All of creation."

Sean studied the papers. He entered some figures on the adding machine, then looked up at Nancy. "It appears we have almost enough credit in the mission account to get us to Aria, hopefully by January. The mission association may have received some credit for us. I haven't checked with them since last month. Even if it doesn't happen in January, I have faith that we'll have enough to get there by spring of next year."

Nancy took a sip of her coffee without looking up from her Bible. "One day at a time, hun. His timing is always perfect."

"I know, I know. I'm just eager to get there. There's so much that has to come together for this trip. You know me; I like to have all of my ducks in a row."

"That's why you have me," Nancy replied, smiling. "I don't have any ducks."

"Yes, always the calm in the middle of my storm," Sean replied, returning her smile.

"Have you heard from the linguist you contacted?"

He nodded. "Yes, he emailed me yesterday. They have had little success working on communication avenues. This tribe is so remote, their language doesn't derive from any other known language. The guy has been working on a picture alphabet. We know nothing about their vernacular or their culture, so it's hard to break the code."

"I know someone who speaks the language of every tribe and tongue," Nancy said.

"Well, thank goodness. Maybe you could call Him up," Sean joked.

"I'm just saying, is all." Nancy waved her hand and then picked up her coffee cup. "He's been in this from the beginning, Sean, and He won't leave us now—or ever. Don't do so much planning that you let anxiety take over your mind. Be prepared, yes, but trust your source for all the things, even the language part."

"Yes, dear," Sean said as he picked up the papers, straightened them with a few taps on the table, and then tucked them back into the manila folder labeled "Aria." "But you may have to remind me tomorrow—and the next day and the day after that."

Nancy shrugged, then raised her cup for another sip. "That's what I'm here for."

Codill lifted the basket hanging from his arm. "Now for the fun part."

"I'm excited to see what Eve sent," Aadiel said. "I assume she put together some things to help Sean and Nancy. Am I right?"

"From the first time this family was called, the Holy Spirit has been cultivating a legacy. Every generation has faced a different scheme from the enemy. I heard you and Eve took a stroll down memory lane."

Aadiel nodded. "Yes. It was painful but necessary."

"You used each one of those weapons for the family's destruction, but the Father saw fit to preserve these people. In their weakness, He was their strength. The Pathrose generations used every gift here in this basket. In this last mission on Earth, Nancy and Sean will need all of them."

Codill walked over to the kitchen island, then removed the linen cloth from the basket. The gift was wrapped in butcher paper and tied with a twine. "You might remember this one. I put it here in the kitchen because Sean can use it even now. This one is 'peace.'" Codill turned to Aadiel. "Paulk and Sarah found this glorious prize when they came into the faith. It replaced the fear and anxiety with which you had bound them so completely. Remember?"

"Oh, I remember. I employed fear, deceit, panic, and hopelessness. Those weapons worked flawlessly until that fateful night when they heard the gospel message. Sarah went from a fearful coward hiding in her room to a thriving member of the church, boldly loving and serving her family and neighbors. Her transformation blew my mind. That gift of peace was the beginning of my end."

Codill smiled, then reached into the basket as he walked into the living room. He placed the next gift on the coffee table. "Durane and Amira shone with this one. Remember how they had 'joy' that made no sense?"

"I could never understand how their joy remained no matter what weapon I used against them. Despair never took root. I even taunted them with lies about good works. Joy was present in their lives no matter how dark things seemed. I didn't understand it then," Aadiel said, gazing at the gift on the table, "but I do now."

The great missionary moved from room to room, placing the gifts and explaining each one to Aadiel. Patience, goodness, and kindness were all placed neatly around the house, ready to be found. Aadiel walked through his memories of the family members as they placed the gifts. His thoughts paid tribute to their long suffering and honor to the King.

"Just as he did for the previous generations, the Holy Spirit has provided all the gifts our young missionaries will need now and in the future. As they pray, study, and prepare for their journey, they'll find these gifts, and the Holy Spirit will make each one available to them as needed. No weapon formed against them shall prosper."

"May I place the last few gifts?" Aadiel asked. "After centuries of attacking this family with the dark weapons, I would love nothing more than to replace those with the ones given by His Spirit."

"Absolutely. That's a great idea," Codill said as he handed Aadiel the basket.

He looked inside and saw that six gifts remained.

As Aadiel placed the first of the six on the counter beside the sink in the washroom, Codill spoke. "Wisdom is a magnificent gift. The light of the Holy Spirit shines on their intelligence and will. May it illuminate their mind and instill an attraction to everything that's divine. Worldliness and a focus on self will fade away."

As Aadiel placed 'understanding' on the bedside table, Codill spoke again. "These final missionaries have immersed themselves in holy scripture. His Spirit will now illuminate the truth and understanding of the supernatural purpose set before them."

On the table by the bathtub, Aadiel placed the next gift. "Judging correctly requires knowing God's perfect will," Codill continued. "They will require the gift of 'counsel' to navigate this responsibility."

As Aadiel lifted the next gift out of the basket, Codill pointed to it. "Ah, now that is very important. Do you remember when John the Baptizer came and said he baptized with water, but one would come after him who was more powerful than him?"

"I'll be honest. I avoided people like John. He was so crazy. We weren't all that concerned that anyone in their right mind was listening to him anyway," Aadiel admitted.

Codill chuckled. "Well, to catch you up, John baptized people in water for repentance. He was making the way straight for the more powerful One to come after him. Jesus would baptize them with the Holy Spirit and with fire."

He reached down and took the gift from Aadiel's hand. "'Power' will bathe Sean and Nancy in His courage, giving them endurance and a firm mind. They will know who they are in our Lord, so when they enter the deceiver's last stronghold, they'll go in bearing the Holy Spirit's unlimited power."

"Wow, that one is super important. Where should we put it?"

Codill walked over to the closet and lifted a suitcase from the bottom shelf. "How about we pack this one up for them? They will never leave, forget, or misplace it. It's that important. Regrettably, so many saints do."

Codill lifted out the last two gifts from the basket and handed the first one to Aadiel. "Here is knowledge. It's not Sean and Nancy's gained knowledge but 'knowledge' from the Father, knowledge of what His son did at Calvary.

"And finally, the most misunderstood of all the gifts: 'fear of the Lord'. Sean and Nancy must never rely on any other power. They must never offend the Father but always have hearts that fear Him. Although they'll travel to lands where people worship other gods, the fear of the Lord must always be their anchor."

Aadiel pondered everything he had just heard. "As Thort, I was familiar with these gifts. They were the stuff of my nightmares. Seeing them grow in bounty in the garden with Eve was amazing, but giving them to Sean and Nancy to use for the Kingdom provides me with a completely different perspective."

As they finished their task, Codill and Aadiel stepped back into the kitchen for another look at Sean and Nancy. "Do they have any idea that the people of Aria are the last people alive who have not heard about Jesus?" Aadiel asked.

Codill shook his head. "No, they don't know, nor do they have a need to know. Just like you and me, they just need to be obedient." Codill brushed his hands together with finality. "And now, He has provided them with everything they'll need for these last days."

"I can't wait to see it," Aadiel exclaimed.

"You, me, and the rest of creation, my friend," Codill replied, placing his hand on Aadiel's shoulder. "Sean and Nancy are ready. Now it's time to equip you."

"Me?" Aadiel asked, wondering what was next.

CHAPTER 26
SEAN AND NANCY

Love and seeds only grow when planted.

Sean and Nancy Pathrose arrived at the final checkpoint at a remote airstrip in South America in late February. They had met their cash reserves and travel requirement goals, with the final funds being raised by an anonymous donation arriving in late November. All the waiting and tedious preparation was over. Now the unknown aspects of the adventure lay in front of them.

Nancy was good at traveling light. Sean, however, being a meticulous planner, always struggled with the packing. His motto was "Be ready for anything." That would be impossible on this trip considering the small plane's weight restrictions. He packed a limited amount of clothing and personal items, so they would have room for toys, books, medicine, Bibles, and, of course, the sacred manuscript.

Sean was concerned about traveling with it, but he believed it was crucial to keep it with them when he and Nancy were in the field. It felt like he was bringing a part of his legacy and anointing for the mission. He took his mother's words seriously when she told him to always be ready for the next instruction.

Sean had taken great care to protect the ancient clay container, wrapping it in several layers of clothing. He also didn't want to be questioned about the contents at border security and forced to open it. Every time they placed his carry-on bag in the plastic bin to be scanned, Sean and Nancy prayed silently. This would be the third time it had passed through the airport scanners on this trip. Sean held his breath as he waited for his bag after the guard searched him with the body wand.

A loud buzzer sounded, and the conveyor belt came to a sudden halt. Sean's heart jumped in his chest. He looked back at Nancy, who was still waiting to pass through the metal detector.

She stared back at him with wide eyes.

"Whose bag is this?" the security officer asked, holding up a black satchel.

"It's mine," Sean replied, raising his hand.

"Please approach the table," the security officer said.

Blood rushed to Sean's head as he grabbed his shoes from the plastic bin and walked over to the table where the officer was unzipping his bag. The officer rifled through Sean's bag with a gloved hand for a few minutes. Then he zipped it up, threw it into a large sorting bin, and ordered the couple to sit down.

Sean and Nancy took a seat in the holding area and started praying for mercy and protection.

After an uncomfortable amount of time, Nancy turned to her husband. "Sean, it's been forty-five minutes. Maybe you should ask them what the holdup is."

Sean looked over and saw that the same officer who had checked their paperwork was now behind the desk. Across the waiting area was a room labeled "Immigration Office." He got up from his chair and approached the desk.

"Sir, we've been waiting for quite a while. Can you give us an update on why we're being detained?"

The immigration officer took a long drag on his cigarette and glared at Sean. "We're looking for your visas," he said.

Sean frowned. "What do you mean? We gave them to you before we went through security." He failed to keep the nervousness from his voice.

The officer looked up at Sean through the smoke from his cigarette. "Are you sure we have them?"

"Yes, I'm sure. We gave them to you, sir. Don't you remember us?"

The official leaned back in his chair and looked to his left and then his right to see if anyone was listening. Then he leaned forward again and lowered his voice. "I don't remember you, sir. But I'm sure you, being an American, could jog my memory."

Suddenly, it dawned on Sean. The man wanted money. He was holding them hostage because he knew they were from America and assumed they were wealthy.

"Sir, we're missionaries headed into your country, as I'm sure you gathered from our visas. We're not wealthy Americans. We don't have any money to give you."

The official leaned over the desk and blew his cigarette smoke into Sean's face. "No visa, no entry. Sorry."

Sean sighed in despair, then turned and walked back to Nancy, plunking down in his chair. "Apparently, this fine gentleman claims we never gave him our visas when we checked in. He has no memory of us."

Nancy scoffed. "You know, I thought it was odd that he kept them after looking over all our paperwork. No one has done that before. I just assumed they had different protocols in this country."

"They have different protocols alright," Sean replied. "He says we can 'jog his memory,' if you know what I mean. If I offer this guy money and his buddy finds out, he could throw us in jail for bribing an official. Who knows where the extortion ends?"

As calm as ever, Nancy took her husband's hand in hers. "God sent us here, and none of Hell's obstacles, not even this crooked officer, will keep us from His mission. Let's just pray that God will move in the officer's heart. We must trust Him, Sean. This is beyond anything we could have prepared for. We have been obedient, and I know God will be faithful."

Sean was tired. They were so close. Why did everything have to be difficult before they even arrived in Aria? He knew Nancy was right, but so much was on the line. Not only were they delayed dealing with this greedy immigration officer, but the man had also confiscated his luggage and the manuscript as well. Months of well-laid plans were useless at that moment. He and Nancy were on the other side of the world, stranded and empty-handed.

Sean needed some time. Nancy knew that hounding him to make her point was never the way to reach him. He processed situations much better when he had time to allow the Holy Spirit to speak to him directly. She visited the restroom, got a drink of water, then ambled around the dismal waiting room to give Sean some space.

When she returned to her seat, Nancy saw a difference in her husband's face. His heart had softened. The Holy Spirit had worked fast.

"You're right," he said. "He has never left us, and He won't forsake us here in this airport. I'm at the end of myself and my abilities to help us here, but that's right where He wants us. He doesn't want us to deliver ourselves. He wants to do it. Thank you for reminding me, dear. You always keep me grounded."

Nancy and Sean joined hands, bowed their heads, and began praying.

Aadiel had been with Sean and Nancy for each one of the last fifty-two days. He had moved when instructed to move, and he had waited when he was told to wait. He longed to make things easier for Sean and Nancy, but God was at work in the entire process. Aadiel remained obedient and ready, but he still wondered what Codill had meant when he said, "Now it's time to equip you."

Sitting next to the faithful couple, he listened to Sean's prayers of repentance for growing weary and self-dependent. As he heard their prayers and petitions go before the Father, he knew that was his cue.

Aadiel walked over to the officer's desk and tipped the lukewarm cup of old coffee over on the desk, spilling it into the officer's lap.

Shoving his chair back from his desk, the officer huffed in irritation and grabbed the paperwork and file folders in front of him before they could get soaked. Looking down at his trousers, which now bore a wet coffee stain right in front, he rolled his eyes, threw the files into a basket on the desk, and tore off toward the restroom. Sean noticed the commotion but stayed focused in prayer with Nancy.

Behind the wall where the immigration desk sat was a small office with a window looking out over the waiting area. Aadiel entered through the closed door of the stuffy office where a tall, slender man with reading glasses sat drinking his coffee and staring at his computer. The man was the chief immigration officer, and he managed all the other officers in the security department. He rarely left his office, however, swamped with paperwork and meetings. Behind him on the wall, Aadiel noticed a picture of Mary holding the baby Jesus in her arms. Under the collar of the man's uniform, the beads of his rosary were just visible. A smile broke across Aadiel's face. This man knew King Jesus! Moving over beside the man's desk, Aadiel leaned down and whispered into his ear.

The chief looked up from his computer, then placed his coffee cup on the desk. Checking his watch, he was surprised to find that most of the morning had slipped away while he responded to emails. He pushed his chair back from his desk and stood, stretching his stiff muscles. Looking out the office window and into the waiting area, he noticed that the deputy officer had stepped away from his desk. He also noticed a couple huddled together in a desperate posture, holding hands. Immediately, the chief recognized they were praying.

When the office door swung open on its creaky hinges, Nancy looked up. A uniformed man was approaching. She stirred Sean, whose eyes remained closed in prayer.

"Excuse me," the man said. "I don't mean to interrupt your prayer, but I couldn't help but notice you. This may sound strange, but I felt led to come over and speak. I'm the chief immigration officer for this airport. Is there anything that I might help you with?"

Sean smiled up at the man. "Actually, there is."

The couple introduced themselves and explained their situation. They refrained from revealing the name of the officer who had pressured them, uncertain of how the chief might respond. He asked them several questions about their mission and their destination. Sean was hesitant to share so much with a stranger, but he also felt a peace about it, as if he were speaking to a friend. When he was finished, the officer motioned for them to follow him.

"Mr. and Mrs. Pathrose, please come with me."

They followed the chief over to the immigration desk, where he riffed through the disheveled paperwork. There in the wire basket sat a file with Sean and Nancy's visas. The officer took them from the file and held them up. "I assume these are the items in question?"

Sean nodded, accepting the visas.

The chief bent down and pulled out a bag from under the desk. "And is this the bag you're looking for?" Sean nodded again, holding his breath.

The chief handed the bag to Sean and the visas to Nancy. "I apologize on behalf of my department for your detainment here. To make it up to you, I would like to arrange protective transportation to your next destination."

Sean let out a sigh of relief. "You're the answer to our prayers, sir. Thank you so much."

"Many years ago when I was a young boy, missionaries like you ministered to my community, and we received the Good News of Jesus Christ. It was difficult for me growing up here, but God has been faithful to bless me and my family. I remain in His service, and it would be an honor to assist you as you move on to your destination."

* * *

SEAN HELD the car door open as Nancy stepped out. The driver that the chief had assigned to transport them removed their luggage from the trunk, then walked around and held his hand out to Sean. "Are you sure this is as far as I can take you?" he asked.

"Yes, thank you. You've done so much. We really appreciate it," Sean replied, shaking his hand.

They were in a small town about two and a half miles outside the village they would soon visit. It was the closest community to Aria. It had been almost three years since Sean and Nancy had agreed to dedicate their time, talents, and resources to the calling of remote work.

Aria was a village of approximately 300 men, women, and children who had remained hidden from civilization until recently. By some miracle, the village had gone undiscovered. It was located between two mountains in a remote pass covered by thick jungle foliage. Locals believed evil spirits haunted the area. There were legends of strange disappearances and deaths, which led to great superstition and avoidance of that part of the jungle.

It turned out there was a growing population of people living on the other side of that thicket with their own legends and superstitions. The villagers of Aria were not hostile; they were a group of indigenous people who had relied on courage and cunning to keep their village secret from the rest of the world. Out of fear, they avoided all outsiders and rejected other cultures.

Two years ago, one of the local townspeople had been traveling along a trade road near the Arian Pass when he noticed a young boy. A jaguar had mauled him and dragged his half-dead body out near the road.

The boy was transported into town, clinging to life, and doctors treated his wounds. His injuries were extensive, and the doctors didn't expect him to pull through. He remained unconscious for over three weeks. No one knew where he had come from. His shredded clothing and the markings on his skin were strange and unrecognizable to the townspeople. The boy spent over six months in the hospital being nursed back to health.

One of the missionary nurses assigned to the hospital took a particular interest in his care. She gave him the name "Found." While he was unconscious, no one could communicate with him. That barrier remained in place when he woke up. The language he used was unrecognizable to anyone in the hospital.

The nurse was so happy when Found finally awakened from his coma. As for Found, he was disoriented and afraid. She worked tirelessly to comfort him through the shock of waking up in a strange place. The jaguar broke both of his legs in the attack, so he could not get out of bed. The nurse spent all her spare time by his side. She attempted to communicate with him, using pictures at first. She would show Found a picture of a tree, and he would respond in a language she could not understand. The nurse was determined to discover more about him. Over the months, she worked with flash cards and showed many pictures to Found. Pictures of local birds, water, fire, sun, stars, monkeys, and hundreds more flashed before him as he continued to recover. The nurse recorded his responses and taught him several English words. They were making great progress. She even established a crude alphabet with the help of her husband, who was a missionary linguist at the local school.

Upon realization that Found was a member of a completely unknown tribe of people known as Aria, the missionary organization that employed the nurse and her husband offered resources to aid Found's recovery. During the latter part of his convalescence, they sent translators to help decode the Arian language. It was so unique that it was difficult to navigate. Working diligently for months, the missionary scholars translated part of the New Testament as well as the creation story and a few passages from the Old Testament into Arian.

Sean and Nancy had heard about the remote village through the mission's communications and felt led to go there. The couple had worked with the linguists on Zoom calls, learning all that they could about Found, his culture, and his language.

The culmination of two years of hard work would soon open the door to spread the gospel to a brand-new people. Sean wondered how long it had been since a missionary had such an opportunity. So many people had poured their lives into this mission already. Soon he and his wife would meet Found, make the journey through the secret pass, and attempt to make contact with the tribe of Aria.

Since their arrival, the gift of love had overwhelmed Sean and Nancy. Sean grew less concerned about the details, feeling more equipped and more at peace than ever. They realized this was significantly more than just an ordinary mission trip. What Sean and Nancy didn't know was that all of Heaven and Hell were also anticipating this crucial encounter.

CHAPTER 27

THE FINAL TRIBE AND TONGUE

Soon after Sean and Nancy agreed to take the assignment, the missions group connected them with Paul Stinson, a twenty-year missionary veteran. Paul had been living and working in the area for over seven years and was familiar with the recent developments in Aria. He had met with Found several times over the past year, learning everything he could about the remote village and its customs. He was excited to meet the Pathroses in person and to take the next steps in reaching the tribe.

Paul spent several weeks preparing for Sean and Nancy's arrival. He purchased their supplies and made arrangements for their room and board. The team would be required to travel on foot when they eventually entered Aria, so Paul had purchased a couple of donkeys to help carry supplies. He had also gathered rations, medical supplies, and other items that had been donated from his church. Every item on his list had been checked and checked again.

Paul was surprised to see Sean and Nancy arrive by official motorcade that morning. When Sean explained what had taken place back at the airport, Paul laughed. "You had an escort alright—a heavenly one."

After unloading their luggage and freshening up from the long travel, Sean and Nancy met with the team in the camp's dining hall. They were informed they would be required to quarantine for six weeks before attempting contact with Aria. This would ensure that no outside illness would be unintentionally spread to the tribe. Sean had anticipated this would be the case, so it wasn't surprising. This would also give Paul time to brief the team on the information gathered from communications with Found and teach them what little he knew about the people and their customs. They would study the topography of the land and decide on which route they would take.

After a few weeks at the mission, Sean and Nancy had settled in and familiarized themselves with the area. Sean had imagined things would be much more antiquated, so he was surprised to find the technology and most of the amenities of life there similar to those at home.

It amazed Sean and Nancy even more that a village of people could have remained undiscovered in the modern age of cell phones, drones, and satellites.

"There's no explanation for it," Sean said one morning while marveling at the phenomenon over breakfast with Paul.

"I believe there is an explanation for it," Paul replied, smiling. "A heavenly explanation."

Sean inquired about the possibility of Found returning to the village to make the introductions and translations for them. "Wouldn't that make the most sense?"

"It would make things much easier," Paul agreed, "but Found has refused to return. He fears for his safety after divulging the tribe's location. To his people, he is now a traitor. They would probably kill him if he returned with us. We have agreed not to mention him."

"So, we'll just walk in and pretend like we have found them by chance?" Nancy asked.

"We will come bearing gifts," Paul said. "That's what all the supplies are for. I know that the two of you also brought items from America. Found has warned us that his people may not accept the items, but we feel like it will at least give the message that we come in peace and don't wish to harm them."

"God help us. It seems risky," Sean said.

"It is risky, but we won't be going in alone," Paul replied, patting Sean on the back.

The weeks of quarantine flew by. Sean and Nancy used the time to learn as much as they could in preparation for the mission. On the morning of their departure, Sean, Nancy, and Paul rose early to pray together and to go over the last-minute preparations. Then they loaded the donkeys with all the supplies they would offer to the Arians.

So many thoughts were swirling through Sean's mind as he tightened the straps on the saddlebags. He and Nancy might never return from the village. If the tribe was set on maintaining their obscurity, they might kill any intruders. Who knew if they had already killed people who had stumbled upon their village? Sean and Nancy had worked in the mission field before but with established bases and people who had already accepted outside influences and the Word. Neither of them had any experience with initial contact. No missionary alive did. Sean had come to terms with all the possibilities, though, and he knew Nancy had as well.

Sean thanked God that he had been called to this task. As he shifted the backpack strap on his shoulder, he thought about the manuscript inside of his bag. How magnificent was it that his family had been so key in the Father's plans over the years? They were the keepers of the manuscript, and now they were the messengers to this hidden and quite possibly last unknown tribe of people on Earth.

Aadiel stood on the other side of the donkey from Sean and smiled. He was proud of them and so grateful to be on this important assignment. He wondered what Hell Ops was scheming against the mission.

Aadiel knew Sean must be feeling uneasy about what was to come. He wished he could reveal himself to assure him that no harm would befall them. After all, the Father, who knew the end from the beginning, had set these events in motion. The One whose words never returned to Him void had spoken the directive. There could be no failure.

"Don't worry, my friend. You're part of the glorious plan, and Paul is right. You won't be going alone," Aadiel said.

Sean didn't hear the words with his ears, but the message comforted his spirit.

Suddenly, a bright white light shone on Aadiel, and a huge angelic being stood at his side. The angel was much larger than Aadiel. He had a golden sash around his waist and a sword in a sheath that glistened like a diamond. This angel was neither a messenger nor a servant; he was an angel of war.

"Aadiel, our King of Armies has sent me here to empower you with a portion of His authority."

Aadiel's mind flashed to Codill's words. *This must be what he was talking about,* he thought.

"Our adversaries are gathering in great numbers above Aria," the angel continued. "The enemy knows this battleground is the most strategic place on Earth. Hell Ops has made every weapon of destruction and death available to them. To defeat them and carry out your mission, you will need His authority."

The angel unbuckled the golden sash from his waist and handed it to Aadiel. The sheath that contained the mighty sword hung from it. "Wear this authority around your waist. It will be a sign to everyone who sees it that His authority is supreme. No power will overcome you. Those who accompany you will know no fear or trembling and will experience peace and confidence as you walk with them in His authority."

Aadiel took the sash and cinched it around his robe.

"Now you are equipped," the warrior angel said and then he disappeared.

Aadiel placed his hand on the hilt of the sword. "Now I am equipped."

The walk in was grueling. That part of the jungle was wild and untamed. As they worked their way toward the pass, it felt as if they were exploring a part of the world where no person had walked. It was as if nature had built a tremendous barrier between civilization and the village. The natural camouflage was wild and untamed, yet it seemed intentional. The thick foliage barred the entrance to the pass from sight. Sean and Paul used machetes to widen the path for the donkeys. The jungle leaned in on them like a thick curtain. It didn't clear at all before dumping them at the foot of two sheer cliffs that shot into the sky. When they finally emerged from the thicket, the sight was incredible. The rocks on each side were immense. The rock walls were jagged and intimidating. Portions jutted out on crude ledges that looked as if they could drop boulders on the group at any moment. The pass between the two rocks was only about as wide as a Greyhound bus.

The donkeys, which had been quite compliant so far, stopped in their tracks as if sensing some unknown entity. It took a good bit of coaxing to get the animals moving again through the narrow pass.

Suddenly, a great wind spun up from beyond the walkway and tore through the opening between the cliffs. The wind picked up the sand, swirling it in every direction. It blinded them and beat against their skin like tiny needles. The whirlwind also spooked the donkeys. They bucked, and one of them dumped a few of the supplies that Sean had tied to its back. Acting fast, Nancy pulled some blankets from the pack that had dropped to the ground and threw them over the donkeys' heads, which calmed the animals. After the three of them had covered their faces and eyes from the beating sand, they worked to secure the supplies. They knew they needed to move forward, not knowing how long the windstorm would last. It was disorienting and required persistence and persuasion to get the donkeys moving again. It was grueling trying to traverse the rocky terrain blinded by their head coverings and deafened by the wind. The storm persisted and beat down on the team through the entire pass.

What Sean had planned to be a few hours' journey turned into a brutal six-hour haul, and by the time they made it through the pass, the team was weary, filthy, and thirsty.

Only after they reentered the thick jungle on the other side did they find some reprieve.

Now Sean understood how the Arians had remained undiscovered. He was thankful for the extra water bottles he had stowed in his backpack, but that burden plus the weight of the clay container holding the manuscript had added even more to his load, causing his back to ache as he shifted his pack off his shoulders.

"That wind was brutal," Sean said.

"And where did it come from?" Nancy asked. "It was so sudden."

"Seemed supernatural to me," Paul replied. "It seems quite apparent that something doesn't want us to make it to Aria."

Sean nodded as he took a drink. "No doubt about it. Fortunately, that something is not in charge here."

Sean noticed the excitement in Nancy's eyes as she removed her head covering and sunglasses. She shook the dust out of her hair, then wiped her face with her scarf. He smiled and handed her one of the water bottles from his backpack.

Nancy removed the blankets from the donkeys' head. She beat the dust out of them, then folded them and stowed them in the saddlebags. "I'm sure thankful for these guys," she said, smiling as she stroked one of the donkeys. "Even though this one is super stubborn."

Sean's spirit was renewed and uplifted in response to his wife's resiliency. He was thankful to have a partner who shared his passion for the mission but who brought different strengths to the effort.

Paul reached into his jacket pocket and pulled out the crude map that Found had drawn for them. "I know this map isn't to scale, but it doesn't look like we have too much farther to go." He pulled out his compass and established which direction was northwest.

After continuing through a dense thicket made of different shorter shrubs, the team arrived at an overgrown meadow with thick sawgrass that reached over their heads.

"We're definitely in the right place," Paul said. "I can see this on the map. The path should be to our right."

They walked around the edge of the meadow until they found a path with the tall grass laid down just wide enough for one person. They were completely blind except for the narrow path in front of them. Paul went in first. Nancy led one donkey in, and Sean brought up the rear, the second donkey following him.

Feeling vulnerable as they walked through the grass, one in front of the other, Nancy prayed again for safety.

They walked for what felt like a long time before the path emptied into a large, cleared portion of the meadow. As their eyes adjusted to the sun, just across the meadow a small village came into view. A few dozen small yurt-style huts set in a circle were nestled in a carved-out area of the jungle. Larger structures were scattered throughout the huts. The focal point of the village was a tall structure positioned in the center of the habitations.

Aadiel had been walking in front of the group. He stepped out into the clearing and scanned the tree line, spotting a multitude of dark demons. Some were perched in the trees, some were standing in the village, and others were standing guard in the meadow. Many of them were high-ranking demons, but there were representatives from the lower legions as well.

Every dark eye turned on him in an instant, and a frenzy of sounds came from the village.

"Who is that with them?" a demon hissed.

"I've never seen that one before," another replied. "What's that blue robe he's wearing?"

"It can't be," a demon in one of the trees exclaimed.

"Can't be what, you idiot?"

"Don't we know that face?" the demon in the tree asked the group.

A hush fell over them as they focused on Aadiel's face, searching for recognition.

Then one of the demons fell out of the tree and hit the ground with a thud. It was followed by hissing, gasping, cursing, clawing, and a roar of confusion throughout the ranks of the fallen.

"Kill them all!" the head demon shouted, hatred dripping off his tongue.

Before the demonic ranks could assemble themselves into action, however, Aadiel pulled the lapel of his robe aside, revealing the great sword.

The demons gasped in unison. They dared not employ a single demonic tactic. Evil seldom knew fear among its ranks, but Aadiel could see it in their dark eyes. He placed his hand on the great sword of authority's hilt and glared back at them.

The first thing that Paul, Sean, and Nancy noticed was that the village looked abandoned.

"I don't see any people," Nancy said.

Sean ran several scenarios through his mind as they continued toward the village. Had something happened to the people since Found left there? Had a plague hit the community and wiped them out? He realized that could not be the case because someone had maintained the land around the village. Had the villagers detected the missionaries' approach and gone into hiding? Were they waiting in ambush?

As they entered the village, they marveled at the detail of the small habitations. The intricate huts impressed Sean with their engineering and efficiency. Earthen pipes ran from gutters on each roof into a cistern and back into the huts' foundations.

"These people have running water," Sean said in amazement.

"I see that," Paul replied. "And look at the tools they're using." He pointed to a scythe leaning against one of the huts.

"I guess I was expecting them to be much more primitive, being so isolated and living out here on their own," Sean said.

"This is amazing," Nancy exclaimed. "They're so self-sufficient. I need the Internet and YouTube to figure out how to work my microwave!"

In the center of the huts was an ornate structure that looked like a large gazebo. Its thatched roof was roughly twenty by thirty feet with no walls, supported by eight pillars. Sean approached the structure and touched one of the massive poles created from a multitude of two-inch-thick vines woven together. The pillar was about eighteen inches in diameter and stood nearly seven feet tall. The intricacy of each pillar amazed Sean. Each one looked identical in width and height, which was impressive considering each one was made of hundreds, if not thousands, of individual vines. As he stared up at the underside of the thatched roof, he noticed they had used some of the same vines as joists and rafters. Each one was engineered and weaved together, reaching back into each pillar. It was an architectural design that defied logic. Sean wondered whether modern-day technology and construction tools could replicate it.

"How could they have built this?" Nancy asked, marveling at the architecture.

"It doesn't look like anything human beings could engineer," Paul replied. "I've never seen anything like this."

Under the structure were several beautifully crafted tables and stools. The tables were bare except for small lamps made of an earthen material sitting in the middle of each table. Each lamp was full of oil with a brand-new wick made from mullein leaf sticking out of a hole in the nozzle.

"The world may know nothing about these people, and they may know nothing about Jesus yet, but His Spirit has been their inspiration and guide," Sean said. "There's no other explanation."

Paul chuckled. "I think some distant kin of Bezalel must have been here at some point. Seriously."

It took Nancy a minute to make the connection. "Ah, Bezalel, the chief builder of the tabernacle. I had to dig for that one, Paul. Good one."

After the three marveled at the details of the structure, Nancy looked over at Paul. "So, where do you think everyone could be?"

Paul shrugged. "I'm not sure, but they haven't been gone for long. This place is immaculate, and someone is taking excellent care of everything. I can only assume they're all hiding in their huts."

Nancy paused and listened for any sounds of life. She looked over at the small huts again but didn't see or hear anything. "What should we do? Should we approach one and knock?"

Sean shook his head. "No, I don't think we should be overly intrusive on our first visit. Let's just put the toys for the children on these tables. Maybe they'll recognize it as a peace offering. We'll keep the toiletries and medicines and present them later if we get the opportunity. Maybe the bright colors will interest the children, hopefully causing the adults to be more open when we return. I pray these small gifts will break the ice, so maybe they won't hide the next time we come."

Paul and Nancy agreed with the plan, then walked over to the donkey that held the large bag of toys. Paul had organized a toy drive as a youth activity at his home church, collecting simple handheld toys. The bag held forty to fifty of the collected items. Paul carried the bag over to a table and pulled the toys out one by one. Sean and Nancy spread them out, covering two of the small tables.

When all the toys had been arranged on the tables, Nancy looked at their finished work. "I sure would like to be here when these children see all of this. I bet their faces will light up like it's Christmas."

"I hope you're right," Sean replied. "And I hope we brought enough toys for each child to have one."

"When we come back, if some children didn't get something, we'll make sure we return with more, right, Paul?" Nancy said.

"Yes, we can always find more if needed. Found told us there were about forty children when he left the village, so hopefully we have enough." He folded up the empty toy bag and secured it to the donkey. "I'll say this. In all my years of ministry—and I have served in many remote villages—I've never experienced a 'no contact' visit."

"I'm sure there's a great deal of fear and reluctance among the people," Nancy said. "Otherwise, they wouldn't be living out here on their own."

"I'm just glad they weren't lying in wait intending to harm us," Sean said, glancing around just in case. "Even though we haven't officially contacted the villagers, I would call this progress."

He grabbed his donkey's rein and took one last look at the village, searching again for signs of life. The village remained eerily silent.

The team headed back toward the path across the grassy meadow, hoping to make it back to the missionary camp before dark.

Aadiel took one last gaze across the meadow toward the village. Many of the demons had fled, though a few remained to stand guard. No doubt they would report what they had witnessed to Hell Ops. He was sure Hell Ops would deploy heavy backup before the next visit, but he didn't care. No weapon in Hell's arsenal could harm Sean and Nancy. Hell's minions could come and gawk, but Aadiel would be there, and his God had equipped him with everything he needed for victory.

When the trio of intruders were well out of sight, the Arian elder and his son emerged from their hut. They had given strict instructions for everyone in the village to stay sheltered in place. They approached the agora or gazebo and found the tables filled with an assortment of strange items. The men didn't recognize any of them. The collection included several types of dolls, carved wooden cars and trucks, tractors, and airplanes. There were also plastic balls, baseball bats, and gloves, puzzles, beaded necklaces, crayons, coloring books, a slinky, a plastic flute, paint-by-numbers booklets, and much more. The elder and his son regarded the assortment of items with troubled looks on their faces.

With growing curiosity, some of the other villagers peeked out of their hiding places. Although the elder had not yet given permission, a few ventured out, followed by a few more until all the villagers were standing under the agora. They marveled at the strange, colorful objects on the tables.

One of the little girls approached the table with her eyes set on a baby doll. Before she could pick it up, the elder slapped her hand. "Don't touch! Get back!"

The girl drew back, ashamed, and hid her face in her mother's apron.

"Touch nothing," the elder's son said, reinforcing his father's order.

The crowd shuffled back as the adults secured their children.

Just then an older child jumped up and down and pointed at the slinky. "Mika, Mika!" he shouted.

"Mika, Mika!" another girl exclaimed, pointing to a plastic doll wearing a dress.

The villagers whispered to each other, wondering how the elder would respond.

He held up his hand for silence. Then, walking over to the first table, he picked up the slinky and turned it sideways to inspect it. As he did, the bottom of the slinky fell out of his hand and coiled down toward the ground, startling him. He almost dropped it but then swooped the toy back up into his hand. After a thorough inspection of the item, the elder smiled and held the slinky up in the air like a trophy. "Mika, Mika!" he shouted.

He moved to the second table and picked up the doll. He handed it to his son and smiled at him. His son held the doll up and showed it to the villagers. "Mika, Mika!" he exclaimed.

The two toys had nothing in common except for their color, which was exactly the same.

The elder took the doll from his son, then stuffed it and the slinky into his robe. He turned to two of the other leaders. "Light the altar!"

The villagers fell into a state of confusion as the two men scrambled to gather wood. Many of them asked questions in hushed tones, and the children pleaded with their parents to touch the toys.

As soon as the fire was roaring, the elder ordered the two men to gather all the toys from the tables and set them on the altar. As the villagers and their children buzzed in a confused frenzy, the two men picked up the toys and threw them into the orange blaze. The elder recited a prayer to their god as black smoke billowed into the sky.

A hush fell over the crowd as the colorful plastic melted, giving off a toxic chemical smell. The other dolls' clothing ignited quickly, though the wooden toys and other items took longer to burn. Eventually, the fire claimed even the leather of the baseball glove and balls. It consumed everything except the slinky and the doll.

The entire village witnessed the sacrifice. As the fire died down, the elder took the remaining two toys from his robe and walked toward his hut. He stood at the threshold and lifted the doll and the slinky into the air toward the doorpost. "Mika, Mika!" he proclaimed. Then he lowered the toys, bowed, and passed under the mark painted at the top of the doorpost. Every doorpost in Aria bore the same mark, which just happened to be the same color as the doll's dress and the slinky.

CHAPTER 28
THE LAST MISSIO

When Sean, Nancy, and Paul arrived back at the missionary camp late that evening, the excitement was palpable. Even though they had not made official contact with the people, everyone wanted to hear about the "lost village" of Aria.

While Paul went back to his living quarters to check emails and clean up, Sean sat in the common area and recounted the events that occurred during their travel to the village. He explained what it was like to see the remote village for the first time and how eerie and quiet everything was. The group was just as astounded as Sean and Nancy by the villagers' advanced engineering capabilities.

"I don't know what I was expecting," Sean admitted.

"I guess since it took so long to break the language barrier with Found, I assumed they would be much more primitive, just living in the dirt," an older missionary said.

"Thinking about it now, we should have known they would have to be very smart and cunning to have remained hidden for centuries," Sean replied. "That requires a great deal of willful intent."

"Or maybe God sheltered them," Nancy said. "This is His timing."

"When will you guys head back?" another man asked.

"As soon as we can get supplies loaded up and turned around," Sean replied.

"We have to get some rest, of course, dear," Nancy said, placing her hand on Sean's shoulder.

"Speaking of which, let me get you all some tea," a lady toward the back of the room said.

"Thank you!" Sean replied. "Tea sounds wonderful. So, Paul is checking the weather forecast for us now. After the dust devil we experienced on a cloudless day in that mountain pass, I certainly wouldn't want to be caught in a storm. We can't risk losing the donkeys, or worse, each other."

"What's your plan if the villagers continue to stay hidden?" someone asked.

Nancy had been wondering about that herself. She wasn't sure they had a plan.

"My thought is to pull up a stool in that magnificent meeting hut, or whatever you want to call it, and wait 'em out," Sean said. "They have to come out sometime, right?"

The group laughed, and Nancy smirked and looked over at Sean. "Sometimes you make me wonder why God chose you for this work. You're so non-confrontational. Just sit and wait? *That's* your plan?"

"I hope you pack some snacks," the older missionary said.

The group laughed as Sean shrugged at Nancy. "Well . . ."

Before he could continue, Paul came running into the room, out of breath. "Guys, I have some wonderful news!" He bent over and sucked in air, trying to slow his heart rate. "I just got off the phone with Mary, the nurse who spent the last two years with Found, nursing him back to health and learning his language. She told Found that we had traveled into the village without incident. It surprised him that we found it so easily. But guess what? Found has agreed to accompany us back to Aria when we return!" A huge smile spread across Paul's face.

Sean bolted out of his seat. "What? Are you serious? That's fantastic!"

Everyone in the room was excited by the news.

"Wait, but I thought he refused to return for fear of his life," Sean said.

"He did. Apparently, Arian hunters have orders to take their own lives before falling into the hands of outsiders. Found would have done so had they not found him unconscious. He didn't know where he was when he woke up weeks later in the hospital.

Frankly, we're very fortunate that his injuries were so severe. If he had all of his faculties, he would have attempted suicide before Mary established contact with him."

"What changed his mind about going back?" Nancy asked.

"After Mary told him about our initial visit to his village and our safe return, he told her that he had some sort of dream last night. He said he wants to share what he has learned about Jesus with his people. He told Mary that if he loses his life while doing it, it will be an honorable death."

"Well, praise God for that dream," Sean said. "This changes everything. We need to make plans right away. How's the weather looking, Paul?"

"Unfortunately, tomorrow is a no go, and so is the next. High winds and a storm are expected at around midmorning and will continue, on and off, for twenty-four to thirty-six hours. We need a good long travel window when we go back now that we know what we're dealing with. It looks like Thursday will be our next cloudless day. Found will arrive here at camp tomorrow. I'm going to make the arrangements tonight, and Mary is going to accompany him to make introductions. He's comfortable with her, and she communicates with him better than anyone else."

"Thursday works," Sean replied. "That gives us plenty of time to rest, meet with Found, and get everything packed up and ready to go. This is such good news. Thank you, brother."

The next day, the same driver who had delivered Sean and Nancy from the airport agreed to drive Found, Mary, and her husband to the missionary camp. Although Found had lived in the city for months, his time had been spent in the hospital and rehabilitation facility on the same property. He could not recall his transportation in the ambulance to the hospital all those months ago because he had been unconscious, clinging to life. Today would be Found's first car ride.

Mary rode in the SUV's front seat making small talk with the driver as they drove through town. She kept turning to check on Found, attempting to comfort him with a smile. She knew this was a lot for him.

Found had no words to describe the cold air machine blowing in his face. The seats, which were covered in animal skin, were amazing, and he could not understand how they were moving under the power of invisible horses. Despite his wonder, he remained stoic for the duration of the ride, rubbing his hand over the smooth leather seat and staring out the window as trees, buildings, and other vehicles whizzed by.

When they arrived at the village, the driver came around and opened the door for Mary. She stepped out, noticing that Found hadn't moved from his seat. He was looking down at the strange buttons and door handle in confusion.

Paul, who had been waiting with anticipation for this moment, walked over to the SUV and opened the door. "Good afternoon, Found," he said with a big smile.

Found smiled back and then got out of the SUV and looked around. "Good," he said as he pointed back to the vehicle.

Paul chuckled. "Yes, quite good indeed. I'm sure." He closed the door. "Come please. Meet my friends." The two of them walked inside the camp's main building where Sean and Nancy were waiting at the conference table to meet the boy who they hoped would soon change everything.

After introductions, Mary expounded on some of the information she had given Sean and Nancy earlier about the Arian culture.

"Arians have always been polytheistic, paying homage to many gods. They worship different deities depending on the weather, their crops, their health, and superstitions. They offer sacrifices to these gods often. Their worship is an attempt to find favor for the harvest, for fertility, for longevity, and all sorts of other things. The people also believe in a prophecy that was given long ago and passed down through ages. An ancient Arian seer foretold that the 'One' would someday travel to their village to give them immortality and take them to a new village where they would live happily forever."

"That's interesting," Nancy said, smiling at Found.

"He told me that his elders believe that the 'One' will come very soon, so they have increased their sacrifices and have been preparing the village in expectation. And get this: apparently, the Arians have a sacred color." Sean frowned. "A sacred color?"

"Unless I'm misunderstanding him, Found tells me that the prophecy speaks of a particular color symbolizing the coming 'One.' They mark themselves with it and worship any idol that bears its hue."

Sean considered the prophecy. "So the 'One' will offer them immortality and take them to paradise forever. That sounds very familiar."

Here was a group of people who didn't know who Jesus was. They worshiped many gods, but the Father had given them a message and a promise of truth that would soon come to them.

"Thank you, Found. Your story gives me so much hope," Sean said. "Thank you for sharing it with us."

Mary helped the team communicate their plans for return to Aria with Found. His fear and reluctance about returning to the village were gone. Now he was full of courage and hope, ready to share the message of Jesus with his people.

"I have a third donkey to help carry the additional supplies that were dropped off today," Sean said. "What time do you think we should start out tomorrow morning, Paul?"

"Let's leave at sunrise. The forecast is showing favorable conditions, but I want to have extra time in case we experience any more trouble on the way in."

As the team discussed a few more details about the trip, Mary translated for Found.

"Found, do you understand everything?" Paul asked. "Are you comfortable with all of this?"

Found smiled and nodded. "Found ready. Go, good."

"Yes, go, good. Okay then," Paul said as he stood up.

"Everyone, be sure to get some rest," Sean added, standing up as well. "Mary, we've made arrangements for Found to stay here with us at the mission. You are more than welcome to stay here too unless you need to get back to the hospital."

"Found says he feels good about staying without me. Plus, I'm scheduled to work tomorrow afternoon."

The group prayed together and said goodnight. After Mary departed with the driver, Nancy showed Found to the room they had prepared for him. The anticipation was thick, but she hoped they could all get a good night's rest. They were going to need it.

Early the next morning, after a light breakfast, the team met with the other missionaries to pray together. Paul also seized the opportunity to double check the weather forecast.

Aadiel stood behind the group with his head bowed as they prayed. He would go before them again, bearing the sword of authority to ward off any threats. He knew the forces of darkness would have had plenty of time to regroup. He also knew they didn't stand a chance.

Sean threw on his backpack and grabbed his donkey's rein. "I guess we're ready."

Found smiled at him. "Go, good."

To the team's pleasant surprise, the mountain pass didn't prove difficult that morning. It was like a completely different journey. As they exited the jungle, the cliffs stood like sentinels guarding the path. Everything was quiet as the team walked through. There was no wind, and all they heard were birds singing in the trees around them. They strolled along at a leisurely pace, arriving at the meadow ahead of schedule.

As the group walked through the meadow and approached the clearing, Aadiel detected a sweet scent on the breeze. It blew from behind him, encompassing his spirit in perfect peace. He knew exactly what that scent was. He also knew that he would never get used to it. The Spirit of God was present. He closed his eyes and took a deep breath.

Placing his hand on the sword's hilt, Aadiel broke through the tall grass and stepped into the clearing. Scanning the tree line that surrounded the village, he saw multitudes of dark forces staged throughout the area. A demon stood guard over every hut, and another team of minions stood at the center of the village. An entire platoon patrolled the perimeter with their heads on a swivel. Aadiel looked at the sky and saw higher-ranking demons circling the village like vultures waiting to devour. Just as he had expected, Hell Ops had intensified its forces since their last visit.

"What audacity," he mumbled.

Strangely enough, the legion had not picked up on Aadiel and the team's presence as they entered the field. The aroma of the Spirit wafted through Aadiel's nostrils once again. He felt a powerful feeling of authority rise in his spirit. Then he drew the sword from its sheath and held it in the air. A bright light pierced the sky.

"Be gone!" he thundered with a voice that shook the atmosphere.

At that moment, confusion and chaos enshrouded the dark beings. They jumped from their perches and stations as if an electric charge had shot through their veins. The demons bolted in every direction like cockroaches, shrieking in terror.

The sheer power and authority took Aadiel by surprise. The words had come from his own mouth, but the force came from the Holy Spirit.

Aadiel placed the sword back into its sheath. "Here one minute and gone the next," he said with a chuckle, noting that not one demon remained. Oh, how he wished the precious missionaries standing behind him could have witnessed what he had just seen.

Sean stared across the meadow at the empty village. Not a person or animal was in sight. Only a line of smoke rising into the sky from an ash heap gave any hint that someone had once been there.

As they approached the structure in the center of the village, Nancy noted the eerie silence. It was as if all life had suddenly vanished from existence. *I wonder if this is what it will be like when Jesus returns,* she thought. *Here one minute and gone the next.*

Sean walked over to the tables where they had left the toys. The tables were empty except for the lamps. Although lamps showed signs of use, they were full of oil with freshly trimmed wicks, just like before. Every toy was gone.

Paul walked toward the remains of the fire. He realized it was a shrine or altar. He motioned to Sean and Nancy, pointing to the ashes. "What does that look like to you?"

Sean bent down and picked up a stick. Sifting through the ash, he turned over a melted piece of yellow plastic. He also found several charred fragments of carved wood and melted metal. Sean looked up at Nancy. "It appears they didn't appreciate our gifts."

Nancy put her hand over her mouth in disbelief. "Oh, no. I hope we didn't offend them."

Sean looked back in the direction they had come. "Where's Found?"

As the three of them looked around, Nancy spotted him making his way toward a hut in the center of the village. Suddenly, an older man appeared in the hut's doorway and stepped out, spear in hand. Nancy noticed a much younger man standing in the same doorway staring out at them.

Sean instinctively stepped in front of his wife, holding his breath as they watched the interaction.

Found fell to his knees and bowed his face to the ground before the old man.

Not knowing what to do, Sean, Nancy, and Paul bowed low and pressed their faces to the ground as well.

After a few seconds of uncomfortable silence, Found stood up, and he and the older man exchanged words in their native tongue. Then the elder grabbed Found by the wrist and dragged him into the hut, closing the door behind them.

Nancy, Sean, and Paul looked at one another in bewilderment as they stood up.

"What now?" Nancy asked.

Paul shrugged. "I have no idea."

"Like I said before, we can always pull up a stool and wait," Sean said, smiling at his wife.

Nancy rolled her eyes as she smiled back. "You win. I guess we'll wait after all."

Over the next hour, the three discussed their theories about what might be going on in the hut with Found. They debated whether to unload their supplies or bring them back to the camp with them, considering what had happened to the toys.

Then the door to the elder's hut swung open. The three missionaries stood up. Found came out first, followed by the elder, his son, and two small children. The elder called out in Arian, and soon more of the villagers ventured out of hiding, though they kept their distance from the strangers.

Found walked toward the missionaries, followed closely by the elder and his family. His expression was perplexing. Sean could not tell if he was sad, afraid, or hopeful.

"Sit," Found said, pointing to the ground.

The three missionaries plopped into the dirt.

The elder and his family stood several paces behind Found.

Found spoke in broken English, explaining as best as he could what had happened after Sean, Nancy, and Paul had left the village on their previous trip. The villagers had never seen toys. At first the elder had assumed that the items were totems carrying various curses against the tribe. As a result, he wouldn't allow any of the villagers, especially the children, to touch them. Then he had the items sacrificed to one of their gods, requesting protection from curses.

There were, however, two items among the lot that he held back from the sacrifice. Found pulled the slinky and the doll from his robe and showed them to the missionaries. He had noticed the toys in the elder's hut upon entering and immediately understood why they didn't destroy them.

"Mika," Found said, holding them up.

"Mika," the villagers repeated in unison, bowing in reverence.

Sean remembered what Mary had told them. "Ah, yes, Mika, the coming deity."

Found pointed at the huts. Sean hadn't noticed it before, but each hut had a painted swath over the doorpost. It was the same color as the slinky and the doll's dress.

Sean didn't know what a slinky, a child's doll, and the markings over the doors had in common, but apparently, it was important to the elder.

Found had explained to the chief what had happened to him while hunting. He told him of his near-death experience and the life-saving care that he had received from the missionaries at the hospital. He also informed the elder and his family that the missionaries were not there to harm them or to curse them. They were not there to attack their beliefs or interrupt their culture either. Instead, they were there to learn from them.

Found pleaded with the elder not to fear Sean, Nancy, and Paul. It took some heavy persuasion, but to Found's surprise, the elder was open to the idea.

"Trust, time, long," Found said, imploring the missionary team to temper their expectations.

That was the first contact with the remote village of Aria. The team journeyed back to the village many times over the next several months. Their interactions with the people were short and simple, and the villagers remained guarded. Sean and Nancy decided not to push their gifts or supplies on the people. They understood the inroad with these people would be slow, one small step at a time.

After the fourth visit, the elder permitted Found to return to the village full time. The young man was clearly different. During his stay at the missionary hospital, Found not only received salvation but was also baptized in water and filled with the Holy Spirit. The Spirit radiated through him and drew his family and friends, who wanted to hear more about his experiences. After their initial hesitancy faded, the villagers could not get enough of Found's story. He was allowed to share openly, even with the children.

Sean and Nancy noticed the influence Found was having with the people when they visited. He had opened the door for a trusting relationship between them and the people of Aria. They were so grateful for him.

One afternoon while sitting at a table in the common space, Nancy watched the children dancing around Found in a circle as they came over to listen to him speak. They loved being with him, and he loved them.

"Found is a missio," Sean said to his wife.

"A missio?" She had never heard of that term.

"A missio is 'one who is sent or dispatched as an agent.'"

"That he is," Nancy said, smiling. "Possibly the most important missio since Jesus."

"You might be right," Sean replied.

Six more months passed as Sean and Nancy visited the Arians at least once a week. There was much to be thankful for, but sometimes it didn't appear they were making any real headway for the Kingdom. The elders were open to surface relationships with the missionaries. They would listen to Found's stories of the gospel, but they remained persistent in their belief system, holding fast to the ancient prophecies they had received and continuing with their ritual sacrifices.

While sitting with Sean one rainy afternoon, Found discussed the elder's reluctance and attempted to explain the challenge with their beliefs.

"Come soon," he said.

"Who is coming?" Sean asked.

"Color, come to take us."

"Color? They believe color is coming soon to take you where, Found? Did you tell them that Jesus is coming soon?"

Found shook his head. "No Jesus. Not Jesus." He turned and pointed to one of the huts. "Chief says color come to Aria, take us. Mika, Mika."

Sean was at a loss. He didn't understand what Found was trying to tell him. Whatever it was, the expectation was preventing the elder and his village from accepting the message of Jesus. Feeling frustrated, Sean changed the subject to a matter concerning needed supplies.

That night, Sean spoke to Nancy back at the missionary camp.

"Found is so amazing. I appreciate his gift of patience with his people. I could use more of it."

"What do you mean, hun? What's wrong?"

"I have always believed Jesus saved and empowered Found in the perfect time to bring salvation to his village. I realize that I just assumed 'now' was the perfect time. It's been months, and I'm not sure we're any closer to reaching them than we were the first day we walked into the village."

"Patience is available to you, just like everything else we need to accomplish this mission. It's such an incredible story. I know things are moving slowly, so it is difficult to see the progress." Nancy brushed her fingers through Sean's hair.

"I know. I know. But not one soul besides Found has been won in this village yet. They listen, but the words don't hit. Something is holding them back, and I'm not sure what it is. I tried to talk with Found about it today. He went on about some color coming for them. I don't know. Sometimes I just don't understand what he's saying."

"You remember what Mary told us about the tribe's sacred color, don't you?" Nancy asked.

"I guess not. I had no idea what he was talking about."

"I'll call Mary in the morning," Nancy replied. "I don't remember specific details, but she mentioned their belief structure being tied to the color they have painted on their doors, something to do with the prophecy."

Sean sighed. "If only we could communicate better."

"Just think back to the day when they wouldn't even come out of their huts," Nancy said. "Patience, my love. I'm hearing the words 'Don't get frustrated.'"

Sean shook his head, still not ready to relent on his frustration. "I feel like some days we're just going through the same motions, day in and day out."

His eyes trailed down to the backpack beside his feet. "It's just like this heavy bag I carry around every day. I'll carry it to the ends of the planet because that's my commission, but I would love to see something happen with it. I guess I'm just ready to get on with things. I want to see the Arians come to know Christ." He tapped the bag with his foot. "And I want to find out what 'this' is all about?"

"Have you asked?"

"Asked for the souls in Aria? Of course I have. We do that together every night."

"No. Have you asked if you could be the one who carries the manuscript to its purpose?"

"Well . . ." The question caught Sean off guard. He had never even considered asking for that. His family had carried the clay urn around for thousands of years. Had any of them asked?

Nancy opened her Bible to Hebrews 11:1. "Now faith is the assurance of things hoped for, the conviction of things not seen." She closed her Bible. "I feel like we're standing on a precipice. Something big is about to happen. Aria feels it too. We have hoped earnestly for these people, and I know something is coming. Even though we don't have a single convert yet, through faith, I see it!"

Sean sat and contemplated it all, including what Found had said about the color coming and Nancy's anticipation of impending change.

"Well, dear. Sounds like you have a lot to ask for," Nancy said as she stood up and put her hands on her husband's shoulders. She looked out the window into the night, toward Aria. "I see a field white with harvest. Let's ask Him to open our ears and eyes."

That night Sean lay in bed, and prayed for Aria's conversion just as he had every night for almost three years. He also recalled every gift of the spirit that was available to him: love, joy, peace, patience, kindness, goodness, faithfulness, gentleness, and self-control. He and Nancy had needed every one of those gifts to get to where they were. Sean also gave thanks to his Lord's generous Spirit, surrendering yet again and vowing to depend more on the never-ending source of life.

Then Sean prayed a different prayer, a prayer he had never considered before. He requested God's permission to witness the ultimate purpose of the sacred manuscript with which his family had been entrusted. Could he be the one to see the task to fruition?

CHAPTER 29

THE PURPOSE

Aadiel sat on his front porch, staring out at the never-ending new day. He expected Kafziel to arrive at any minute with instructions for his next commission.

Thinking over the past few days with Sean and Nancy flooded him with thanksgiving. The opportunity to go before them bearing the King's authority to drive out the dark forces was his greatest honor. The excitement of what would come next was hard to contain. He couldn't wait for Kafziel to arrive.

He didn't have to wait long. Aadiel spotted the quirky angel from far off walking down the road from the North gate. He could tell by the awkward shuffling gait, it was Kafziel, but two others walked beside him. It was not until the threesome walked a good bit closer that Aadiel recognized the two other angels, Ramiel and Joam.

"Hey, do I know you?" Kafziel yelled as they entered the front lawn garden, his eyes squinted in a playful taunt.

"I certainly hope so," Aadiel said, smiling back at him. "Joam, Ramiel, it is good to see you both again. Welcome."

"It's good to be here with you, old friend," Ramiel responded.

The four of them made their way onto the porch. Aadiel offered his special chair to Kafziel. Joam took a seat on the second stair of the stoop, while Ramiel leaned back on one of the two columns supporting the overhang of the porch.

"Can I get you anything," Aadiel offered.

Kafziel sat back in the chair and rubbed his rotund belly. "Thank you, Aadiel, but we just left the Bistro. I couldn't eat or drink another thing."

Aadiel smiled and leaned back, propping his foot against the opposite column facing Ramiel. It was so good to be counted in the presence of these angels, to feel at ease and connected with them. Aadiel still felt the need to pinch himself sometimes.

"The three of you may wonder why I have called you here together this morning. Aadiel, you know I'm here with instructions. What you don't know is that I'll deploy you along with Ramiel and Joam for this next assignment," Kafziel said.

Aadiel made eye contact with the two and tipped his chin. "An honor."

Ramiel said, "I agree, it will be good to be back in the field with you, Aadiel."

"I look forward to it," Joam added.

Kafziel began, "Aadiel, as you now know, Ramiel here spent a very long tour of duty on assignment for your protection during your ops as Thort. Joam, on the other hand, spent his tour guarding the manuscript during the dark ages. They both received those direct orders from the King Himself."

"I know now, yes. I had no idea what was going on before that fateful day beside James's stream."

"All by design," Kafziel said. "With the culmination of this mission, it makes perfect sense that the three of you will serve together. Aadiel, your assignment: the Pathroses. Ramiel's assignment: you, and Joam's assignment: the manuscript. The three of you together will serve one purpose."

Kafziel stood and walked over to Aadiel. He grabbed the sleeve of his blue robe and turned it over. Aadiel looked down at the word stitched into the fabric, PURPOSE. Ramiel and Joam joined them, each holding out the sleeve of their own robes bearing the same word.

"The wait is over. The final showdown on Earth is about to begin. It will take place between the two majestic mountains. The dark kingdom will make its last stand for the 300 souls in Aria. As you all know, there will be no battle, no draw, no flesh and blood spilled, quite the one-sided event, but then we do serve the Lord of Armies who proclaimed victory long ago," Kafziel said with a proud smirk.

"For the three of you, your purpose will be to declare the three eternal messages. You know, the ones foretold by John the Revelator."

The three angels looked at each other, acknowledging what was about to take place.

Kafziel stood back from them and took a more formal stance.

"Joam, you will go first. You will herald the message of Good News to the peoples of Earth, to every race, tribe, language, and nation."

Looking then to Aadiel, he said, "Your message will be next. You will address the fallen, the realm you once swore your allegiance to. You wear the symbol of God's sovereignty around your neck. You will stand side by side with Sean and Nancy Pathrose and bear witness to the everlasting Love to the Arians. Finally, you will announce the ultimate defeat of Satan and all his followers before the King sentences them to the Lake of Fire." Aadiel's eyes got big.

"Oh, and one more thing." Kafziel reached into the pocket of his garment. "You will need this." He handed Aadiel a shiny silver key. "Everything has been prepared."

"Yes, sir." Aadiel took the key from Kafziel and then stepped back.

"Finally, Ramiel, you will announce the day of judgment for Earth, just as you did that day for Thort. Then you will summon the King's bride, those who obey God's commandments and have remained faithful to Him."

Kafziel finished with the assignments, and the three angels stood on the porch in silence. The moment all creation was looking for had finally come. The Father had given his consent for the Son to gather his bride.

It was time.

CHAPTER 30

MIKA

The morning arrived just like any other day. Sean rose early to gather more supplies and prepare the donkeys for another journey into the heart of the jungle. It was a journey that he and Nancy had made time and time again, hoping and praying for a breakthrough. He had packed their bags and walked that path so many times, he could do it in his sleep.

Nancy stepped out of the mission house with a steaming cup of tea in her hand and smiled at her husband. "Today could be the day, you know," she said.

He nodded. "It could be. You never know. Maybe we'll get there and discover that Found led them all to Christ while we were gone."

"Wouldn't that be something? I'm almost ready. I just need to wash my face and use the restroom one more time."

"Okay, hun, could you grab my backpack from the bedroom on your way back?"

"Sure, no problem," she said as she went inside.

Little did the missionaries know that this was not just the day they had been praying for in Aria. It was also the day for all of creation, and their final trek into the jungle would take them into the divine destiny for all humanity.

Aadiel, Joam, and Ramiel stood at the mouth of the Arian pass. They had passed the time imagining the surprise of the enemy army, which was soon to come.

"They have no idea what's coming," Ramiel said.

Aadiel nodded. "I wonder how long it will take for them to realize it."

"They probably won't get it until you make the official announcement, Aadiel," Joam replied.

"I don't know. Fluto is pretty quick on the uptake. I think he'll probably swallow his tongue when he sees the three of us assembled here. He'll know something is up."

"I can't wait to see it," Ramiel said, rubbing his hands together in excitement.

Just then they heard footsteps approaching from around the bend, and they readied themselves. "Here they come," Joam said.

Nancy led her donkey in front of Sean as they entered the clearing to the meadow. She saw the villagers buzzing around the huts and fire pits doing morning chores. She and Sean were halfway through the meadow before anyone noticed them approaching.

A young pregnant woman who had been tending to a pot of boiling water over a fire noticed them first. She stood up, her mouth dropped open, and the spoon she was holding fell to the dirt.

A child shrieked, piercing the divide between spirit and flesh.

"Mika! Mika!" the child proclaimed.

There were gasps and screams of surprise as the villagers froze in their tracks, turning their attention toward Sean and Nancy Pathrose.

The child was still shouting when the chief elder stepped out of his hut to see what the commotion was about. His son and Found almost tripped over him, frozen on the bottom step of the hut. Eyes widened, and jaws dropped open in awe.

Feeling a significant presence behind him, Sean turned.

Standing there was a mighty angel robed in the deepest, most pure blue he had ever seen. The same blue as the dress of the doll and the toy slinky and the same blue that marked the doorpost of every home in Aria. The same blue color, Mika.

Sean and Nancy fell to their knees.

"Mika," Sean said in realization. "Color has come. Mika."

He glanced over and noticed the entire village had bowed in reverent fear. Found lifted his head, making eye contact with Sean, a knowing smile on his face.

"Mika," Sean mouthed to Found.

Found nodded and mouthed the same word silently back at him.

Aadiel took Sean and Nancy by the hands and helped them to their feet. He pointed to Found and motioned for him to join him. It was terrifying. Sean's knees trembled, threatening to buckle, but Aadiel steadied him. "Don't be afraid, Sean."

The three missionaries and the great angel stood facing the village. Aadiel opened his mouth and spoke in perfect Arian dialect. "I'm the one whom your ancestors prophesied would come to you. I stand as proof that these missionaries preach the truth. Your only salvation is found in surrender to Christ Jesus, the God who was born to a human virgin, suffered, was crucified, and died, so you don't have to. He rose from the dead, ascended to His Father in Heaven to sit on the throne as King. He comes today to judge the living and the dead. He offers eternal life to replace the evil hearts of men and the sin that leads to death. He gives you the choice."

When Aadiel finished speaking, he nudged Sean and Found toward the village. Then he looked at Nancy. "I see a field white with harvest."

Ramiel and Joam emerged from the tall grass and took their place on either side of Aadiel.

Time fractured. The veil that concealed the chasm between two realms lifted. The eyes of the flesh, held captive from the moment Adam stepped out of the garden, blinked open again. The overlapping dimensions of the kingdom of Earth and the Kingdom of Heaven bled past the barrier.

In the distance on the western mountain, the dark lord Satan stood flanked by his hordes of demons, standing rank by rank in battle formation. Aadiel recognized Blastus and Sorpine among the other fallen sons standing at Satan's side. Fluto was there too, bearing the proud star that proclaimed him a captain of the armies. His glare locked on Aadiel, full of hate and disgust.

Opposite them the great armies of the Lord stood amassed, blazing with the blinding, pure light of His glory. The saints were present, that great cloud of witnesses, looking down over the valley at Aria. Although their numbers were unfathomable, each one was recognizable and unique.

Aadiel picked out Paulk, Codill, and James Pathrose right away—his people. Simon Peter stood among them. Kafziel was gathered with the other council members toward the front. Aadiel smiled up at him, and Kafziel winked back.

All of creation stood silent, facing off, locked in anticipation. Every human soul, every angelic and demonic being, the birds of the air, the fish of the sea, the beasts of the land, every tree, every rock, and every created element of the cosmos paused in wait.

The three angels turned their heads to the east.

The mighty King nodded.

Joam rose into the air. He swept off the ground, swirling the dust beneath him as he ascended. His voice thundered like a trumpet. "Honor God and praise His greatness! Every race, tribe, language, and nation, bend the knee to the Almighty One who created the heavens and the Earth."

Aadiel rose from the ground in a fury and positioned himself above the western mountain. The silver medallion hung from his neck for all of Hell's armies to see. Beside it, another item hung glistening as the light caught it: the key to a bottomless pit, which lay open, waiting, ready. From Aadiel's right hand hung a mighty chain. He glared at Satan and the dark legions standing on the ridge as he spoke in a commanding voice. "Today is the day of disaster. Disaster for all enemies who set themselves against God, His Son, and His sheep. You caused God's people to drink the wine of immortal lust, bringing shame to the ones He loved."

Aadiel pointed at Satan's twisted face. "Evil dragon of deception, the King comes today to deliver the sentence of your miserable eternity. All of you who serve this master will follow him to his fate."

With a deafening crash of thunder, white lightning burst forth from the heavens. The mountain the hordes were standing on split from east to west. Aadiel sliced through the expanse with a swing of the mighty chain, laying hold of the great serpent of old. It was as if a huge star imploded, swallowing the entire legion. All who served the master of darkness followed him like water swirling down a drain. They were consumed in a gaping inferno of darkness, not only the demons of every rank, the principalities, powers, and their prince, but all unrighteousness on the entire planet. Gone in an instant.

Finally, the great Ramiel took to flight. He soared over the crowds of Hell, crossed the valley of the pass, then circled behind the great gathering of saints. All eyes were fixed on the messenger as he joined Joam and Aadiel in the air between the armies.

He opened his mouth and declared his message throughout the world. "The day of judgment is at hand. He comes this day to judge the living and the dead."

Then Ramiel rose above the other messengers to proclaim his last message. "Now, I call forth the Church, the betrothed Bride of the Son of Man. All who obey God's commandments and have remained faithful to Him, I am here to proclaim the return of the King."

EPILOGUE

As Ramiel sat on the stone wall outside the entry gate to the great hall, deep in contemplation, Joam approached. One look at his friend's countenance proved they shared the same sentiment.

"Well, here we are again," Joam said.

Ramiel looked up and smiled at his friend. "Yes, here we are. Big day."

Joam stuck his finger in the collar of his formal dress robe and tugged. "Do I have this thing on right? I don't know if I do."

Ramiel glanced at the back of Joam's collar. "Yeah, you're good."

"Thanks."

"I remember the last time we sat on this wall together."

"Yeah, it's been a minute," Joam replied, nodding. "That was the day He promised us He had a plan."

"And, boy, did He ever," Ramiel said. "And now it's time. Here we are."

Joam looked through the gate at the massive double doors leading into the hall. "It shouldn't be long now."

"Yeah, I expect He will arrive any moment," Ramiel said, glancing toward the wall.

Joam detected a different tone in Ramiel's voice. He knew what it was. He put his hand on his friend's shoulder. "Hey, I know. I get it. I wish he was here too. But he's not missing it. He feels this glorious day with us."

Joam pointed toward the high knoll overlooking the western wall. "Just think, he has the best seat in the house."

Ramiel turned and gazed up at the knoll where the Memorial of Free Will once stood. A pillar of black smoke billowed into the sky like the plume from an erupting volcano, visible from every part of the Celestial City. No trace of the memorial grove existed. On the day of Earth's reaping, the ground beneath the memorial had opened up, swallowing every herb, shrub, and tree. Every climbing and creeping vine was incinerated in an instant as the cauldron of fire and brimstone seared up from the pit beneath. The smoke of torment would never cease to spew from that gaping hole, the exact footprint of the garden of trickery that once existed. In the molten bowels below, Satan, the dragon of deceit who corrupted Earth with immorality, and the entire army of Hell was in chains. He had marked throngs of people with the weapons of his destruction, and they had refused to accept the ransom paid by the Blood of the Lamb. There the entire lot existed, submerged beneath the suffocating surface of an eternal lake of fire. There would be no rest for them day or night. The evidence of their torment would rise from that pit in the presence of the King and his holy angels forever.

"I know he can see it. We all see it," Ramiel said.

Joam nodded. "If Aadiel has ears, the Lord knows he can hear the celebration from out there."

Ramiel's face broke into a grin. "That's the truth. Who can't?"

The sky above them thundered like the roar of a rushing waterfall, filling the Kingdom with a splendid proclamation. The chants and praises of the saints roared from the assembly of the great hall, filling every space. "Praise God! Salvation, glory, and power belong to our King!"

Just then, Carley and Casey skipped up the sidewalk, holding hands. They were wearing beautiful white dresses tied at the waist with satin sashes. Their hair was braided, each one wearing an intricate headpiece woven from the stems of beautiful flowers. Each of them held a basket full of rose petals, harvested from Eve's garden. The twins were humming in perfect harmony as they walked up to the gate, a tune never heard before by anyone but the two of them. It was lovely. When they finished rehearsing their chorale masterpiece, they stopped and looked at each other. Carley crinkled her nose and smiled. "I think He's gonna like it," She said.

Casey tilted her forehead to touch her sister's. "He'll love it."

Behind the girls stood a mass of children clothed in white from the crystal waterfalls. Each of them sang a different melody, creating the most precious music that Ramiel and Joam had ever heard.

The girls looked up at Ramiel and Joam and then over at the big doors, which remained closed. "Are they ready for us?" Carley asked.

"I'm sure they are. Ladies, you look and sound beautiful," Ramiel said, bowing as he motioned them to continue through the gate.

The girls smiled, then linked arms and skipped past the angels, their white slippers padding in unison against the glass-like finish of the golden path. Then the girls parted ways, each standing at the open doors, welcoming the other children. They stood there until every child passed through the entrance and then followed them in.

"Perfect little flower girls, those two," Joam said, smiling at Ramiel.

Then the atmosphere shifted. A brand-new fragrance filled the air and their lungs with gladness and thanksgiving.

King Jesus approached.

Ramiel and Joam stood at attention until He was standing before them. Then they bowed low.

"Look at you, guys. Looking spiffy," Jesus said. "At ease, fellas."

"My King, you are perfection itself," Joam said.

"Yes, and thank you for allowing us to be a part of your ceremony," Ramiel added. "There's no greater honor in the Kingdom than to stand beside You today."

Jesus smiled, his countenance giddy. "It's exciting, isn't it?"

"It is sir," Ramiel replied. "Are you ready?"

"I am, but before we go in, I have something for you."

"For us?" Joam crinkled his brow and then looked at Ramiel for a clue.

"You know me," Jesus said. "I love to give gifts." He smiled at the angels and then took one step to his right. Behind Him stood Aadiel, gleaming with joy.

"Aadiel!" Ramiel shouted, bolting forward to hug his friend.

"You didn't think I would let one of the three amigos miss out on my big day, did you?" Jesus said.

Aadiel smiled, tears streaming down his face as his friends wrapped their arms around him.

Thort's epiphany and the Father's mighty sovereign hand had brought him full circle, surrounded by his friends, marked with purpose, and restored to his King.

His resting place outside the city wall was perfect. That morning, he had relished every sound, every smell, every breeze, and every shout of praise coming from inside the Celestial City. From his porch the pillar of smoke was visible, reminding him of salvation from that eternity of suffering. Aadiel was at peace, satisfied and fulfilled in every way.

Love and appreciation superseding any emotion he had ever experienced came that morning when Kafziel handed him an invitation sealed in royal wax—special permission from King Jesus to take part in the greatest event in eternity.

He had entered the gate by the explicit order and authority of the King. He didn't deserve to be there. He knew it, and so did everyone else, but he was a guest of the Groom, invited into the Kingdom on that glorious day. Why? He didn't know, but Aadiel would love and serve the King forever, never doubting his position or questioning his Lord's love or decisions again.

The three of them embraced Jesus.

"I love you guys, and I'm proud of you," Jesus said, patting them on the back. Then He took a step back and adjusted his belt and sash.

"Now I'm ready."

The great doors swung open, and trumpets blasted, announcing the King's royal presence.

Aadiel, Joam, and Ramiel followed Jesus, watching in admiration as He ascended the stairway and entered the great hall. He smiled down at the scattered rose petals. As the King passed through the masses, the crowd erupted in a deafening roar that echoed throughout the new Heaven and the new Earth.

Then a loud voice superseded the crowd's cheers, proclaiming His glory. "Behold, Christ, the Son of the living God, the Word who became flesh, was crucified, buried and rose on the third day."

All of the inhabitants of Heaven bowed in reverence and awe.

As Jesus approached the Father's throne, He smiled, nodded, and turned to face to all of creation.

In that instant, Earth burst forth new Eden, its glories no longer restricted, once again basking in the streams from the fountainhead of its Creator. Galaxies known and unknown and stars far and near danced in unison. Black holes from every universe burst into colors never witnessed by any created being. Rotating stars from every galaxy formed rings, blasting glaring light and producing brilliant beacons amidst a sea of the Father's galaxies. On Earth, rocks cried out. "Hosanna! Hosanna!" The trees, now full of ripe fruit, clapped their branches with joy. The seas became crystal clear, and all their creatures, great and small, roared from the depths the name of the King of Kings and the Lord of Lords. New crystal rivers flowed in unison with the sounds from Heaven's choirs. Mountains swayed in the clouds as redemption filled every particle of sand and every flake of snow. Volcanoes were sucked into the new Earth and replaced by windswept meadows swaying with the beauty of twelve different species of flower, celebrating twelve new seasons, each an eternity unto themselves. The new Mika sky held teams of angelic hosts, and Kafziel stood with God's faithful Divine Council, witnessing the new birth. "Glory and honor to the One who has overcome!" they proclaimed.

The King turned to His Father. His glorious Bride also stood united, the many having become one, their filthy rags traded for the

Kingdom's royal white linen, the same white linen that Sam and Spencer Pathrose had pulled back from the rock crevasse in that tiny cave on Patmos.

Jesus smiled down at the generations of the Pathrose family as they stood before Him, perfect and spotless.

Knowing what was coming, Ramiel looked over at John the beloved and wondered what must be going through his mind. So long ago he had put pen to paper, transcribing the secret words of his Rabbi, then seeing that the sacred writings stayed tucked away, miraculously preserved, and now presented for that very moment in that very hall. John smiled at his Master.

"Peter," Jesus said, "the precious rock on whom I built my Church."

"Yes, my Lord," Peter replied from the center of the Pathrose family.

"Who has my love letter?"

"Sean Pathrose still has it, Sir," Peter replied.

"May I have it now, please?" the King asked.

Sean bowed, then handed the clay container to his distant cousin, Saint Peter.

Peter ascended the steps and handed the container to Jesus, then they embraced.

Jesus turned to face the saints His Father had given him. Then He broke the seven seals that held the lid on the clay container.

Reaching in, he removed the bronze cylinder.

Paulk smiled as he recalled the day he had fired those seals.

Jesus ran his thumb through the beeswax, breaking open the last protective barrier to reveal the rolled scroll.

"You all did a great job. This looks just like it did the day John wrote it all down," Jesus said, smiling at Paulk. "Thank you all for holding onto it for me, and Joam, thank you for watching over it."

Jesus unrolled the scroll, made eye contact with the saints, then began to read. "My Bride, you were presented to me at Calvary in a betrothal period designed by my Father awaiting this day—the fulfillment of faithfulness and divine jealousy that you had for me with the purest hearts. From this day forward, you will live with me for eternity in New Jerusalem, a city adorned for you as my most glorious and radiant love. You have become my one, although you are many. This day you share my name, 'Wisdom,' as you become one with me. I write my name on your foreheads, for you have overcome death, just as I have. You were once lost like a harlot, abused by my adversary, left to rot and decay. But you took my Spirit's hand and rose from the darkness into my Father's delight. You became pure of heart as the fear of my Father took root and grew in your heart. You have become mother to twins, Righteousness and Peace. Your days are now consumed with gentleness, patience, and kindness. You died daily so that others could join me in eternity. You submitted yourselves to others, feeding them My bread of life and partaking in the drinking of My water, which never runs dry. Unending mercy and the good fruits of my Spirit follow you as you seek my face. I find no hypocrisy in you as you dwell on my approval, just as I dwell only on my Father's. In eternity, I'll nourish and cherish you in everything. You will never be alone, nor will you ever need anything. With my blood you have been set free from the stains of sin. You have become a shining light of my love, for you have confessed your sin. Now you have no stain or wrinkle. Through my blood, you have made yourself ready."

Jesus smiled at His Father and then turned to the host of Heaven and his bride. "Rejoice, new Heaven and new Earth! We invite you to the marriage supper of the Lamb."

AFTERWORD

When we first embarked on the journey of creating the storyline and plots for Thort's Epiphany, we kept asking ourselves, why write such an outlandish tale? First, perfect families don't exist in our world. Plus, telling a story about a demon's renunciation is a daunting task, even for the most skilled wordsmith.

Yet, we sought solace in fiction, recognizing that it can often illuminate paths that are dimly lit or entirely obscured by life's adversities. In the realm of non-fiction, our Bible stands as the ultimate guide. Verses like Matthew 5:48 provide a brilliant light: "But you are to be perfect, even as your Father in Heaven is perfect." While considering those words, we wondered if we could weave a story about a lineage of devout followers who thwart the adversary's schemes at every turn and, if so, what impact that would have on the forces of evil. Could this family be sinless, or would they merely be a family walking in complete righteousness, shaped by our Lord's grace atonement? The conclusion was obvious. We live in a fallen world. Sin is present, but perfection is attainable. The Pathroses' faith in the Lord would be unwavering. So, we depicted a family who defeats darkness with perfect righteousness, showing our Father's power.

For over 2,000 years, the Pathroses were not without sin, but they were exemplars of a perfect walk, a daily portrayal of unwavering righteousness. The prince of this world might deceive many into believing that no one can be perfect, but, as always, he is mistaken.

This family was perfect. They had unwavering loyalty, faith, and service that dismantled every evil scheme that Hell could concoct against them. As a result, the enemy saw his end, and our sovereign God, who specializes in the impossible, embarked on a divine plan that had never entered the minds of men or angels.

Let us not forget, His work is far from over, and so is ours. As long as we have breath, it is never too late. No sin is too evil, and no story unredeemable to a sovereign God whose very nature is love. Jesus purchased our path from eternal decay to the throne room by His side.

Finally, be not deceived. This is not fiction promoting universalism. It is the author's way of showing readers the limitless ways God could use the angels He created, even the ones who turned their backs on Him.

Don't miss out on that glorious day when the thousands of generations bow down in worship, and all creation joins with the angels singing, "Holy is the Lamb!"

ABOUT THE AUTHORS

E. Carey Slay, Jr. was born in small industrial town in north Alabama. After graduating from high school, he left home to attend Samford University in Birmingham, Alabama, on a ministerial scholarship. After a couple of unsuccessful years in college, due primarily to immaturity, the armed forces called. Four years later, an appreciation for what college could do for a young man, Carey rejoined the college ranks, changed his career to business and did not stop until his VA benefits ran out. The results were a BA Degree in Finance and MA in Personnel Management. He began his career in banking as a trust officer and many years later served as Founding Director and eventual Chairman of a community bank. However, most of his professional career was in the retail automobile business where he began as a salesman, then CFO of several dealerships and was blessed to eventually become a minor owner of a successful Toyota dealership.

Although Carey had made a career in finance and banking, he also enjoys teaching Christian themed material. After leading small groups through books like C.S. Lewis' "The Screwtape Letters" and Young's "The Shack", he decided to pen his own Christian speculative fiction story.

* * *

Cara Slay Coleman is the daughter of E. Carey Slay, Jr. and his wife Janice Slay. She was born in Jacksonville, Florida and raised in south Alabama where she currently resides as a mother of four children with her husband, Jonathan Coleman. She graduated from Troy University of Dothan with a bachelor's degree in finance but has spent most of her life serving as a stay-at-home mother. As a connoisseur of fiction, Cara was intrigued by the concept of Thort's Epiphany when her father introduced it to the family. Following the lead of the Holy Spirit, she began the work of fleshing out the characters and bringing life to the plot and story line.

* * *

When the writing personalities of a teacher and a visionary collide, there is great challenge. One wants to teach an important lesson, and the other wants to tell a good story. Carey and Cara team up to create a book which does both.